THE FEVER CALLED LIVING

Also by Barbara Moore
 HARD ON THE ROAD

The Fever Called Living

BARBARA MOORE

Doubleday & Company, Inc., Garden City, New York
1976

ST. PHILIPS COLLEGE LIBRARY

COPYRIGHT © 1976 BY BARBARA MOORE
ALL RIGHTS RESERVED
PRINTED IN THE UNITED STATES OF AMERICA
FIRST EDITION

Library of Congress Cataloging in Publication Data

Moore, Barbara, 1934–
The fever called living.

1. Poe, Edgar Allan, 1809–1849, in fiction, drama, poetry, etc. I. Title.
PZ4.M8186Fe   [PS3563.057]   813'.5'4
ISBN: 0-385-12081-8
Library of Congress Catalog Card Number: 76-2807

For Cassandra and Segundo

CONTENTS

Prologue—*October 8, 1849*	1
BOOK I NEW YORK	13
BOOK II FANNY	97
BOOK III VIRGINIA	203
BOOK IV THE LADIES	245
BOOK V HOME AGAIN	299
Epilogue—*October 8, 1849*	337
Author's Note	344

*Thank Heaven! the crisis—
  The danger is past,
And the lingering illness
  Is over at last—
And the fever called "Living"
  Is conquered at last.*
For Annie

THE FEVER CALLED LIVING

PROLOGUE

October 8, 1849

i

"Poe? Dead?" said the Reverend Dr. Rufus Wilmot Griswold. "By God!"

Horace Greeley, interrupted by his friend's exclamation, finished the sentence he was writing and put his right forefinger on the last word before looking up. "Yes, dead," he said. With a practiced motion he stuck his pen between his teeth and dug with his free hand into the debris that covered his desk: piles of newspaper clippings and pamphlets, a paste pot, sealing wafers, unopened letters and six large turnips wrapped in yesterday's copy of the New York *Tribune*. He looked exasperated when he didn't find what he was seeking and said, "The news came by the telegraph this evening from Baltimore." He dug some more. "I've got it here somewhere. Apparently Poe died yesterday."

"Was it foul play?" the Reverend Dr. Griswold asked softly.

Greeley blinked. "What an imagination you've got, Gris. Why should there have been foul play? Poe died suddenly in some hospital. Don't ask me for details. Nothing has come through yet. The point is, you knew him well, and despite his irregular habits and peculiar temperament Poe was a well-known man. I want you to knock something out on him for me. And fast. I'll use it in tomorrow morning's edition." Still marking his place on the editorial he was writing, the publisher swept several dozen tattered magazines and a slashed copy of a rival paper, the *Herald*, from a rickety table next to his desk. "You can write it right here. The typesetters are already caught up and calling for copy. Here. Pen. Ink pot. Sand box. Paper. Oh, by all that's holy, where's the paper? Boy! Paper! Do you hear me, boy? I'm out of paper!"

Greeley roared the last into a speaking tube on the wall, then serenely resumed his chair, snatched the pen from his teeth and continued writing. Down a short flight of stairs in the editorial offices, there was a commotion and cries of "Mr. Greeley wants writing paper!" The Reverend Dr. Rufus Griswold, sometimes Baptist preacher and full-time littérateur, turned sharp, trenchant gray eyes to the third man in the office, old Dr. John Francis, sometimes littérateur and full-time physician, who had accompanied him to call on the publisher. Although Horace Greeley's powers of concentration were renowned, the Reverend Griswold automatically lowered his voice to avoid disturbing him, whispering to Francis, "I've always said Poe would die one of these days in a fit of delirium tremens. I lay odds he was off on one of his binges."

"I wonder," Dr. Francis mused. "He had an ailing heart too, although I don't suppose that was generally known."

A boy, perhaps twelve, rushed in with an armload of foolscap. The Reverend Griswold took the paper and said again, wonderingly, gloatingly, "Dead, by God."

Greeley looked up impatiently. "Write!" he commanded. "And give me a good obituary. After all, the man lived in this city for the last five years."

"Shall I sign the account?" the Reverend Griswold asked. "I'd really rather not."

"All right, use a pseudonym. But write!"

The Reverend Griswold obeyed. He began slowly to scrawl:

Edgar Allan Poe is dead. He died in Baltimore yesterday. He paused, struggling with his lead, then the pen moved again, more rapidly: *This announcement will startle many, but few will be grieved by it. The poet was known, personally or by reputation, in all this country; he had readers in England, and in several of the states of Continental Europe; but he had few or no friends; and the regrets for his death will be suggested principally by the consideration that in him literary art has lost one of its most brilliant but erratic stars.*

Dr. Francis leaned over the Reverend Griswold's shoulder to read, his bushy gray locks brushing Griswold's broad, balding forehead. Dr. Francis promptly snorted. "For shame, Dr. Griswold," he said. "Will you stab away at poor Poe so, now that he's dead and can't defend himself? Poe had many friends who will mourn him. Indeed, I thought you were one of them."

The Reverend Griswold gazed up at Dr. Francis with a familiar expression of cocksure defiance. "Poe was not my friend, nor I his," he said. "I'll do him justice in my account, but you can't expect me to conceal facts, sir."

"Facts?" Francis said. "Why, you've even got his name wrong. What's this 'Allan'? I never heard him call himself such. Poe despised double-barreled literary names."

"It was his name, nevertheless," the Reverend Griswold said. "But anything to satisfy a friend . . ." At the head of the sheet, he wrote, *Death of Edgar A. Poe.* "There," he said. "And now to get in a gentle puff for one of my favorite books." He dipped his pen in the ink pot and began a new paragraph:

The family of Mr. Poe, we learn from Griswold's Poets and Poetry of America, from which a considerable portion of the facts in this notice are derived, was one of the oldest and most respectable in Baltimore. David Poe, his paternal grandfather, was a Quartermaster-General in the Maryland line during the Revolution, and the intimate friend of Lafayette, who . . .

Dr. Francis threw himself on a leather bed lounge that crowded the little office to the popping point. Horace Greeley's white cotton overcoat, the kind that only draymen or fishmongers usually wore, and a straw hat, out of season now that it was October, lay on the foot of the lounge, but the publisher was a messy man and Francis had no qualms about nudging them onto the floor with the toe of his boot. He took up a tract from some abolition society, then laid it aside again and listened to the busy scratching of the two pens.

Edgar Poe dead. In ways, it was predictable. The last time Dr. Francis had had occasion to examine Poe, the dysrhythmia of the pulse had been alarming. Ten regular beats of the poet's heart, only ten, after which the pulse intermitted, then finally beat again, ten times more. But although a Methuselahn life could by no means have been predicted for Poe, with care and any kind of luck at all he might have lived for some years yet. No, it was all too impossible that Edgar Poe should be dead. New York couldn't be the same without its Raven.

New York, princess and whore—Dr. Francis loved her in both her manifestations, and he loved her citizens, particularly the vivid ones like Edgar Poe. For five years he had run into Poe on the streets or in drawing rooms, sometimes his own. Five years of glimpses and memories, and Dr. Francis was getting old and the memories would die with him. Memories of Poe, noticed fleetingly in a crowd on the roof of Barnum's, flushed and laughing like a boy when a cable broke and some balloonist's gondola slowly disappeared over the Astor House roofs during a routine ascension. Memories of Poe, in his cups and quarrelsome, staggering out of Sandy Welsh's Cellar nearby on Ann Street. Memories of Poe, on the wagon, declining brandy and talking trochees and pentameters over cigars at Dr. Francis's, while Griswold, genial, sarcastic, whispered scandal in the corner as was his wont, and young Melville, when he was in town, sat like a stone in another corner or, depending on his mood, related racy stories, his laughter ringing out. Memories of Poe, walking alone along Greenwich Street eating hot gingerbread bought from a vendor, looking happy for a change. Memories of Poe at the theater, looking judicious and full of self-esteem. Memories of winter nights at some fool reception, with little Fanny Osgood gazing adoringly at Poe, and Griswold, jealous as a snake, glowering on the other side of the room. Well, Griswold now had Fanny at last, or what was left of her, and Poe had the closed coffin that, if you judged from his writings, always so terrified him.

It was Fanny's business, in fact, that had brought them to the *Tribune* tonight. The Reverend Dr. Griswold was getting up a volume of her poems, and the *Tribune*'s publisher was always co-operative about puffing his friends' works if they didn't overdo their requests. Not overdoing would be a problem for Griswold. He was working up two or three other anthologies on which he would want notices. But, then, he always was. Griswold was a hard worker. A facile writer, too, although not a very good one. Dr. Francis watched him, scribbling away, pulling material out of a prodigious memory that served him in place of talent, and served him better than talent had served many a man.

As if aware that he was being watched, the Reverend Griswold paused: man thinking. Elbow propped on table. Cheek propped on fist. One forefinger on temple, as if to emphasize its lofty height. Poe's forehead had been loftier. That must have galled the reverend doctor. But then, rivals in both love and literature, the two men had probably always galled one another. Had they had less in common, they might not have quarreled so often.

The flow of the Reverend Griswold's pen seemed to be sticking seriously. He said, "Dr. Francis, won't you help me? It occurs to me that there's some absolutely vital material in my rooms that should be included in the death notice."

"Send a boy," Dr. Francis suggested. "My own plans run to beef and brandy at Delmonico's, then home to bed. There's nothing like beef and brandy in cholera weather."

The Reverend Griswold's severe mouth stretched itself into a charming smile. "Come, sir, there have been no new cholera reports for weeks. And I daren't trust a boy to rummage in my papers. Poe gave me a copy of a new poem right before he left for the South. It's a beauty, the last thing he had written, and I've seen it published nowhere as yet."

Dr. Francis rose from the couch. "But surely Poe sold it to someone or other. He always sold his poems the minute he wrote them. Or tried to. Poor devil, he was always poor as Lazarus."

"It doesn't matter if the poem runs elsewhere, now that he's dead," the Reverend Griswold said. "Come now, Dr. Francis, we must properly illustrate his honorable rank as a poet. Won't you help me—and Poe?"

Dr. Francis stretched lazily, but his stout, vigorous body gave the lie to his pose of lassitude. He possessed great vitality and energy and could never sit still very long. "By God, you'll pay the hack hire," he said, "or I won't stir."

"Of course. And while you're there, get me a copy of Bulwer's *Caxtons*. There's a passage in it I can use."

"About Poe?" Dr. Francis said, but his eye was caught by the sheets of foolscap Griswold had already filled, and he didn't really listen to the answer. Biographical stuff. True or untrue? With Poe—not to mention with Griswold—one could never really be certain. While the Reverend Griswold gave instructions on where to look for the materials he wanted, Dr. Francis skimmed quickly. He wanted to sit down and read the whole manuscript, but Griswold was sighing and looking strained, and Dr. Francis arched shaggy eyebrows at him. Griswold's health was dubious too, poor fellow. It showed, for one thing, in his eyes. Were they unusually dilated tonight? Opium? Another fit coming on? Both? The Reverend Griswold was not Dr. Francis's patient, but the old physician was aware, from town gossip, that Griswold had had some sort of epileptic fit the previous autumn, and another that spring, and somewhere in between had had a bad bout as a result of acting as his own physician. These amateurs, they'd do it every time. Run to the pharmacy for opium pills to try to secure a temporary animation, then wonder why they felt utterly smitten after ravaging their systems. Dr. Francis put down the sheets, put on his tall hat and reassured Griswold he would return promptly.

There were no cabs on Nassau Street, and he had to walk over to Broadway before a cabman roared out the familiar, "Cab, surrrr?" The city was becoming impossible. All the activity and wealth were moving uptown. Why, new mansions were rising almost daily on the Fifth Avenue, and it was built up almost to Twentieth Street. The Fifth Avenue gave itself airs too, but to Dr. Francis, only Broadway —the Broad Way, it had been in his youth—was and always would be the artery through which throbbed the life's blood of his city.

Poe had wandered these streets. Wandered, never uttering a word of complaint about his poverty, from publisher to publisher, with famine dogging his heels and little but misery ahead for his young wife and that formidable old beggar of a mother-in-law. Wended his way down newspaper row, his old black frock coat scrupulously clean and brushed, his fine, print-like manuscripts neatly rolled, finding no market for his work.

Well, of course, Poe wasn't the first starveling writer to learn that authorship as a profession was a very good walking stick, but very bad crutches. It certainly wasn't sensible of him to focus all his energies on writing, to the exclusion of the wholesome pursuit of other sources of wealth. And it wasn't as if he could possibly have hoped ever to rise to the level of the greats whose names would ring through the ages. What other period of letters had known a Halleck, a Willis, a Whittier? A Bryant, a Holmes, a Sprague, a Dana, a Percival, much less Professor Longfellow? There was even, perhaps, Dr. John Francis to be considered.

Poor Poe. Too obsessed with finnicking literary ideals. Too proud. Too scornful. Heaven only knew, although Poe endured enough misfortunes to last six lifetimes, any man with eyes in his head could see that he brought many of them on himself. Yet, could Poe have swallowed his pride and toadied the editors as assiduously as a Griswold, he might have been alive and well this night, well, and well praised and well paid.

But, no, this modern world was in the grip of reformists. Morals must triumph! Up with temperance, with abolition, with woman's right, with Graham bread. Down with an eccentric writer of queer verse and queerer tales who despised an age and a society that thought wealth the *only* gauge of man's success.

Dr. Francis ruminated his way to Griswold's rooms at the New York Hotel and kept the cab waiting for the return journey. The hotel was temptingly close to Bond Street and Dr. Francis's house, but he conscientiously ran his errand, if for no other reason than to keep an eye on Griswold and what he was writing. By the time he returned to the *Tribune* offices, he saw that Griswold's previously written sheets had disappeared, and proof sheets had taken their place. The paper's morgue must have come up with clippings on Poe, because a pile teetered precariously on the edge of Griswold's borrowed table. An old copy of *Union Magazine* was folded open, and Griswold was busily copying some poem. At his own desk, Horace Greeley was still writing rapidly, endlessly. Had he sent Griswold's copy through without even reading it?

"Ah, at last!" the Reverend Griswold cried upon catching sight of Dr. Francis. "You brought the Caxton novel? I've been sadly held up without it." He flipped rapidly through the pages. "Good, here it is. Bulwer's description of his character Francis Vivian: envious, arrogant, ambitious. Meaty stuff, eh?"

"Surely you're not going to use that," Dr. Francis said.

"Why not? It fits Poe to a T."

Dr. Francis frowned but said nothing. Griswold could be a good friend and an amusing companion, but, if attacked, he could also be one of the most vindictive of men. No point in stirring him up needlessly. But the need became immediately apparent when Dr. Francis picked up the proof sheets and tried to find the more contemporary stuff on Poe's life. His eye fell on . . . *this period, Mr. Poe had to be confined at regular intervals in the Insane Retreat at Utica, where* . . .

The old physician's piercingly bright eyes shot fire, and he thumped on Griswold's table with his fist. Clippings, foolscap and the sand box fell to the floor. "Now, by God, this is a damnable lie, and you can't write this sort of thing. I won't stand for it," he roared.

"See here, see here," the Reverend Griswold stuttered, taken aback.

Behind the big desk, Horace Greeley also exploded into a sudden storm of temper. "By all that's holy!" he bellowed. "Dr. Francis, I allow no censors on this newspaper other than myself. If you can't control your meddling, I'll have to ask you to leave."

"Meddling, by God!" Francis roared back. "There are libel laws in this state. You permit this jealous fool here to write this kind of canard, and—"

The publisher's attention, finally, was fully captured. "Canard? What's this?"

"Poe was never in the Insane Retreat at Utica in his life," Francis said. "Nor Bedlam either. That's just a filthy example of the kind of lurid stories that have always attached themselves to Poe. What else are you writing, my oh so reverend friend? That Poe was a monster? A demon? A great sot? Or have you settled for smaller beer and merely made that old claim he was a great womanizer? Oh, by no means worry about the truth of your stories. There are so many to choose from. Write that Poe had three wives, that's always a good one. Write that he broke up homes. Write that he borrowed money from ladies without returning it, now that's a perennial favorite. Oh, and here's one you may not have heard: that he tried to seduce his foster father's second wife, and that's why he was disinherited. And of course everyone knows that he killed his own poor little wife to provide material for his stories. Good God, what else have I heard whispered about Poe? Help me out, Dr. Griswold. Jog my memory."

"Dr. Francis, you go too far," the Reverend Griswold said.

"And you, sir? The stories about Poe are endless, but anyone but a fool would take them *cum grano salis*. I am all too aware that to deny canards is to dignify them, but this is ridiculous. Poe mad? Next you'll tell me he was an opium chewer. But I think you might know rather more about such practices than he, Dr. Griswold."

The Reverend Griswold paled and jolted to his feet. Horace Greeley hastened clumsily around his desk and stepped between the two men. "Come now," he said soothingly. "This is all just a misunderstanding."

"It is Dr. Francis who misunderstands," the Reverend Griswold said coldly. "I have it on the best authority that Poe was taken to the Insane Retreat at Utica three times in the winter of—"

"Whose authority?" Francis demanded, bristling like a gamecock. "I am personally acquainted with the directors at both Bedlam and Utica. They can assure you, gentlemen, that the name of Edgar Poe has never been entered on their books."

"Then he must have been entered under an assumed name," the Reverend Griswold insisted stubbornly.

"Indeed, sir," Dr. Francis said, "and do you think so prominent a person as Edgar Poe could escape notice so easily? I tell you no. Poe mad? Nervous, I'll grant you. A bad heritage there somewhere. But not mad. I'll also grant you his occasional bouts of drinking, but need that sort of thing go into a man's obituary? *De mortuis nil nisi bonum,* I say."

The Reverend Griswold's Latin was shaky, even on common phrases. Knowing this, Dr. Francis used it deliberately. The sting hit target. Griswold lost his head. "And Poe's women?" he demanded. "If he was so pure, what of all his women? My God, man, not a month ago he got engaged to some woman in Richmond, for her money, but I have it on unimpeachable authority that he was planning to move her to Massachusetts near a certain creature he was in love with there, so as to continue to have intercourse with his mistress. And that's not even the worst of it. That mother-in-law of his was going to live *with* them, and it's commonly understood and believed in neighborhoods where they lived that he had criminal relations even with *her*. What a delightful ménage! What a pity your dear friend died before he could effect it!"

Dr. Francis turned away in disgust, and Horace Greeley also looked offended. "Enough, Gris," the publisher said. "Dr. Francis, I remind you that Poe is dead and can sue no one for libel. And as for you, Gris, I'm sure you had no intention of writing about such matters in Poe's obituary."

"No, of course not," the Reverend Griswold said sulkily. "I mentioned that he was to have been married this week, nothing more."

"Then come, I cannot see two such good friends fall out over a swine like Poe. No, Dr. Francis, don't attack me next. I confess that I didn't care for Poe, but that is neither here nor there. Gris, let's just take out that part about the Insane Retreat. Dr. Francis, will that satisfy you?"

"My intention wasn't to carp about factual material," Dr. Francis said stiffly. "But I also advise caution in writing about Poe's, um, women friends. That's touchy stuff, that. It should be treated carefully."

"Of course," Horace Greeley said. His eyes were wandering back to his own desk and the stack of foolscap he had been working on.

"Well, let's get on with it. Give me your proof sheets, friend Gris, and I'll correct them. Here, you say Poe died yesterday, but the paper won't be on the streets until tomorrow. It must read 'day before yesterday.' And by all that's holy, bring it to a conclusion soon. Poe is an important story, but the paper's awfully crowded."

"I've written the ending already," the Reverend Griswold said. "I need only insert a few things, such as the other poem Dr. Francis was so kind as to bring me." Placatingly, he added, "Did you read it, Dr. Francis? It's really lovely. Believe it or not, I'm anxious to show Poe in his best light. I'll feel reassured if you'd go over the entire piece for me. I would not wish deliberately to fall into error. Here is the ending. Then you might look over the proof sheets when Horace is through with them."

The two men regarded one another. Dr. Francis bobbed a little bow at the Reverend Dr. Griswold and took the sheets offered him.

On top was the poem he had fetched from Griswold's rooms. Poe's own, familiar, copperplate hand. Untitled. *It was many and many a year ago,/In this kingdom by the sea* . . . Nice beginning. He would read that later. And what was this? Griswold must have unearthed the telegraphed notice of Poe's death from the debris of Greeley's nightly literary battleground, but it was pretty uninformative. *We have not learned of the circumstances of his death. It was sudden, and from the fact that it occurred in Baltimore, it is presumed that he was on his return to New York.* "After life's fitful fever he sleeps well." Fair enough, and not an unpleasant ending sentiment.

It was getting late. Dr. Francis was hungry, and he would find beef and brandy at home as easily as at Delmonico's. He considered pushing Griswold no further, but then an underlined sentence leaped off an earlier page. *As a critic, Mr. Poe was little better than a carping grammarian. As a poet* . . . Damn and double damn. No telling what else Griswold had written.

He might as well learn the worst. He picked up the proof sheets the publisher had finished editing and reclined once more on the leather couch. He shuffled the pages, passing rapidly over Poe's early life. He couldn't vouch personally for any of that. Where did the stuff about Poe in New York begin? Yes, here, this was the place:

Near the end of 1844, Poe removed to New York, where . . .

Book I

NEW YORK

. . . but this
Is a world of sweets and sours;
Our flowers are merely—flowers . . .
                    Israfel

1

Bells ringing and two great, flickering columns of pale fire pouring from its flues, the steam ferry shot across the bows of a huge Indiaman making majestically for the open sea, and a fat man at the railing beside Poe gasped and closed his eyes. Amboy, Arthur Kill, Kill Van Kull—after the slow trip by train from Philadelphia to Amboy, they had made good time. It was not much past five o'clock on April 6, 1844, as the ferry neared journey's end. It was a raw, shivery day. It was raining heavily, but despite the rain most of the passengers had rushed up to the hurricane deck, there to swat at clouds of early New Jersey mosquitoes and gawk as the ferry wallowed relentlessly onward to plunge through a flotilla of anchored clippers and join the steamboats and steamships, barges and canal boats, sailing vessels and local ferries, all busy as insects, that comprised the customary traffic of New York harbor.

Poe, sharing with Virginia his old West Point greatcoat, pulled its folds tighter around her plump shoulders and studied the rapidly nearing cityscape. From the harbor, New York merged with the sea. A jungle of bowsprits and masts threatened the bulging warehouses that everywhere lined the docks, and the city's smells and sounds rushed out to meet them: the usual mephitis of molasses, spices, roasting coffee, evil-smelling drugs, garbage, reeking slips; the usual bedlam of steamboat bells ringing and longshoremen shouting and dogs barking and iron cartwheels crashing against the cobblestones. Clots of immigrants, huddled on the docks beside boxes and ragged bundles tied with rope, added shrill cries in German, Swedish and English to the din. They looked emaciated from dysentery and seasickness. They looked stunned. They looked upon the city with a heady combination of excitement and fear.

Near Poe and Virginia, on the other side of the fat man, was a younger man with that dashing, casual air that made Westerners unmistakable. Staring at the immigrants, he drawled under his breath, "My God, the poor creatures." Then he saw that Virginia had heard him, and he raised his hat. "I beg your pardon."

"Why 'poor creatures'?" she said. She glanced up at Poe. "They've come to make their fortunes. And perhaps they will."

The Westerner said, "Then I wish them luck." He eyed Virginia admiringly. It was her own fault, of course, for replying to him, but Virginia habitually drew admiring glances anyway. Although always smaller in person and younger looking than her real age, Virginia had a round, full figure and face, with a little, pouting mouth and a big, merry eye. Her hair was raven-black, contrasting startlingly with her white complexion, and she impressed observers as sweet, smiling, simple and shy. Her voice was as soft and appealing as her person—small, lisping, childlike—and it obviously struck the Westerner as charming. He looked more than ready to continue the conversation and Poe began to frown, but there was a heavy thump and both the dashing Westerner and the timid fat man gasped loudly. The ferry had docked. A handful of roustabouts with burlap sacking thrown over their heads scurried through the rain to secure the lines thrown them by the ferrymen. Poe turned his young wife toward the lower deck and the ladies' salon.

"There's nothing more to see here," Poe said to her. He had to raise his voice to be heard over the screaming of a sullen flock of herring gulls that wheeled overhead. "You'll start coughing if you stay out in this wet."

She hung back. "Let me come with you," she said. "I can help you look for a boarding house."

Poe shook his head and hurried her along. Two black-dressed women peering out at the rain made way for Virginia at the door of the cabin but looked disapprovingly at the black-dressed Poe as he started in after her. The women rustled through a curtained alcove into the inner sanctum. Virginia laughed softly.

"At least you'll have company," Poe said. "Just stay right here and keep an eye on the trunks, and I'll be back for you directly."

"Give me my medicine, Eddy."

"Do you need it right now?"

"Well, Muddy said to take it just in case."

He looked at her eyes, deep blue, violet in certain lights. The pupils were slightly contracted. The medicine bottle in the pocket of Poe's seedy, black flair-tail coat proclaimed itself to be Dr. Merrill's Patented Bronchial Deactivator. For the past several weeks Virginia's mother had sworn by it, but any chemist could have mixed the same formula for a quarter of the cost. Opium, oil of wintergreen, a touch of quicklime, 60 per cent alcohol—a standard medication, except for the quicklime, but a strong one. Poe was dubious about Virginia's taking another dose so quickly, and as she sipped, delicately but straight from the bottle, his face lost the faint smile that it usually wore when he looked at her. "I'll buy an umbrella," he said. "There's nothing to worry about. I won't let you get wet."

"You mustn't waste the money," she said.

"Don't worry about the money. Don't worry about anything."

"I'm not a bit worried," she said. "Everything is going to be just lovely." Her sweet, rounded face was calmer now. Her breathing, too, was calm and regular. "Do hurry back," she said. "I'm hungry. It'll be time for supper soon. Find a place with something good for supper. If it isn't too expensive. Find oysters, they're cheap. Or find bread and butter. You can't go wrong with bread and butter."

"I'll certainly try to do better than that," Poe said. He went out into the rain, jamming the old military cap that matched the cloak more firmly onto his head. The fat man had already rushed down to the dock, but the Westerner, Poe saw, still lingered hesitantly in the eddies of disembarking passengers. The two men nodded at one another.

"Nasty day," said the Westerner.

"Yes, isn't it," said Poe.

"Is your sister not getting off?"

"No, I'll come back for her when I've chosen our lodgings," Poe said. It was a common mistake, and he didn't bother correcting it. Virginia was his first cousin, and they shared certain family traits: the same dark, curly hair, the same unusually high, broad forehead. At least the man hadn't said "daughter." That mistake had been made too, not only when Poe first married her—Virginia then being thirteen but looking even younger, Poe being an aging "youth" of twenty-seven—but even more recently. Virginia still looked like a very young girl, not a grown woman of twenty-two, and Poe, to his dismay, had lately begun to look even older than his thirty-five years.

The Westerner said to Poe with the air of a man making a confession, "I'm not quite sure where to go myself. Friends in Philadelphia told me to try the Astor House. But it's a pretty old place, isn't it?"

"Not very, I believe. And I believe it's still regarded as New York's finest," Poe said.

"Then it's in a good part of town?" The man chuckled, a little shamefacedly, and gestured with his cane. "Sword stick," he said. "I got it in Philadelphia. I thought we had plenty of rowdies out where I come from, but they tell me there's someone waiting to murder you here on every street corner. They said to watch out for press gangs too. Maybe you didn't know, there's some kind of election Tuesday. They say the gangs roam the streets and grab strangers and drag them from poll to poll to vote when election day comes around. Do you suppose that's true?"

"Well, it's not too unusual in any large city on the seaboard," Poe said. "But you should be safe enough. Just use a little care in going about the city."

They reached the splintered wooden planks of the wharfs. Foot traffic and noise tugged at them like a heavy current. Poe's hearing had always been overly sensitive, and he winced as a placard-bearing man rushed past them shouting, "Palace steamboats to the West!" Among the milling crowds, other touters competed:

"Cheap hacks!"

"One million acres of superior farming lands!"

"Come to the cheapest hotel in all New York!"

A land agent shoved his way to them, quickly assessing their clothing, and pulled a set of handbills from his flapping waistcoat. "Speak English?" he bawled. "You're English, right? Here's an opportunity you won't want to miss. Palermo, Missouri, it's building right this minute on the beautiful banks of the Gasconade River and the great Mississippi."

"Get along with you," the Westerner said. "I never even heard of a town by that name. Besides, the Gasconade runs into the Missouri, not the Mississippi."

"How would you know?" the agent cried indignantly. "Why, Palermo looks forward to a great commercial future as a river town! And it's got an inexhaustible coal mine that will make it one of the greatest places for steam works on the whole river!"

A drenched Irish family with a litter of weeping, red-haired children moved closer, listening, and the land agent veered away to them. A surge of drays, wagons and carriages rattled past, each wheel equipped with an iron hoop to grate against the uneven cobbles. A clutter of longshoremen cut between Poe and the Westerner with antlike determination, wrestling bales and barrels toward the street, and brief panic flooded the Westerner's face. He fought his way back to Poe. "Listen, why don't we go someplace quiet and have a drink?" he said. "You'd be doing me a considerable favor."

"I wish I could," Poe said, "but I must see to getting us settled."

"You're not planning to *live* here, are you?"

Poe smiled suddenly. "Yes."

"Good God," the Westerner said. Then another wave of traffic thundered by, and Poe could not catch what else he said. A hotel stage turned the corner by Battery Place, and Poe saw the name Astor House on its side. He directed his companion's attention to it.

"What?" the Westerner shouted. Poe turned the man by the elbow and pointed. "Oh," the man said. "Oh, yes. Many thanks. Well, I hope you enjoy your stay here, but if you change your mind and decide to come West instead, come to St. Louis. And be sure to look me up. Thaddeus K. Perley's the name. Here, here's my card."

"Edgar Poe, at your service."

"What?"

"Edgar A. Poe," Poe shouted.

The crowd cut them off. "Pleasure to meet you, Poe," the Westerner called.

Poe waved. The breach between them widened. The Westerner hesitated a moment, then gripped his cane and struck out stoutly for the stage. Poe also hesitated, reluctant to commit himself to the city. He wished the man had recognized his name. But, then, so few people did, unless they were members of the interlocking circles of critics, professional magazinists and writers such as himself. Or such as he would like to be considered. The literary circles were closed circles, self-serving, difficult of access. But that's why he was here. To mount a siege against New York's walls.

Alone now, alone as always, Poe straightened his shoulders, which were already military-straight, and plunged into the street. Bread and butter or a shilling's worth of oysters for Virginia's supper. There he would begin.

2

By the spring of 1844, the narrow, muddy streets of New York had proved a greater lure than the fenceless frontiers for a swelling population of four hundred thousand souls—ragged children sent off to work twelve-hour shifts at shoe factories for a salary of eleven cents a day, dandified but desperate roughs who infested the lower part of town, phlegmatic Germans who crowded into windowless back rooms rented for four dollars a month, unruly Irish immigrants, fashionable ladies in crinolines, merchants in tight tail coats and an assortment of flotsam that the rest of the nation claimed could be recognized anywhere as citizens of New York by the fact that they all wore goatees, smoked nasty seegars and read the *Tribune*.

By the spring of 1844, the consumption of alcohol was beginning to go down, thanks to the temperance movement, and, some thought for the same reason, the prevalence of ether sniffing and opium chewing was going up; women were boldly beginning to demand "rights" that both the Bible and the state denied they possessed; the rappers, with their leaping tables and floating tambourines, were learning how to communicate with the spirit world; politicians were predicting war with a jealous England if the nation was fool enough to annex Texas; angry men in the South were beginning to speak more frequently of secession; and hotheads in the North were contemplating their own promising plans for secession, such as controlling the workers by confining suffrage to the owners of at least five thousand dollars' worth of property, kicking out the mayor and council, declaring New York and Brooklyn a free port, annexing the adjoining counties of Kings and Westchester and becoming an independent principality.

By the spring of 1844, Edgar Poe was a thirty-five-year-old pauper adrift on the streets of New York, with run-down boots, a rip in his trousers and $11.82 in his pocket—his reward for a lifetime of desperately hard work, during which he had produced three small volumes of poetry and one of collected tales; he had written enough additional tales to fill four more big volumes, if he could only persuade some publisher to publish them; he had guided three highly successful magazines to their success; and he had written enough literary articles, reviews and critical essays to earn the admiration of every man of genius and the enmity of every untalented hack in every literary center in America.

As far as these literary centers went, Poe was hated in Boston, thanks to his outspoken belief that all talent and genius did not reside exclusively in New England. He was *persona non grata* in his boyhood home, Richmond, where he had raised the circulation of the *Southern Literary Messenger* from seven hundred to over five thousand—considered astonishing for the place and the times before he fell out with the owner over wine, women and literary standards. And as of yesterday, he was also quits with Philadelphia, where the same pattern basically repeated itself, but on a slightly larger scale. There, he again boosted circulations on his last publication, *Graham's Lady's and Gentleman's Magazine*, from five thousand on its subscription list when Poe assumed his editorial chair to fifty thousand, the largest in the world, when Poe left it. Again he dipped his critical pen in prussic acid as often as ink and accumulated new enemies as a consequence. Again he became notorious as a drinker. Again he fell out with the owner.

So that left to Poe this little island of Manhattan, and although Poe knew that because of past literary feuds he could not expect a uniformly warm welcome here, it was his last remaining hope. Here he had to make his mark. That the city was potentially hostile bothered him far less than the fact that it did not recognize him at all, and, hopping from cobblestone to cobblestone, avoiding the puddles as best he could, he bitterly envied those comfortable souls who passed him in carriages, splashing mud with democratic vigor upon Poe, upon a ragged little girl selling songs and upon a half-dozen roughs rushing into Battery Park, where shouting and cursing could suddenly be heard.

It was the city's usual election fever. A mayor was to be chosen the following week, and marches, meetings and mayhem were progressing at their customary rate. Poe turned up Greenwich Street to avoid what sounded like a scuttle, and he grimaced absently to himself when, with his broken boots, he was forced to wade through a slimy, yard-wide swamp to the curbing. But now that his boots were wet he could ignore other puddles. His mind busied itself with rapidly shifting impressions of the city and with rapidly shifting thoughts—with concern for money, with worry about Virginia and with pondering Thaddeus K. Perley of St. Louis and his hearty advice to go West.

Go West instead of East. Go to new country and new hopes instead of old. Every man thinks and wonders. But Poe was thirty-five. Thirty-five, and any man, particularly a poet, had not much youth left. Perhaps not even much time left. Thirty-five, and pounding at the gate of last hope. He who enters here and fails winds up in the refuse pile. That one by the curbing, for instance. Coal ashes. Poe could also make out beet tops and cabbage leaves.

But he would soon be writing again. He had to. He also had to watch for boarding-house signs. None here. DRUGS & DYES . . . HAVANA SEGARS . . . Gray and white speckled pigeons huddled under an eave. Even with the traffic sounds he could hear them cooing. Feathered weather vanes. Pigeons always cooed when it was going to rain.

The trouble was, a poem was bothering him. Not one that sang its way into his head with urgent, rhythmical excitement, but an old poem, nagging, nostalgia for a love song gone sour. Virginia's mother —Muddy, they always called her—wouldn't like that. Poe wasn't good with money and he knew it, and if he hadn't known it, Muddy would have reminded him. But he knew that if a man had to earn his living by his pen, poems didn't pay well enough. Especially not when you considered the months or years of work that often went into them. Only the Longfellows of the world could get as much as fifty dollars a poem, and they couldn't get it always. For the rest, it was only a few dollars paid whenever the magazine got around to it, six months after publication sometimes, and often no offer of pay at all, for behind every bush was some silly rhymester with literary aspirations for whom the joy of seeing his work in print was payment aplenty.

No, forget about poems. Write articles and tales. Once a writer's name was worth anything at all, he could count on at least two to three dollars per printed page for an article, and a three-page article would give them roof and food for a week.

He passed a butcher shop and paused. Food. Dressed pheasants and ducks in a little square-paned window. God knew, they needed money desperately. The last months in Philadelphia had been very bad. Whatever he and Muddy could muster in the way of delicacies and comfort had always gone first to Virginia, especially since she had become ill, but lately there had been too little even of rough, plain fare. This was not a good moment for poetry or dreaming. Nor was it a good place for it. Lower Greenwich at one time was a fashionable street, and the comfortable brick houses of many merchants still graced it, but an aura of change was all too evident to Poe's nostrils. The gutters were ankle-deep in mire and garbage so foul that it had been rejected by the city's vagrant pigs. A portly pair of these four-legged citizens brushed past him, trotting to inspect a decayed tea chest that leaned drunkenly into the gutter, but the chest contained only more ashes and the pigs trotted on.

Poe, too, was in search of provender, he reminded himself, and farther up Greenwich, almost to Cedar Street, he spotted an enclave of elderly dwellings that kept their sidewalks reasonably clean. He stopped in the rain to study one old house with a "Boarders Wanted" card in the window and the name Morrison on the door.

It was a plain, three-storied brick house, with brownstone steps and a porch with brown pillars. As he inspected it, a woman and a little girl, boarders he assumed, came out and hurried toward the corner, where a balloon vendor had taken refuge from the rain under the awning of a store. The little girl frowned with determination as she ran.

Another vendor, this one of umbrellas, safe from the rain under one of his own samples, came by on the opposite side of the street. Poe thought of the $11.82 that was his fortune, but he also thought of Virginia waiting for him back at the ferry. He crossed the street and bartered briskly, returning with a black, second-hand umbrella for sixty-two cents and, for nothing, the information that Morrison's was a good, cheap house.

The woman with the little girl had looked respectable. Poe went in. Although the foyer was shabby, he was further reassured by the appearance of a tidy Irish serving girl and, as he waited for the landlady, the two middle-aged clerks who entered quietly and went immediately upstairs. They looked adequately dressed and, better yet, well fed; New York landladies were notorious for feeding well in October, when the city began filling up after the summer exodus, but less and less well as the boarding-house year rolled toward May, when people started leaving again.

And yes, the landlady, Mrs. Morrison, had rooms. Only in the garret, the rest of the house was already taken up by eight or ten boarders, several of them ladies, he had to understand. But, then, the garret rooms were comfortable. Would he care to look?

Poe followed her up two flights of carpeted stairs and a short flight that was bare wood. He glanced about him. The room was small. Just a bed, a table that would do for writing, several chairs, a coal stove, a slop tub and a huge wardrobe. Although there was hardly space enough left to move around, there was also an old, soft red carpet on the floor and cheerful red curtains on the front and back windows. Poe was partial to red. The price wasn't as good as he had hoped, but he could cover it: seven dollars a week for the pair of them, boots and laundry thrown in.

The money went quickly, but so did the time, and he did not dare leave Virginia alone for long. He paid Mrs. Morrison a week in advance and walked quickly back to the Camden and Amboy Railway Company pier, where he again stopped and bargained, this time for a hack, before collecting Virginia and their trunks. The whip stuck at fifty cents because of the trunks, and Poe had to accept it. New York, he was already finding, was an expensive city to live in.

The whip followed the North River to take them home, past the piers of the great European steamship lines, past those of the coast steamers and the steamboats plying between the city and the neighboring towns, and Virginia leaned from one side of the hack to the other, as if uncertain whether to stare at the busy river or at the glimpses of the city afforded by the side streets. While Five Points and Water Street boasted the worst hells of the city, all the streets near rivers, in order to attract sailors, had their share of dance houses and sailors' boarding houses, with the usual entourage of runners and ropers-in and women who populated such places. Virginia peeped at the women with fascination, while Poe prosaically occupied himself only with worrying whether she and, more to the point, Muddy, would like the house he had chosen.

Their garret room was not yet dusted and ready when he arrived at Number 130 Greenwich Street with Virginia, but the landlady's husband helped Poe bring in the trunks, and a fragrant odor of teacakes greeted them as he ushered Virginia into the dark foyer. Virginia, following her nose, ran to the door of the dining room and slid it open a crack. "Oh!" she said. "Oh, Eddy, come see!"

"We're to wait in the parlor, Virginia," Poe said.

She came away from the dining room reluctantly. "But there's a mountain of ham, and another of veal, and cheese and two kinds of bread—" Suddenly, she started coughing, a deep, tearing cough that turned her white face gray.

"Oh my!" clucked the landlord, a beslippered, good-natured old fellow. "Oh my, she's fair choked herself with drooling, poor little thing."

"It's all right," Poe said quickly. He pressed his handkerchief into Virginia's hand and turned her shoulders slightly away from Mr. Morrison. "She's had a bad cold, but she's getting over it now."

Mrs. Morrison, flour on the front of an apron she was hastily removing, appeared in the door from the kitchen. "Is she sick?" she said sharply. "We don't keep sick people here."

Virginia threw Poe a look full of dread, but she was coughing too hard to speak. Poe said, "No, it's nothing. A touch of bronchitis after a cold." He groped in Virginia's reticule. "Here, Sissy. Here's your bronchitis medicine."

She waved it away helplessly with one hand, tears streaming from her eyes, still coughing into the handkerchief. Poe's own pale face paled still further. He watched apprehensively for what he feared: blood, cherry-red arterial blood flooding out onto the handkerchief. But there was no blood, and soon the coughing spasm ebbed. Virginia reached blindly for the medicine bottle and took a deep swallow.

"Are you sure it's just the bronchitis?" the landlady said.

Virginia was able to answer for herself. "I get it every winter," she said in a choked, apprehensive voice. "Ah, that's better. No, no more medicine, Eddy. It makes me sleepy, and I want my supper. I'll be just fine now, Mrs. Morrison. Really and truly."

"The bronchitis," the landlady said, still suspiciously. "Well, if it's just the bronchitis . . ."

"I always get over it when the weather warms up," Virginia said timidly.

Mr. Morrison said, "Best buy a penny pan to set on the stove tonight. It helps the bronchitis no end if you keep vapor in the room."

"Vapor? Nonsense," said Mrs. Morrison. She sniffed like an intelligent dog in the direction of her kitchen and added hurriedly, "A turpentine and lard plaster applied to the chest, that's the thing. Be sure to cover it with a square of red flannel, Mrs. Poe. There's nothing like red flannel for a plaster. Mr. Morrison, fetch up the rag bag.

I'll attend to the plaster right after tea." She went back to her baking.

When the door of the kitchen closed, Mr. Morrison said softly, "Poor little thing, she's in consumption, isn't she? That chalky complexion. You can always tell. My own little mother died of consumption."

"As did mine," Poe said. "But my wife is not in consumption, I assure you."

"And don't I know?" Mr. Morrison said. "My own little father, now, he died of a carbuncle. There are those as think both are catching, but I'm fifty-seven years old and I'd have long been dead if they was catching, now wouldn't I? Just try not to let the poor little thing cough too much, and Mrs. Morrison will never know. Now, into the parlor with you. But watch out for the canary. He's loose. Mrs. Morrison thinks he's got to have his exercise every day. I'll just find the rag bag. Down in the cellar, I expect. Wouldn't you know she'd send me down to the cellar, and me with the rheumatiz? Doesn't that just make you chuckle?"

He puttered off down the back hall. "Are you all right?" Poe asked Virginia in a low voice.

"Oh yes. Oh, Eddy, they won't throw us out, will they?"

"Of course not," he said. He eyed the medicine bottle. There was almost three fourths of the bottle left, but soon, he saw, he would have to find the money to buy more.

"That horrid old man," Virginia whispered. "Why do people say things like that? Just wait until Muddy gets here. She'll tell him it's only the bronchitis, won't she?"

"Of course she will."

But their eyes met, and in them there was knowledge. Virginia looked away first, and she swallowed and said quickly, "When you go out to buy the pan, get two buttons and a skein of thread. I'll mend your trousers tomorrow."

"Yes, fine," he said. He looked away also.

Virginia yawned. "I suppose I must have a skein of silk and a skein of cotton too. Can we afford them both?"

"Of course," he said, but he counted mentally. How much was thread? The silk would be expensive, maybe two pennies, maybe even more. But he must not reveal to Virginia that they were only a hair from starvation. He led her into the parlor. It was warm and smelled of geraniums and would have been comfortable, except for the canary, which was very loud. So much trilling din from such a tiny bird. The canary paid them no attention at all, but, between bursts of warbling, flew busily about the room. Poe's eyes followed it as it perched on a velvet chair here, on the window there, next above the door. One bullet and a fowling piece, and, bird, farewell. He was a good shot. He used to teach the smaller boys to shoot, out in the fields and woods beyond the cemetery. That time they'd practiced on Judge Bushrod Washington's domestic fowls, got carried away. So much blood. No, forget the blood. Pa caning him endlessly for killing the birds. No, forget the canings. Don't look toward Virginia, watch the canary. Her big, dark eyes so dark with fear and . . . guilt? She knew her sieges of illness maddened him. But it was not her fault. No, forget it all, forget it all, forget it all.

To Poe's relief, another of the Irish help soon appeared and announced that their room was ready, and shortly afterward Mrs. Morrison, flushed from her baking, climbed the stairs to ask if they were settled in comfortably and to say that tea would be served immediately. The medicine had done its work. Virginia coughed very little in the dining room, and, urged by Mrs. Morrison, she filled her plate once, twice, then a third time. Later, when Poe got back to their room with the water pan and the other small purchases, the level of the medicine bottle was lower, the room smelled of turpentine and Virginia was sleeping soundly.

Wearily, he pulled off his wet boots and set them near the stove. Maybe they would be dry by tomorrow. He unhooked the chain of the small leather purse tucked in his waistcoat and carefully counted the big Mexican pesos and the assorted pennies and five-penny pieces that, if one's assets were too small to be measured by bank notes, were a standard currency of an age that had not yet decided whether to reckon in shillings, "bits" or quarter-dollars. There was rain on the roof and $4.53 left in the palm of his hand. Tomorrow was Sunday. There was no way to start looking for a job on Sunday. But he could start making preliminary inquiries, and there would be time to write something. It would be enough. It had to be enough.

3

The New Yorker habitually tore down his city and rebuilt it every ten years or so, which accounted for the ever present litter of brickbats, rafters and slates that helped make traversing the sidewalks such a hazard, and also helped account for the city's galvanic feeling of constant change. The New Yorker changed his customs too, but in 1844 the majority of the citizenry still dined two hours early on Sunday afternoons, at one o'clock instead of three, to allow their servants that one afternoon off in honor of the Sabbath. After dinner, the New Yorker thought of recreation. If the weather was fair, the working classes rushed to the ferries and went to Hoboken to commune with wild flowers in season and gin from convenient rustic taverns in all seasons, returning reluctantly only in time for the night church services. The fashionable promenaded Broadway, which, on this one day of the week, was so empty of the dense and rapidly moving mass of men, animals, omnibuses, carriages and carts which usually thronged it that one could actually make an audible answer to "How do you do?" without having to draw one's friend into a side street or shop to speak to him. Toward three o'clock, the church bells rang out hopefully for afternoon services, but few people answered the summons. The New Yorker grudged even the few hours in the morning and again at night that decency required him to pass in church.

At three o'clock, then, on the day after Poe arrived in New York, church bells were tolling unavailingly and, the rain clouds having cleared, the entire length of Broadway, from the Battery Park to the Union Square, was afloat with strollers as Poe paced by the Croton Fountain, waiting for an old friend he hoped to meet there. He had spent the morning working, with a few minutes out to leave a note for his friend J. Augustus Shea. Although he was glad to have the present break and the prospect of an hour's fresh air, he knew he soon had to get back to Virginia and his writing table.

Yet there were compensations in his temporary state of idleness: here came brown eyes and light brown curls peeping from a mauve glacé silk bonnet; there, in blue-black silk poplin, went glossy black hair and a wistful face, a face that reminded him fleetingly of the first love of his young manhood. Elmira. A young, adoring girl, and

Richmond, and a walled rose garden. The fragrance of white violets and honeysuckle, and Richmond, and dreams of love and poetry. The yellow river, and Richmond. The red brick mansions, and Richmond. The tobacco-dusty air, and the only real home he had ever known: Richmond.

First for Poe, almost remembered, there had been a doll-like mother with a childlike figure and great, wide eyes, a strolling player, dying of consumption on a straw mattress in an upstairs room of Richmond's old Washington Tavern under the bewildered eyes of a two-year-old boy. Then there was a hired hack rattling over the cobbled streets of that Virginia city bearing another woman, this one doting and childless, and, on her lap, the pretty little boy, already suffused with a feeling of loneliness that would follow him to his grave. Then, at the other end of the short ride, a charitable resident of the city, John Allan, opened wide the door of his house.

John Allan—Jock, they called him in Richmond—was a merchant and proud of it, and a Scot and even prouder of that. He put a price tag on everything, including love, and his Scottish frugality and foresight kept him from ever opening fully his purse or his heart. For the next sixteen years, Poe matured under the stunting dominance of John Allan's stubborn will. Young Edgar was carefully schooled, but there was time enough away from lessons for him to serve in the warehouse and behind the dry goods counter once in a while. To run occasional errands for the store. To be coddled and slipped pocket money by ailing "Ma" and her plump sister. To be caned judiciously by "Pa" when he was unruly, which he was from time to time, for Poe had a will of his own. To scribble on the store paper: *Last night with many cares and toils oppress'd/ Weary I laid me on a couch to rest*— To watch the sheet picked up by a thrifty hand that turned it upside down to put it to more momentous use: "Cash in chest— about $1000. Bank share—$6120. May collect in 60 days—$1375.48."

For a while, John Allan called the handsome youngster "Edgar Allan," for he was thinking about legally adopting him. Then Poe went by "Edgar Allan Poe," for John Allan never followed through with the adoption idea. By and by John Allan was calling him "Ungrateful." Then—John Allan never ceased reminding the willful young devil that he ate the bread of charity—it became "Ungrateful Villain," and finally "Black-Heart," with an ultimatum: no more idling around the house scribbling poetry, no return to the university with a literary career in view, but home study and eventually the law. Self-prophecies of future greatness as a poet were as disgusting as the gambling debts he had brought home from his one year at the university, disgusting and disgraceful, that's what. John Allan had a lame foot, and his black cane pounded on the floor and his black eyebrows frowned in his dour hawk's face, and young Edgar Allan Black-Heart flung out of the house with nothing but the clothes on his back. The door of the house slammed behind him. Teary Ma smuggled money. Proud Edgar left the mansions, the river, the air heavy with the syrupy fragrance of Virginia leaf and went into exile, working his way north on a coal ship under another, self-chosen name: Henri Le Rennét. Henry the Reborn.

It was the first of many restless journeys for Poe and, from time to time, of assumed names. For this rebirth he chose the first name of his much-admired but scarcely known older brother, Henry Poe. He chose the city of his actual birth, Boston. There, the childlike mother with the huge eyes had played Cordelia in *King Lear* while carrying the child for whom she later drew a little sketch of Boston Harbor that he would treasure all his life. Before she died, vomiting blood, she inscribed it on the back, "For my little son Edgar, who should ever love Boston, the place of his birth, and where his mother found her best and most sympathetic friends."

The eighteen-year-old exile succeeded in finding not sympathetic friends but a printer for his first volume of verse, which, bitterly, he signed only, "By a Bostonian." It sold, when it sold, for twelve and a half cents a volume. Soon poverty and a complete lack of critical notice drove him from the cold and careless arms of art to the first of many brief ventures into other occupations, this time as a clerk. Then reporter on a Boston newspaper? Next fledgling actor? Lithographer, printer, bricklayer? He never cared to talk of all the odd jobs he took to earn a few shillings. After being starved out of chilly Boston, he entered the U. S. Army as Private Edgar A. Perry, but he didn't like to admit that either. Instead, he told adventurous stories of his having spent those years in European travel.

Poe next tried West Point. A future General Edgar A. Poe was forever lost to the world when, despairing of a reconciliation with John Allan, he mounted a campaign to get himself expelled. He had then contemplated becoming a soldier of fortune and joining the Polish

Army, but failed to follow through, just as he tried unsuccessfully for a schoolmastering post, and hopefully pursued a will-o'-the-wisp that would have seen him landing a government sinecure and starting his own magazine with the leisure and financial security it would have afforded him. Once, shades of John Allan, he even desultorily studied law a few months. Between and through it all he wrote. Through joy and through sorrow, he wrote. Through hunger and through thirst, he wrote. Through good report and ill report, he wrote. Through sunshine and through moonshine, he wrote. Tales of terror carefully crafted to please prevailing taste, romances, satires, poetry, one try at a book-length adventure story, a hack job on conchology—whether the subject matter came from within or grew out of the necessity to earn his bread, always he wrote.

Today, Poe had been writing hard not on some black tale but on a hoax. The world had rarely awarded much applause to his attempts at humor, but he himself thought highly of them and enjoyed writing them. At least he usually managed to place them for a few dollars. The friend for whom he was waiting, he hoped, would help him place this one once he got it polished to his satisfaction. Poe felt at ease and almost optimistic, on that sunny Sabbath in April, as he sighed after a lithe phantom in blue-black silk poplin floating away from him. He made a mental note of the fact that her skirt was trimmed all around with scarlet velvet. Charming. He would mention it to Virginia and her mother. Muddy had once supported herself by dressmaking, with Virginia as her helper, and Muddy retained the interest of the professional. Poor old Muddy. Poe had had to leave her behind in Philadelphia with the cat and the parrot and the last of their household possessions to sell or pawn for whatever she could get. There hadn't been enough money to bring her with them to New York. But she would come soon. She lived with them, and always had. He would send for her as soon as he could find work or sell an article.

Only God and their dressmakers knew the investment these slowly strolling New York women represented. A ball dress would feed Poe for a year. An entire wardrobe, and he could take Virginia on a long sea voyage, which some thought might benefit the lungs, and have enough left over to support a comfortable household for a few decades. But Poe enjoyed the view and was smiling over a slender little thing, surely not more than sixteen, who had rushed the season in white Swiss muslin, when his friend came rushing up to him, hallooing and puffing, like a ship pushing against a heavy wind.

"Poe!" Shea exclaimed. "When did you get here? How long have you been here? Why didn't you wait until I got out of church? Why . . . ?" But he had run out of why's, and the two men wrung one another's hands heartily.

Augustus Shea was an old friend from Poe's brief tenure at West Point, where Shea had run the commissary. Older than Poe, Shea now wrote poetry with small success and fancied himself something of a literary influence, with larger success, supporting himself meanwhile with the law. Freckled, sandy-haired, portly and robust, he looked like an Anglo-Saxon Napoleon, or perhaps a pirate. Fierce, friendly eyes peered out under freckled eyelids at Poe. "I'm late," Shea proclaimed. "Sorry, Poe, but I stopped to glance at the reconstruction work they're doing on Trinity Church. Do you know that the vestry has voted to complete the tower at once? Put on the spire? They're going to use a steam engine to raise the stone. But how are you? How is that delightful little wife? Better?"

"Not yet," Poe said. "Sometimes it seems that she's getting a little better, and then she has another attack. Dr. Mitchell, of Philadelphia, says she has the bronchitis."

"Ah!" Shea said shrewdly. "You should move her out to the country, my young friend. Move her to a farm. Have her take the breath of the cows at milking time. There's nothing better for chest complaints. Some say goat's whey, of course, but cow's breath and country air are a sure cure."

"It's something to consider," Poe murmured.

Shea peered at him, then took out his purse. "Meanwhile, I assume you're a little short of funds," he said.

Poe's gray eyes widened, startled, then he laughed. "Well, of course I'm short, but that's not the reason I called on you."

"Touchy, touchy," Shea said. "You haven't changed a bit. But don't be a fool, my boy. Five dollars? More?"

"Give me three," Poe said. "With what I have, that will keep me going for a fortnight. I promise you, I'll pay it back. My luck must be changing—being offered a loan, instead of having to ask someone for it."

"Don't give it a thought," Shea said. "By God, Poe, it's grand to see you. How long are you going to be in New York?"

"Permanently—with any luck at all."

"Ah," Shea said, again shrewdly. He looked around. People were staring at them as the money changed hands, but then people always stared at Poe, without being sure just why. A well-knit, well-formed body of medium height, held with military erectness. Nothing too unusual there. The clothing, that was a bit more out-of-the-way. Except for Poe's white linen, he habitually wore black, black meticulously neat but slightly frayed, black from his black ascot to the black broadcloth pantaloons strapped under the boot. But it was Poe's face they really stared at. The mouth was sensitive, perhaps overly delicate, and the forehead was extremely high and broad in a head that was large, at first view almost too large for the frame. Regular features, though, and magnificent, dark gray eyes, large and luminous and utterly alive, even as he absently put Shea's money in his purse.

"Are you still such a fanatic for exercise?" Shea said. He gestured with his crooked-headed hickory cane. "We can walk. What will it be? The country or downtown?"

"The country," Poe said gratefully, and so they headed up Broadway.

Broadway's cobblestones turned to dirt when they got as far north as Fourteenth Street. There, the city's most important thoroughfare became a country road to the village of Bloomingdale, which lay six miles from town at what dreamers predicted would one day be a One-Hundredth Street. The entire island of Manhattan, even then, had been divided into future streets and would-be city lots that were only a greedy dream of land speculators and a crosshatch on the city planners' maps. The muddy wash of Bloomingdale Road already had a little straggle of north-reaching buildings, but these soon faded into shacks and shanties and lean-to's that only a newly arrived Irishman or a pig would live in. Then there was just the road and an occasional carriage or young man-about-town out putting his trotting horse through its paces in an area of rolling meadows and farms. Somewhere a mourning dove called. Poe listened eagerly. It was like cool, soothing oil poured on irritated eardrums, and his spirits rose in proportion to the distance he put between himself and the city. Eventually, however, Shea pleaded for a stop, and they walked only a few paces farther, out of the shade of old elms from which small new leaves still sprinkled droplets from yesterday's rainstorm. Shea led Poe to a fence in the pale sunshine, draped his handkerchief on the top rail and clambered up to arrange his portly bottom thereon. Poe leaned on the fence beside him.

"We must talk seriously," Shea said. "I must hear your plans."

Poe shrugged boyishly. "Oh, well, plans."

"Will you look for a new editorial post?"

"I'll look, naturally. I must."

Shea shook his head. "As I feared," he said. "I hate to tell you this, but the prospects aren't very bright. Oh, money is getting a little looser here. New York is finally struggling out of the doldrums of the Panic, and new journals have been starting up almost as often as they go broke. But there are twenty applicants for every chair even so. Besides, what about your hopes for your own magazine? Have you given that up?"

Poe was surprised. "Never," he said. "I must be my own master, Shea, and my own editor. My God, do you think I want to be a mere writer of stories all my life?"

"No, my boy, I thought you wanted to be a poet." Shea's voice was hushed as he pronounced the word that he considered holy.

Perhaps because Poe's parents had been of the theater, in him the actor was never far submerged beneath the critic, the writer, the man. In response to Shea's tone, Poe lifted his chin, fingered his broad ascot and struck a characteristic pose: "Poetry is my passion!" he declared ringingly. Then he relaxed, as he could only with an old friend, and added, "But really, Shea, there are some events that can't be controlled—events that have prevented me from making any serious effort as a poet. Under happier circumstances, poetry would of course have been the field of my choice."

"But your poetry could make you a famous man. Tell me the truth, Poe. Wouldn't you care for fame?"

Poe began to frown at the decaying mat of last year's leaves beneath his feet. "Fame?" he said slowly, like a man tasting the wine of the word. Then bitterly he repeated it. "Fame? I idolize it. I would drink fame to its very dregs. Call me a fool, Shea, but I'd like to have incense ascend in my honor from every hill and hamlet, from every town and city in this country. Fame? Glory? They would be life-giving breath, and living blood. Surely no man really lives, unless he is famous."

"Then set your cap for it. Let nothing stand in your way. God knows, I've never known a man more able. You should have been famous long before now."

Poe laughed grimly. "Yes, I am thirty-three years old," he said, ignoring the fact that he was, of course, thirty-five. "Think of it, thirty-three! And what do I have to show for it? A trunk full of manuscripts, and another bale or so rotting away in the desk drawers of editors who can't make up their minds whether to accept or reject. My God, to be twenty again. Remember back at the Point, Shea? Remember Room Number 28 in the old South Barracks? After taps, Tommy Gibson already snoring and old Locke snooping around to make sure we hadn't replenished the brandy bottle? And writing like a madman by the light of my last candle."

Shea nodded. "Your finest poems. You must never neglect your poetry, Poe."

"There *is* one poem. A long one. I've been thinking of dragging it back out again. Perhaps I could get it to come out right this time."

"That's my lad!" Shea said. Then the piratical look came back into his eyes, and he mused, "But you must simultaneously consider strategy. You're at a crucial step in your career now, my young friend. Strategy is all-important."

Poe watched the older man like an attentive schoolboy. A guilty look, like that of a schoolboy who has not been innocent of mischief, stole over his face.

"What do you mean?" he said.

"I mean now is no time for false steps," Shea said.

"Has someone been telling you tales about me?" Poe said cautiously.

Shea pursed his mouth. "No-o-o. Not directly. But one hears things. It's odd, but one seems to hear things every time your friend Rufus Griswold has been in town."

Poe grimaced and said, "No friend of mine."

"No, an enemy. Attend me now, Poe. I don't know the truth of the tales that have been circulating about you, but I know this for sure: there must be an end to them if you hope to make your way in New York."

"What kind of tales?" Poe demanded.

"Drinking," Shea said promptly. Poe looked away, but Shea persisted. "There was also talk of your leaving your family destitute.

Leaving your wife and her mother, in fact, while you went off to Saratoga with some woman."

Poe said nothing.

Shea said, "Well?"

"Such talk cannot be dignified with an answer," Poe said.

"There was no woman?"

"Not . . . not in any compromising sense. There may have been a friend, a kind friend, who . . . Dammit, Shea, I was ill for over a year. Seriously ill. And penniless, if you want to know the truth of it. If there was a kind friend with an establishment in Saratoga, a friend who kindly extended an invitation, an opportunity for rest and sun and a careful diet . . . ?"

"It's not an act of friendship to cause a man to forget his wife."

Poe shook his head wearily. "I can assure you, Shea, I have never for one hour, for one instant, forgotten my wife."

"Well then, there's the drinking," Shea went on more gently. But Poe looked so miserable that the older man slid off the fence and said, "Come, we can talk as we stroll back. I think the only point I need make is that, other friends aside, Rufe Griswold *is* no friend of yours. He's in New York frequently, you know. Oh yes, I know he's jobbing together books in Philadelphia as fast as he can scissor and glue other men's work, but his two little girls stayed here with relatives after his wife died, and he pops in and out to visit them. You might be interested to know that he's also been canvassing the town for an editorial job, looking for some way of settling in New York permanently. And he's been toadying Lewis Clark lately, Poe. They're thicker than thieves, and I fear Griswold has been tale-carrying. Please, please don't give him and Clark's clique anything new to whisper. You've irritated them, anyway. Too many adverse reviews. I shouldn't have to remind you that they can ruin an author they don't like as quickly as they can make the fortune of one they're in league with. If Clark can't do it by taking potshots at you in the *Knickerbocker*, they'll do it by nasty anonymous reviews. Or they have means that are even more underhanded. This story they've been whispering about Saratoga, now. Do you see what I mean? Clark and Griswold are two of a kind, the only difference being that Griswold's incapable of direct attack. But he'd be capable of anything behind your back."

"Then I must guard my back."

"Precisely. As for the rest of your strategy, if you're really serious about starting your magazine, Poe, it's essential that you make the right impression. You don't know New York. It's infected with the merchant mentality. If New Yorkers think you really need money, they'll never pony up the backing I assume you'll need to get the magazine under way."

"I know that much," Poe said worriedly. He hesitated, then, progressing pell-mell from worry to gloom, blurted out, "I'll never have the magazine, will I, Shea? It's always money. Why is it that in America, more than anywhere else in the world, to be poor is to be despised?"

"Now, now, my boy. Dreams can come true, if you help them on a bit."

"Not mine."

"Don't give way to pessimism. But you must also temper your flights of optimism, Poe, and fully consider all the facts. The problem of making the right impression applies both to obtaining eventual backing for your magazine and to obtaining a more immediate editorial chair to help out with the daily expenses. You know how it is: the good jobs are never offered to men who apply for them, but only to those who put up a good pretense of not wanting or needing them."

"That leaves my pen, then," Poe sighed. "I have a humorous piece just completed. Well, it's a hoax, actually. It occurred to me you might be willing to talk to one of the daily papers about taking it."

"Ah, it's of the popular type?"

Poe smiled wryly. "Yes, I hope so. I've cast it as an express news story about the successful crossing of the Atlantic by a steering balloon. I think the quidnuncs will find it most convincing."

"Prodigious!" Shea said. "It sounds perfect for the *Sun*. I have a great deal of influence there. I know there's no fame to be gained from the penny papers, but we might consider a useful little trick—since it's to be a hoax you must publish it anonymously, and then if it creates a big enough sensation we'll let the word get out that it was really Edgar Poe who wrote the story. That'll set the town to buzzing."

"I had hoped for something of the sort. It might work."

"Of course it will work. And I'll see to it that the *Sun* pays you adequately, you can rely on that. Meanwhile, I can look around for other bits of hack work for you to keep you going while you write the poem. The senior editor of the *Columbia Spy* in Pittsburgh is a good friend. He pays three dollars a column. Maybe I could do something for you there too."

"Mr. Bowen? Yes, I know him. And I can't say no. But the *Spy* is hardly more notable than the penny papers, Shea. There's no fame to be gained there."

"That's the point!" Shea said triumphantly. "Our strategy will be for you generally to lay low until you can burst into the public eye with a great head of steam. What about a new collection of your tales? Have you thought of trying to get one published?"

"Constantly," Poe said. "If I only had the money, I'd publish them myself. They demonstrate my variety as a magazinist as nothing else could."

"You know I have contacts in England," Shea said. "There'd probably be no money in it for you, but what would you say to a British collection?"

"I'd say yes, instantly. There seems more glory than money in collections anyway. Lea & Blanchard only gave me twenty copies as payment for my *Tales of the Grotesque and Arabesque*. Not what I'd call a princely profit."

"I tell you, my boy, if we build up our steam carefully, you'll have your damned magazine yet, and a suitable income at last. And then, Poe, ah, and then. And then without these daily cares that confront you, we'll see what kind of poetry you can really write! The poems, my boy! Everything for the poems! Try for something that will meet both critical and popular success. Why, you can write rings around any of the crew that people run after so. I know as sure as we're standing here that our children's children will look back to our time and say, 'This was the time of Poe.' Yet must your fame wait for our children's children? We must make the world awake and say, 'This *is* the time of Poe!' "

Poe gave himself over to the refreshing waves of his friend's enthusiasm. "Your advice seems very sound," he said. "I'm more than willing to try."

Across the road in front of them, a possum slowly ambled, and as slowly disappeared into a tangle of wild grapes, the fruits of which were only a spring's dream of harvest. Shea looked after it thoughtfully and added, "I'm serious about all this, Poe."

"So am I. I'll dig out the old manuscript of the poem I mentioned and start to work this very afternoon."

4

In back of Morrison's boarding house, two Sundays after, a few drunken Germans could be heard singing, and an ailing horse stabled under the open windows of the second garret room that Poe had rented for his mother-in-law went into heavy spasms of wheezing at regular intervals. Muddy smiled tolerantly and fended off the eager hugs of Virginia with manlike strength. The closest Poe had ever had to a real mother, Maria Clemm was also his aunt. Like Virginia, she resembled him, but in her case it was the same fine gray eyes and the same plumage: black, always tidy black, always well-worn black, but with an immaculate white collar and a white widow's cap that she was never seen without. She stooped and unfastened the lid of her big wicker basket, and out stepped a large, angry cat. Its tortoise-colored fur, usually sleek and smooth, was spiky, and it jumped immediately to the windowsill and looked down at the horse. Then the cat started to bathe.

"Oh, she's mad at us," Virginia said. "Did she hate the train?" She began to coax, "Catarina, Catarina, don't be mad. Catarina, won't you even say hello?"

"Leave her alone awhile," Poe said. "Wait until she decides to forgive us." He kissed his Aunt Maria's broad, homely face. She was a big woman, as tall as Poe, and he had to tilt his chin up to reach her cheek. "It's so late, Muddy. Was there trouble with the ferry connection? I waited on the docks all afternoon."

"I took the cars through Trenton, not Perth Amboy," Muddy said. "It's longer, but it was a dollar cheaper."

"But, Muddy, a dollar isn't important where your comfort is concerned."

"A whole dollar? A few more hours on the train were well worth it." She looked around the little room. A wooden bed. Two wooden chairs. A wardrobe and a dresser with a wavy mirror. "My, how nice," she said.

"I know the house looks buggy," Poe said defensively, "but it's really very clean."

"No rats? This close to the river you're bound to have rats. I do hate rats."

"No, certainly not. We haven't even seen a mouse."

"Then it will do beautifully until we can all work very hard, and all do beautifully, and all get ourselves out of trouble. Have you been drinking, Eddy? Tell your old Muddy the truth now. Have you kept your promise to your poor old Muddy?"

Virginia came to hang on her mother. "Of course he's kept his promise," she said. "He hasn't drunk a drop since we got here. He's been very good, and he's been working so hard. I've been good too. And, Muddy, oh, all the good things we've had to eat! You'll get fat, like me."

As unselfconsciously as a nursemaid inspecting a two-year-old charge, Muddy anxiously ran her big hands over her daughter's body, then peered at her eyes and pried open her mouth. "Your gums are almost as white as your teeth," she said. "You'll never get well, my girl. Stop that coughing now. You know good and well what I've told you."

"She's not doing it on purpose," Poe protested. "She's coughed almost none since we first arrived, and she's had no night sweats."

"Well she's coughing now. Pick her up, Eddy, there's a good boy. Is your room next door? Carefully now. Wait, I'll throw back the covers. Where's her nightie? Her medicine? Ah, she hasn't been taking enough of her medicine. No wonder she's sick again. Just leave her to me. There's a good girl. There's a poor little Sissy. You're safe with Muddy now, my poor little girl."

Poe backed out of the room, fighting down the familiar terror. Virginia struggled for breath, but the paroxysm of coughing shook her with convulsions so severe that it sounded as if she were strangling. Choosing that moment to greet him, the cat slipped out into the hall and sniffed the cuffs of his trousers thoughtfully as if to detect what places he had been and what adventures he had undergone. Poe's own nose and eyes did similar detective work through the doorway. No blood? No spots of fresh crimson?

Muddy closed the door. The cat stiffened, taking umbrage, Poe thought, but then he saw that she was staring at the top of the stairs. There, staring back at them with sharp, shiny eyes, crouched a big, brown rat. It was fully ten inches long, with a tail almost as long again, and it looked at them nervously but fearlessly.

"No," Poe said warningly to the cat, and after a few seconds she turned her head away with apparent indifference. At the top of the stairs there was now nothing. Suddenly, with no sound and no movement detectable to Poe, there was nothing at all. Had there ever been a rat? Yes, the cat had seen it. It wasn't just a specter of a rat conjured up by Muddy's fears, but a denizen of the city.

The brown rat, like so many of the city's population, was not indigenous, but an immigrant. Initially from Central Asia, its ancestors had migrated westward, spreading to Europe along the trade routes, slipping into America from a ship during the War for Independence. It was a latecomer to a city already inhabited by the black rat, whose homeland, long ago, was India, and the Alexandrian rat, originally from Egypt. Poe had it somewhere in his commonplace book where he jotted lines and stuck clippings and kept the miscellany from his wide-ranging readings. Now the three tribes were moving westward, as the nation itself moved West.

So might he. It might not yet be too late. Move Virginia West to kinder climes. Move South, and go home again. But without access to editors, how could he peddle his wares?

The cat rubbed herself against his legs, then led the way to the next room. She leaped up on Muddy's trunk and gazed at a covered birdcage Muddy had put on the dresser, but she made no attempt to go close to it. Poe uncovered the parrot and watched it stretch its gaudy wings. He stood there quietly, listening to the horse and, now, Virginia, as they both labored loudly to breathe.

Later he sat listening to Muddy sipping tea and tried not to listen to the moist chewing sounds as she finished off a cold mutton chop. Muddy said, "Did you ask at the *American* or the *Commercial Advertiser*, son? Did you ask at the *Knickerbocker?*"

"I can't ask at those journals, Muddy. Those men aren't friendly to me."

"We can't let pride stand in our way. Just leave everything to your old Muddy, my poor boy. I'll go out tomorrow and ask everywhere for you. I'll soon find you a proper job."

"It's not pride, Muddy. It's strategy. If I play my hand correctly, I won't have to settle for a desk in someone else's office. We'll have *The Stylus* at last. We'll be rich. Shea and I have been working at the figures. Do you realize that if I could circulate only twenty thousand copies at five dollars a year, the expenses, even if you estimate all contingencies at the highest possible rate, would not exceed about thirty thousand dollars? That leaves a balance of seventy thousand dollars a year in profits, Muddy. Think of it!"

Muddy inspected the bone of the mutton chop. It was bare. She put it on her plate and said, "My, that would be lovely. But we can't eat pie in the sky, now can we, son? Mr. Leary would give me only six dollars and seventy cents for all your books. That won't take us very far."

"But, Muddy, I've been writing very well since the moment we got here. A change was just what we needed. I've got another story almost finished. Now that you're here, you'll copy it for me, won't you?"

Muddy could copy Poe's beautiful, clear handwriting so closely that a stranger couldn't tell it from Poe's, and she often served as his secretary. "Of course," she said, "and I'm sure it's a lovely story. But you know how long they take to place. By the way, your 'Purloined Letter' came back again. I hardly know where to send that one next."

Poe began to rub together the thumb and little finger of his right hand, a habit when he was nervous or thinking hard. "You see what I mean?" he said glumly. "Just because a story is a little out of the ordinary run, the editors are afraid to chance it. I *must* have my own magazine."

Muddy patted his hand comfortingly, but she went inexorably on. "But what of now, son? If you refuse to let editors know of your availability, how will we even be able to get books for you to review? I'm sure that I could sell them at a better price here than in Philadelphia. Only six dollars and seventy cents for all those books. Why, the bound volume of the *Messenger* alone should have been worth more than that."

"But, Muddy, you didn't sell that one! You know I borrowed it. Didn't I ask you to return it? I'm sure I did."

Muddy looked down at her plate. "Certainly, and I did as you asked."

"Are you sure? It would make me look very bad, Muddy, to have sold another man's book."

She raised her gray eyes and looked at him unblinkingly. "I said I returned it. Don't you trust your poor old Muddy?"

"Of course. I'm sorry."

"My poor boy, brought up in luxury and extravagance. How should you know anything about money transactions? You must let me advise you, Eddy. Haven't I always attended to your literary business for you?"

"I assure you I'll call upon all the more likely editors," Poe said unhappily. "Discreetly, you understand, just so they'll become aware that I'm now in New York and can start thinking favorably of me. It's part of the strategy Shea and I have worked out."

She studied his stubborn face for a moment, then sighed and refilled her teacup. "Very well, then, we'll try your plan. I'm sure I can find some sewing. All the ladies will be wanting summer dresses soon. Then, if we can get enough money ahead, I can buy yarn and knit some little purses. You know my fancy knitting always pays very well."

Poe began to relax. He said carefully, "If we can manage that summer in the country, I might even have time to work on a major poem. Something popular for a change. Shea and I decided it might not be a bad idea. I've already written one new poem, a short one. It's just the right length for *Graham's*. I've called it *Dreamland*. And I've been tinkering a little with a long one. You know, the one about the raven."

"I thought it was an owl."

"No, I changed it."

"But, son, I thought you'd decided that one was hopeless. You said you were sick to death of it."

"Well, maybe not."

Muddy looked dubious, but she didn't press the point directly. Besides, it was her policy never to criticize Poe's work, only to praise it. "I do believe I'll ask Mrs. Morrison about finding some sewing," she said. "I could surely get some work shirts to do. Why, even at home they paid six cents a shirt. Of course, you had to furnish your own thread."

"Don't worry, Muddy. I know that I must take care of us, and I shall. But let me do it my own way. It's important. This time it will work. This time I know I can get *The Stylus*."

She nodded. "Dear Eddy, I can't wait until we begin to make some money. The first thing I shall buy you is a new pair of boots. I just know everything is going to work out beautifully."

5

In May, the new Trinity Church tower developed cracks around the south front window as the heavy stones of the edifice settled. Repair work was started and, thanks to steam, the spire itself was under way and rising rapidly. In June, the ailing horse that lived in back of Morrison's boarding house died. Virginia was beginning to wilt under the onslaught of the city's heat. In July, Muddy's ever anxious face turned questioningly to Poe's weary one, and she asked him one more time about a farm he had encountered out near the village of Bloomingdale while gathering material for his weekly column on New York's sights for the Pittsburgh paper. Was the farm really so cheap? Was there really milk fresh from the cow instead of half soured from the milk peddler who rattled his cans through Greenwich Street? Did he really think his articles would continue to sell well enough for him to risk not looking for a job?

The stage fare was a shilling apiece and there were raised eyebrows at the unhappy sounds of a nervous cat coming from Muddy's wicker basket, but the ever present mosquitoes dwindled noticeably and a little breeze was blowing as the stage stopped in the roadway in back of Patrick Brennan's farmhouse, a roomy frame building on a rocky rise overlooking the Hudson. Ten young children, one bulldog and a madly barking terrier rushed down a long flight of wooden steps that straggled up the knoll to the house. "Askine!" the children screamed at the terrier, "Askine, be quiet!" Muddy clucked and tutted and held her basket high in the air. Virginia, too weak to laugh with the children, too weak to walk and therefore carried by Poe, gazed up at three tall, green willows that towered over the house, and felt a little breath of summer's green peace whiff into her tortured lungs.

Schemes, plans, letters and manuscripts kept Poe hard at work through the summer months. The goldenrod bloomed, hummingbirds harvested bee balm and goldfinches waited expectantly for the purple pasture thistles to come to a full ripening. By the time the air hinted of the turning of the season, Virginia recovered strength, but even after the high-bush cranberries growing along the river achieved their glowing September red, Poe achieved no tangible harvest of his own for the daily drift of pale blue sheets of paper that he dropped to the floor around his writing table, page by page, script side down, as he completed them.

Pasted together in a continuous strip, rolled neatly into a scroll, these were Poe's stock in trade, and from time to time Muddy would take a scroll and a shilling for the stage fare and go into the city to leave a manuscript for one editor, to pick up a rejected one from another, to drop in at the post office, to make the standard rounds. But the shillings grew scarcer, and Poe, more capable than Muddy of the long walk each way, began to be seen from time to time trudging along the Bloomingdale Road and thence the city streets, musing, deeply absorbed and often apparently unconscious of his surroundings.

One rainy night in late September, the season's first easterly blew into the city. A blow as chill and savage as it had been sudden, it rattled the square panes of Gabriel Harrison's shop window, causing him to start and look up. Outside, a black-dressed man without an umbrella was peering at the window display of twist and plug tobacco. Gabriel stepped quickly toward the door. In lieu of a friend, a customer would be a welcome interruption.

But the man did not enter. Gabriel looked past him politely, out at the darkening street. The evening crush of Broadway traffic had dwindled to a sporadic rush of yellow and red omnibuses. It would be a hard night for the horses, all that slippery mud. The horses' coats steamed visibly in the wet air. It was rapidly getting colder. The lamplighters were late, holed up somewhere waiting for the rain to slacken, damn their eyes. Lights were cheerful. There was nothing now but hateful gloom.

Gabriel peeped again at the man taking shelter under his awning. He seemed rather a seedy-looking young fellow, standing there, gazing with an odd expression at the Virginia leaf. There was something vaguely foreign about the man, something about the way he wore his rain-spattered black cloak. Spanish? No. Maybe he had more the air of an actor. That was it. A fellow actor.

Gabriel brightened. He opened the door. "Won't you come in, sir?" he said to the stranger. "I've just decided to light a fire. Pouring buckets, isn't it?"

"I thank you, sir," the stranger said, "but I think the rain is stopping now." He had an unusual voice, melodious and with fine articulation. He added, "I must be getting on."

"Nonsense," Gabriel said, "it's apt to rain all night." He made a wry face. "The fact is you'd be doing me a favor. Have you ever just ached for an excuse to postpone a chore? Come, here is the stove, behind the tea boxes. Take off your cloak. We'll soon have it dry. Will you join me in a drop of something? What will you have, some of this old port?"

The stranger's nose wrinkled appreciatively at the mingled odors of wines, cheeses, jams and other comestibles that littered the shelves of Gabriel's small shop. All was laced with the heavy, syrupy smell of tobacco. He smiled faintly but shook his head. "A fire would be tonic enough," he said. "I've walked five miles through the rain and now must walk five miles back."

"What, in this weather? It's damned unseasonable for September. I fear we must say good-by to summer. Just reach me some of those wads of paper there, can you? That's all it's good for, tinder." Gabriel stopped bustling for a moment and smiled confidingly at his guest. "This will be the first fire I've made this year," he said.

"Ah," said the stranger. He drew closer to the big iron stove.

Last winter's ashes were still in the grate. Last winter's kindling was nearby, wild black cherry, bought from a sawyer who boated it over from Staten Island. The stranger smoothed out a fistful of wadded sheets of paper from Gabriel's desk and handed them over one by one. He must have seen Gabriel's varied attempts at a song—*See the daring white eagle flying high . . . See the daring white eagle fly to the sky . . . battle cry . . . victory nigh*—but Gabriel busied himself noisily with the coal scuttle, and the man said nothing.

The paper caught, curled. Splinters on a stick of kindling suddenly flared into flame. The pungent odor of stale summer's dust, heating, slowly filled the room. It was the altar of autumn, the signal, so much clearer than the faint beginnings of rust on the oak trees in nearby Washington Square, that change was once again coming and a new time would begin. The two men turned and smiled at each other.

"I noticed you were inspecting the plug tobacco," Gabriel said impulsively. "You must permit me to present you with a sample."

"Thank you, but I'm a very small user of the solace. Your leaf is beautiful, though. The best Virginia, isn't it?"

"Indeed, sir, it is. Are you in tobacco, by any chance?"

"No," the man said. The odd look came back into his eyes. "I once knew someone who was. In Richmond, when I was a boy. I used to play in a warehouse filled with great tuns of fragrant tobacco. You know how smells take you back."

"Well, then, you really must have a piece," Gabriel said. "Everybody chews *some*time. Here, here's a tasty bit. Put it in your pocket if you don't care to try it now. I really insist."

The man eyed Gabriel's open, eager face, and a suggestion of hauteur that had flared into his manner faded and was replaced by a smile, again faint, briefly lighting what may have been a habitual melancholy. "You're very kind," he said. "Perhaps I'll try it on my way home. The rain seems to have let up considerably."

Gabriel flinched. The man couldn't go yet. He would be left alone with those damned wads of paper. The man apparently followed Gabriel's eyes as they went worriedly to the cluttered desk.

"Were you composing when I interrupted you?" he asked. "Is that the chore you were interested in postponing?"

"Ah, well, just a little thing I've been working on," Gabriel said. "I'm president of the White Eagle Political Club, as it happens, and we need a campaign song. I trust I won't offend you, sir, if I say that the fate of the nation depends on getting Mr. Clay elected. Why, annex Texas, and what will we have? War with Mexico, as sure as we're standing here. And another slave state on the mutilated conscience of union. —Oh, Lord, sir, forgive me. I take it you're a Southerner. I forgot."

The man reached one of the remaining wadded papers from Gabriel's pile and uncrumpled it. "One gets rather accustomed to anti-southern sentiments in New York," he said absently. He took another wad and studied it.

Gabriel turned red. In silence he looked over the man's shoulder. He hadn't gotten very far. Not through a satisfactory first line, actually. He said hopefully, "It's supposed to be to the measure of 'The Star Spangled Banner.' You aren't perchance musically inclined, are you, sir?"

"You would not think so if you heard me exercising my one talent —playing the flute," the man said. "But may I try my hand? It would be a small return for your gift of tobacco."

"Oh, sir, no, no return is necessary," Gabriel protested, but he ended by sweeping the litter on his desk to one side to provide a clear working space. The man sat down in Gabriel's chair and reached for a quill. "A white eagle," he mused. "Something of a coincidence. I've been working with a somewhat darker bird. Hmmm. Perhaps . . ."

He began to write rapidly in a clear copperplate: *See the white eagle soaring aloft to the sky,/Wakening the broad welkin with his loud battle cry.*

"Why that's wonderful!" Gabriel exclaimed. "'Wakening the broad welkin.' Welkin. Now, that's . . ."

"Just another word for sky," the man said. He picked through Gabriel's discards, noting a conceit here, pondering a word there. He wrote two more lines while Gabriel read over his shoulder. *Then here's the White Eagle, full daring is he,/As he sails on his pinions o'er valley and sea.*

"Wonderful, wonderful!" Gabriel said.

"Hardly that," the man said. "But you want a campaign song, not great poetry. Besides, it's all your own material. I'm just rearranging it a bit. Too bad it doesn't scan better. Maybe I can correct it."

"No, it's perfect as is. And 'welkin,' that's a touch of elegance. That's just what it needs. Welkin. Now, why didn't I think of that?"

A customer came in, and Gabriel went to wait on him. When he came back, the man was writing the second verse. The quill rarely hesitated. Gabriel tiptoed away and put more coal on the fire. The stove had scarcely begun to glow before the man put down the quill and leaned back to peruse the completed song.

Gabriel was in a quandary. He was delighted with his new campaign song, and it was only fair to pay his new acquaintance something for his trouble. Those old boots, those neatly mended gloves. It was all too easy to guess why the man had walked such a distance in the rain instead of catching a stage: couldn't afford the two bits for the fare. But when Gabriel broached the subject of a fee, the man's face grew cold. "I thank you, sir, but I could not accept," the man replied firmly.

"Oh, but, please, you must allow me to express my appreciation by some token," Gabriel said, flustered. "A bottle or two of wine, then? Or brandy. Here, have you tried London Dock? A very unusual brandy, strong and black." The man kept shaking his head, and Gabriel grew more flustered. "Then at least accept a packet of tea.

Here's a fine one: bohea, the real thing. Or . . ." Gabriel stopped and looked shyly at the man. "Please," he said. "I would still be tearing up paper and tearing out my hair if it weren't for you."

The man's dark gray eyes softened. "Then give me a small bag of coffee, my friend, and I will be in your debt, not you in mine. I must confess that my affairs have not been running smoothly of late, and a cup of fine coffee is something my mother lately has not enjoyed."

"It's a privilege, sir," Gabriel said happily. "My compliments to your mother, and a bag of this genuine mocha. It's the finest in the shop, in the city. Will you tell me your name, sir? I should like to know your name."

"Certainly," the man answered. But he hesitated, before continuing, "Thaddeus K. Perley, at your service."

"Gabriel Harrison, at yours," Gabriel said. Gabriel occasionally acted in minor professional roles. He also drew and painted, was a friend to no end of authors and newspapermen who regularly gathered at the cluttered shop at Broadway and Prince and was active in both local and national politics, and he liked to think of himself as one of the better-known men in New York. But the man only offered his hand and a warm how-do-you-do, and Gabriel concluded he was obviously a newcomer to New York.

The front door banged open. Gabriel was almost annoyed. His new friend absorbed all his attention. But he beamed as he recognized an old friend, Fitz-Greene Halleck, who was not only a prominent banker and John Jacob Astor's secretary, but, by avocation, one of the nation's foremost poets, now gazing at him and Mr. Perley through gold-rimmed spectacles that were dappled with raindrops.

"Why, welcome, Mr. Halleck," Gabriel began.

Halleck interrupted him. "Great heavens, Poe, is this you?" he exclaimed.

"Poe?" said Gabriel. "This is Mr. Perley."

The man who had warmed himself at Gabriel's fire looked at Halleck, then at Gabriel, and after a moment's pause he said, "The fact of the matter is, Halleck, I have made this gentleman's acquaintance under the name of Perley. No harm was intended and none done. I knew the facts would develop of themselves."

"Another hoax, Poe?" Halleck said. "Surely you recognized Edgar Poe, Gabriel. Why, he's the author of that 'scoop' the *Sun* ran last spring about that transatlantic balloon trip. You set the town on its ear with that one, Poe. Where have you been? No one's seen you all summer. I thought perhaps you'd gone back to Philadelphia."

"No. I suppose you might say I've been playing the hermit. We moved out to the country for the summer. The place is a perfect heaven. I've hardly seen a living soul outside of my family."

Gabriel wasn't sure whether to be offended or what, to learn that the friend he had just met as Thaddeus Perley was someone named Edgar Poe. Poe. Come to think of it, he had heard of the fellow. A militant critic, Gabriel's writer-friends said. And Poe did some writing himself. Edgar A. Poe. Why, of course, he'd read a Poe story in *Godey's* that very week, some bleak thing about a bereaved husband trying to transport the body of his dead wife to New York. A writer, not an actor then. But no matter. Gabriel liked the man, his courtly manners, his grave ways. He bustled to his shelves, saying, "Seat yourselves, gentlemen. Do put your boots up, Mr. Halleck, they'll dry faster. I have an old English pineapple cheese somewhere. And one of the finest old ports in the city. In the world. We'll nibble and bend our elbows in homage to his majesty the port."

"You've lit the stove, Gabriel?" Halleck said. "Make us a dish of tea then. Tea would go down well on an evening like this. It feels like December outside."

"That's why it's a night for port," Gabriel said. He found the bottle he was looking for and turned back to his guests. Behind Poe, Halleck shook his head and mouthed something at Gabriel. "What?" Gabriel said.

Halleck looked uncomfortable. "A cracker," he said vaguely. "A cracker or two might go well with the cheese."

The stove by now was muttering cheerfully. Gabriel arranged chairs and glasses and set a tea box where all could reach easily for the cheese and crackers. Halleck still looked uncomfortable, but he seemed to relax when, in spite of Gabriel's urgings, Poe declined the port.

"Well, Poe, and what have you been writing there in your hermit's den?" Halleck asked. "Some new adventure of M. Dupin?"

Poe waved a negligent hand, as if to dismiss such matters. "*Gift* has taken a new Dupin, I believe," he said. "No, I've gone back to poetry, like it or not. You know how a poem can keep after you, Halleck, until you get it right. But I've also been arranging material for an anthology, a critical history of American literature."

Halleck smiled, a sweet, enthusiastic smile. To the world, Halleck was reserved, but with his friends he was all cordiality. "Competition for Rufe Griswold?" he said. "Griswold isn't going to like that. I saw him the other day at the *Tribune* office, by the by. I suppose he was back in town for a visit."

"The Reverend Rufus Griswold?" Gabriel said. "I beg pardon, Mr. Poe, but weren't you editor of *Graham's* a few years ago, and didn't he replace you?"

Poe's face stiffened, but he said courteously, "Only for a brief period, I believe."

"Yes, just long enough to drop the circulation to half," Halleck said wryly. "I hear it's down to not more than twenty-five thousand, Poe. There goes all your good work down the drain." Poe looked at the port bottle, and Halleck added hastily, "I know one shouldn't gossip, but there's been some interesting talk about those circulation figures. It seems that Mr. Graham accused the Reverend Mr. Griswold of jiggling them. Pocketing the money from new subscriptions, you know, and sliding the names onto the circulation lists without mentioning them to Graham. I don't know whether to believe it or not."

"Nor I," Poe said. "I believe I will have just a small glass of port, Mr. Harrison."

"Have you supped, Poe?" Halleck said. "Come to my house, why don't you? I think the housekeeper said something about sausages and potato salad and walnut cake with applesauce."

"Oh, please, don't go," Gabriel said. "Have more cheese. More port. Or I can open some tins." He was puzzled. Something was obviously disturbing Halleck, but he had no idea what. He pressed them to stay, looking forward to a literary conversation, and his two visitors did not disappoint him. Poe became more and more animated as the port bottle went around, and soon was telling Halleck about a biographical sketch of him that was to have appeared in *Graham's* that month by no less of a personage than the poet James Russell Lowell.

"But Lowell came down with a fit of indolence," Poe said, "and the writing was delayed. Damn the fellow. Yet I can sympathize. Indolence is one of my own besetting failings. I'm either extremely industrious or slothful. It's a fact, Halleck, that I'm only negatively ambitious. I'm only spurred on now and then to excel fools, because I can't bear to let foolish persons imagine they can excel me."

"Then thank heavens for fools," Halleck said, "for if we are ever to create an American literature instead of merely imitating English writers, we need originality such as yours."

"And yours," Poe said courteously.

"Oh, I hardly write any more," Halleck said. "A few translations from the Spanish or German, but I seem to have lost interest in writing my own verse. Getting too old, I suppose."

Gabriel clucked his tongue scoldingly. Halleck was only about fifty. "It's your commercial pursuits that keep you too busy, Mr. Halleck," he said. "Commerce enjoys your leadership, and literature must go begging."

"Leadership! Yes, we must have leadership!" Poe said excitedly. "That's why I'm going ahead with my own magazine. I'm calling it *The Stylus*. Even before I left West Point I knew my ultimate purpose was to found a magazine of my own. A magazine of bold and noble aims, to fight against our general editorial course of corruption. It has been my constant endeavor to establish not a reputation great in itself, but one to further this special object. Criticisms, poems, miscellanies, my tales—I've written them all with the establishment of my journal in mind, and I've formulated literary principles with the same end. *The Stylus* will provide a base, don't you see, from which to fight the power of the entrenched literary cliques. No newcomer to literature has a chance now because of them. They're afraid of newcomers, they're afraid someone will start publishing real literature and leave them with no markets willing to accept their own trivia. A really good journal, insisting on the highest of standards, will help establish conditions favorable for real authorship. God knows, it might even help make it possible for the good newcomers to make a decent living from their writing. You gentlemen authors, Halleck, who sit down and pen a poem or two when you take time from your commercial pursuits, you can't imagine what it's like for the brilliant young author who lacks an independent income and must needs live on what the publishers pay him."

How could it have happened? Mr. Poe was clearly drunk. Yet Gabriel himself had poured for him. Only two glasses of port, yet Mr. Poe was obviously to the staggering point. Halleck heard him out patiently and continued to urge Mr. Poe not to make the long walk to the country in the dark but to stop the night with him, and eventually, after a third port, Mr. Poe agreed and got to his feet.

"Your coffee, Mr. Poe," Gabriel reminded him. "We left the bag on the front counter."

"Ah yes, of course," Poe said. He patted his pocket where he had put the tobacco. "I am most indebted to you, Mr. Harrison." He started for the counter.

"Will he be all right?" Gabriel asked Halleck in a low voice. "Do you need any help in getting him home?"

"No, no. I've seen him this way a few times on visits to Philadelphia. A gentle word, the offer of one's arm, and he's always easy to manage."

"I shouldn't have insisted so on the port," said Gabriel worriedly. "It's my fault."

"You couldn't have known. Some men just don't take well to spirits. But he's a good man. Be his friend, Gabriel, and he will be a friend to you."

"With the greatest of pleasure," Gabriel said.

He went forward with Halleck to say his good-nights. On the streets, puddles among the cobblestones gleamed in the gas light. Broadway was quiet, but not empty. People returning from the different theaters picked their way gingerly along the slippery, uneven sidewalks. Cabs and carriages rolled swiftly by. Down the block, a baked-potato vendor turned his back to a splatter of thin, cold rain that still oozed from the clouds. Until the moment that the carts, the donkeys plodding under loads of apples and late lettuces, the heavy wagons bearing grain began to creep toward the markets at dawn, the city would come as close as it ever came to sleep.

Gabriel said shyly, "Mr. Poe, I thank you for my song."

Poe grasped his hand. "I haven't . . . I hope I haven't inconvenienced you in any way tonight," he said.

"Indeed not, not in the slightest. Meeting you has made the night memorable."

"Ah," said Poe, and as shyly as Gabriel he added, "I suppose any night that men can make any song can't be a night totally wasted."

Long after they left, sharing Halleck's umbrella, Gabriel lingered at the door of his shop, watching the mud puddles dimple under the almost invisible dance of the rain. You couldn't see the mud. In the dark the puddles were jet black, and in the rays of lamplight a pure and shimmering gold. The wind had died. The clouds seemed to be passing. Tomorrow would be a beautiful, golden day, Gabriel decided. Then he locked the door, and wondered if he were only wishing.

6

One day of chilly rain, and already sounds were different. The branches of the elms Poe passed under as he walked home early the next afternoon creaked more loudly in the breeze, and their leaves, drying slowly, had a more brittle rustle. In October they would fall. The leaves they were withering and sere. Crisped and sere?

He neared the last small colony of shanties, built largely of mud with the inevitable pigsty attached. Irish squatters. The city would soon push them elsewhere. Some men predicted that the cities of the East had already outlived their day, that foxes would soon stare from the windows of the crumbled buildings. Others predicted that the cities would continue to grow. Although he deplored it, Poe agreed with the latter. Within thirty years, he himself predicted, every wild, noble cliff on the island of Manhattan would be leveled for a pier; the whole island would be densely desecrated by brick buildings with pretentious facades of brownstone; all would be withered by the spirit of improvement. Even towering buildings, as high as twenty stories, would eventually rear into the skies.

But for now, the upper portions of Mannahatta—he preferred the rhythmic sound of the "true" name—had a certain air of rocky, barren loneliness which was compatible to his state of mind. Poe felt a little ill. Surely not the wine. Had he drunk more than one glass last night? The sausages he had eaten at Halleck's house, that might be it. One shouldn't eat pork in cholera weather. Pork, some people said, was responsible for spreading the cholera, although other people said oysters. Cholera! God, he shivered at the thought. But the cold wave that blew in yesterday would surely blow any cholera from the city. In these northern climes, cholera was only a summer disease.

Poe walked rapidly, swinging his cane a bit, trying to put the shanties behind him. A pack of dogs ran out of ragged gardens to bark, obviously enjoying the opportunity to make a show of their ferocity, and a twelve-year-old girl ran after them. She was a slim little thing, barefooted, with auburn hair and deep brown eyes. She called off the dogs and stood staring at Poe. She didn't beg. Even in the outskirts of the city, far from Mayor Harper's new uniformed police—"cops," people were calling them, after their prominent copper buttons—few people begged in New York. But she looked at him appealingly, and Poe felt his pale face redden. He had nothing to give her. He gallantly raised his tall, well-brushed hat, and the little girl blushed in turn and turned away. When well beyond her, alone once more on the rain-washed road, Poe slowly smiled.

But the smile faded as he fell into a reverie that had become habitual. Poems were not made in rooms, they were only written down in them, and Poe often worried out problems when walking. The thirteenth stanza, predictably, was bad. Of course there was "gloated," that was a marvelous touch. *On the cushion's velvet lining that the lamplight gloated o'er,/ But whose velvet violet lining with the lamplight gloating o'er,/ She shall press, ah, nevermore!* The double meaning of those two "gloatings" would probably remain a private treasure, as who but himself could be counted upon to know the rare usage of "gloated" in the sense of "to refract light"? But verbal treasures, whether private or public, must go into a poem as plums into pudding. The problem was that damned "lining." Sounded like the upholstery was turned inside out. But he had to have the "violet velvet" chair. It went with the silken purple curtains of the third stanza. The two touches of picturesqueness served as a relief to the other, more somber surroundings. But *lining*? Damnation, there must be something more appropriate.

Would he have to give up the chair? Never. Violet velvet. Just saying the words aloud was sensual pleasure. Purple silk and violet velvet. Luxurious. More luxurious by far than the fine linen sheets he had slept on last night in Halleck's well-run bachelor digs. He had awakened to hazy sunlight through rich lace curtains and, faintly heard, the rattle of shutters being taken down by yawning housemaids. The young housemaid who had later brought up his coffee hadn't been bad-looking, either. He suspected that Halleck found little use for women, but the man knew how to surround himself with beauty. Poe had idled much of the morning, long after Halleck had left for Mr. Astor's office, feeling just ill enough to ease his conscience and enjoying his surroundings. But Muddy would be worried, and Virginia, and he had finally embarked upon his return journey.

The walk was a long one, but Poe had plenty to keep him occupied. This poem, this *Raven*, would bring to poetic flower the great theme of death and lost love explored in so many of his stories, and it had to be right. The palpitant quality of the meter—found in one of Elizabeth Barrett's poems, it was true, but meter was the common possession of all poets, wasn't it?—was perfect, and so must be the rest of the poem. The problem was, a poet had to keep his hand in by continuous practice, and his was rusty. Not for years had he had the leisure to write and rewrite, to give time to the many poetic experiments that interested him. So as he walked his mind worked forward and backward, picking at the knots of his present poetic problems, and he was brooding over the ninth stanza and its *Bird or beast upon the sculptured bust above his chamber door* when he fetched up at the Brennan farm. Bird, yes, but a *beast* sitting upon a bust? Ridiculous.

A handful of the younger Brennan children rushed down to the road to greet him, but Virginia stayed on the back stoop and waited for Poe to approach her. Her worried eyes assessed him for any signs of damage. Dried mud on his trouser legs, yes, mud caked thickly on his boots, but Poe leaned to kiss her confidently, feeling sure that she would not be able to detect the eighteen-hour-old aura of one little glass of port.

"I must get rid of that word," he told Virginia absently. "Whoever heard of a beast sitting on a sculptured bust above a man's chamber door? No beast could occupy such a position."

She looked bewildered, but she said, "Oh yes, a mouse, for instance."

Poe gave her one of his rare humorous smiles. "A mouse? Get along with you." He fished into his tail coat pocket and drew out Gabriel's bag of coffee. "Where's Muddy? I wrote a ridiculous song for a friend last night, and he sent her this bag of real mocha."

Poe's favorite among the Brennan children, young Tom Brennan, who found the dashing gentleman so fascinating that his mother scolded him for constantly following Poe around, succeeded in wresting Poe's cane and cloak from him and rushed to carry them into the house, shouting, "Did you get caught in the storm? It blew down a white oak by the pond. There were three nests, but all the birds were gone!"

"Fitz-Greene Halleck took me in," Poe told Virginia. "The city was a swamp."

The anxiety began to fade from Virginia's round face. "Poor Eddy, you must have been drenched," she said. "Come right upstairs and change. Mrs. Brennan, may I have a bucket of hot water? You must soak your feet in hot water, Eddy. You know how easily you catch cold."

"Leave it, I'm fine. And you? Did you have an easy night? Did the storm frighten you badly? Did you keep Muddy upstairs with you? Where *is* Muddy?"

"She went to the city to look for you," Virginia said. "We were so worried."

Poe felt shame mount to his cheeks and a bubble of exasperation sink to his stomach. "Mr. Halleck was insistent that I not walk home in the rain," he said. "There was nothing to worry about."

"I'm glad," Virginia said softly. "I kept telling Muddy it was just the storm." Her natural gaiety reasserted itself. "It was a wonderful storm. The wind made the whole house shake. But it harvested apples galore for us. We've been making apple butter all morning, haven't we, Mrs. Brennan?"

The amiable, still-handsome Irishwoman nodded. "Yes, and dinner's running late because of it." The family kept country hours, and usually dined at one in the afternoon. "I hope you're not starving to death, Mr. Poe. Would you take a little buttermilk? Perhaps a couple of fried eggs to keep you going? It'll be an hour or more."

But Poe declined and went up the stairs of the old farmhouse, leaving behind him the murmuring women's voices, which, like the hum of bees outside the windows, created a reassuring rhythm that he did not consciously listen to. Muddy had a little room of her own downstairs, but Poe and Virginia slept in the garret and, on the second floor for Poe to work, they had another big, airy room, where they could watch the sunsets over the Hudson River. Two hundred acres of fruit trees, flowers and vegetables raised for the city markets sloped down to the river, across which the wild cliffs of the New Jersey shore loomed above passing side wheel steamers. Surveying this domain, the Poes' tortoise-shell cat, Catarina, was lying in one of the open windows in a pool of bright green sunshine that filtered through the leaves of the willow trees sheltering the house. She turned and stared at him calmly with eyes the color of the sun, green-yellow, except for the black, vertical slits of her spindle-shaped pupils. Poe paused to greet her gravely and pass a hand over her lazy, smooth body.

The room had once been occupied by another boarder, a French officer who fled into exile after the collapse of Napoleon, and who later journeyed onward, leaving behind parts of his past: French military prints, heavy Empire draperies, a big desk and, on a shelf above the door, a little plaster bust of the goddess of arts and wisdom, Pallas Athena. Stroking the cat, Poe studied the bust, still worrying over the ninth stanza. *Bird or beast upon the sculptured bust above his chamber door.* Bird or mouse? Great gods. Such a line would indeed make him famous.

Virginia entered the room after him, carrying a bowl. "Eddy, you haven't changed yet," she scolded him. "At least take off those boots and give them to me. It'll take an hour to scrape all the mud off of them."

"Leave them for Muddy," Poe said, punning mildly. Poe enjoyed a low fondness for puns. "When is she coming back, anyway?"

"I don't know," Virginia said. "It might be hours and hours yet." She joined Poe and the cat by the window and added, smiling, "Look, I brought you some apples. I saved you the nicest ones."

"Then we're all alone?"

She nodded. "Except for Catarina."

He looked at her questioningly. Perhaps, if she weren't too tired . . . ? She had been feeling much better since their move to the Brennans, and she rarely looked as healthy and blooming as she looked today.

Poe knew, without ever having discussed it with his young wife, that women did not feel carnal pleasure. Even after she had grown up a little and he did not feel like an utter cad in imposing on her the marital duty, even before she had become ill, they limited their love-making to six or eight times a year, despite the fact that Poe privately thought that once a month would not be unhealthful or too frequent. But perhaps the time might not be entirely inappropriate, perhaps this very night. Or even, he thought daringly, perhaps this very afternoon. Muddy had yet another new patent medicine for Virginia that she now insisted her daughter take nightly, and Virginia was usually stuporous afterward. When Virginia was fully awake and sentient, they were alone together so rarely. He looked discreetly at her woman's full hips and breasts, seeking the childlike form of the very young girl he had married. His little cousin. Little, childlike Mrs. Poe, with the great wide eyes. How charming she looked even now in the white voile dress Muddy had sewn for her. Black-haired, blue-eyed, laughing self-consciously up at him, fully aware of the charming contrast between her light, white dress and the glistening red apples she held out to him, offering.

"Sweet little Sissy," Poe breathed.

Her eyelashes began to flutter involuntarily, and he smiled, flattered.

But the cat's ears pricked suddenly toward the open door behind them. Voices murmured downstairs. Even Poe's keen hearing could not make out whose. Then, immediately, heavy footsteps began to labor up the stairs, and the cat's ears relaxed and Poe flushed. Muddy.

Poe and Virginia moved apart guiltily. Too guiltily. Muddy looked at them alertly as she entered the room. "Oh, Eddy, your poor boots!" she exclaimed. "Give them to me immediately. There'll be barely time to clean them before dinner. Are your clothes still damp? Mrs. Brennan told me everything. That horrible storm. My poor Eddy, are you feverish? We were out of our minds with worry about you. Ufh, take my basket, Sissy. Be careful, it's heavy. Mrs. Shea insisted that I bring you home six jars of her potted shad. It won't taste like the shad I used to pot in Maryland, my children, but how could I tell her it's a specialty of my own?"

"You saw Mrs. Shea?" Poe said. "Why?"

"I was looking for news of you, my poor boy. I was terrified that you had become . . . ill while you were in the city. Where else would I look if not at the Sheas? But you hadn't even been there. Mr. Shea asked all over town after you, and finally discovered you had been benighted at a Mr. Halleck's. Such a relief. It gave me heart to go about my other errands. Darling Eddy, I've brought you your mail. There was quite a stack of it at the post office. That Dr. Chivers from Georgia has written you again. You'd think as rich as he is he'd at least pay his own postage, but as always the letter came postage due. I was tempted to leave it."

Virginia hugged her mother. "You've sold something!" she said. "You had to, if you could pay for any letters. Which article did they buy? Which? Which?"

Muddy shook her head. "No, I fear not. I only borrowed a few shillings from Mrs. Shea. Now, don't start frowning, Eddy. I'll repay her myself from my knitting money. Should I have walked? I fear I should have. But I was so anxious to see you, I took a steamer to Stryker's Bay instead of the stage coming home. Sissy, I want you to lie down until Mrs. Brennan finally gets dinner ready. And don't forget to get out of that dress before you stretch out."

"But, Muddy, I'm not a bit tired."

"Certainly you are. You're an invalid. Go upstairs now, and don't talk back to me. That's my good girl. Now, Eddy, give me those boots, and sit down. Your letters can wait. I have a lovely surprise for you."

Both Poe and Virginia did as she instructed them, albeit reluctantly. Obedience was the price they paid for Muddy's boundless love. In his stocking feet, Poe sat at his desk and watched Muddy tackle his boots with an old case knife, scraping the mud into the empty fireplace. The manuscript of his poem, what there was of it, lay at hand. He itched to pick it up. The poem was still sticking badly, and he wanted to get on with it. But he waited patiently for Muddy's "surprise."

"Son, I went by to see that nice Mr. Willis at the New York *Mirror*," she said.

"And?"

Muddy's homely face beamed. "Now, don't get too excited, Eddy. It's good news. I've found you a job!"

"A . . . what?"

"A job, darling boy. A real job. I told Mr. Willis frankly how things are with us. Sissy sick. And you've been feeling none too well yourself, my poor boy. I knew you wouldn't mind my confiding in him, Eddy. You've always spoken so highly of dear Mr. Willis."

"But my God, Muddy, I've only corresponded with the man about articles. I've never even met him. He could have no interest in my affairs. Besides, I . . . I don't want a job. I didn't want to get your hopes up, but Shea is almost sure he is going to be able to persuade Charles Astor Bristed to put up the backing for *The Stylus*."

"Mr. Astor's grandson?" Muddy said. "I wouldn't count on it, dear. You surely know by now that the rich are far less generous with their money than the poor."

"I'm not counting on it, Muddy, but you know what Shea and I decided. To get my magazine under way I first must have uninterrupted time for my own work. I need the time more than ever now that things are going so well."

"But, Eddy, they're not going well at all. Whatever are you thinking of? We've barely been able to pay our board bill here, and even if we could afford it we can't possibly stay here through the winter. This place is a barn. It's drafty. We have Virginia to think about, you know."

"Of course," said Poe, more agitatedly, "but you've forgotten the plan. I have every hope that Harper's is going to take a collection of my tales, and the biography that Lowell is doing of me will enhance my reputation hugely. I must do nothing to jeopardize my reputation, Muddy, not now of all times. Why, Muddy, I can demonstrate for you that I'm not counting upon Mr. Bristed or his wealthy friends for money for *The Stylus*. I have a brand-new idea, one that wouldn't call for waiting until everything jells. I'm going to propose to Lowell that we club together with a group of other, carefully chosen authors and raise the backing for the magazine among ourselves. That'll get *Stylus* under way even sooner than we'd hoped. And then there's the poem. I can finish it any week now, I think."

Muddy shook her head sorrowfully, and Poe leaped to his feet with a wordless cry. The cat, startled, bounded from the windowsill to safety on the mantelpiece. Both cat and Muddy stared at Poe with alarm in their eyes, and he choked back his exasperation. He had never lost his temper at Muddy. "You don't understand," Poe told her. "Let me explain it to you again."

"My poor boy," she said, "it's true, I don't understand how you can go on struggling so long with one poem. I'm sure it's going to be lovely, but I only understand that we must have bread. Not for me, Eddy, oh no, not for me. For you. And for Virginia."

"But I'm thinking of Virginia," Poe said. He began to pace. "If I take this job with Mr. Willis, we'd have to move her back into the city. That could be fatal for her."

"Is it worse than doing without food and medicine for her?" Muddy asked humbly.

"Of course not, but . . . this poem will make all the difference to my reputation. I'm so close to finishing. And Virginia feels better, much better since we moved her to the country."

Muddy nodded. "She always gets better in nice weather, but she'll get worse again this winter, whether we move her into the city or not. Eddy, I know how hard it is for you to face, but you *must* face it. All we can do is give Virginia the best care that we possibly can, but no matter what we can do, she's not always going to be with us. You must prepare yourself for it. You must accept it."

"She's not going to die!" Poe said. "Oh, God. God, help me."

"Darling Eddy, our prayers have gone unheeded. Try to bear it. I know you can, if I can. But I can't lose you too, son. You can't live on air. You must let me look after you. I know Mr. Shea has your best interests at heart, but he isn't the most practical of advisors. I'm only trying to do what's right. Mr. Willis speaks of you so enthusiastically. And it's not as though he wants you to start work immediately. He wants you to contribute at column rates for a few weeks. That will give you plenty of time to finish your lovely poem, now won't it? The *Mirror* is going to go daily in the first week of October, you see. That's why Mr. Willis so badly needs a mechanical paragraphist."

Poe sank into the chair by his desk. "A mechanical paragraphist," he said with a bitter little laugh. He had assumed, naturally, that Willis wanted to take him on as editor. Chained to the oar of a mere daily journal, that would be bad enough, but the fates had prepared for him an even more poisonous dose. A mechanical paragraphist. To sit in an office waiting to be called on for any miscellaneous work of the day, scissoring other journals, digging up tidbits of news to be turned into one-paragraph fillers. The only step lower was to be a lowly reporter.

"Of course Mr. Willis also wants you to do book reviews," Muddy said hastily.

"Of course," Poe said. "It's all right, Muddy."

"Darling Eddy, it's not what I would have wanted for you. I know it's a sacrifice, a young man of your genius working in a subordinate position after being editor of the biggest magazine in the whole United States, but it pays well."

"How well?"

"Well, much better than we're doing now. Fifteen dollars a week. Eddy, believe me, I'm only trying to do what's best for you and Sissy."

"It's all right. I . . . I think I'll try to work a little now before dinner, Muddy. I had some ideas for the poem while I was walking home from the city. I think I'll just try to get them on paper now before I forget them."

Muddy left reluctantly, but she finally left. The cat returned to her pool of sunshine in the window. Poe picked up the sheets of manuscript before him and gazed at the title, *The Raven*, trying to reconstruct the fragile edifice he had been building. Nothing came. The ideas had flown like a flock of frightened birds. He tried hard to remember, to think of the poem and nothing else. Don't think of mechanical paragraphing. Above all, don't think of what Muddy had said about Virginia.

But the words so neatly written on the first of the pale blue pages were almost too brutal to take: *Vainly I had sought to borrow/ From my books surcease of sorrow—sorrow for the lost Lenore—/ For the rare and radiant maiden whom the angels name Lenore—/ Nameless here for evermore.*

He had always known it would come. Sometimes he thought he had known from the day his brother Henry died, Henry, that cherished older brother, almost unknown until he was on the verge of dying. Dying of consumption, like their actress mother. Dying, cared for by their Aunt Maria, Muddy, who had taken him into her household and her heart, just as she later took in the younger brother. Dying, coughing his life away in that attic room shared for a brief while by Poe, while a little girl they both called Sissy peeped at them apprehensively through the door.

"There are those as think the consumption's catching." Who had said that? Never mind. Don't think of it. Don't think of Virginia just now.

But . . . lost? For evermore? Poe sank his head into his hands. No point in trying to work. He wished to hell he had a drink. Just one glass of port, like last night. But it was better not to think of port, either. It was almost time for dinner. He sat quietly, waiting.

7

After this, Poe's poem went cold on him for the remaining weeks he spent in the country, but, refusing to come to life on paper, it nevertheless refused to die in his imagination. As golden September burned to red October, all manner of flying things raised Poe's eyes from his halted pen. He couldn't look from the window of the Brennans' farmhouse at night without encountering the silent flight of a tiny, tuftless saw-whet owl, couldn't walk through the fields for a chilly swim in the river without flushing the plover and the bobolink into whirring flight from beneath his feet. His feet were newly shod, for Muddy had anticipated what she regarded as a change for the better in their fortunes and had bought him an elegant new pair of gaitered shoes. So he walked in greater comfort one morning in early October along the Bloomingdale Road to the city, listening to the scream of jays and watching the gyre of a pair of goshawks overhead. In the city, the ever present jays still cursed and conversed, and through a soot-covered fourth-floor window at the Hoe Building on the corner of Nassau and Ann streets Poe watched a large, weather-beaten, orange-and-black butterfly sail past, rapidly losing the elevation it had gained to top the neighboring buildings. A migrating monarch, it was weeks behind the gay and gaudy clouds of its fellows that had already fluttered through the city, heading south. Would to God that he could follow them, Poe thought, but he carefully kept any expression of the thought off his face as he listened to the co-owner of the New York *Mirror* apologize, with deferential courtesy, for the smallness of the desk he pointed out to Poe in a corner of the editorial room.

"Editorial closet is more like it," Nathaniel Willis said. It was a small room. Two rough brick walls, two unpainted partitions, the one window. "We're just camping out here, you might say. If the daily edition goes well, I suppose we'll move into larger quarters. But one always hopes that, doesn't one?"

Poe quietly murmured an appropriate answer, and Willis smiled at him hesitantly, showing fine teeth set in a well-cut mouth. He was a sunny-tempered man, impulsive, generous, energetic, but so deferent that it was obvious to Poe that Willis and his partner were both gratified and edgy to have captured him as their employee. His reputation, or some version of it, must have preceded him, Poe thought. What were they expecting? Some display of not only genius but temperament? The shirking of duties, daily storms, fits of sulks and arrogance whenever they called upon him for some bit of hack work? What nonsense. In for a penny, in for a pound. He would do the job Muddy had hired him out to do, and teach them a thing or two about running a journal in the process.

"You'll have the usual contributions sent in by mail, I suppose,"

Poe said. "I'll be glad to look them over. Amateurs' pieces usually want a bit of retouching, at best."

"You're very kind, Mr. Poe," said Willis.

"Not at all," Poe said. "What time have you decided to go to press, if I might ask?"

"I thought two o'clock, with a stop-press at three to add any southern mail news and late Wall Street news. That should make home delivery possible between five and six o'clock."

"Very sound," Poe said.

"Naturally, as soon as the stop-press items are in, you'll be, er, free for the day. The artist must have time to pursue his own writings, eh, Mr. Poe? But I believe I understood from your mother-in-law that you're planning to move back into the city soon, and occasional evenings, I wondered, would you mind very much taking on some of the play and concert reviews? I'll try to do most of them, but I'm sometimes engaged in the evenings. You'll agree, I'm sure, that an active social life is the curse of the writer."

"No doubt. By my own is none too active, and I'll enjoy seeing something more of the theater. My wife is a confirmed invalid, and we live very quietly. Once we get resettled in the city, I'll be free for any evening events you deem appropriate. That should be within a week or two."

"You're *very* kind," Willis said. He hesitated, then added, "May I say that your mother-in-law impressed me as one of those rare angels upon the earth that women can sometimes be? That saintly face. That gentle and mournful voice. A veritable angel, Mr. Poe."

"I thank you on her behalf," Poe said gravely. "To my great good fortune, she has been a true mother to me for many years now. I call her by that dear name."

Willis's eyes moistened with the ready emotion of a romantic and chivalrous man, and Poe suppressed a smile. His own praise of Muddy had been perfectly sincere, but he knew Muddy's dignified but well-practiced begging act too well to feel much sympathy for her victims. And here was Willis, obviously touched, as well, by his own big-heartedness in heeding a distressed old widow's plea. Indeed, it was very big-hearted of Willis to hire the best editor in the United States for such a trifling salary.

But Poe found it impossible to feel irritable toward the fellow. Admiration and warmth shone from Willis's bluish-gray eyes, and the eyes went endearingly modest as Willis stammeringly asked him, "Would you, er, I've written an essay for the first edition on Monday, just to, er, set the tone of this business of going daily, you might say. I wonder, would you mind awfully looking it over for me? I mean, if you have time. But perhaps you're busy this morning. There'll be plenty of time Monday morning, when we actually start to work."

"I'm not busy at all," Poe said. "In fact, I only came into the city today with the object of gaining a little familiarity with the journal's materials and aims. Your essay will make an excellent starting place for the morning."

Someone, Willis or the other partner, George Morris, had already carefully equipped Poe's little desk with the necessary accouterments of the magazinist—paper, steel pens, a big scissors for clipping items from other papers on the exchange list, the usual array of writer's tools. Poe hung up his hat, straightened his ascot and prepared to apply himself conscientiously to his employer's first request. He saw that Willis's essay had obviously cost him effort. Numerous erasures and interlineations. But the end result was simple and to the point: Cheap, shilling copies of books had proliferated to the point that they lay about every parlor, rail car and steamboat. Literature today was an everyday matter, and the long pilgrimages made to it by quarterlies and monthlies were as much behind the time as stagecoaches on rail routes and sloop passage on the Hudson. In order to keep up with the literature of the time, everyone should read the daily New York *Mirror*.

Not too bad. He'd let it go without retouching. Editing one's editor was a thankless task anyway. Not that the essay wouldn't benefit by finer phrasing. To think that Willis was one of the most popular writers in America, if not *the* most popular, all on the basis of some sentimental little poems and a fashionable preoccupation with incest. But at least he had little to do with the usual grinning skulls and hooded figures and coffinlike shadows that were so much the literary mode. Not that it was bad, per se, to write within the fashion. Poe did a fair business with death's heads and coffins himself. Touches of incest too. Perhaps all writers had to write to their readers' faddish expectations, but Poe was convinced that he himself brought a vigor and an effective style to the same old subject matter, in a manner that a Willis could not hope to rival.

Willis seemed to be composing laboriously now at his own desk. No easy worker, he, for all that his finished products read easily. He was a remarkably fine-looking man, Poe decided, studying him out of the corner of his eye. Tall, graceful of carriage, with curly brown hair that he arranged a little foppishly. Poe had heard odds and ends about Nat Willis through the years, just as Willis had apparently heard odds and ends about him. Willis seemed to be making a career not just of writing, but out of being A Writer. He went much into the world, traveled, delivered poetical addresses, sought the intimacy of noted women and got into quarrels with notorious men. It was one way to gain acclaim. Unite the éclat of the littérateur with that of the man of society. But no, nonsense, that sort of running around, pushing oneself, would consume time that one needed for writing. Wouldn't it?

The other partner, George Morris, came into the room, and Poe heard the footsteps just in time to discipline his eyes and present, for Morris's appreciation, a picture of a hard-working assistant editor studiously reading a manuscript. So he was disagreeably surprised when he heard a voice other than Morris's and looked up to see the man who came in with him.

It was Lewis Gaylord Clark, editor and publisher of *Knickerbocker Magazine*. Certainly not a friend to Poe. Not for years. Not since Poe had first applied his critic's tomahawk to a book written by one of the members of Clark's mutual admiration society. Morris and Willis both looked puzzled by the arrival of the newcomer, but Willis rose to his feet to greet him. Poe also rose, but stood silently as Willis said, "Why, Clark, have you come to wish us luck on our new venture?"

"Precisely," Clark said. He smiled with smooth bonhomie. "I shall be expecting great things of you. Although I must say that I don't envy you the task of getting out a daily paper on literary matters. Finding enough good material for a monthly edition is almost more than I can manage." Clark had drooping eyelids, which made his eyes look cunning and secretive. He looked slyly at Poe. Clark and his *Knickerbocker* had never been given the opportunity to turn down any of Poe's articles, because Poe knew all too well what Clark's reception would be to any of his works, but Clark seemed to Poe to be insinuating just the opposite.

Willis said cheerfully, "I was worried myself about material until we were fortunate enough to enlist the aid of Mr. Poe. Mr. Poe, Mr. Clark, surely the two of you have already met. They tell me the population keeps growing, but it seems to me I always keep running across the same few hundred people everywhere I go on the eastern seaboard."

Poe waited. The literary circles were indeed small, and he had met Clark, had dined in his company several times at the George Grahams' in Philadelphia, as a matter of fact, but he was damned if he was going to acknowledge this if Clark didn't. But Clark held out his hand and said, "Poe, what a pleasant surprise. Why, no one told me you were in town."

"How are you, Clark?" Poe said politely. "How are things at the magazine?"

"Quite well," Clark said. "Booming, to tell the truth. The way circulation is growing, it looks as though I'll have to put on a new editor or two."

Poe flushed. Obviously Clark knew good and well that Poe was not only in New York but might have hoped for a good position somewhere. It was humiliating, to have his nose rubbed into the lowliness of a little job on a little daily, but Poe refused to rise to Clark's bait. "Yes, new editors can be a problem," he said. "Qualified men must be hard to attract."

"Oh, I wouldn't say that," Clark said. "If he weren't such a good friend, I might latch onto Rufe Griswold, for instance, but friendship and business are best kept separate. By the way, Poe, whatever happened to your scheme for starting your own magazine in Philadelphia? Changed your mind, did you?"

"I've merely postponed the plan," Poe said stiffly.

"Pity," Clark said. "I was looking forward to the competition. We don't have much in the monthly field, you know."

Poe counterattacked. "Indeed not," he said. "It's often commented that New York falls short as a literary center due to its lack of any . . . shall we say, leading magazine? I'm interested to learn that the *Knickerbocker* is prospering so. I seem to have heard contrary reports. Perhaps I'll consider New York as the locale when I resume the plans for my *Stylus*."

Now it was Clark's turn to flush, but he answered cautiously. Dueling was illegal but not uncommon, and, failing pistols, more than one editor had found both his printed and private opinions opposed by a stout cane. "Come, Poe, a new journal opens every other week in New York, and they go broke as regularly. It usually comes down to a matter of backing." His glance wandered from Poe's new, gaitered shoes to his old, turned collar. "But perhaps money is no problem for you, eh?"

Poe said quietly, "To the contrary. I am poor."

Nathaniel Willis, thoroughly uncomfortable by now, intervened. "I would never want to dissuade a man of Mr. Poe's extraordinary abilities from working on his own projects, Clark, but I sincerely hope he won't be leaving us too quickly. I have the highest admiration for Mr. Poe's genius, and I'm relying on him to help the *Mirror* off to a running start."

"Well, ah, of course, of course," Clark said. "Well, gentlemen, I'd best be getting back to my sanctum. I just wanted to drop by to wish you luck. Pleasure to see you, Poe."

"My pleasure," Poe said calmly. But he stood nervously rubbing his little finger against his thumb as his two new employers saw the visitor out. Damn the smug cur. He would show Clark. He would show all the fools. What a piece of sorry luck that Nat Willis and this foolish job had come along to stifle the flow of his poem. He would finish it somehow, and somehow he would get *Stylus*, and invitations would come pouring in from all of New York's social leaders, and he would look coldly down his fine, straight nose at them all. They would see. They would all see what a man of genius could do when he made up his mind to excel.

8

"Wait in my room!" Muddy said sharply. "I can take care of her. Out!"

Poe closed the door and leaned against it, panting. Blood, good God, he was sure this time. It was blood, blood suddenly gushing forth from its hidden channels, spreading, staining her nightgown, dyeing the sheets, blood flinging its sharp and salty smell into the air. Was there blood on his white shirt front? Specks of cheerful red, slowly turning rusty brown? Oh, God, it was maddening. He would surely go mad this time.

Poe looked wildly around the squalid room, Muddy's room in the dingy boarding house they had found a block off Washington

Square. He jumped as the door to his own room opened a crack. The cat slipped through, then the door closed again. The cat jumped onto Muddy's bed and tucked her paws tightly under her. Was there snow on the wind? A cat could tell.

The cat looked calm. What else could it tell? Was this the time Virginia would die? He couldn't endure it. He couldn't endure the blood. He shuddered. Blood, wet, trickling from her mouth back in Philadelphia, a vessel ruptured while she was singing, they thought at first, but it was the first certain indication of an illness that could be misdiagnosed and misnamed but no longer ignored. She recovered partially, but there had been blood since, and now blood again, in these cold, cramped little rooms, already the second hemorrhage since he had moved Virginia back to the filthy air of the city.

The door opened again, and Muddy hurried in. Was that blood on her big hands? No, they were always red and chapped, like a washerwoman's, poor Muddy. Poe gulped and said, "Shall I go for Dr. Francis? Is she still . . . ?"

"No, no, she's quiet now," Muddy said. "I gave her a grain of morphine. It helps her stop coughing, and that helps the bleeding stop. All she needs to do is keep quiet."

"But the doctor . . ."

"We don't need him again. He told me what to do. Opiates. They lower the respiratory irritability, and they help her breathe deeper too. Besides, it wasn't a real hemorrhage. She just coughed too hard. I've done it myself. Broken some little vessel when I had a cold."

"Are you sure?" Poe said.

"Of course I'm sure. You must go review the play, Eddy. It's the best thing for you, to get your mind off Sissy."

"It's only some trivial play," Poe said nervously. "I think I'd better stay here. Do we need more morphine? Have we enough money for it?"

"I saved two dollars back from last week. That's plenty. The landlady can send one of the servants to the pharmacy if I need anything. You'll be late for the theater if you don't leave now. Be sure to go straight there. Mr. Willis will be depending on your review. And promise me, Eddy, to come straight home. Won't you promise your poor old Muddy?"

She looked at him with concern. Ah, she must be worried that he would go to some barroom. Perhaps she was telling the truth about

Virginia, if she had unused anxiety enough to trouble about that. Poe began to feel calmer. He felt calmer still when Muddy allowed him to look in on Virginia briefly and he saw no telltale traces of blood. He paused, watching her slow breathing. White cotton sheet from toe to hip, white cotton nightgown from hip to chin, heavy white eyelids calmly closed, pale mouth slightly open, flickering blue shadows from the gas jet playing over all. She looked like a drowned girl at the bottom of a dark, blue ocean. She looked like his dreams and his nightmares combined into one.

Poe leaned forward, almost unwillingly, and touched Virginia's rounded cheek. Could he be sure she even breathed? The flesh was warm. She sighed and stirred, and Poe, panicked, pulled his hand away. But the white eyelids remained closed and the pale mouth only sighed and didn't speak. Embraced by morphia, her sleeping spirit was ensnared by dreams, by nightmares of her own.

Poe gazed bleakly at the small table by the window that was all he had to use at the moment as a writing desk. Buried in the stacks of pale blue paper there was still a raven, sitting above the door of a chamber that Poe reluctantly had had to leave but which his own ensnared imagination inhabited still. Sitting on a pallid bust of Pallas. Pallas Athena, goddess of arts. A bust of white plaster, white like Virginia's drugged face. As much of a wife. More.

Poe sighed without realizing that he sighed. The particular stack of paper headed *The Raven* was fatter now, but the damned poem was still not what he wanted. How could it be, he thought jealously, when other tasks demanded so much of him? The last stanza was only the latest mess. *And the lamplight o'er him streaming casts his shadow on the floor.* How could light get up there behind the door, the bust and the raven? Hopeless.

But forget it. There was no hope of working on revisions tonight. Even a man possessed could not work with his stricken wife lying unconscious not two feet from his pen. Go out. The curtains of the Park Theatre raised nightly at seven-thirty, and Muddy seemed determined that he should go. Besides, he faced a twenty-block walk down to the theater from this most recent abode, two rooms on the second floor of a nondescript building on Amity Street, and he would just have time to make it if he walked fast.

Feeling tired and depressed, Poe went out into the city. No snow, but it looked, as always, like rain. A shifty east wind was blowing again, rattling the swinging signs along Broadway, and Poe drew the flaps of his old West Point greatcoat closer to his body.

The gaslights shivered and danced with each freak of the wind. All cities were ugly, Poe knew, but how he hated this particular city. Crowded, dirty, few trees, no grass, no sky, no view, no stars, no space. Stumbling over furniture in rooms that were too small. Living cheek by jowl with hundreds of other people in each little block. No place for the cat to go outside. No sunshine. Nowhere to plant a seed and watch it grow. Nowhere to be alone. Constant noise. Fire bells ringing nightly. Soot in the air and grime on the streets, and now Virginia's recurring illness in their tawdry quarters. Why, why, couldn't he make up his mind to take her somewhere to warm, dry, healing air? How could he stay here, scurrying and scrambling for five dollars for a poem, blinking at death and winking at ambition? But he couldn't leave New York now.

Three blocks down Broadway, Poe slowed as he passed Gabriel Harrison's tea and tobacco shop. On a night like this, Gabriel's stove would be glowing cherry red. Turn in? He had been back several times to chat with his new friend. Gabriel would welcome one with his usual enthusiasm and perhaps one of the bottles that were always so conveniently near at hand on his shelves. But no, he'd promised Muddy. And there was the ridiculous play to review. He hastened on.

No, he couldn't leave these crowded streets now, not when his grand scheme was finally beginning to build up the steam that he and Shea had worked so hard to engineer. True, any interest that John Jacob Astor's grandson might have had in sponsoring *The Stylus* seemed to have faded since Poe went to work for the *Mirror*, and true, his hope that Harper's might publish a new American collection of his tales hadn't materialized, but at least the biographical sketch that James Russell Lowell had been so slowly writing for *Graham's* was finally finished. Although Poe's "life" wouldn't run until the February edition, word of it was already getting around. Edgar A. Poe, *the most discriminating, philosophical, and fearless critic upon imaginative works who has written in America*. Edgar A. Poe, the writer of tales, possessor of *a faculty of vigorous, yet minute analysis and a wonderful fecundity of imagination*. Edgar A. Poe, the poet whose works had *the smack of ambrosia*, and Edgar A. Poe, possessor, furthermore, of *that indescribable something which men have agreed to call genius.* Poe cherished not only the compliments but the hint of more tangible rewards due to Lowell's good services. One Charles Briggs, better known on newspaper row as Harry Franco after a popular novel he had written, was trying to find a monied publisher to help him start a new weekly literary paper in January, and Franco had recently started showing a flattering interest in Poe on the strength of Lowell's recommendation and praise. If only there was some way he could get part interest in the journal. God knew, it wouldn't be the same as his very own *Stylus*, but, while awaiting the appearance of monied backers of his own, it might be the next best thing.

Why, when things were just starting to work, did Virginia have to choose this particular moment to get sick again? A gust of panicky wrath blew down his neck with the gusting wind. Poe's hurrying feet had brought him even with City Hall Park, and there was no windbreak here, only the bare branches of elm, poplar and catalpa, pathetic little city groves that pretended to be a forest.

The park meant that Poe was almost to his destination. He hurried to outstrip the wind, past the Doric columns of the Astor House. Even in this freezing easterly, a few men lounged on the hotel's front steps, as they always did, watching the busy bustle of Broadway, whittling and reading newspapers in the daytime, smoking at night, eyeing women's ankles. A good night for it, with the wind whipping so. From a hundred windows of the hotel the warm flare of candles blazed. Nat Willis lived here, lived in a luxurious suite, held court in the public dining rooms and parlors. Daily, from nine in the morning until press time, Poe worked quietly and industriously at his corner desk at the *Mirror*, and daily, since they had moved back into town, he trudged drearily home to his boarding house, while daily Nat Willis blithely strolled the couple of blocks up to the noisy elegance of the Astor House. If Willis weren't so eternally friendly and helpful, Poe could easily learn to hate him. But Poe's time would come.

And now, at last, here were the hissing gas jets of the theater lights. Just in time. The night was living up to its promise, and a few preliminary spatters of rain leaked from the cold murk that was the sky. Poe showed his journalist's pass and hurried inside. The theater was cold. The management relied upon the body heat of its audience to warm it. But at least it was well lighted and dry, and Poe took his seat, shivering. He must have walked even faster than usual. He was early.

On the front benches in the pit, a few newsboys, shine boys and match-and-toothpick boys had apparently forsaken their customary evening haunt, the Bowery Theatre, and were settling in for a few hours' oblivion, like Poe. Children of the streets, they would sleep later, in this cold night of early winter, on the stairways of the newspaper offices or in old barrels and boxes under doorsteps, but they always seemed able to find a few coins somehow for their three passions—the theater, tobacco and gin. A distinct odor of gin wafted now from the pit, and Poe looked at the raggedy boys almost enviously. Then he saw a face on the bench right in front of him smiling at him eagerly, and he recognized an acquaintance, a writer, like most of Poe's acquaintances.

Distracted by his thoughts and slightly dazed by the buffeting of the cold wind, Poe had to seek for the man's name. The fellow had a fat, round face and a body to match, and like many fat men often played the clown. Cornelius Mathews, that was it. A good friend of a man who held promise of being a good friend to Poe, Evert Duyckinck, one of the most influential of the New York littérateurs. And Mathews was not without power himself in the city's chronic literary wars. Poe roused himself. It was only politic to be nice to the man.

Mathews reached a cold hand across the bench to shake Poe's, saying, "What a pleasure! I wish I'd known you were here, Mr. Poe, we could have sat together. But I only dashed in by impulse. The theater suddenly beckoned imperiously. You know how it is. I've a play of my own in my desk, into which I have put my very best, and now I must compare it with the wares of others."

"Ah, a play," Poe said politely. "What are you calling it?"

"*Witchcraft*," Mathews proclaimed. It was obviously the only opening he needed, for he proceeded immediately to tell Poe all about it. Poe chose an attentive expression to arrange on his face and listened patiently, knowing that the rising of the curtain would shortly save him. But although Mathews's play sounded like silly mishmash his interest was finally caught. What was the fellow saying? Something about the horror of the hero when convinced that his mother was a witch. His thoughts flew back to his raven.

"I suppose it might be difficult to train one," Poe said, "but why don't you at this point have a raven, bird of ill omen, flit across the stage over the witch's head?"

"A raven?" Mathews said. "What an interesting thought."

"Well, it might be an effective bit of stage business." Poe's eyes stared at the drawn curtain, but his mind was turned inward. "Do you know," he said, "that bird, that imp bird, has begun pursuing me mentally, perpetually. I cannot rid myself of its presence. As I sit here I hear its croak and the flap of its wings in my ear, as I used to hear them when I was a boy." He blinked, remembering Mathews, and added a word of explanation: "My foster father moved to England for a few years when I was a child. He put me in school at Stoke Newington. The place was thick with ravens. I don't know why. Maybe all of England is."

"Are you working with a raven yourself?" Mathews said.

"A poem," Poe murmured.

"How *very* interesting. Inspired by Dickens's raven in *Barnaby*?"

Poe smiled. "Perhaps. The poem's lain in my desk so long I've forgotten. Yes, it probably was Dickens's raven. I was going to have an owl, a night bird, bird of wisdom, with its ghostly presence and inscrutable gaze, entering the window of a vault where a man sat beside a bier. But I changed it for the sake of the raven's ability to speak. You know how some poems can change. You take them out occasionally, you add a line or two, you put them away again. It was going to be only a short poem, but through the years it's grown despite me. I shall blame it on the bird. Do you think that Dickens was similarly haunted by Barnaby's raven?"

"Oh, I doubt that," Mathews said. "Dickens writes too fast. He doesn't allow himself time to be haunted by anything. I think . . . Damn, the curtain's going up. I suppose we must be quiet. Shall I see you after the play? You must share a hot oyster supper with me. And a hot whiskey or two, what do you say? Then we can talk comfortably."

On the benches near them, other spectators began to look at Mathews indignantly, and one elderly man hissed a "Shhhhh!" Mathews grinned and turned around to face the stage, and Poe took a lead pencil and a few sheets of folded paper from his coat pocket and quietly prepared to do his duty as theater critic. Hot oysters and hot whiskeys. Now, that had a true smack of ambrosia. But he couldn't accept Mathews's hospitality without returning it, and with money needed for Virginia's morphine, there would be none to spare for enjoyment. And whiskey, hot or cold, no, a pity, but no. He'd had nothing to drink since he left Philadelphia. Well, nothing to speak of. One little glass of port that night at Gabriel Harrison's. Best leave well enough alone.

Attend, now. The actors had begun their lines. Poe had a special feeling for actors. His own mother had played the Park in light comedy when Poe was a baby. His father too, according to brother Henry, Henry reared by the Poe family rather than wealthy strangers and therefore more familiar than he with the tales told of their parents. His parents. His father. When Poe tried to remember him, there was nothing but the frowning brows and Scottish burr of John Allan. His own father had simply disappeared into the shadows of time. Dead, some of the Baltimore Poes said. Dead of drink, said others, while still others preferred dead of consumption. No, don't think of consumption. Think of salty old Grandmother Poe's favorite theory: her son, Poe's father, wasn't dead at all, but run off with some other woman. Run off, discouraged by unfavorable press notices, perhaps while acting in this very theater, to Scotland, from whence he would someday return.

But attend. Poe's now was the duty of writing the night's press notices. At minimum, the actors deserved his attention.

Later, hanging on the edges of the crowd leaving the theater, Cornelius Mathews reluctantly accepted Mr. Poe's excuse that his wife was ill and he'd best be getting straight home instead of stopping for supper. Why, Mr. Poe was one of the most courteous, attentive listeners he'd ever encountered, and he was eager to tell him more about his play. Cornelius detained Mr. Poe a few moments, chatting. Outside, the rain was turning to ice. Cornelius wasn't eager to brave the tempest, and the theater crowd always presented an interesting spectacle. Besides, at intermission, Cornelius had spotted a party of ladies, to his surprise, for the habit of theatergoing was frowned upon even for gentlemen. He wanted to satisfy his curiosity as to the identity of the bold ladies.

Good, there they came. He recognized two of them as a Mrs. Mowatt and a Mrs. Ellet. That explained it. Anna Mowatt was one of those women's emancipation types, and it was even rumored that she was planning to defy society to the point of writing and staging a play. What kind of play? Not about witchcraft, surely. That would be the end of life, if the silly woman had suddenly decided to write about witchcraft.

"Excuse me just a moment," Cornelius said to Mr. Poe, and he turned toward Mrs. Mowatt, calling her name. The other woman that he knew in the party, the poetess Mrs. Ellet, looked at Cornelius coldly. A blundering gaucherie, that, to call Mrs. Mowatt's name loudly among a throng of strangers. "I beg your pardon, Mrs. Ellet," Cornelius said. "I just wanted to say good evening to Mrs. Mowatt."

Mrs. Ellet arched an eyebrow and, without replying, continued to stare coldly at Cornelius and his companion. He blundered on.

"Uh, Mrs. Ellet, here is someone you simply must meet. May I introduce Mr. Edgar Poe to your acquaintance? Mr. Poe, Mrs. Elizabeth Ellet."

Mr. Poe immediately doffed his hat and bowed. But Mrs. Ellet only looked outraged and swept by them wordlessly.

"Oh dear, Mr. Poe," Cornelius said. "Oh dear, I'm truly sorry. I suppose I shouldn't have tried to introduce you in such a public place."

"No matter," Mr. Poe said with gentle courtesy. He looked after the departing Mrs. Ellet. "Rather a handsome lady," he said. "Haven't I encountered her name? She writes, doesn't she?"

"Indeed yes, she's both an authoress and a poetess. She moved to South Carolina after she married, but I think her husband rarely sees her. She always seems to be in New York. Ordinarily she's a very pleasant lady. Decorous, but pleasant. I suppose she felt a little . . . you know, conspicuous, coming to the theater. Please forgive me, Mr. Poe."

Mr. Poe murmured new reassurances that he was not offended by the snub. Cornelius finally allowed himself to say good night. It was a pity. Cornelius *would* have liked to talk more about his play, but he bethought himself of his supper and took consolation in the form of two dozen baked saddle rocks at the nearest red lantern marking an oyster cellar.

The night was truly foul. Cornelius next indulged himself in only a couple of hot spiced rums and, bought from a shivering street vendor, a single meat pie before boarding a northbound omnibus and rattling homeward along Broadway. He was astounded, as the bus reached the corner of Bleecker Street, to see none other than his own Mr. Poe, standing in a circle of sickly light thrown by a streetlamp, writing on the margin of a paper and utterly lost to all about him.

Cornelius dashed off the bus. He slipped and almost fell under the wheels of a two-horse hackney coach, which swerved and collided with a brewery wagon. Their wheels locked, and the whole traffic of the street came to a noisy, cursing standstill. Mr. Poe never looked up, even as Cornelius panted up to him. Frozen raindrops sparkled in Mr. Poe's black hair, and his feet were in a freezing puddle.

"Mr. Poe, whatever are you doing here!" Cornelius said. "Quickly, come under my umbrella. I thought you were going straight home. Why did you flee from a friend and supper?"

"Ah, Mr. Mathews," Mr. Poe said distractedly. The wind snatched at his words, and Cornelius had to bend close to hear him. "Forgive me. I intended to go home, but I couldn't have eaten, drunk or slept or gone a step farther than this, or waited a moment longer than now. It is *The Raven*."

"Your poem? Of course. You had an inspiration." Cornelius was thrilled. How supremely artistic! He filed away the picture of the-haunted-artist-in-the-storm for possible use of his own sometime, but he added, "I understand perfectly, but the height of a storm is no proper time for writing, Mr. Poe. You'll catch your death."

Mr. Poe looked at Cornelius despondently, as if dying weren't such a bad idea. "My God, but I'm heartily disgusted with this poem," he said. "Sometimes I think it's good, but many times I've so poor an opinion of it that I've been on the point of destroying it."

"Oh, you mustn't do that," Cornelius said. "I'm sure it must be excellent. You're just tired of it. One gets that way, toward the end. Won't you read it to me?"

Mr. Poe shook his head. "I haven't the manuscript with me."

"But surely you remember it. Why, I could recite you my *Witchcraft* word for word after laboring with it so long. How does it start? Just recite me the first stanzas."

Not at all forgetting the storm, conscious of the romantic picture he himself surely now presented of the playwright bravely encouraging a fellow artist no matter what the consequences to himself, Cornelius coaxed until his companion began to recite in a strained voice. The first line was decidedly appropriate: "Once upon a midnight dreary . . ."

Then Cornelius did forget himself. Great, black wings fanned him like the cruel east wind, and an inhuman voice began croaking grief and madness. Cornelius stood with Poe in the puddle, clutching the wind-beaten umbrella over their heads, until Poe came to the words "Perched and sat, and nothing more."

A sheer lack of strength seemed to make Mr. Poe stop. With a slight tremor, he said, "It is cold."

Indeed it was. Cornelius suddenly realized that the drip of the umbrella was running down the back of his collar. "The poem is superb," he said sincerely, "but it is madness to stay out in the storm. Come, let me walk you to your door."

The spell was broken. Mr. Poe's lips continued to frame snatches of more verses as they walked on together, but the wind was so noisy and Cornelius was so conscious of the wet coldness of his collar that it was very hard to follow. Rather a long poem too.

When they reached the steps of Mr. Poe's home at 15 Amity, Mr. Poe turned and thanked Cornelius with the peculiar grace and charm of manner that always seemed to distinguish him.

"Be sure and finish this Raven poem," Cornelius said.

With a sigh, Mr. Poe answered, "I shall have to. It seems to have reached the point where it will not let me rest. Perhaps if I get it all on paper the ill-omened fowl will quit my ear and leave me in peace."

They said good night, and Cornelius turned his steps back toward Broadway. No, despite Mr. Poe's earlier suggestion, he wouldn't add a raven to his beloved play. If his strange friend succeeded in finishing his poem, ravens would surely become too closely identified with the name of Edgar A. Poe. What an odd man he was. Standing under a streetlight in the rain to write. Good heavens, a snug study, after all, was far the better place. Well, Mr. Poe would find such comforts up his stairs, and a hot spiced rum, no doubt, to take the chill off the night. That's exactly what Cornelius would have when he got to his own digs, a couple more spiced rums. Better hurry. Art was all very well, but there was no sense in catching cold.

9

Compared to London with its population of two million people, New York with its four hundred thousand was a small town. It was small in area too, and since the vast but inconsequential foreign scum and domestic dregs kept largely to their own purlieus, an important fellow such as the Reverend Rufus Griswold could confidently count upon running across numerous acquaintances when he chanced to visit the city. So, on a snowy afternoon soon after Edgar Poe concluded he could make no more improvements, at least for now, on the poem that had come to obsess him, the Reverend Griswold was dismayed but not surprised to bounce into Horace Greeley's New York *Tribune* and encounter, leaving, no less a person than Edgar A. Poe. Griswold flushed a vivid red and stood stock-still, whereas Poe turned paler and drew his chin up proudly. Griswold opened his mouth to speak—to say what, he hadn't the faintest idea —but Poe walked past him as though he didn't exist, leaving Griswold rooted to the floor and redder than ever.

Griswold glanced quickly around. In the busy bustle of the newspaper office the slight had apparently gone unnoticed. But there was no denying it to himself; he had just been cut, by God, by Edgar Poe. It was the depth of something or other, to be snubbed by a man worthy of no man's notice. Griswold therefore clenched his fists, to express his anger, and took several deep breaths, to calm it, before running up the stairs to the publisher's private office.

There was, however, an observer in the *Tribune* newsroom—a penny-a-liner waiting to try to peddle a paragraph about an illegal sixty-three-round boxing match he had witnessed. He blinked in bored bewilderment at Griswold's disappearing back and thought how much the man resembled the poet he had stared at a few moments before. Slender, nervous-looking men, both of them, of medium height, with unusually large heads. The two might be brothers. But if so, why didn't they speak?

The penny-a-liner went back to waiting impatiently for the city editor's attention and dismissed the thought. Yet there were grounds for his brief confusion. Except that Griswold's shoulders were slightly stooped and Poe's were habitually straight—Poe's years as Private Perry, then West Point Cadet Poe, stayed in his posture forever—the Reverend Rufus Griswold, like the double in Poe's "William Wilson," was enough like Poe in many ways to be not just a brother but a second self.

Poe had another doppelgänger, a zany Georgian named Thomas Holley Chivers, who just happened to be something of a genius, but he was at his home in Georgia that afternoon working on a play and wouldn't be in New York until the following June.

Griswold was not a genius. It was cause enough for his initial dissatisfaction with Poe. Too, Griswold only dreamed what Poe really lived, and lived what Poe only dreamed in nightmares. For example, on the day his beloved wife died, Griswold sat for thirty hours by the side of her coffin, kissing the cold, dead lips and embracing her every time the watchers urged him to try to sleep. His grief would not subside. On the day she was buried, at the moment the body was placed in the tomb, he shrieked and fell on the coffin with agonized weeping. Nor, after he was finally dragged away, could he forget. Forty days after the funeral, he still could not believe his wife was dead. He dreamed of their reunion night after night. In a fit of madness, he went again to the vault wherein she lay. The sexton unclosed it, and Griswold went alone, down, down, into that silent chamber. He kneeled by her side and prayed. Then, with a trembling hand, he unfastened the coffin lid, and turned aside the drapery that hid her face—only to see the hideous changes wrought by death and time and rot.

Beside himself, he kissed the forehead that had been so warm and white in life but which now was black and cold. He cut off a lock of the beautiful, still luxuriant hair that was damp with the dew of death. Then he sank down in senseless agony beside the ruin of all that was dearest to him in the world. In the evening, a friend found him there, his face still resting upon her own, and his body almost as lifeless and cold as that before him.

It was the stuff of the day's bad poetry, surely, and, like Poe, Rufus Griswold had dreamed in his youth of becoming a great poet. He tried, in fact, but he had no creative ability. Failing poetry, Griswold dreamed in his young manhood, also like Poe, of becoming a great critic. Like Poe, throughout his life he often regarded himself as a solitary soul, homeless, joyless, an outcast, wandering through the world with only his wits to depend upon. Like Poe, Griswold journeyed hopefully between New York, Philadelphia and Boston, trying to find work. After Poe had made the *Southern Literary Messenger* in Richmond the best literary magazine of its time, then left, Griswold tried unsuccessfully to land the post of editor. After Poe helped make *Graham's Lady's and Gentleman's Magazine* in Philadelphia the largest magazine in America, then left, temporarily he thought, he walked back into the offices one day to find Rufus Griswold occupying his chair, whereupon Poe turned on his heel and left permanently. They knew the same men, and the time came when they loved the same woman.

As to their dissimilarities, Griswold was a farmer's son, though he would have liked to conceal it, and he spent his boyhood on a barren little Vermont farm. Poe was the son of players, but his father's people had been gentlefolk, and he was reared in a genteel setting. Griswold was a Northerner, Poe was a Southerner. Griswold had a few months' schooling here and there in little country schools. Poe was educated in private schools in England and Richmond, and although he had only a year at the University of Virginia before his gambling debts and John Allan's parsimony forced him out, Poe had the necessary educational trappings of a gentleman. Both read widely, but Poe had the benefit of a creative mind to apply to his readings. Lastly, Griswold pursued what he termed "theological studies" after the Panic in '37 spurred him to cast about for some way to supplement his income, whereas Poe was the adherent of no religion. This was scarcely regarded as being to Poe's credit in an era in which to be irreligious was to be considered a lunatic, but then preaching solely for money wasn't much to anybody's credit either.

At the time Poe had moved his little household to New York, Griswold was working in Philadelphia, doing several hundred things at once, as was his custom. Griswold was involved in editing a quarterly review for an anti-Catholic Protestant association, jobbing together books on just about any subject one can name, proclaiming the need for a copyright system to protect the works of Americans from being swamped by a sea of pirated editions of British books and simultaneously pirating the works of as many British writers as he could scrape up. He also preached occasionally.

But the pertinent fact is that Griswold's daughters lived in New York with their dead mother's wealthy relatives—Griswold was never foolish enough to marry poor women—and not only literary business but family duty brought him frequently to the city. So it was inevitable that he would meet Poe sooner or later, and characteristic that he would then bound up the stairs at the *Tribune,* burst into Horace Greeley's office and, unable to resist telling a piquant bit of gossip even if it was on himself, burst out, "I've just been cut by the lowest cur in the world. Think of it! Cut by Edgar Poe!"

Greeley, as always, was writing with a great noise as his nib scratched away at the paper. As always, he finished his sentence and marked his place before looking up impatiently. But his scowl changed to a smile as he recognized his young friend and protégé Rufe Gris, as he called him. "Friend Gris!" he said. "Welcome."

"Did you hear me? Why, he cut me cold! And after all I've done for the ingrate! But it's just like Poe. Did I ever tell you about the time he cheated me out of seven dollars and a half for a review on my *Poets and Poetry*? There we were, talking about the book not long after it came out, and Poe said he'd thought of reviewing it for the *Democratic Review* but someone else had beat him to it. So I told him, naturally, that he needn't trouble himself about the publication of his critique should he decide to write it, for I would attend to all that—get it in some reputable journal and see that he got their usual pay. But if you know Poe, you must know that he's always penniless. I paid him his fee out of my own pocket, so he wouldn't have to wait, and I knew he could use the double payment. So what does Poe do? He accepts my offer, writes the review, hands it to me, and I hand over seven-fifty. Naturally, I didn't dream of looking over the manuscript in his presence. I just took it for granted that all was right. But do you know what he'd had the nerve to say? He'd cut the book to pieces! Said I'd shown rotten judgment and partiality to my friends! Now, what do you think of a cur like that?"

Greeley astonished him by bursting into helpless laughter. He laughed so long and merrily that he had to put down his pen. Finally, he said, "Gris, Gris. And did you think you'd bribed Poe nicely to write you a puff?"

"Well, it was a perfectly standard transaction," Griswold said defensively.

The editor dredged a dubious-looking handkerchief from his crammed coat pockets and wiped his eyes. "I would never have guessed Poe had a sense of humor," he said. "Augustus Shea's been after me to pick up the most marvelously morbid poem, a thing Poe's given to the *American Review* for February. No humor there, believe me."

"What poem?" Griswold said jealously. "Poe has scarcely written any poetry for years."

Greeley shrugged. His eyes wandered back to his editorial. "Well, he seems to be writing it now," he said. "Gris, sup with me tonight, and tell me all your news. And scoot in the meantime. I'm busy."

"You're always busy," Griswold said. He removed a rusty garden rake from a chair by his friend's desk and sat down. "Besides, I'm engaged tonight. So listen to me for a moment, but first tell me about this poem of Poe's. You're not really going to reprint it, are you?"

"Why not?" Greeley said. "Shea swears it's great. The *Mirror* plans to reprint it too, and apparently Shea is trying to get all sorts of other people lined up. He and Poe have concocted some kind of publicity scheme. Run it anonymously at first, and start everyone guessing who wrote it. Too clever by half, but you know what the holiday season's like. There's never any solid news, so I've got to print what I can get. And this Poe is a comer, or I miss my guess. He's been doing quite a nice job of work for the *Mirror*, and Bisco and Harry Franco are thinking of taking him on for their new *Broadway Journal*, had you heard?"

"Hire a ruthless scoundrel like that? I don't believe it," Griswold said.

"Believe it. And they're not just hiring him. Somebody said something about a partnership, in exchange for the privilege of listing his name on the masthead. But enough of Poe. Tell me about yourself. Are you going to be around over Christmas?"

"I don't know. Yes, probably. But I may have to go out to Illinois."

"What in heaven's name for?"

"Don't you read your own paper? I sent you a notice, and you ran it. I've been appointed professor of belles lettres at Shurtleff College. Not that I'll have to spend any time out there, of course. But now they're going to award me an honorary Doctor of Divinity degree. What do you think of that? You'll have to start calling me Dr. Griswold."

"Stuff," said Greeley.

Griswold's feelings were hurt. For two long years he had campaigned as a crusading clergyman-editor against the growing menace of Catholicism (those incoming tides of dangerous Irishmen!) and the reward of an honorary degree from the little Baptist college seemed only appropriate. He had looked forward to a more enthusiastic reception to his news, not to mention a paragraph in the *Trib*. He rose and replaced the rusty rake on the chair. "Well, I must be off," he said. "I've got a thousand people to see. Will you be at Miss Lynch's soirée tomorrow night?"

"She sent a card. I suppose I must," Greeley said. "Ice cream and pâtés and all sorts of horrors. I don't know how people's stomachs stand these affairs. But if you're going, all the better. We can finish our chat there."

As Griswold left the publisher's office, Greeley's pen was already scratching away, with a noise like the frantic feet of a large insect trying to escape the page. So much for the *Trib*. Griswold would somehow get his paragraph about the degree in the paper yet. Meantime, there were less pleasant things to contemplate. This possibility of Poe's being presented with a partnership in a new journal, it made his chest go all hot and tight. Poe's arrogance was already impossible. What kind of lordly airs would the man give himself if he lucked into a position of real power? Worst of all, Poe would be happily ensconced in New York, while he, Griswold, remained stuck in Philadelphia.

But once out on Nassau Street, in the heart of newspaper row, Griswold's spirits rose. The city was dressed in winter white. Snow on the sidewalks, snow on the streets. Runners had replaced wheels on carriages, and the silvery jangle of sleigh bells was everywhere on the air. What a glorious, merry city! How much more exhilarating than stodgy old Philadelphia!

Walking carefully so as not to slip, Griswold proceeded along Nassau, bowing to occasional acquaintances. At the corner of Ann Street, where the New York *Mirror* and, temporarily at least, Edgar Poe had offices, Griswold frowned briefly and hurried his footsteps, but within a quarter-block he regained his smile as he saw one of his more charming literary acquaintances, Fanny Osgood, hurrying toward him. He stopped and made a low bow.

"My dear Mrs. Osgood," he said. "What brings you out on such a day? And on foot in all this ice. Tsk. It's foolhardy."

Fanny blinked at him with pretended myopia, perhaps to give herself a moment to place him, and perhaps also aware that the rapid fluttering of her dark lashes called complimentary attention to her large gray eyes. Their acquaintance was closer by correspondence than in person. Frances Sargent Osgood, writer of many graceful little poems and wife of the portrait painter Samuel S. Osgood, had been a consistent contributor to *Graham's* during Griswold's brief turn as editor there, and he found her both whimsical and delightful. Pleasant to look at too, with her black hair and slender, almost fragile figure. She was all wrapped up on this winter's day in dark fur—fur cape, fur muff, fur boa, from which her pale little face peeped gaily.

"Reverend Griswold, well met," she said. "Alas, I've been summoned to the *Knickerbocker* to retrieve a small effort that Mr. Clark deemed unworthy of his pages. Tell me whom to send it to next. To you? Have you any influence at *Godey's*?"

"Certainly," Griswold lied, "and more with Clark. Leave it with him, and let me see what I can do."

"How wonderful it is to have friends," she sighed. "I shall indeed leave it all in your capable hands and go home. Have you ever seen such snow? And there'll be more, I warrant. Look at those slate-colored clouds. They'll be dumping on us at any moment."

"You must let me find you a cab," Griswold said gallantly.

"No use," Fanny said. "The city's bogged up to its neck. I just saw the most wonderful accident befall a party of sleighers. They turned a corner too fast, and hats, buffalo robes and people all tumbled into the gutter, while the horse and sleigh decamped up the street. It was splendid."

Griswold laughed, as she apparently meant him to do. "Then you must allow me to walk you home, if that is our one form of transportation," he said. "The footing is very dangerous. I've seen a half-dozen pedestrians take a fall already this afternoon."

"My grateful thanks, Reverend Griswold, but I'm to meet Samuel shortly, and he'll see to me. He popped over to look in at Trinity. They got the first flying buttress up before the cold set in, have you seen? And the spire, well! A friend has somehow gotten hold of the tower key, and Samuel's hoping to go up. It's well over two hundred feet tall by now, I understand. Just think what a glorious view of the city he'll have, not to mention of all this horrid snow."

"You don't care for snow?" Griswold said. "Neither do I, usually. I dream of sunshine and a temperate climate."

Fanny pursed her lips. "So I've heard," she said, "and I'm not at all pleased. Are you really going to marry some wealthy widow from Charleston and abandon all your friends here in the frozen North?"

Griswold flushed. "Certainly not," he said.

"No? I could have sworn I heard there was a lady who had engaged your interest, although someone did say that she was, er, Jewish, I believe. That will teach me to listen to idle talk. But you must not blame me. All the other talk I hear recently is about war with Mexico, and you cannot blame me for wearying of that."

Griswold looked suitably somber at the mention of war and hastened to steer the conversation from the rumor Fanny had heard. "I fear that particular bit of talk may be true," he said. "We're trembling on the brink of war, and for what? For the sinful extension of slavery and in order to pay the debts of a desert called Texas."

"Oh no, Reverend Griswold, I forbid you to tell me anything about the war. I detest war. Surely all civilized people do. Tell me . . . oh, about your little daughters? Are they well? Tell me about your latest book, whatever that may be. I have a good idea. Why don't you do an anthology of female poets of America, and refrain from consigning me to the appendix this time?"

Fanny laughed openly at his discomfort, normally not a good tack with Griswold, but he ended by laughing with her. She had teased him before about his ranking of her poetry in his *Poets and Poetry of America*, by which, naturally, he meant male poets and men's poetry. He had included few women, even in the appendix, and a few other literary ladies had been bold enough to let him know of their displeasure. But Fanny's teasing was perfectly good-natured, with none of the nagging sulkiness that characterized so many of these would-be poetesses. And besides, Mrs. Osgood looked so very pretty today. Why had he never noticed before that she was quite so pretty? But he was keeping her here in the snow. That would never do. Her health was said to be delicate.

Feeling very much the cavalier, Griswold said, "I think you may have given me an extraordinarily good idea. We must talk about it. But I will never forgive myself if I let you get chilled. You're coming to Miss Lynch's soirée tomorrow night? You must promise me that we can discuss the book there."

Fanny smiled. "I fear we're not important enough to have been invited to Miss Lynch's soirée. She has us to afternoon affairs from time to time, but we haven't graduated to her grand evening affairs, so I cannot give you the promise. But you must give me your arm in crossing this street. Then I must let you get on about your business."

How lightly her gloved hand rested in the crook of his arm. How small and dainty the glove. Griswold helped her solicitously and felt sincerely distressed when the charmingly furred young woman declined his offer to walk her to her destination, a friend's house en route to the Astor House, where he learned she was staying this winter. Safely on the curb, he paused, prolonging the moment. "You must allow me to have a word with Miss Anna Lynch. Her salon can only benefit by your presence. It amazes me to discover that she has not asked you to the soirée. She is fond of the best people, and how could you and Mr. Osgood possibly not qualify? I will welcome the opportunity to be your sponsor."

"Pray don't, Reverend Griswold. I'd feel such a fool."

"I insist. How can I forbid myself the pleasurable possibility of seeing you more often? And Mr. Osgood, of course."

Fanny chuckled, a low, throaty little chuckle. "Are you flirting with me, sir?" she demanded saucily. "No, surely not. I'll start disbelieving in your Charleston widow if you don't take care, and your engagement was such an interesting topic. No, you mustn't walk me any farther. Not a step. I forbid it. Where were you going next? I'm sure you're going out of your way, Reverend Griswold, and I won't have it."

"I had no other errands," Griswold murmured.

"I don't believe you."

"Well, it had occurred to me to stop and see Harry Franco and John Bisco, but . . ."

"Franco and Mr. Bisco and their new *Broadway Journal*? You must go immediately, and be very nice to them so they'll welcome future contributions from your friends. Now, where are they? Oh yes, on Beekman in Clinton Hall, I believe, so you must go that way, and I must go this. Good afternoon, Reverend Griswold. I'll tell Samuel I saw you. Good-by. Good-by."

Griswold stood in the snow and watched her out of sight. She moved gracefully, with a light, quick step, like a bird skimming over the snow. Amusing little thing, unpretentious and gay. Yet somehow arresting today. Perhaps it was the furs. Her husband must be doing well, putting up at the Astor House and buying such furs for his wife. They looked like Russian sable, and a set like that could cost up to a hundred dollars. Or one's attention had been caught just by her smile, so ready and artless, even though her words were sometimes artful. What must it be like to be blessed with a happy temperament like hers?

There, she was gone. Griswold became aware that, quietly, vertically, thick snowflakes were falling. On a sudden impulse he ran a few steps and caught a flying flake in his mouth. It melted instantly, leaving a tiny aftertaste of dust. Good heavens, he hoped no one had seen him, a dignified man of the cloth chasing snowflakes like a boy. But he felt queerly light and alert and somehow more alive than he'd felt ten minutes before.

Happier, too. He'd been a little out of sorts recently. Fanny's rumor had a solid basis of fact, even though it was a wealthy Jewish spinster, not a wealthy Jewish widow, to whom he had lately been giving troubled thought. To have a luxurious home, to be able to travel, to buy expensive books, to stop working so damnably hard—it sounded so very peaceful. But, on the other hand, he strongly suspected that the lady was more than ten years older than he, and she was far from pretty. Was he ready to settle for a life merely of peace when there could be even . . . love?

Griswold grinned at himself. What foolishness. While perhaps reasonably well off, dark Fanny certainly wasn't wealthy, and she was already married, to boot. There was no reason to start thinking suddenly of Fanny Osgood in terms of love. No, surely he was happy because of an idea that had occurred to him back in Greeley's office: he would go see the new proprietors of the *Broadway Journal* and tactfully let them in on a thing or two about the man they were apparently becoming entangled with, one Edgar A. Poe. Poe's goings-on had been the scandal of Philadelphia. If one wanted to, there were shocking bad things one might relate.

Griswold stood a moment longer, refining his idea. Better, he would draw Harry Franco aside, without John Bisco, and have a little chat just with him. Franco's greatest interest was self-interest, but he had a grudgeful, spleenful side that one might be able to turn to one's own advantage. Besides, Franco had written quite a lot for the *Knickerbocker* over the years and was friendly with Lewis Gaylord Clark, one's own great friend and Poe's great enemy, whereas John Bisco had edited the *Knickerbocker* before Clark got his hands on it, and could not be counted upon for a sympathetic hearing to any of Clark's friends. Interesting, the way men always dislike their successors and predecessors.

Griswold made a mental note also to talk to Clark about Poe while he was in town. One wouldn't want Clark to forget that he *was* Poe's great enemy. If need must, one could relate some new insult Poe had dropped about Clark. Poe always made insulting remarks about people he was on the outs with, so surely he had said something ugly about Clark recently, it wouldn't really be lying.

But be discreet. Poe was somehow pushing himself into the limelight these days, and one had one's own interests to look after. There was the new book one was working up on prose writers of America. Much as one regretted the necessity, one would be forced to include some Poe material there. Well, where business was concerned, one could not let personal prejudices stand in the way. Poe was too self-centered to be aware of other people's true feelings about him, and he could be counted upon to respond warmly to a friendly approach. One would simply write the arrogant bastard and ask for a sampling of those strange tales.

But first, a little detour to Beekman Street for a chat with Poe's would-be partner. Griswold kicked off the snow that was freezing around his boots and started on his way, feeling keenly happy for no reason that he could clearly define. But revenge, like the sudden, irrational dawning of love, is sweet.

10

"Yes, but dammit, Shea, it's impossible to utter an uninterrupted sentence in Harry Franco's hearing," Poe said. "The man has a perfect mania for contradiction."

Gabriel Harrison poured fresh coffee into both men's cups. "If you ask me, Mr. Poe, Mr. Harry Franco is just green with jealousy of you," Gabriel said.

Poe brightened and looked at his two friends. How cozy. How warm to sit for a few minutes beside Gabriel's sizzling hot stove behind the tea boxes, when all was gray slush outside. "I must say, that possibility hadn't occurred to me," Poe lied, addressing the remark to both Gabriel and Augustus Shea. "Yet it's true, Harry Franco has been acting downright queer lately. Almost as though he wanted to back out of the *Broadway Journal* arrangement."

"No, no," Gabriel said enthusiastically. "It's your *Raven*. He envies you the fame that he well knows is on your horizon."

Shea looked thoughtful, but he nodded. "It's a great poem," he said. "I envy you myself."

"Come now, Shea, you're just sending me up," Poe said. Then he sat back and basked as Gabriel expostulated and Shea assured. Poe sipped the good coffee, despising himself mildly. It wasn't like him to bid so obviously for compliments on any of his work. But, God, how marvelous it was, that the poem already seemed to be creating talk. How marvelous it would be if their publication scheme only succeeded in fulfilling itself completely. No money in it, as usual, aside from the fee—Poe hoped for fifteen dollars, but it looked as though the *Review* was going to stick at ten—for the first official printing of *The Raven*. But if the poem only received as many reprints as he and Shea had planned and worked for. Then, given the attention that could come his way . . .

Poe sighed, a sudden mood change. "If only I could have gotten those alterations on the eleventh stanza done in time for the *Tribune*," he lamented. "Then the poem might have had a decent chance."

"Oh, but the stanza is wonderful as it stands," Gabriel said. He quoted proudly, like a schoolboy secure in intimate knowledge of his text:

"Wondering at the stillness broken by reply so aptly spoken
'Doubtless,' said I, 'what it utters is its only stock and store
Caught from some unhappy master whom unmerciful Disaster
Followed fast and followed faster—so, when Hope he would adjure,
Stern Despair returned, instead of the sweet Hope he dared adjure—
That sad answer, "Nevermore!" ' "

"But how much better the alteration!" Poe said. He rolled it off in a singsong:

"Startled at the stillness broken by reply so aptly spoken,
'Doubtless,' said I, 'what it utters is its only stock and store
Caught from some unhappy master whom unmerciful Disaster
Followed fast and followed faster till his song one burden bore,
"Nevermore—oh Nevermore!" ' "

"A minor point," said Shea.

"There are no minor points in a poem," Poe said gloomily. "But then, again, the stanza still isn't right, is it? Why, it's a full line short. How could I have overlooked that, Shea, when I sent you the change for the *Trib*? Not that any change wouldn't have been for the better. I still can't understand—"

"Poe, Poe, at the rate you're going you'll be revising your *Raven* until the day of your death," Shea said. "Leave it, man. It's perfect. Settle back and enjoy its run. For run it will."

Poe tried to relax. "Well, of course, I wrote it for the express purpose of running, just as I did 'The Gold Bug,' you know."

"The bird will beat the bug all hollow," Shea predicted. "Success is assured."

"It's odd," Poe said. "I don't *feel* successful. All I feel is nervous about it all."

Shea laughed at Poe's confession. "There speaks one writer for all," he said. He raised his coffee cup. "To lacerate one's nerves needlessly. To invent worries when only happiness should exist. Gentlemen, let's drink to the life of all writers."

11

While the sale of New York's morning newspapers was largely a monopoly of the newsstands, the afternoon papers, the weeklies and the extras were the stock in trade of the packs of homeless young boys who howled and bellowed like eager, half-grown hounds in pursuit of pedestrians on the city's streets. Fights between a pair of ten-year-olds to see who could sell a potential customer a paper were not uncommon, so the trade was considered too rough for homeless young girls, of whom there was also a plentiful supply. They were left to sell flowers, matches, cigars, songs or themselves. Wall Street and the big hotels were favorite sites of the street vendors, and the customer could buy anything from a canary to the latest Dickens novel, which often appeared in the shape of extras. It didn't matter whether he wanted to buy. He would suddenly be surrounded by a yelling throng of waist-high competitors crying, "He-e-ere's the *New World Extra*, get *Martin Chuzzlewit!*" and "He-e-ere's the *New World*, Dick's new work, buy *Marty Ch'zzl'wit*, sir?" and they wouldn't disperse or let the reluctant buyer pass until he parted with a penny and accepted the paper.

Despite a heavy and regular fall of snow, the winter of 1844, turning into the new year of 1845, was a lucrative winter for O'Neill the Great, Wandering Jew and Horace Greeley. This was a different

Horace Greeley. Like many of the paper boys, he didn't know his own name, but he slept more or less regularly at the *Tribune* and therefore borrowed a name from its publisher. His friends, O'Neill the Great and Wandering Jew, did know their names, but they never told them, and, learning early that all crafts have their own traditions, Horace Greeley the younger never asked. At any rate, the three boys had done a fair business over Christmas in the latest Boz, and in late January a weekly called the *American Review* had sold unexpectedly well, thanks to a queer poem about a raven by someone called "Quarles." Then the same poem turned up in the *Evening Mirror* on January 29, and the rush was really on. The whole town suddenly went raven-mad. Everybody was wondering who the author was and repeating bits of the poem on the streets. Wandering Jew could read a little, and after shouting, "He-e-ere's *The Raven*, get *The Raven*, here it is!" all up and down Broadway, the boys eventually even spelled out for themselves what they'd been shouting about.

Well, then the *Trib* reprinted the thing on February 4, and the *Weekly Mirror*, the Saturday wrap-up of the daily *Evening Mirror*, ran it again on February 8, and business was so wonderfully brisk that it looked as if the raven was edging out the eagle as the national bird. All bubbles eventually had to burst, though. Both Horace Greeleys knew that, and when the nine-year-old Horace fetched up in front of the New York Hotel one still snowy afternoon to find an obvious out-of-towner perusing *The Raven* in an obviously out-of-town paper, he knew that thieving editors all over the country had been busy with their editorial scissors, and the poem had had its run.

Horace was depressed. He'd just been thrown bodily off an omnibus by a conductor who objected to anyone else making a shilling, honest or dishonest, on his crate. He had a devil of a cold, and last night on the *Tribune* stairs someone had stolen his socks off his sleeping feet, and now he would have to wait until some other fad burst into the public print before he could anticipate making enough spare money to replace them. He hung about in front of the hotel, trying half-heartedly to peddle a shoe-latch or two to the syrup-spoken Southerners who favored the dump, until Wandering Jew and O'Neill the Great showed up. Wandering Jew was eleven, and wirily strong, and he could usually be counted upon to keep ahold of a certain marmalade jar full of gin.

"Hey, Jew," Horace Greeley cried shrilly when he saw him. "You got the jar?"

Wandering Jew swaggered up to Horace, O'Neill close behind. They were both grinning triumphantly. "Sure I got the jar," Wandering Jew said. "Got something else too. News. The snow's melting a little. We made twopence apiece sweeping the puddle down at Broadway and Pearl afore Round Hearts edged us out."

"Gimme a swig, Jew," Horace pleaded. "This has not been my lucky day, and I'm fair perishing w' th' cold."

A tall, shivering man with a malarial complexion, coming out the hotel door with a companion, looked at them with distaste as the raw odor of gin bit into his nostrils. "Little thugs," he said. "Ought we call a policeman?"

"There's never one to be seen in New York when you need one," drawled his companion. "They say if you do manage to find a policeman, you have to bribe him to investigate any crime. Listen, Jeffers, did you chance to see that *Raven* poem in the *Howard District Press*? People are saying that Nathaniel Willis wrote it."

"Nonsense, it was his partner, Morris, I have it on good authority. You know General Morris's works, of course? Why, he's the man who wrote *Woodman, Spare That Tree*."

"Impossible," declared the companion. "If it wasn't Willis, it was another man, a New Yorker named Shea. *I* have it on good authority."

Young Horace Greeley, warmed by gin, guffawed. But quietly. The boys were run off promptly from the hotel doorways by the footmen if they showed undue impudence to paying guests. But when he spotted a black-dressed man walking rapdily toward them down Broadway, he couldn't resist crying out, "Where're you from, gents, the sticks? There comes the Raven himself, Mr. Edgar A. Poe. Everybody knows that."

"Poe?" said the second Southerner. "Good God, I know the man. The second Mrs. John Allan was an acquaintance of my wife's. Quick, Jeffers, step back into the hotel with me. I'd never hear the last of it if I had to speak to him."

But the first man, Jeffers, lingered until Poe came abreast of the hotel, staring avidly at a strange face that he perceived instantly was romantic, diabolic, tragic.

Nine-year-old Horace Greeley did not possess the adjectives to apply to Poe, but he too felt the fascination of the figure and paid it the most fitting tribute that he could. "Hey, Bard," he yelped. "Bard, over here." He waved Wandering Jew's gin bottle at Poe. "Here, Bard, have a nip!"

Jolted from his reverie, Poe glanced about. He had gone home to dine, as the afternoon meal was included in his board, and had stolen a few freezing minutes for a brisk walk around Washington Square before going back to newspaper row. He saw no one he knew in front of the hotel, only a tall gentleman staring at him curiously and three waifs. One boy held out to him, eagerly outstretched, a jar filled with a cloudy white liquid and called again, "Bard, Bard, share a round with us!"

By God! Recognized on the street by a trio of little urchins! A warm glow, starting from his stomach and climbing to his throat, suffused Poe.

Poe bowed to the boys and knew that in so bowing he bowed to sudden fame—for *The Raven* was indeed proving a swift, complete, roaring success. And what did he find on these condor heights? A jar full of gin proffered by three ragged boys, boys not too much younger than he had been himself when he first crystallized the ambition of becoming a poet.

Well, he must scorn the gin, but he would not scorn these small, pale children. A smile briefly lit his face, and he said to the boys, "Gentlemen, I thank you, but I've found that drink does not agree with me."

"Nevermore?" quavered one of the trio, the smallest boy, but the one with the biggest smile.

"No, nevermore," Poe agreed gravely. "However, each man to his own pastime." He dug into his pocket. Yes, thank heavens, he had a shilling. "Won't you instead have a round on me?"

The quickest open palm belonged to a red-haired boy with the look of the Irish about him. Poe dropped the shilling therein, tipped his hat and resumed his journey.

They shouldn't drink, they were so little, but what other fleeting comfort had they on these cold streets? He shouldn't give away money, he had so little, but wasn't it only appropriate to pour a few drops on the altar when the gods finally allotted one such a heady potion?

Flushed, happy, soaring with raven's wings, Poe hurried down Broadway. As he walked, he noticed for the first time that other passersby were staring at him, as if they saw a real live despairing poet, a regular Lord Byron, in front of their very eyes. And from Episcopalian deacon to loafing gambler, from lady with heavy looped coiffure to weary shopgirl, they all stared avidly.

Damn, there went privacy. But here came solace—fame! At last!

Book II

FANNY

*Thou wouldst be loved?
To F——s S. O——d*

1

As the lecture audience swarmed around him, a Unitarian divine newly returned home on the *Britannia*, reported, "Your *Raven* has produced a sensation in England, Mr. Poe." A stripling studying law decreed, "Half my friends are taken by the fear of the poem, and half by the music, Mr. Poe." One of the swarm of literary women confided, "Oh, Mr. Poe, I've been absolutely *haunted* by the 'Nevermore.'" A brawny sculptor gushed, "One of my acquaintances who has the misfortune of possessing a bust of Pallas can never bear to look at it in the twilight, Mr. Poe." Dr. John Francis, who knew everyone and was known by everyone, boomed, "Poe, you must give me the pleasure of presenting you to one of your greatest fans. Why, my hand is fair bruised, the way she clasped it in pleading for an introduction to you. Elizabeth, my dear—'the Raven!'"

Genially but without punctilio, Dr. Francis threw back his head, puffed out his chest and waved his hand with an elaborate gesture so all-encompassing that it might have indicated Nat Willis lounging smilingly beside Poe, the library of the New York Historical Society, in which they stood, the lectern that Poe had just vacated or the rest of the audience of editors and intelligentsia moving slowly toward the doors. Poe would not have known to whom he had just been introduced had not Dr. Francis, in a habitual gesture, patted one of the ladies crowding about Poe on the head. She recoiled like a snake, and Poe recognized her instantly—dark, rather aloof good looks, dark brown hair carefully arranged in symmetrical ringlets. It was Mrs. Elizabeth Ellet, the woman who had snubbed him and Cornelius Mathews at the theater early in the winter.

Poe bowed slightly and slowly, fixing upon Mrs. Ellet's embarrassed face a look of ceremonious gravity. She apparently decided that ignoring Dr. Francis's indiscretion was her best tactic, for she rustled forward a step, curtsied and said graciously, "How I wish you had recited your own poem to us, Mr. Poe. It would have been a thing to tell our grandchildren. Surely no American poem has ever harvested so instantaneous and so complete a success, and surely no American poet has ever found himself so instantaneously famous."

It was no more than the simple truth, but it was nice of her to say it. Poe concluded he would be merciful to the woman. "You're too kind," he said. "Yet if, as I mentioned in my lecture, our American poetesses awaken one happy day to their full potential, and if I am someday fortunate enough to have grandchildren, I trust I may be able to tell them of having heard far more important poems from the fair poetesses' lips."

The ladies in the group all murmured and looked pleased, even Horace Greeley's old-maid literary critic from the *Tribune*, conceited, prim-mouthed Margaret Fuller. Poe permitted himself to smile, but at his private thoughts. No doubt half the women waiting to congratulate him on his lecture wrote poetry, at least in the secrecy of their bedrooms, and no doubt each immediately visualized herself as the fair poetess who would pen the famous poem. Poe swept his eyes over the bonneted heads of the nearest ranks, seeking one particular fair face that he had noticed in the audience as he talked—one with delicate but unremarkable features that could by no means be termed beautiful, but so attentive, so engrossed in his every word, so . . . well, utterly charming, that he had found himself in danger of forgetting the rest of his audience and lecturing only to that one expressive face. Poe experienced a mild disappointment when he did not see his fair admirer among the people surrounding him, but Dr. Francis grasped him vigorously by the arm and turned him toward the next lady to be introduced.

"Miss Anna Lynch," Dr. Francis boomed, "I have the honor of presenting to you Mr. Edgar Poe." More formal this time, but the irrepressible little physician ruined the effect by another pat on the head. He had to stretch a bit to do it, as Miss Lynch was above the usual height, but her composure was unruffled. She made Dr. Francis and Poe a dignified curtsy and gazed at Poe with calm, intelligent eyes. Poe's eyes, as he bowed back, sparkled. Miss Lynch was renowned as a hostess to visiting bluestockings and the New York literati, and an introduction to her had been something he had hopefully anticipated on this night of triumph.

"I am indebted to you for your lecture," Miss Lynch murmured to Poe. "I came expecting to see Mr. Poe the poet, but you have allowed us, as well, to become acquainted with Mr. Poe the critic. I was especially taken with your point that indiscriminate laudation of American books has tended to the depression of American literature. I don't believe I'd ever encountered that particular point of criticism before."

"I would certainly hope not, Miss Lynch," Poe said. "The critic, like the poet, should not belabor his audience with imitative thought."

Everyone around him tittered appreciatively, to show they had been listening to the lecture, as Poe, speaking on American poetry, had taken a good whack at Longfellow for diluting genius with an alacrity for imitation. Miss Lynch looked as though she would like to pursue the conversation, but she gave way to the next in line after murmuring that she hoped Mr. Poe, "and Mrs. Poe, of course," would come to call. The invitation, casual though it was, was exactly what Poe had hoped for, and it was with an even brighter countenance that he turned to smile at his unofficial sponsor at this debut to the New York literati, Nat Willis. But Willis was gone from his side, Poe feared because of jealousy, and Poe himself suffered a twinge of jealousy soon after. Near the doors, he spotted Willis talking to the same attentive lady who had so captured his own attention, and, damn it all, the lady looked every bit as attentive now that she was talking to Willis!

Poe disengaged himself from an unlikely pair, a stuttering mathematician and an intellectual-sounding stockbroker's wife. The room was emptying at last. Poe contemplated going over to Willis and wangling an introduction to the pretty brunette, but freckle-faced Augustus Shea, friend and benefactor, his yawning little son leaning against his legs, stood beaming by the lectern, and Poe approached him to receive the final and perhaps most meaningful congratulation on his well-received lecture.

"My boy, you were a roaring success," Shea pronounced. "I think you'll find that you'll be able to augment your income very nicely in the future by lecturing. I counted between two and three hundred people."

"Nearer three hundred, don't you think?" Poe said anxiously.

"We'll find out when the ticket-takers settle up. And your

honorarium aside, it's not the number but the quality of the audience that counts. The most intellectual and refined people in the entire city turned out—fertile soil, my boy, for the seeds you have sown tonight! Does Willis plan to report for the *Mirror?* I believe I noticed representatives from all the better papers. Definitely a man from the *New World* and another from the *Morning News* and, counting Miss Fuller, two from the *Tribune.* Oh, how Rufe Griswold will writhe! He's scheduled to lecture the Historical Society here next week, you know."

Poe had to laugh. He did indeed know. Although, since Griswold was being so friendly these days, he had left any uncomplimentary references to Griswold's appraisal of American poets out of his lecture, he had deliberately chosen as his title "The Poets and Poetry of America," that same unimaginative designation Griswold had used for his anthology. Let Griswold try to follow that act!

Poe was pointing this out to Shea, and both were laughing, when Nat Willis joined them, smiling sunnily and looking elated. He shook hands with Shea.

"What a triumph, eh?" Willis said. "You would have drawn an even larger audience, Poe, had the weather been better. Next time. You must repeat the lecture, of course. But damn it, man, you've presented me with a nice problem for my review. How can I write that you praised my *Unseen Spirits* without seeming to praise myself?"

Shea promptly began advising Willis on what to write, but the sleepy little boy tugged on his pants leg and Shea forsook literature for fatherhood. He took the child up into his arms. "I must get this young man home to bed," he said. "Poe, call when you have a chance. You too, Willis. You both know your way to my door."

"But won't you have a bite to eat with us?" Willis said. "We've no need to wait here. One can trust the Historical Society for the fee, Poe. It's one of the few places one can. For the most, it's best to have the money in your pocket as you go out the door."

Willis smiled cheerfully at Poe. The warm respect and friendship he had offered his former assistant at the *Mirror* had changed not a whit now that Poe had gone on to a one-third partnership in another journal. As they concluded they must all go their separate ways and Poe gathered up the manuscript of his lecture, Poe decided he must have been wrong earlier when he suspected Willis of jealousy. But it was hard to comprehend—a literary lion of seasons past, not resenting the appearance of a new and more imposing lion. The increasing sullenness of one of Poe's new partners, Harry Franco, was more in line with Poe's expectations. Harry Franco and his dull novel were in eclipse, and the Raven was on the rise!

Shea left. A deferential young attendant peeped curiously at the Raven, alias Edgar Poe, as he went about turning off the gas jets, and the Raven, wide awake, keyed up, flushed with the first full bloom of his new fame, took a last look at the scene of his triumph, then moved reluctantly toward the door. Virginia's nightly dose of medicine, pure laudanum at the moment, would have done its work, and although Muddy would be waiting impatiently to ask how the lecture went, he was reluctant for the evening to end.

"By the by," he asked Willis lightly, "who was the lady with the black hair that I saw you talking with right before the crowd cleared off?"

Willis's laughter rang out. "But didn't you know? That was Fanny Osgood—she for whose poems you prophesied such a rosy future in your lecture. I watched her as you talked. She was veritably abloom with modest blushes. I told her to come meet you, but she was too shy."

"Good Lord," Poe said, "that was Mrs. Osgood? But I should have known. The faultless grammar, the delicate grace of her verse—how could the poetess not be as charming as her poems?"

Willis laughed again. "What's this?" he said. "Has our Fanny a new conquest? But she's equally impressed with you, Poe. Shall I make *you* blush by telling you of the praise the good lady heaped upon your head? But no, you must hear it in person. I shall insist that you meet. Come to me this Sunday at the Astor House. I shall command Fanny to be present also."

Poe smiled a little, wistfully. But he said, "No, Willis, even if I had the inclination I'd have no time for amours. Wiley & Putnam wants to issue a new edition of my tales, and if I am to rework them to my satisfaction, every minute of my time for the next few months is committed to my pen."

"A new volume of tales? Good heavens, man, why didn't you tell me?"

Poe raised his eyebrows in vague surprise. "I must have forgotten. Anyway, it's not very important. I want the volume, of course, but what I'd like even better is a new volume of collected poetry. It's been, um, some years since my last volume came out, and that was largely juvenilia."

"You must have both volumes," Willis said heartily, "but you must also have an introduction to Fanny. Rufe Griswold has fallen madly in love with her, my spies tell me. Will you let him run away with the prize?"

"Do you mean that she, ah . . . ?"

"No, no, of course not. Fanny may not be above encouraging a gentleman's respectful attentions, but she would always draw the line at a platonic friendship."

"Does Griswold know that?"

"Who knows? I only know that he's been in New York more than in Philadelphia since about, oh, since Christmas, and one sees him often in the Osgoods' company. Don't you really want a closer look at the little black-haired magnet that draws him so?"

"Well . . ."

"Sunday, then. It's settled. I'll have a few other people in also. It would be good for you to get out into the world a little more, Poe. A literary man's career is not created solely by his pen, not in New York anyway. You know?"

Poe knew. Indeed, the man at his elbow was the model he had been studying with ever increasing interest. He shook Willis's hand and said good night, and turned his solitary steps toward his boarding house. To deliver poetical addresses, to get into quarrels with notorious men, to seek the intimacy of noted women. He was not sure how his master strategist, Shea, would regard the full prescription, but a newly fledged bird must try his own wings. Yes, he would go to meet this ladylove of the Reverend Mr. Griswold's, the Reverend Doctor Griswold as the fool was calling himself now. In fact, he would write her out a copy of *The Raven* in his own hand and send it to her between now and Sunday. That would be a graceful gesture.

And what a pleasure it might be, to hear those words of praise that Willis would not repeat, from the fair lady's own fair lips.

2

Frances Sargent Osgood, née Locke, was the daugher of a Boston merchant who had encouraged his children toward belletristic achievement and had reason to be pleased enough with the results. Her sister wrote prose and verse. A brother was a popular journalist. Fanny's bent was poetry, sometimes issued in tiny, decorative books with titles like *A Wreath of Wild Flowers from New England,* and sometimes published (but too infrequently paid for) by magazines and journals whose mailboxes overflowed with the pressed-violet passions of a generation of suppressed women who sought some outlet, any outlet, from their appointed rounds as daughters, wives, mothers and pressers of violets.

Fanny was a wife, having married a young painter who captured her interest and eventually her hand while painting her portrait. She was a mother, having given birth to two daughters, now aged five and ten. Fanny was also a buccaneer, having an unladylike gusto for Life, by which she meant something she had not yet succeeded in defining but which was the same thing Napoleon meant when, asked what he wanted from life, he replied, "More!"

Like a good painter's wife, she had followed her husband to London, where she erected a conjugal establishment around his easel, sautéed aubergines in his oil and, their succession of hired rooms having only one possible reception room, his atelier, entertained visitors on the stairs when the atelier was occupied by a sitter. Gay, witty, unaffected, she entertained them so well that the atelier was occupied more and more often. Her husband's career flourished in a minor way, and so did her own, but her enjoyment of the artistic world of Europe was eventually curtailed when her husband decided to return to Boston in hopes of greater success. Coincidentally, Fanny turned thirty, at which age, like most young people, she had planned to die, but, like most thirty-year-old people, she restlessly began thinking it was time to start to live. Walking one street, she would wonder what was happening on the next street over. What was on the other side of that hill? Should she cut off her yard and a half of black hair? Should she try to persuade Samuel to move to Italy? Should she take a lover?

But no one in Boston took lovers—nor in New York, New Haven, Providence, Philadelphia or the other eastern cities to which her husband wandered in search of commissions, taking rooms by the week or month in hotels when sitters were abundant, staying with relatives when things went less well. Fanny easily charmed all the men, and the women as well. The men all flirted with her ponderously and she flirted back, but the times permitted no greater display of ardor than the jotting of some sentimental bit of verse.

She had one with her now, on the cold but bright Sunday morning following Poe's Tuesday lecture, as she swept down the Astor House stairs, shivering in the draft from the front entrance. It having occurred to her on the spur of the moment that Dr. Rufus Griswold might be useful to her, she had deliberately set herself the task of charming him one snowy day, and he had just sent his seventh or eighth avowal of devotion, inscribed in pencil in a copy of Leigh Hunt's *Poems*. Only two lines this time. *Would I were anything that thou dost love./ A flower, a bird, a wavelet or a gem,* mailed along with a note lamenting that the press of duties made it necessary for him to cancel his lecture next week at the Historical Society but hoping he would see her soon.

"Better that he'd sent the gem," Samuel had laughed when she'd shown the two lines to him. Then he'd turned back to his easel and the rosy bloom he was trying to coax to the pale chin of a browbeaten coffee merchant's wife who was due for her final sitting the next day. Perhaps to the detriment of their marriage, Fanny sometimes thought, she and her husband were good friends, and "Fanny's beaux" were a standing household joke. But she found the lines flattering, if a bit clumsy, and determined to show them to Willis, for love-by-versification was traditionally made in public. It was often the only fun in it, anyway, and Fanny had not hesitated to show about an acrostic valentine, a popular fad, that she had sent to Griswold with the names of Osgood and Griswold interwoven.

But another poem had also been handed to Fanny that week at the hotel's table d'hôte, and she entered the main drawing room that morning in response to it. Amid young marrieds who preferred boarding to housekeeping, expensively dressed virgins shopping the marriage market and well-off widows whose little dogs permeated the hallways of the hotel with the faint but permanent smell of urine, Willis and his daughter awaited her. He was a widower, and his young daughter, Imogene, often played hostess for him. Fanny waved them closer to the fireplace. "What, am I the first?" she said. "And I waited so patiently so I could be last. Don't tell me your Mr. Poe has come and gone."

"No, he's late," Willis admitted. "It's very unlike Poe. But you've already missed the Duyckincks and Stella Lewis and her spouse. Does that please you?"

Fanny touched the stuff of Imogene's morning dress. Fanny always touched. Life came to her through her fingertips as well as through her eyes and ears, and her fingertips told her of intricate embroidery on French cambric and the cool slickness of heavy satin ribbons. Pretty, pretty. She wrinkled her nose, not at the gown but at the thought of the fat Brooklyn poetess, Stella Lewis, and said, "Thank heavens I waited then. But I don't know what to think of your Raven. I thought you told me he wanted my opinion on his poem."

"He does indeed. But you'd read it before, of course?"

"Of course, everybody reads it. Its effect on me is singular, like weird, unearthly music. It was with almost dread, Willis, that I heard you say he desired an introduction. Note, I do not refuse to receive him. How could I, without seeming ungrateful for his enthusiastic eulogy of my writings? But on the other hand, how can I receive him if he refuses to come?"

"He'll be here," Willis said. "Ah, here comes another friend. Have you met young Mat Brady, Fanny? Good, and Mrs. Oakes Smith and Mary Gove right on his heels. Let's move to a sofa. The ladies will want to sit."

The ladies were obviously making a series of morning calls, for they only stayed a few minutes, but shy little Mathew Brady lingered, hoping to see Poe, whom he said he knew, and Fanny automatically set out to enchant the youth. It was easily done. She soon had him telling them about his new daguerreotype gallery, and teased the pleasant twenty-one-year-old to a blush by accusing him of providing unfair competition for her husband's portraits.

Then Willis was on his feet and gesturing, and the black-dressed poet whose lecture she had listened to so attentively the previous Tuesday was hurrying across the drawing room to them, looking upset and breathless.

"Poe," Willis said, "I'm glad you could come. Is something wrong? Your wife . . . ?"

"No, she is fairly well today," Poe said. He greeted Imogene, then turned to Fanny.

Involuntarily, she rose. The man's proud and beautiful head was erect, and his dark eyes looked at her with a peculiar expression of sweetness and hauteur. Acknowledging Willis's introduction, he greeted her calmly, gravely, almost coldly, yet with so marked an earnestness that Fanny could not help being deeply impressed.

"I apologize most humbly for my tardiness," Poe said softly. "I have looked forward to this occasion all week."

"Do put it out of your mind, Mr. Poe," Fanny said.

"At least you're here at last," Willis said, good-naturedly, as always. "Poe, here is a young rascal who claims he's a friend of yours. You remember Mathew Brady, don't you?"

"Why, of course," Poe said, but he gave the young man a puzzled look along with his hand. "What are you doing in New York, Brady?"

The youth smiled at him shyly. "I live here. It's a great pleasure to see you again, Mr. Poe."

Fanny said, "Mr. Brady has opened a daguerreotype gallery across the way. I'm drumming up business for him. Mr. Poe, you must go and sit for your portrait immediately. For that matter, you must also come sit for my noble husband. There, gentlemen, don't you agree that I did that well? I have fairly divided Mr. Poe between the newest and the oldest of the portrait arts."

The men relaxed, and Poe's face lightened a little, as she had hoped it would, but young Brady blurted out, "And you must also allow me the pleasure of buying you a drink one of these afternoons, Mr. Poe. I owe you a julep. Several, in fact." Fanny allowed her doe's eyes to widen more fully, and the boy turned crimson. "I met Mr. Poe in Washington one night in the middle of a roaring party," he tried to explain. "I don't know whether it was the juleps or the port or the rummy coffee we washed it down with, but I certainly had a head the next morning!"

Fanny burst into laughter at Poe's expression. "There, now," she said to Imogene, "now you know how gentlemen comport themselves without the restraining presence of a lady. I assume, Mr. Brady, there were no ladies in your party?"

The boy's rout was complete. "N-no," he stuttered, "only a Spanish don with sweeping mustachios whom Mr. Poe teased until . . . until . . ."

Poe intervened. "Until he was on the verge of challenging me," he said to young Brady. "Of course, how could I have forgotten? But you've pinpointed the reason well. Rummy coffee, Mrs. Osgood, does interesting things to one's memory, although a lady, I am sure, would not know that."

"Then this lady must try it," she said. "In turn, I might recommend chloroform, Mr. Brady, Mr. Poe. Half the people I know have been dissipating on it lately. It's very curious, the effect it has on one's system. One's mind is filled with the strangest dreams, and the sensations of a week seem to be crowded into a minute. The last time a young friend of mine, George Strong, dosed himself, he reported he distinctly heard the performance of most of Mozart's 'Requiem,' but, as he noticed at the time, not by a very good orchestra. Except for the quality of the orchestras one dreams, it seems an innocent kind of amusement. Best of all, unlike your rummy coffees, one doesn't seem to wake up the next morning with a head."

Both Brady and Poe looked at her hopefully as she chattered, as if hoping she could dissipate the embarrassment in which they were sunk, and Willis soon took an oar and rowed them to the shoals of New York University, inquiring about Brady's studies of daguerreotyping there with a pair of experimentally inclined professors. But the youth soon took his departure, still looking faintly red around the ears.

Fanny turned the full power of her expressive gray eyes on Poe and demanded bluntly, "Is something troubling you this morning, Mr. Poe? You looked so worried when you came in."

"No," he said. "Yes. Well, to tell the truth, I suppose it sounds like nothing, but—my cat has run away. Don't laugh at me, Mrs. Osgood. I beg you."

"Why, I wouldn't dream of laughing," she said. "Your cat? Poor creature, lost in a giant city. What can we do? Have you looked?"

"Since early this morning," Poe said. His finely cut mouth seemed to tremble. "I scoured all the streets for blocks around our lodgings. I kept fearing I would see her dead body in the gutter, run over by one of these filthy carriages."

"You mustn't despair," Fanny said. "Surely she's just hiding somewhere. We'll all help you look, won't we? Mr. Willis, must you stay on here? Are you expecting more callers?"

"I fear so," Willis said, "but I could leave word at the desk that I was called away unexpectedly."

"No, you cannot disappoint your guests. Mr. Poe and I will find the cat. Wait for me just a minute, Mr. Poe. I'll run upstairs and get a wrap."

She was gone before Poe could find words to gainsay her. "Generous heart!" he exclaimed to Willis as he watched her slight figure rustle quickly from the drawing room. "Yet I cannot allow her to accompany me. I spent the morning clambering about in coal yards. Such a search would be ruinous for her gown."

Willis patted his arm consolingly. "There's never any stopping Fanny from what she wants to do," he said. "Resign yourself to having an assistant. Is the cat your special pet, Poe?"

"My wife's, but I must admit that I'm very attached to the beast, and she to me. Please forgive me, Willis, for running off this way. It's an insult to your other guests."

"But not to the most important one," Willis said. "Take heart. Fanny has a lucky touch. She'll surely help you find your tabby."

With repeated expressions of his sincere regret, Poe took his leave of Willis and Willis's young daughter and went to await Fanny at the foot of the broad stairs. What an establishment. A crystal fountain and a flower market's plunder of fresh flowers in its splendid inner quadrangle, and, somewhere in its viscera, it was said, even a steam engine and a force-pump that provided every floor with water closets and running water. And what a woman. Seen at close quarters, Mrs. Fanny Osgood looked as fresh as a twenty-year-old, Mrs. Fanny Osgood had beautiful eyes, Mrs. Fanny Osgood had a charming voice, gay and melodious. The most that could be said for her lips were that they looked sweet, and the most for her soft little nose that it was witty, but she had an extraordinary complexion, clear and fine-grained, and, beneath the delicate curve of her bosom, she obviously had a sensitive, impulsive, ardent heart. What foul luck that the Brady boy had so far forgotten himself as to blurt out that damaging recollection of their first meeting. Poe's clearest memory of the night was making a fool of himself by wearing his cloak inside out. He closed his eyes and tried to shut away the thought. Whatever must the lady think of him?

But the lady, as she rejoined him bundled up most prettily in furs, seemed to have nothing but cats on her mind, and as they boarded a ponderous Broadway omnibus she questioned him closely about Catarina. When did they last see her? The previous night, when

Muddy let her out the back steps of the boarding house, exasperated by her continued caterwauling. Had she ever run away before? Never. Had she been allowed to go outside on her own in New York before? Occasionally, though she usually seemed content enough inside. Why had she been caterwauling? No one knew. Had she been rolling about on her back? Why yes, how could Fanny have known that?

Fanny shot Poe a startled look, then smiled at him, a funny, patient smile, as though he were a little dense. "Why, it's simple," she said. "Haven't you noticed? The wind is acid, but the sun is bright. The trees are bare, but they have little brown buds that will soon be leaves. It's nearly spring, and your cat's in love."

Poe stammered as badly as young Brady had. "But . . . but good heavens," he said, "with whom? I told you, she almost never goes outside, and she only spits at the landlady's . . . how can I put it? . . . disabled tom. So who could it be?"

Fanny compressed her mouth, but her eyes laughed. "Mark my words, when an Iseult decides to fall in love, chance always manages to provide a Tristram. Have you noticed any other tomcats in the neighborhood? No? Then what about serenades, unearthly howls in the dark of night? Yes? Really, Mr. Poe, I'm surprised at you. For a man who invented a detective like M. Dupin, you've shown surprisingly little deductive ability."

The omnibus groaned to a stop at the corner of Amity Street, but Fanny counseled that they should double back to mid-block and try any back gardens to which they could gain access, with particular attention to barns and any livery stables in the neighborhood. Poe felt inordinately foolish as they paced along, calling, at Fanny's urging, "Catar-i-i-i-ina, Catar-i-i-i-ina, cat, cat, cat, cat." He was wishing desperately that Virginia's pet had been taught to respond to the more traditional call of "Here, kitty, kitty," when only three doors away from his boarding house Fanny spotted a big, gray tiger-striped tomcat, and they went in pursuit as the tom slipped through a broken board in a fence and dashed through an open lot to Bleecker Street.

They ran. Fanny was laughing. "There!" she said. "There!" The tom crossed the street on the fly and disappeared into a private stable through a frowning gate surmounted with jagged iron spikes.

"Damn," Poe muttered, and stopped, but Fanny ran straight through the gate. He followed, to find his panting companion explaining to a groom whose frown matched the gate, "You must let us through, my man. We're looking for our cat."

"Nar, missus, there's naught here but our own barn cats," the groom protested.

"I insist on looking," Fanny said. "Step aside." She pushed past the man, who turned his frown on Poe, but Poe stared back at him haughtily and charged after Fanny. Daintily holding up her skirts, she ran through the stable to a large shed in the rear, where a phaeton and a gig stood next to sacks of grain and bales of hay.

"Now call again," she instructed Poe.

The groom followed, staring at them suspiciously. Poe hesitated.

"Call," Fanny insisted. "She'd never come to me, only to you."

"Uh," he said. "Uh, Catarina. Catar-i-i-i-ina, cat, cat, cat, cat!"

There were rustlings among the bales. An entirely different tomcat, this one orange, suddenly materialized and made a break for it over the sloping roof of the shed. And Catarina strolled out from behind the phaeton wearing an earnest, serious expression, not quite looking at them, as though to disassociate herself from such unseemly proceedings.

"Catarina!" Poe said. She allowed him to scoop her off the manure-caked floor of the shed and looked inquiringly over his shoulder at Fanny and the groom.

"There," Fanny said graciously to the groom, "I told you our cat was here." She reached to touch Catarina's soft fur lightly. "Come, Mr. Poe, shall we take her home?"

The cat squirmed in Poe's arms as they retraced their steps, but he held her firmly, and as they emerged to face the foot traffic on Bleecker Street, she ducked her head and pushed it into the crook of his arm as if to hide from the horrors of the busy street.

"Through the open lot?" Fanny inquired.

"No, there's no outlet to Amity. We'd best go around. You must come in with me, at least for a cup of coffee, you know. My wife will want to thank you. And then I'll see you home."

"No, this time you must stay with Catarina, to console her," she said.

Our cat? *This* time? Poe glanced at the woman beside him, and his body made known to him his response to the implied intimacy of her words—a simultaneous tightening of the larynx and the testes, a sudden rush of blood. Good God, could it be that chance also might manage to provide a restless human Tristram—a Tristram flushed with new fame, hopeful, eager to reach out to life after the long winterchill of despair—with his Iseult?

But despite a sense of slight levitation, the habit of cautious pessimism kept his feet on the ground, and Poe walked Fanny sedately to his boarding house and up narrow stairs to the second-floor back and his bedroom, which had to double today as a parlor. Virginia, sitting pale and sad by the window, turned upon them reddened violet eyes, and at the first sight of Catarina she ran to Poe with a sharp cry and buried her face into the cat's furry side.

"Oh, Eddy," Virginia gasped. "Oh, Eddy, you found her! Where was she? Oh, you naughty, naughty cat. How could you frighten us that way? Oh, oh." And she burst into tears.

Muddy hurried in from the connecting room and added her own exclamations to the confusion of Poe's trying to introduce his new acquaintance to his family.

"It was Mrs. Osgood who found Catarina," he told a queerly apprehensive-looking Muddy and a Virginia hugging the wriggling cat and weeping into his shirt front.

"Pooh, I did nothing of the sort," Fanny said. "I only helped Mr. Poe deduce her whereabouts. We always had cats at home when I was a girl, and I flatter myself that I understand something of their mysteries. There now, Mrs. Poe, don't cry. Your naughty cat is safe at home again."

Muddy said, "It's Sissy's medication. It makes her overly sensitive. Now, Sissy, stop that. There's no need for all that crying. Can't you see that Catarina is safe and sound?"

The cat had had quite enough. Poe winced as, using her claws freely, she struggled out of his arms, up his coat and to his shoulder, from whence she jumped to his writing table and began washing her feet. Virginia wept on, although with decreasing intensity; daily fits of weeping and sudden descents into sleep had become common for her ever since the pharmacist's pint bottle of laudanum—10 per cent opium infused in 120-proof grain alcohol—had entered their lives. Fanny seemed unperturbed and merely gazed at the cat admiringly.

"How strange that she's not black," she said of Catarina. "I was somehow convinced that you would have a black cat."

"She's a tortoise shell," Virginia hiccuped, leaning on Poe's vacated arm. "At least that's what we call her. Don't you think she looks like some beautiful tortoise-shell comb, with her mottledy gray?"

"Indeed I do," Fanny said agreeably. "And I also think that I should leave you alone to scold her in peace. But don't scold her too much. It would only offend her. Ah, Catarina, you're the queen of the universe, that I can readily see. Do you suppose she would permit me to come visit her again sometime?"

Virginia let go of Poe's arm and childishly clasped Fanny's hand with both of hers. "Oh, please don't go," she said.

"No, please," Poe said. "I promised you coffee and . . . cakes? Do we have any cakes, Muddy?"

"No, I really must be getting back," Fanny said, "but I'll look forward to seeing you again. No, Mr. Poe, you needn't walk me down. I can find the door with ease. I'm so happy that our detective story had a happy ending. I shall tell 'The Case of Catarina' to my daughters, to put them to sleep tonight." She smiled at Poe, and he surely didn't imagine it: there was a quickening of her breath, and she looked searchingly at him for a heartbeat of time, then dropped her eyes as she added, "Although, as it's basically a love story, perhaps they're too young to be told everything."

Muddy insisted on walking Mrs. Osgood to the street door. In the silence between Virginia's hiccups, Poe listened until the footsteps disappeared, then turned and said to Virginia, "Shouldn't you lie down awhile? All this excitement couldn't be good for you."

"No, Catarina must be starving. I must tell Muddy to give her something to eat," Virginia said. "Eddy, what did Mrs. Osgood mean, that it's a love story?"

"Nothing," Poe said.

"But she must have meant something."

"Well . . . how would you feel if there were kittens in prospect?"

"Kittens!" Virginia laughed, suddenly understanding. "Kittens, how lovely! Could we keep them?"

"I don't know. Maybe one," he said absently.

"Oh, Eddy, I can't bear it when Muddy drowns them."

"Shhh, I know," he said.

"Oh, Eddy, isn't Mrs. Osgood charming?"

"Yes," he said.

"I do hope she meant it—that we'll see her again."

"Yes."

3

The problem, as Poe told Shea the following week while scrubbing the ink off his fingers, was time. Now that he had moved to the *Broadway Journal*, he not only had its general superintendence to attend to, but he also did the theater and book reviews and, by the terms of his contract with the publisher, wrote a printed page or more of assorted material every week. Then there were his plan to start lecturing regularly, and the revisions of his old tales that he needed to do for the Wiley & Putnam edition, and the critical history of American literature he'd begun in '44, and the literary war he had started in Willis's *Mirror* and moved to the *Broadway Journal* over the prevailing American practice of imitation and plagiarism, on top of all of which Poe still had his living to earn. The *Journal* would hand over a third share of its profits every four weeks, but it first had to start showing profits before he could collect. This meant that new tales and articles had to be written regularly for other magazines.

"So I've been working fourteen and fifteen hours a day, hard at it all the time," he concluded with a sigh. He emptied the basin of water into the slop tub—Clinton Hall, where the *Broadway Journal* had taken cramped offices, offered no such amenities as running water on all floors—and reached for a towel. "I never knew what it was to be a slave before."

Shea leaned patiently on his hickory cane, waiting for Poe to finish tidying up so they could leave for the theater. "It seems to agree with you," Shea said judiciously. "I've never seen you looking happier. But you do look tired. Are you saving enough time out of your busy life to sleep?"

Poe shook his head. "My poor wife coughs so much at night that we none of us get much rest. So I write a good deal at night now. Might as well, and God knows we need the ready money. Shea, I am as poor now as ever I was in my life—except in hope, which is by no means bankable. Everything I write for the *BJ* will be, of course, just so much out of pocket."

"In the end it will pay you well," Shea predicted.

"At least the prospects are good," Poe agreed. He glanced at his black ascot in the tiny mirror of the washroom and arranged it more neatly. "There," he said. "Just come back to my desk with me for a pair of sharp pencils. The sharper the better. The Park's doing *Antigone* tonight, and I strongly suspect I'll have to rip it to shreds."

On this one evening of the week the twelve-man staff of the *BJ* was particularly busy, for the weekly edition would be off the press the next day. The publisher, not a man to stand on formality, leaned in his shirt sleeves over a stone, worrying about the length of an article with the head printer, William Baxter. The other partner, Harry Franco, who did stand on formality, worked busily at his desk, as did the music critic. The ink-stained young devil-in-waiting, a twelve-year-old named Bob, dashed from a typecase, where he had been helping a pair of compositors, to a proof press and started clanking away, while the office boy, a lanky, sallow fourteen-year-old named Alex, rushed three steps forward when he saw Poe and Shea, then hesitated, gazing at Poe half defensively, half adoringly. Harry Franco also looked up, but, Poe was not completely displeased to see, without any adoration at all on his sharp, thin face.

"Well, Alex," Poe said to the office boy, "is that something for me?"

The boy clutched a sheet of paper in his bony hand. "Oh no, sir," he said. "I mean . . . you're busy right now, sir. I'll catch you another time."

"We're not in that much of a rush," Poe said. "What is it?" He was uniformly kind and courteous around the office, and he saw no reason to deny courtesy to an office boy or, for that matter, to the young chatterbox of a printer's devil.

"No, sir, it's nothing really. Another time. Any time at all."

Poe gently took the sheet of paper from the boy and glanced at it. He looked up smiling. "Why, Alex," he said, "you've written a poem."

"Oh, no, Mr. Poe, it's not a real poem. I mean, it's nothing like *your* poems. I mean . . ."

Shea, who was much about the office and knew all its inhabitants, said, "I didn't know you wrote poetry, Alex."

"Well, sir, I've been trying," Alex mumbled.

"Good boy," said Shea. "With Mr. Poe here as your model, you can't go wrong. Has Mr. Poe told you he's going to repeat his lecture on poetry in a couple of weeks? I picked up no end of pointers myself from listening to him last time. What about it, Poe? Couldn't you arrange a complimentary ticket for a young pupil?"

"Of course," Poe said. "Would you like to go, Alex?"

"Yes, *sir!*" Alex said.

"Good, I'll see to it," Poe said. Reading, he added, "Hmmm, a temperance poem. Alex, do you drink a great deal?"

"No, sir, never!" the boy said. Then he seemed to realize he was being chafed, and he grinned nervously. "I just thought it was a popular subject, Mr. Poe, so I just thought I'd try a . . . I'd try to . . ."

The youngster's eyes kept wandering anxiously from his poem to Poe, and Poe kept him waiting no longer for his reaction. "There's just a little matter of the meter, right here," he told the boy. "Shall I fix it for you? And then, Alex, you must have it printed in 'The Youth's Cabinet.' It's a very nice poem indeed." The youngster went rigid, and he stared speechlessly at his idol, eyes full of doubt and hope. Poe said to Shea, "Would you mind waiting just another minute or two? There's plenty of time before the curtain."

"Far be it from me to deter a budding poet," Shea said. "Take your time. I'll just step over and speak to Franco."

It was more than a minute or two, for the publisher and the foreman called to Poe to ask his approval on a make-up change on the front page. Then the foreman kept him a little longer to discuss the size of the hole he would be holding open for Poe's *Antigone* review. Then the publisher, John Bisco, a New Englander who was determined that his new journal should reflect high literary quality, buttonholed Poe for a whispered consultation about a galley proof he showed Poe. Finally Poe was allowed to get his greatcoat, and he and Shea left to brave the muds of March. The office boy stared after them worshipfully, and Harry Franco again raised deep-set eyes warily as they departed. Franco waved half-heartedly when Poe waved a good night, and Poe ducked his head to suppress a grin and went down the stairs humming his favorite song, "Come Rest in This Bosom."

Outside, Poe gazed up at the cold clouds covering the city and said to his companion, "Great news, Shea! I saw a skein of geese fly over town yesterday morning. Geese flying north means spring is finally here, doesn't it?"

"We'll probably have a few more foul spells," Shea said, "and it looks like you're in for a squall with Harry Franco. Poe, what have you been doing to that fellow?"

"Nothing," Poe said. "Why? What did he say?"

"Why, he immediately began complaining to me about this 'fol-de-rol plagiarism spat' you've been pursuing, but then he promptly turned around and told me he thought it would do the paper good by attracting attention to it. He can't seem to make up his mind. Next thing, he was telling me that you're only an assistant to him on the *BJ*, but in the same breath he tells me how the paper's been gaining strength since they announced you were to be associated with it. It's as if he can't decide whether to love you or loathe you."

Poe laughed. "Franco should be worrying about himself, not me. Our shrewd Yankee publisher is none too satisfied with him, it seems. I fear poor Franco has never in his life composed three consecutive sentences of grammatical English, and Bisco's getting progressively unhappy with his copy. What do you think, Shea? Since I'm having to do all the work anyway, should I aim for a full half interest in the *BJ* instead of a mere third?"

"And cut Franco out? I'd be careful about that, Poe. A man should choose his enemies with the same care he chooses his friends."

"Oh, I wouldn't cut him out. Given time, he'll cut his own throat with Bisco. They can't seem to agree on anything, whereas Bisco and I get along together very well. I must say Bisco endeared himself to me from the very start. Have you ever thought, he had his choice of the whole *Knickerbocker* staff that used to work under him, yet it was me to whom he offered the partnership, just for the authority of my name?"

"Yes, and I've thought you're in danger of getting a very swelled head from all the admiration that's been coming your way."

"Why, Shea!" Poe said. He stopped in his tracks, sincerely hurt that his old friend would criticize him, and a hurrying man with his hat well down on his forehead bumped into him on the sidewalk. The man scowled and muttered something, but then his face suddenly cleared and he said, "It's Mr. Poe, isn't it? Pardon me, Mr. Poe, I should have looked where I was going."

Poe bowed and walked on with Shea, who asked, "Who was that?"

"I don't know," Poe said. "Some lawyer from Brooklyn. His wife writes poetry, I believe. I met him when I called this week on the Samuel Osgoods. No, it was the other night at Dr. Dewey's."

"Dr. Orville Dewey? You were invited there?"

"Is that so surprising?" Poe said. "Come, it's you who tutored me on New Yorkers. They appear to flap like moths around each new season's luminaries. But, Shea, you mustn't think that my head is swelling just because a few fools have learned my name."

"Just be wary, my boy. The Samuel Osgoods of the world will flatter and fawn and in his case ask to paint your portrait, but they're thinking all the time of the use that your renown can be to them. And Mrs. Osgood, well, forgive me for saying it, but of all our ladies who pursue the man of the hour she is one of the more blatant. I hope that you're not allowing yourself to get mixed up with her."

Poe frowned a little. "Of course not," he said. "I merely paid her a courtesy call, to thank her formally for a kindness she had done me." It was true in a way. Poe had been all formality in making a brief call upon the Osgoods, but, although he didn't say it to Shea, the formality was because he found a chattering crowd in their Astor House rooms and Fanny cozily serving tea to two other admirers—not Rufe Griswold, at least, but a Broad Street merchant and the stuttering mathematician whom he vaguely remembered from his lecture. Both Osgoods had proclaimed their delight in seeing Poe, but the scene had been enough to frost any man's budding ardor.

"Ah, Poe," Shea said, "this business of being invited here and there is the dawn of the fame you so richly deserve. Enjoy it for what it's worth, but don't let them spoil things for you. Remember the plan—to gain a secure income so you can retire to the tranquility and leisure in which you can accomplish such great things. These lion hunters will steal your todays, day by day, that's all they want you for. I want you for tomorrow—for posterity."

They were nearing the theater. Chatham Street boiled with carriages, which splattered forth a sea of young men-about-town in white kid gloves and glittering women who comprised the town's public harem; in the Park's third tier, known as the whispering gallery, the two elements would soon converge to discuss negotiations for post-theater labors of love. Poe looked at the crowds contemptuously. "Don't worry, Shea," he said, "I won't be swayed from our ultimate objective. To be the hero of the moment—what a trivial ambition. What can I care for the judgment of a multitude, every individual of which I despise?"

Shea shrugged his stout shoulders uncomfortably. "Don't despise them," he counseled. "Inspire them, like young Alex at the office. Now, there's a good day's work—to inspire youngsters to try to write as you do. Maybe one of them one day will turn out to be a real poet."

Poe smiled tolerantly at his mentor and went to identify himself as a member of the press to the manager. He and Shea were admitted to the dingy, uncarpeted lobby and passed through a narrow underground passage to the pit, keeping careful guard over their purses to thwart the pickpockets who infested the place. On the second two tiers of boxes, the theater's respectable patrons squirmed uncomfortably on hard settees covered by dark moreen. The pit was even more uncomfortable, what with backless benches and no room to stretch one's legs. But it was here that congregated the inevitable riffraff, with its penchant for disgracing even the holy precincts of the Park by chunking peanut shells and pork chop bones at actors who displeased them—and, even more important, here sat the critics and reporters. The actors were fully aware which part of the house they should play to.

Poe sat quietly, brooding over his old friend's scolding as the play started. He hated criticism. Oh, not of his literary output. Nothing he wrote ever quite came up to his own expectations, and he always listened with patient, sometimes even eager, interest to captious examinations of his works. But he hated it when people took issue with his pronouncements on the literary merits of other people's works, and he hated it even more when they found fault with him personally. Poe shifted restlessly, then sat still again. The man in front was leaning back against his knees, calling none too quietly to an acquaintance in the rows behind Poe. But the whole house was restless that night, perhaps because the revival of Sophocles' *Antigone* that the Park was attempting, complete with choruses, Grecian costumes and all, struck the theatergoers as too refined and too classical to stay away from, but also too refined and too classical to enjoy. Now, as the first scene of the play progressed, everyone still talked to seatmates and gawked at the people around them. Even on the stage the actors' gaze went to the audience more often than to their fellow actors.

Beyond the pit and the eight-piece orchestra, idle that night except for the coming chore of playing intermission music, the actor playing Creon cast despairing eyes at the crowded rows of benches, where the steady buzz of chatter was making it impossible to get proper solemnity into his decree that the body of Polyneices should lie unburied. Only one man in the pit seemed to be sitting quietly, watching the stage, and even his attention seemed to be on the air over Creon's head, not on his face. A man dressed all in black. A man with a lofty forehead and a lock of black curling hair tumbling over it. A man half the other men in the pit seemed to be watching. A man . . . The Raven! Of course!

Then damn the audience. Give them the diversion that they want, and let them get it out of their systems.

Into his lines and into Creon's decree, the actor skillfully but dramatically dropped the interpolation, "Nevermore . . . no, nevermore."

Then in the three tiers and in the pit, there was a sudden hush. A low murmur, like the sighing of the wind, ran through the thrilled audience, and every eye in the house turned slowly to fix upon the black-dressed man in the pit, Edgar Poe, who blinked, looked about him, and sat up straighter on his bench.

Creon paused just long enough for a deep, modest blush to mount from Poe's white collar to his pale forehead. Then Creon attacked his next line with such vigor that the audience automatically, if unwillingly, all looked back at him, as if hoping for a continuance of the profound sensation his interpolation had produced. He had captured them at last, all but a stout, freckled man on the bench next to the Raven, who kept gazing around uneasily, and the Raven himself, who still stared at the spot above Creon's head—but now with a faint smile on his strikingly chiseled face and with wide, proud, supernal eyes.

4

In the last week of March, wet winds blew open the buds of the narcissus and crocus that grew in window boxes and ten-by-ten yards and, not yet content with this handiwork, by mid-week shredded the new petals with wheezy gusts. On Friday evening, the stormy winds brought mingled rain and hail, and at nightfall, winter hurled itself for the last time against the city, disdaining an easy death. As fourteen-year-old Alex Crane half trotted, half ran toward the sanctuary of the Historical Society library, the rain had turned to wind-blown sleet that gnawed his red ears and tweaked his nose blue with cold. Alex had a nice room with a master ironmonger's widow down on Maiden Lane, and he would never have left her cozy fireside, where apples baked in the coals and she often let him pop Indian corn, if he hadn't been so anxious to hear his editor repeat his famous lecture on poets and poetry.

Alex would have braved far more than a mere howling storm for Mr. Poe. As an eighty-year-old farmer in Monona County, Iowa, almost three quarters of a century later, he would still tell the curious how he remembered Mr. Poe as one of the finest, truest, most knightly gentlemen he had ever known. Even now, as a young office boy who currently thought he might become a poet if he could only learn to write as his idol did, he told the curious at his Sunday school and in his letters home, that the famous Mr. Poe was of a highly sensitive type, true, but also honest, generous and kind. Mr. Poe's gentle greetings when he came to the office in the mornings, his inquiries and encouragements, made Alex love and trust his editor. He couldn't resist going to Mr. Poe instead of Mr. Harry Franco every time some matter in the office needed a decision. Neither could anyone else, from the publisher on down to Bob the devil. Despite the fact that Mr. Harry Franco was a co-editor, it had been apparent to everybody from the day Mr. Poe first walked in the door just who was boss of the promising new *Broadway Journal*.

Admiring Mr. Poe as he did, Alex derived a heady feeling of importance from what he regarded as their friendship. He had been trying to get up courage all day for the daring act of seeking Mr. Poe out before the lecture to say casually, "Good luck." Once safely arrived at the Historical Society, he warmed his hands at a coal stove in the cloakroom, just in case Mr. Poe gave him his hand to shake, and went to present his complimentary ticket.

Alex thought at first he was in the wrong room, but he was quickly reassured by the sight of Mr. Poe's friend Mr. Shea. But where was everyone else? Scattered like bits of flotsam in a vast dead sea of empty benches there were only several bonneted ladies, a couple of elderly gentlemen and two younger gentlemen Alex recognized as having called upon Mr. Poe at the office, a Mr. Cornelius Mathews and a Mr. Gabriel Harrison.

Diffidently, Alex approached Mr. Shea, who greeted him warmly but worriedly, and added, "So Mr. Poe remembered your ticket, did he?"

"Yes indeed, sir," Alex said. "Mr. Poe never forgets anything. I thought I might just go around and thank him once again. Do you suppose he'd mind?"

"No, no, go ahead. He's arranging his notes in the librarian's office. But, Alex . . ."

"Yes, sir?"

"Nothing. It's all right. It's a wild night, and the storm is delaying people rather badly, that's all. Surely more will come."

"Oh, surely, sir," Alex said. He was shocked to think otherwise. "Why, Bob at the office said Mr. Bisco at the office said the young ladies of the female institute had received special late permission to hear Mr. Poe."

"Yes, but young ladies aren't always very courageous about getting their boots wet. Was it still sleeting when you came in?"

"Yes, sir."

"Damn. Well, run ahead. The office is right that way. And take off your cap, Alex. There are at least a few ladies present."

Alex whipped off his cap. He'd forgotten it. His hair, he discovered, was dry at the crown but soaking wet at the edges, and he combed it with his fingers before tapping lightly at the closed door Mr. Shea had indicated.

A soft, cheerful voice called, "Come in," and Alex opened the door a crack. Mr. Poe was leafing rapidly through a book of poetry and whistling almost inaudibly under his breath. When he saw Alex, he said, "Ah, just the man I want to see. Come in, Alex, and tell me if by any chance you've taken a close look at the audience tonight."

"Why . . . yes, sir."

"And did you see therein a young woman who . . ." Mr. Poe paused and looked at Alex for a moment, then corrected himself: ". . . a lady not so very young, but with a charming smile, and let me see, on a night like tonight probably bundled up in a pretty set of Russian sables?"

"No, sir," Alex said. "I only saw some older ladies in shawls."

Mr. Poe sighed and fingered a marker of pale blue paper that he had placed in the book. "A pity," he murmured. "I thought I might illustrate a point with a pleasing lyric that, by the way, you should read sometime—*She Comes, the Spirit of the Dance*. Well then, in lieu of Mrs. Osgood, did you chance to see a lady with a rather square jaw but, one might say, classic elegance of form, Mrs. Elizabeth Oakes Smith? She's usually accompanied by one of her sons, boys about your age. No again? Alex, there goes my excerpt from *The Sinless Child*. Remember this when you grow up and give lectures, Alex: if you chance to admire someone's poetry anyway, it does no harm to a friendship to read the poet's work in public. But I suppose tonight I may as well excerpt from Willis and Thomas Holley Chivers. You must read Willis for charm, Alex, and Chivers for sound. I know that people ridicule Chivers. The Duyckinck brothers, I'm sad to say, have a habit of reciting those strange stanzas to each other with shouts of delight. Yet though his figures of speech are metaphor run mad and his grammar often none at all, there are as fine individual passages to be found in the poems of Dr. Chivers as in those of any poet whatsoever."

Mr. Poe was not usually so loquacious, and Alex was pleased, but he was worried, too. He said, "Sir, about the audience . . ."

"No, never mind about the audience," Mr. Poe said. "Willis and Chivers will do very well." He closed his book, took two others from a stack he had apparently borrowed from the library and gathered the pale blue sheets on which his lecture was written. "Well, Alex, I'm glad you could come," he said. "Listen closely when I discuss Professor Longfellow. In poetry it is sometimes difficult not to borrow, but there's a vast difference between inspiration and downright plagiarism."

Mr. Poe gave no signs at all of stage fright, but his pale face was alert and expectant as he opened the door to the lecture hall. Alex, following at his heels, peeped around his shoulder to look at the crowd, and at that moment Poe drew in his breath sharply and stopped.

Even including Alex and the ticket-taker, scarcely a dozen people waited.

"Oh, darn," Alex said, disappointed, but from the look on Mr. Poe's face, he could tell that Mr. Poe was more bitterly disappointed by far.

Mr. Poe's gaze roved slowly over the empty benches of the lecture hall, then slowly went to the north windows. Sleet rattled against them. The storm had worsened.

"I guess maybe you should wait a while, Mr. Poe," Alex said stoutly. "The storm will let up soon."

"I think not," Mr. Poe said. His voice was calm, but his gray eyes, when he turned to look at Alex, were miserable. "I am not a lucky man, Alex," he said softly, almost as if to himself, and then he patted Alex absently on the shoulder and went to speak to Mr. Shea and the ticket-taker.

Alex sat on the nearest bench, feeling conspicuous but small in the big, empty hall. Within a minute, Mr. Poe mounted the lecture platform, but only to announce that due to the circumstances, the lecture would not be given and the money would be refunded at the door. The shawled ladies murmured and one by one the would-be audience stood, and Alex finally stood too, feeling downcast and at a loss as to what to do next. Mr. Cornelius Mathews and Mr. Gabriel Harrison brushed past him, going to speak to Mr. Poe, and Alex lingered to listen to their condolences on the treacherous foulness of the weather.

"Come, Poe," Mr. Mathews said, "a hot whiskey or two is what we all need. Who ever heard of sleet this late in the season? A grog will cheer us up no end. Warm us up too. That damned wind is cold, cold, cold."

"Or a nice hot cup of tea," Mr. Harrison suggested.

"Tea be damned," Mr. Mathews said. "It's hot grog a man needs on a night like this. Come along, Poe. We'll go over to the New York's barroom. It's the closest."

Mr. Poe seemed to hesitate, and Mr. Shea joined the trio and seconded Mr. Harrison's idea of hot tea, but Mr. Mathews sputtered jovial protests and insisted on hot grog.

"Well, then, just one," Mr. Poe said at length. His eyes still held the look of misery. "I'll get my coat."

Alex turned away toward the cloakroom for his own coat. He had hoped the men might decide in favor of tea and maybe even ask him to join them, but, temperance enthusiast that he was, Alex was enough of a man of his world to know that while a lady might find consolation in a cup of tea, a gentleman most often sought it in a bar.

Mr. Shea called after him, and Alex paused until the portly man caught up. "Going home, Alex?" Mr. Shea said. "Ride along with me. It's no night to be afoot."

"Why, thank you, sir," Alex said. "If you're sure it's not out of your way? I live down on Maiden Lane."

"No problem," Mr. Shea said. He glanced back at Mr. Mathews and Mr. Harrison, who stood together, waiting. "I'm afraid Mr. Poe is badly upset about the lecture, Alex. And it's such a trivial thing."

"Maybe to some gentlemen it would be, sir," Alex said understandingly, "but I fear my master is a gentleman easily upset by trivial things."

"Too true by half," Mr. Shea muttered. "Damn the luck, and damn Cornelius Mathews and his grogs."

Alex was not given to profanity, but he silently agreed with Mr. Shea the next morning, when Mr. Poe arrived at the *Broadway Journal* office leaning on Mr. Gabriel Harrison's arm and smelling of what Alex strongly suspected must have been more than one glass of breakfast wine. He'd never known Mr. Poe to drink before, much less drink in the mornings, and although Mr. Poe was as meticulously tidy as ever, his face was brightly flushed over the cheekbones, and Mr. Gabriel Harrison's smile, as he greeted Alex, was apologetic.

Mr. Poe sat quietly at his desk and at length roused himself and took some papers from his drawer, but he was still sitting, staring at the papers, when Alex brought him the morning's mail. Then bad got worse. Mr. Bisco, the publisher, came in and after speaking to Mr. Poe went away with a funny look on his face. Then Mr. Harry Franco, the co-editor, came in wearing a new felt hat and a new velvet coat and looking so much like the artists that he liked to write about that Bob the devil giggled and got a dirty look for his pains. Soon Mr. Franco's quick, nervous steps took him to Mr. Poe's desk, and although Alex wasn't near enough to listen, and Mr. Poe's voice stayed low, Mr. Franco's voice quickly raised. There was a sudden, succinct altercation that ended with Mr. Franco rushing to the publisher's office.

Mr. Poe stayed at his desk, looking haughty, the uncustomary color even higher on his face. He picked up the mail and ripped it open as if he were rending an enemy, but at the fifth or sixth letter he stopped and a change came over his expression. There was apparently only one sheet of paper, and Mr. Poe studied this for a long, long time. A smile began to play at the corner of his lips.

Fanny

Finally, Mr. Poe took his pen and uncapped his ink pot and wrote something on the sheet of paper. He signaled Alex, who dropped the exchange list he had been updating and trotted over.

"Yes, sir?" said Alex breathlessly.

Mr. Poe gave him a look that was almost happy. "I seem to have forgotten, Alex, is page three locked up for this edition? All right, no matter. Have this set for the April fifth edition."

It seemed to be a poem, signed by somebody named Violet Vane, but before Alex could do more than glance at it and take two steps, Mr. Poe called him back.

"Wait a minute," Mr. Poe said. "An answer seems indicated." He rose, reached for a notebook in the secretary above his desk and calmly tore out a page.

Alex gasped. It was Mr. Poe's own notebook containing his old poems that he sometimes carefully copied to go into the paper, a notebook which Alex had often looked at longingly but never dared to touch. "Oh, Mr. Poe!" Alex said. "You've ruined it!"

Mr. Poe looked puzzled, and Alex concluded to his dismay that Mr. Poe was still under the influence of the vine—still or again. "Tut, Alex," Mr. Poe said, "I'll have plenty more if I can ever get a publisher for a new volume. Be very watchful of your publishers when you grow up, Alex. As my friend James Russell Lowell recently put it to me, they must be driven as men drive swine—take your eyes off them for an instant, and they bolt between your legs and leave you in the mire."

At that, Mr. Poe sat back down at his desk, inked his pen and marked through the title of the poem torn from his notebook, *To Mary*, and substituted *To F*——, then rapidly and neatly, with the usual inverted brackets, indicated for the typesetters that the title should be centered, noted "10-point Cheltenham" and circled the instruction. He eared both pieces of copy for April 5, but seemed to think again and marked his own poem for April 12. He handed them to Alex, and began to work quietly and efficiently through the rest of his mail.

Alex stood gawking.

"Well, Alex?" Mr. Poe said, looking up.

"Nothing, Mr. Poe," Alex said hastily, and he scurried off with the copy. He didn't dare stop to read it then, but something had happened, something that apparently encouraged Mr. Poe to put in his usual day of steady work. When Mr. Poe, looking sober and cheerful, left at 4 P.M., as he usually did except on press nights, Alex went immediately to the trays of type that were slowly beginning to accumulate for the following week's edition. There was "Diddling," a satire Mr. Poe had reworked. There was the Violet Vane poem, and, yes, there was Mr. Poe's *To F——* with its ten-point Cheltenham head.

Reading upside down and backwards, which, working around printers, he had learned to do rapidly, Alex glanced first at the pseudonymous poem that had come in the mail. *So Let It Be, To ——*, said its own ten-point Cheltenham title. Seven stanzas, but Alex got the drift immediately with two:

> Perhaps you think it right and just,
> Since you are bound by nearer ties,
> To greet me with that careless tone,
> With those serene and silent eyes.
>
> . . . .
>
> That fair fond girl, who at your side,
> Within your soul's dear light, doth live,
> Could hardly have the heart to chide
> The ray that friendship well might give.

A love poem, of course. The ladies sent so many of them. Why had Mr. Poe looked so tickled when he'd found it in the mail? Mr. Poe's own poem gave no real answer, but Alex liked it immensely better, and he looked forward to the issue of the journal in which it would finally appear. He'd be sure and save a copy. But it was short, so he read it over three times, and he thought he had it pretty well in mind by the time he got off and started home through more wind and cold rain for Maiden Lane and the fireside of the ironmonger's widow, mouthing to himself as he briskly walked:

> Beloved! amid the earnest woes
> That crowd around my earthly path—
> (Drear path, alas! where grows
> Not even one lonely rose)—
> My soul at least a solace hath
> In dreams of thee, and therein knows
> An Eden of bland repose.

And thus thy memory is to me
Like some enchanted far-off isle
In some tumultuous sea—
Some ocean throbbing far and free
With storms—but where meanwhile
Serenest skies continually
Just o'er that one bright island smile.

5

But for the difficulty in equipping himself with dress coat and white kid gloves, Poe could earlier have trod the precincts he entered not long after, the home of Miss Anna Lynch at 116 Waverly Place just east of Washington Square, for the sacred purpose for which he presented himself to a young maid at the door—attending one of Miss Lynch's Saturday night receptions.

Other gentlemen left their tall hats and shawls as they entered. Poe left his black cloak and followed. Tramping up the stairs behind him came Horace Greeley, the publisher Greeley, not the street urchin one, clad in dingy white coat and trousers half tucked into his boots. Poe turned to greet him. Terrible thing, that fire that broke out in the *Trib* building. Yes, but he's rebuilding, and he's bluff and cheerful.

A trio of ladies preceded them, floating up to the drawing-room floor. Marabou feathers in shining hair. Hoopskirted crimson velvet, sky-blue silk, blond lace. Poe followed to the double parlors, warmed at either end by glowing coal fires. Framed by a black mantle which in turn was framed by corded draperies stood Miss Lynch, receiving guests with her elderly mother and her sister, Mrs. Charles Congdon, a lady humorist, of all things. Poe doffed the right-hand kid glove and took the offered hands, theirs warm from the fire, his cool from the night. He quietly apologized for the absence of his wife: "Being an invalid, she dared not risk the night air."

Then he turned slowly and regarded the parlors filled with people. There was one of the old Philadelphia gang who, like Poe, had moved to New York, Thomas Dunn English, something of a hothead and something of an ass, but withal a likable young graduate of the University of Pennsylvania School of Medicine, who wrote his graduation thesis on phrenology, then verses that he used to contribute to the magazine Poe edited and now was trying to get a magazine of his own started. Poe bowed. Yes, and there was Fitz-Greene Halleck, talking with General Morris, one of Poe's former employers at the *Mirror*, whom, with kindhearted Nat Willis, Poe often still met for lunch. Good, and there was Willis himself, tall and smiling, talking to short, shaggy-eyebrowed Dr. Francis, who waved to Poe and mouthed something, but Poe couldn't tell what. Later, Willis would be talking exclusively to the ladies. He was like that.

Speaking of ladies, it looked as if many of the stars in the galaxy of The Starry Sisterhood were out tonight. Mrs. Mary Hewitt, poet, sat on a sofa at the side of the room. Mrs. Elizabeth Oakes Smith, poet and suffragist, strolled in from the other parlor on the arm of one of her young sons, pressed into duty, as always, because her husband refused to attend this kind of do. Margaret Fuller, of the Transcendentalists and the *Tribune*, talked nearby to Mrs. Elizabeth Ellet, the haughty and decorous poet who, Poe had recently heard, was also a dangerous gossip. Mrs. Ellet abruptly ceased her conversation and stared at Poe. He bowed again and watched her drop her head. Good Lord, the woman was blushing. Could it be that she was smitten with him?

Ah, no matter. There *she* was, seated on a footstool at the feet of Mrs. Hewitt, dressed in straw-colored silk trimmed with black velvet, her lovely, lively face upturned to Poe with a welcoming smile that began in her eyes, then reached her delicate lips—Fanny Osgood.

Poe bowed deferentially and started toward Fanny, but Mrs. Oakes Smith tapped his arm with her ivory fan. His eyes, turning reluctantly from Fanny, then discovered the identity of a man sitting above Fanny on the sofa. It was the Reverend Dr. Rufus Griswold, squinting at him apprehensively.

Poe was equally apprehensive at seeing Griswold, but his apprehension quickly changed to pleasure. Miss Lynch was strict in drawing the moral as well as the intellectual line, and it was delightful that Griswold should see him in his new manifestation as a distinguished guest at this distinguished reception. Poe smiled at Griswold in a deliberately kind manner and excused himself to Fanny with his eyes. *Sorry. Got trapped.* To Mrs. Oakes Smith, aloud, he said a grave good evening, then flinched slightly when she squared her imposing jaw and proclaimed, "Mr. Poe, I have a trade-last for you and a bone to pick with you, and I'm not sure which to broach first."

Poe had no idea what grounds the lady might have for grievance, but the mere thought made him tense. He glanced again, unwillingly, at Griswold. Certain curious looks had made him wonder if the Griswold clique were still circulating old tales about him, and from time to time he felt distinctly uneasy among his new friends. Too, there was a minor matter of his having gone to the office drunk one recent morning. He was almost sure Harry Franco had been gossiping about that. Poe tried to keep his face from showing his alarm, and he said in his soft, low voice, "Then dreading the bone and being unsure what a trade-last might be, let me take advantage of your indecision, madam, and first compliment you upon your fresh appearance tonight. How can it be that, while all around us, spring is but a hope, summer's roses are blooming upon your cheeks and lips?"

"Heavens, Mr. Poe," said Mrs. Oakes Smith, "your lovely compliment compels me to bring out my own with no further barter. Had you ever been a child, which I begin to suspect you weren't, you would know that a trade-last is an exchange of compliments that one person has heard about another. I have for you a remark Mr. Charles F. Hoffman has passed to me behind your back about your *Raven*. Shall I tell you how he interprets it?"

As much as Poe loved compliments, he was distracted. On her footstool, Fanny had turned away and seemed to be answering some question Griswold had put to her. Poe willed her to turn her attention back to him, as he said to his companion, "By all means."

"Mr. Hoffman holds, sir, that it is a far greater poem than you realize, and points to the trope of the bust of Athena becoming the perch of the oracular raven, saying, 'It is despair brooding over wisdom.'"

"Exquisite," murmured a new voice, and Poe turned to see that Elizabeth Ellet had drifted up to join them, accompanied by the critic Margaret Fuller. Mrs. Ellet looked meaningfully at Poe, but plain-faced Margaret Fuller, who made a habit of depreciating most people and most things, drawled, "How profound of Mr. Hoffman." Her tone was so sarcastic that Mrs. Oakes Smith raised her dark eyebrows.

"Come, Margaret," she said, "I thought Mr. Hoffman's interpretation very nicely phrased indeed. Since you are feeling so disapprobatory tonight and since modesty forbids, I shall not repeat to you the equally well-turned compliment that Mr. Poe just saw fit to bestow on me. But I shall tell you, Mr. Poe, that if I have shed a little of winter's pallor tonight it's because a friend and I walked ten miles into the country to gather pussy willow and wild iris. They're out, you know, most gloriously. And then we walked ten miles back. I'm by no means fatigued, but I must say it was nicer when we first moved to New York. My boys and I could stroll a few blocks up Sixth Avenue and find pastures then, with a few sheep grazing and masses, absolute masses, of wild flowers. Now one must go miles to enjoy the wilderness."

Poe was still preoccupied with Fanny, but he was by habit and inclination attentive to women, and he said to Mrs. Oakes Smith with his usual grave courtesy, "How delightful that you like to walk in the country. It's one of my favorite modes of exercise."

"And mine," said Elizabeth Ellet. Again she looked meaningfully at Poe, and Fanny suddenly turned her head back to the group, alert, as if sensing danger.

The game was now going Poe's way. With deliberate warmth he said to Mrs. Ellet, "I should have guessed. I suppose all sensitive people tend to steep themselves in nature."

"Not I," said Margaret Fuller. "The countryside around New York abounds in copperheads, doesn't it?"

Mrs. Ellet and Mrs. Oakes Smith both cast the *Tribune* critic despairing looks, but said nothing. The Starry Sisterhood freely criticized one another but not the critics upon whom they depended for literary recognition. Changing the subject, Mrs. Oakes Smith said to Poe, "And now, sir, for the bone I told you I had to pick. It has been reported to me that in your assessment of the English poets you find fault with Mr. Shelley's passion. Can this possibly be true?"

Poe was relieved, and he was also flattered when two more ladies drew nearer to hear his answer. Had Fanny noticed the growing circle around him? Yes, she had turned completely around on her footstool, and her back was now to Griswold, her face to him. Her eyes sparkled at him mischievously. They clearly said, *Yes, I see that you are much admired. But don't you wish you were talking to me instead?*

With his own eyes, he answered, *Yes!* But, in a judicial tone, to Mrs. Oakes Smith he presented his opinion: "In passion, madam, Shelley was supreme, but it was an unfettered enthusiasm ungoverned by the amenities of art."

Mrs. Oakes Smith protested, "Yes, but Shelley's enthusiasm was the clairvoyant fortuitousness of intuition. Don't you agree?"

"Not precisely," Poe said, quite truthfully, for it was hard to make out what the woman meant. He might have become bored, but Fanny was still watching him and the hostess joined the still growing circle of which Poe was the center. He raised his voice a bit to address all of them, beginning to enjoy himself. "I think, rather, that we must agree that Shelley's principal forte was powerful abandon of rhythmical conception. But he lacked just that Tennysonian art necessary to the creation of a perfect poem. You are mistaken if you suppose that passion is the primum mobile of the true poet, for it is just the reverse. A pure poem is one that is wholly destitute of a particle of passion."

Poe's audience buzzed excitedly. What a radical statement! What daring!

"Then you admire Tennyson?" asked Mrs. Oakes Smith.

"Yes, I consider Tennyson one of the greatest poets who ever lived," Poe answered. But he answered inattentively, for he had just noticed, with a small thrill of delight, that Rufus Griswold was now sitting rigidly on his sofa, glowering jealously at Poe over Fanny's head.

Poe smiled back benignly, then, rubbing it in, exchanged a long glance with Fanny. Her eyes asked, *Should you not abandon your admirers and come to me?* He answered, *No, naughty goddess, you should abandon the frowning Reverend Griswold and all of your other admirers and come to me.* But what was this? Dr. Francis came blustering his way to Poe's side with young Dr. Thomas Dunn English in his wake, exclaiming, "My God! Poe, how can you say that? Why, Tennyson's poems are as effeminate as a phlegmatic fat baby. He is the most perfectly Greek statuesque in his conceptions, if you please, of any man who ever lived since the days of Pericles."

"This is just what constitutes Tennyson one of the greatest geniuses who ever lived, Dr. Francis," answered Poe. "Passion has nothing to do with pure poetry. For every drop of passion that you infuse into any poem, just so far do you materialize, deteriorate and render it no-poem. A pure poem is the rhythmical creation of beauty wholly destitute of everything but that which constitutes purity, namely, ethereality."

Interpolated Fanny, *Casanova! You just let Mrs. Ellet brush you with her shoulder!*

Interpolated young English, as if he were eager to draw some of the audience's attention to himself, "Well, Poe, but this would not only bring you in conflict with the time-honored opinions of the world, but be the establishment of a new mode of criticism among the nations."

"True, but that does not give me a moment's concern," blandly answered he. With equal blandness he answered Fanny, *It was an accident. The lady's interest in me is not reciprocated.*

If what you say be true, come to my side, said Fanny.

"If what you say be true, then two thirds of everything that Shakespeare ever wrote is absolutely good for nothing," argued English.

Certainly it is true, but it is you who must come to my side, said Poe to Fanny. To English, he said, "Certainly it is good for nothing. Nothing is good for anything except that which contains within itself the essence of its own vitality. Otherwise it is mortal and ought to die."

Poe's young antagonist was losing confidence, but that only made him argue more hotly. "Then if this be the case, if all the poetical works in the world were pruned of their excrescences, there would be very little real poetry left," English said.

"Very little, indeed—but just enough to show that what I say of poetry is true," pronounced Poe.

"Then Byron, Wordsworth, Coleridge, Montgomery, Southey and many other world-renowned sons of song would fare badly," insisted English.

Fanny rose hesitantly.

A sudden, radiant smile broke out on Poe's face. "But no worse than they deserve," he answered happily. "And now pray pardon me, English. I have monopolized the floor too long, and I see an acquaintance about whose health my wife has asked me to inquire." He bowed to his interlocutor and took a step away from literature and toward love. Griswold jerked forward on the sofa, almost as if he meant to grab at Fanny's silken skirts, but she gracefully controlled their fullness and floated a few steps toward Poe.

They met in the center of the room. With shyness real or feigned, Fanny gave him her hand, and he bent over it solicitously. Young Dr. Thomas Dunn English gazed after him, disgruntled by his conversation and bewildered by his smile. "How rude," he said to Margaret Fuller. "I wanted to ask Poe what he thought of Keats."

The Reverend Dr. Rufus Griswold also gazed after Fanny and Poe. He leaned back slowly against the cushions and sat silently. But his trenchant gray eyes were like those seen above a dueling pistol aimed across twenty paces at a man's heart.

6

Poe was a poor judge of character. Griswold was a good one. It was Griswold's most effective weapon in the discreet, undeclared war upon which he immediately embarked. He first tendered the enemy, Poe, a pressing invitation to dine with him, and enjoyed a long chat about Poe's recent activities. Upon his next trip to New York, Griswold chose the person most susceptible to his machinations. With pleased anticipation, the one-time temperance zealot raised his voice to be heard above the noise in the smoky, crowded Astor House barroom and asked *Broadway Journal* co-editor Harry Franco, "Now what'll you take? Julep, sling, cocktail or sherry cobbler?"

Harry Franco's sharp, thin face swung quickly to Griswold's. He looked suspicious and startled. Griswold smiled.

"Don't you recognize the line?" he asked Franco. "It's from one of my favorite novels."

Now, finally, Franco smiled back. "Well," he said, preening a little. "I did think the wording sounded familiar."

"A very humorous scene," Griswold said. "But, then, the whole book was exceedingly picturesque. I expect I've re-read *The Adventures of Harry Franco*, oh, two or three times since I first ran across the serial form in the *Knickerbocker*. Clark was commenting to me only the other day that he wished you hadn't gotten so tied up with the *Broadway Journal*. I'm afraid he misses your contributions."

A barman interrupted, asking for their order, before Harry Franco could reply. Griswold smothered an exclamation of annoyance. But his bait had been carefully chosen, and Franco snapped at it as soon as a pair of whiskey cobblers stood before them on dark, glistening wood.

"It's true, I'm busy, but perhaps I could accommodate an old friend like Clark," Franco said carefully.

"Hm, hm," Griswold said. He sipped the disagreeably sweet drink, ordered only because Franco had ordered one, and added, "Of course, there is one little problem. The way your journal keeps attacking everyone in sight, I must tell you frankly, not only Clark but certain other splendid men have worried aloud to me recently that your, um, co-editor may be influencing you against them."

"Well, by God!" Franco sputtered. "Will Poe end by costing me every friend I have in New York? I tell you, Griswold, I've done my best to control him, but he has wormed his way into the confidence of the publisher, and, by God, well, by God!"

"Yes, indeed, that sounds just like your friend Poe," Griswold said.

"*My* friend! Claim him yourself, Dr. Griswold, if you can stomach it. Why, he had to be carried home in a wretched condition only a month ago, after you stood him dinner at Brown's. That's twice now that he's come to the office soggy with drink!"

"Tsk," said Griswold. "I'm most sorry to hear that, but then periodic drunkenness always has been one of Poe's problems. And to think that he has the nerve to refer to you constantly as 'the brandy-nosed Mr. Franco.'"

"He does, does he? He refers to you as 'the sycophantic serpent.'"

Franco glared at Griswold. Griswold glared back. Then Griswold forced himself to relax. "Ah well, that's Poe for you," he said. "Strange, how the man eventually turns on everyone who befriends him. As for that dinner at Brown's, well, he wormed himself into that invitation, as well. You'll want to watch him, you know. I understand that he's bragging around the city that he'll also end by pushing you out and having the *Broadway Journal* for his own."

"All right. All right, this is the end!" bawled Franco. Three City Hall politicians turned and stared at him, but Franco didn't bother to lower his voice. "Two can play that game, you know. Perhaps there *will* be only a single name on the masthead of the *BJ*, but I can tell you right now, it won't be that of Poe!"

Now a pair of Wall Street lawyers also turned to stare, and Franco bit off his threat. More quietly, yet suspiciously, he added, "But perhaps I shouldn't have said that, Dr. Griswold. Any plans I might make would be handicapped if word of my intentions were intercepted by Poe."

"No word will come from me," Griswold assured him. "Besides, even though literary business requires me to see Poe from time to time, he well knows that I'll not hear a single word against you. I made that very clear to him the last time I encountered him. You know how Poe goes on behind one's back. What was it that time? Oh yes, that you pretend to a knowledge of French, yet are profoundly ignorant of it. I cut him off. And, of course, he backed down instantly. That's Poe in a nutshell."

Franco seemed to force a smile. "The man's unbelievable," he said. "For you, he provides a pretension to a knowledge of Greek and Latin, and a complete ignorance of same."

That rankled. It still rankled thirty minutes later, when Griswold genially bade Harry Franco good-by and crossed Broadway in a red sunset. Together, he and Franco had provided Poe with pretensions toward German, and had assured one another he couldn't read a word of the language, but still that stab about Latin and Greek rankled. Griswold felt so upset that he turned into City Hall Park and sat down for a moment on a wrought-iron bench. Three gray pigeons waddled toward him hopefully, and he shooed them away with his hat. City vermin. Like rats. To think that some people actually fed the creatures.

Griswold turned his thoughts resolutely toward more pleasant things. Harry Franco, that was a good start. One down. Next . . . hmmmm. If Franco succeeded in ridding himself of Poe, excellent. But since he might fail, it would be good strategy to put a bug in the ear of any potential backers on the Poe side, for Poe could never succeed in running the journal on his own without floating notes.

Griswold decided he would make one exception—Horace Greeley. The *Tribune* publisher should, in fact, be actively encouraged to loan Poe money. It would put Horace's nose out of joint faster than anything else, to have Poe default on a loan. Serve him right. Horace shouldn't have been so insulting that time about his honorary title.

What more? The *Knickerbocker* and Clark must be encouraged to continue denigrating Poe. And was there anything that could be done with Poe's young friend Thomas Dunn English? Some opportunity later, perhaps. The last thing one wanted was for word to get back to Poe that Griswold had mounted a discreet campaign against him.

Mrs. Elizabeth Ellet? No, dangerous. Poe would tear his pants with her eventually, as he did with everyone, and meanwhile the lady was treacherous enough to turn upon a Griswold as well as a Poe.

But Fanny, ah, the lovely Fanny. Even if one opted for marriage with the wealthy Miss Myers, one could *not* bear the thought of Poe's possible victory in their war for her affections. Talk to Fanny frankly about Poe? No, no. Miss Myers would be arriving in Philadelphia soon from the South. He dared not see Fanny just now, for fear that he might change his mind yet again. But . . .

Of course, just for the moment, there was another Fanny suitor with whom one just might be able to accomplish a small thing or two, the merchant who had been so madly in love with her so long. Yes, he'd give thought to that. Every little thing might help. And other ploys would surely occur to him.

Griswold suddenly felt tired and short of breath. If only he could make up his mind whether or not to marry Miss Myers, then small undertakings such as seeing that Poe got his just deserts would not be so taxing. The Myers question took a lot out of one. How *could* one marry her when it was Fanny one loved? And yet, all that money, and the sweet freedom it could afford . . .

The Reverend Dr. Rufus Griswold slumped on the uncomfortable bench, finding life complex. How much simpler it would all have been had one's wife's cousin accepted the proposal one had made her a discreet year after one's dear wife died. The cousin had been both rich and attractive. One would have loved her dearly, one was certain. Then the magic of Fanny would never have occurred, and the necessity of deciding about Miss Myers never need take place.

It was unfair, when one worked so very, very hard, to have to suffer on endlessly, while mere luck raised other, less worthy men effortlessly to the heights.

7

When a man finds that he has arrived at the top of a great height, it behooves him to raise his eyes higher to the filmy heavens, for to turn and peer into the abyss is to grow sick and dizzy. Peering, he first experiences an impulse to shrink from the danger. But, unaccountably, he remains, and slowly, shudderingly, there comes the thought: what would his sensations be if he were to fall from such a height?

Poe knew the answer from his chronic nightmares, but for his present purpose he had only hinted at it—a precipitous sweep . . . a rushing annihilation. And then, if, instead of stepping back, the man looking down from the edge of the abyss feels the sudden, irresistible temptation to step forward . . . ?

Glancing back over the freshly inked sheets of pale blue paper, Poe concluded that his article was going very well. He dipped his pen into a bronze inkstand which he had used since boyhood and which John Allan had accused him of stealing when he first left Richmond, and he wrote rapidly on a new sheet:

I have said thus much that in some measure I may answer your question—that I may explain to you why I am here—that I may assign to you something that shall have at least the faint aspect of a cause for my wearing these fetters, and for my tenanting this cell of the condemned.

He paused. The wick of the candle was sputtering in a pool of melted wax, and he didn't know where more candles were. Probably in Muddy's room, but he didn't want to run the risk of awakening her.

Across the room in which he wrote lay Virginia, sleeping. These were new rooms again, way over on East Broadway. The board bill overdue on Amity Street, the Poes had joined New York in its May Day migration to new quarters—joined the tailors carrying their shop signs, joined the laborers straining to push carts laden with bureaus and bedsteads, joined the jam of refugees in wagons piled high with pots and quilts and crates of chickens and the family cat, moving up in the world or moving down, but moving, as custom demanded, in time for their new addresses to be listed in the annual city directory. So Poe's address was new, although the rooms, musty, moldy, a front and a back room on the third story of an old house, were far from new. So Poe's desk was bigger here, although the bed in which Virginia tonight was sleeping alone was smaller. So Poe's reputation and, true to Shea's fears, his self-esteem were far larger and all was different, but in one way all was the same: when Poe returned home from the offices of the *Broadway Journal,* from the theater and concert hall or from society's salons, there was always the nightly dose of laudanum for Virginia and for him the nightly necessity to write.

Poe's family cat lay on his knee, as she often did, as he wrote. Sometimes she curled herself across his shoulders like a floppy fur collar. She would have preferred to lie upon his papers, but Poe was firm with her on this one point. Kittens had duly appeared, but despite Virginia's pleas Muddy had drowned them all. The new

Broadway Journal might be setting the town on its ear with its controversial articles signed E.A.P., but handsome profits were still to come, and even blind kittens eventually opened their eyes, were weaned by their mothers and had to have food bought for them.

So Poe wrote, working even more rapidly because the candle was burning so low. He wrote:

Had I not been thus prolix, you might either have misunderstood me altogether, or, with the rabble, have fancied me mad. As it is, you will easily perceive that I am one of the many uncounted victims of the Imp of the Perverse.

It is impossible that any deed could have been wrought with a more thorough deliberation. For weeks, for months, I pondered upon the means of the murder. I rejected a thousand schemes, because their accomplishment involved a chance of detection. At length—

The candle flared up as the wick burned through and fell. Poe regarded it for a moment, then wrote on.

At length, in reading some French memoirs, I found an account of a nearly fatal illness that occurred to Madame Pilau, through the agency of a candle accidentally poisoned. The idea struck my fancy at once. I knew—

Damn, there went the light. But never mind, he could wrap it up easily the next morning. Keep it very short. The successful murderer is suddenly overcome by the idea of confessing to his undiscovered crime, and *voilà*. Two or three paragraphs would do it, for the real work, that of explaining the motive, was already done.

It was the temptation of the perverse act, the overwhelming tendency to do wrong to oneself for the wrong's very sake. He'd explained very clearly, he concluded, that with certain minds, under certain conditions, such a temptation becomes absolutely irresistible.

With certain minds, under certain conditions. That was just a sop to the reader, of course. It was man's nature, pure and simple, but his knowledge of human nature also assured him that few readers would care to face this dark side of themselves.

Poe stretched, disturbing Catarina. The stench of the dead candle filled the room, and he rose and went to the window. In New York, even in the stillest hours, there was always someone on the street, and presently he could smell dust, then could make out a man with a huge birch broom slowly sweeping the middle of the cobblestones. Behind him came two other men, who swept into the gutter the day's accumulation of dust, discarded trash and dog dung, and behind them came carts in which the debris was dumped, to be trundled to the nearest dock and thrown in the river. But Poe scarcely noticed what he saw. His mind was still stringing word to word and image to image. It was hard to stop in the middle of a scene, but he knew stopping would make it easier to start again in the morning.

The morning, what was it he must do in the morning? Get this new article finished for *Graham's*. Start reading Dr. Lewis's *Plato Contra Atheos* for a *BJ* review. Drop a note to Elizabeth Ellet thanking her for some books she had just sent. Or drop by to see her. She would be leaving the city soon for her husband's home in South Carolina, and she'd never forgive him if he didn't say good-by. He should see Nat Willis too. Willis was going to England next month, and Poe feared he would feel his friend's absence keenly.

His mind veered to his article. The murderer, he decided, should suddenly be bitten with the idea of confessing while strolling in the streets. He walks faster, then faster still. It's his own thoughts he's trying to escape, but the crowd, seeing a man running, begins to pursue, and then . . . then a heavy hand crashes onto his shoulder and his secret bubbles up to . . .

Everyone was leaving town or had already left. Everyone, and especially the fascinating Fanny, gone to Albany with that ne'er-do-well husband of hers. For the sake of Fanny's health, Osgood said. It was true that she'd picked up a dry little cough during the latter part of this glorious spring, but it was more likely for the sake of Osgood's purse that they had abandoned the city. Fanny had sighed they'd be staying with relatives.

It must be one or two in the morning. He'd feel poorly tomorrow if he didn't get some sleep, and now was the time that sleep was possible, in the silent gap between Virginia's early night siege of coughing and the second seizure that always seemed to begin an hour or two before dawn. But the bed here was so small. It was probably the bed's fault that he'd been having so many nightmares again. "No wonder you dream of suffocating, my poor boy," Muddy had said a half-dozen times lately. "If only we could afford to buy you a nice couch." Yes, if only.

If only Sandy Welsh's Cellar weren't so far downtown, he could get a candle there. The congenial spirits who never seemed to leave the place, journalists and others, would be playing cards by candlelight at the very moment, and it would be, "Poe, take a hand." Of course, it would also be, "Poe, have a cup," and maybe he would even have a glass of wine. Fine, dry sherry. Like that splendid amontillado he'd drunk once at Brown's. Who had he dined with that afternoon? He owed the man a debt. Just one glass, that would be best. He'd endured eighteen months of strict sobriety, then he had let down the barriers the night of the stormed-out lecture. But except for another time or two when perhaps he'd let it get out of hand, it wasn't as though he'd been drinking regularly as of late. Just a glass now and then. He had it under good control, and any man might find himself thinking of a single glass of wine when he needed to get through fifteen-hour days, day after day.

Well, maybe two glasses of sherry, then. Not three, no, never again three. Three glasses of anything were dangerous. He'd never do that again. He'd learned his lesson the last time an old friend from Baltimore, Charlie Burr, had breezed into town, diffidently hoping the now famous Mr. Poe would remember him.

That Dr. Chivers from Georgia was due in New York soon, was it this month or next? That would mean hour after hour wasted in literary babble. The fool seemed to think Poe had nothing to do but write endless letters in answer to Chivers's own. Couldn't the man realize that in the same time it took to write a long letter, he could be writing some article that might bring in ten or fifteen dollars? But Chivers would never think of that. He was rich, rich, a man whose friendship could prove valuable if the way ever looked clear for *Stylus*. And he seemed a good-hearted fellow, for all his babble.

Suddenly resolute, Poe went to the wardrobe for his black cloak and his hat. The East River and its sailors' taverns were only six blocks away. One glass of something, and a candle, and he could finish his story tonight. Then he'd have the jump on tomorrow's chores. Muddy could copy the completed article for him first thing in the morning, and he'd mail it off to *Graham's* before he even went to the office.

He had just the title for it. He would call it, simply, "The Imp of the Perverse."

8

Great God! That looked exactly like his friend Mr. Poe, swaggering along the pavement, tottering from side to side, as drunk as an Indian!

Thomas Holley Chivers, M.D., of Oakey Grove, Georgia, halted his hurricanelike stride down Nassau Street, whence he had gone to discuss the printing of his newest book of poems with Mr. Jenkins the printer, and peered nearsightedly from close-set brown eyes. He almost decided he was mistaken, knowing full well that Mr. Poe had been in bed for the past two days with an illness—hadn't he called on Mr. Poe each day? hadn't he helped the poor invalid while away the tedious hours with sublime literary discussion?—but one of a group of laughing men standing on the steps of a whiskey shop was loudly spouting praise in which the name of Poe prominently figured. The men quite ignored Chivers, although Chivers's tall, lanky figure, draped in the flapping folds of his best gray traveling suit, usually attracted considerable attention from these seegar-smoking New Yorkers as he cantered through their streets. Chivers cocked his head and squinted and looked them all over closely and finally concluded, with a thrill of fascinated horror, that the perambulating drunk was indeed Mr. Poe.

"Poe!" he called, veering to intercept him.

"You're the Shakespeare of America," called the other drunk from the whiskey shop.

Poe bowed vaguely at the drunk, then at Chivers and said, "Afternoon." He started to walk on, so Chivers leaped after him and grabbed his coattails.

"Alas, Poe," he said, "don't you recognize me? Ah, man, look at the state you're in. Why should a man whom God by nature has endowed with such transcendent abilities so degrade himself into the veriest automaton as to be moved only by the poisonous steam of hell fire? Your body is a harp made by the hands of God, not an evil-spirit machine."

Poe looked at Chivers in some bewilderment, but then he grasped him by the coat collar and said, "By God, here is my friend now. Where are you going, Dr. Chivers? Come, you must go home with me."

Chivers took Poe by the arm to steady him. "Why, Poe!" he said. "What under heaven could have put you in this fix?"

"What fix?" Poe asked impatiently, frowning one of his thundercloud frowns.

"Why, I should think you ought to know," Chivers said. "Did you not hear that impudent fellow spouting your name at the top of his voice?"

"To be sure I did," replied Poe. "But what of that? He's nothing but a damned fool."

"But he was insulting you. Polluting your fair name with his stinking breath to that drunken, promiscuous crowd!"

"By God!" Poe said. "He insulted me? Then I'll take my cane to him, as I took it this very day to Lewis Clark!"

Good Lord! said Chivers internally, then aloud said, "No, Poe, you must not do so while walking with me." He held on hard to Poe's arm, and succeeded in turning him in the direction of his home. "Did you *really* cane Mr. Clark?" Chivers asked Poe breathlessly as he steered him onward.

Poe chuckled indignantly. "No, he backed down. He's a damned coward, by God! But he'll think twice before he insults me in his damned magazine again. Do you know what he had the nerve to call me this time? 'An anonymous decrier of American periodicals.' The swine. And all because I wrote that American magazine content is less original than that of British magazines. By God, can anyone deny it? And on top of everything else he compared me unfavorably to Rufus Griswold!"

"Come, Poe, it sounds a tempest in a teapot. Let us talk of important things. Did you get my article today?"

"Your article? I've received no articles from anybody today. But then I've been quite busy. I've great news, Chivers! I think I see a chance to take over the sole proprietorship of the *BJ*, were I to want it. Harry Franco has plotted up a palace coup, to turn me and Bisco out, but Bisco isn't going to let him get away with it. I've talked him into turning the tables on Franco. If I could get the capital together I'm absolutely sure I could persuade Bisco to sell the whole kit and caboodle to me. How would you like to be co-publisher of a New York paper?"

"What?" Chivers exclaimed. "Did you not receive my 'Luciferian Revelation'? I sent it by a boy at the hotel, but I had no change on me, so he would have asked for his tip when he delivered it. Think, Poe. This is of the utmost importance. I was inspired to write the article by reading your 'Mesmeric Revelation.' I wish you to publish it in your paper the *very first thing*, because I think well of it, and think you will also. It gives a death blow to materialism, you see. And I sent you also some poems, which you can publish in your paper the week after."

Poe blinked groggily. "But it's the paper I'm talking about, Chivers," he said. "I have no confidence in Bisco's determination to keep it afloat on his own capital, and it would be a thousand pities to give up just as everything flourishes. It's a splendid investment. I just can't understand why everyone is suddenly so short of money. You haven't heard anything, have you, Chivers? You'd tell me, wouldn't you, if you'd heard any adverse talk floating around about investing in the paper?"

"You're always talking to me about the paper," Chivers complained. "Cuss the paper! What do I care about the paper? For heaven's sake! Do not connect my respect for you with any worldly matter, Poe. Alas, alas, it will mean a full day's work if I must recopy both the article and the poems. Did I tell you that Colton has lost some of my sonnets? They were written right out of my heart, as I write everything. And now Colton swears he never received them, and I brought no copies with me. It's his own fault if he does not get to publish them. I sent the sonnets some time ago, but I had no way to pay the postage, as I gave it to the stage driver in the road."

Poe blinked some more, and with exasperation Chivers saw that there was no point in trying to talk to him of serious things. It was a decided inconvenience, for he had meant to consult Poe about the problem of cloth covers versus paper covers for *The Lost Pleiad*. According to Mr. Jenkins, cloth would cost almost sixty dollars more, and although Chivers had long since resigned himself to publishing his books of poetry at his own expense, surely the critics whose notice he was hopeful of gaining would not hold him in disdain for saving a whole sixty dollars. Would they?

But Poe recaptured his interest immediately by locking his arm with Chivers's and saying, "By heavens! By heavens, Chivers, I am now going to reveal to you the very secrets of my heart. Chivers, I am in the damndest amour you ever knew a fellow to be in in all your life, and I make no hesitation in telling you all about it as though you were my own brother. But, by God, don't say anything about it to my wife, for she is a noble creature whom I wouldn't hurt for all the world."

Chivers's thin-lipped, stubborn mouth opened in an "O" of appalled attention. Could this be? Young Mrs. Poe, whom he had met when calling at Poe's rooms, seemed such a tenderhearted, such an affectionate woman, always addressing Poe with the endearing appellation of "My dear." "My dear, will you have a glass of lemonade?" "My dear, I am going out with Mother to take a small walk, I think it will do me good." Yet she was not a healthy woman, as he perceived after a brief acquaintance with her. That pallor. That terrible cough that attacked her at irregular intervals. Chivers said, enthralled, "Well, what is it, Poe? I am anxious to hear it. Where is the lady with whom you are so in love?"

"In Providence, by God! I've just received a letter from her, in which she requests me to come on there this afternoon on the four o'clock boat. So I must go, but I'll be back tomorrow."

"Wait, Poe," Chivers implored. "You cannot possibly contemplate paying your court of love to a lady in your present condition. Wait until tomorrow, and meanwhile tell me about her. What is her name?"

"My condition? By God, you're right! I haven't a single dollar in my pocket. Be a good fellow, Chivers, and loan me ten. I'll pay it back when I return tomorrow."

"Ten dollars!" Chivers said.

"Yes, ten, and not a penny more. I am determined to be frugal, and you know that I'm good for it. Did I tell you about the *BJ*, Chivers? I think I see a chance—"

"Yes, yes, you told me. Who *is* this lady? What is she like? Ah, I can guess. My thoughts rush back through time to a beautiful blue-eyed girl named Mary with whom I used to gather flowers during play time and to whom, sitting in my lap in the shadow of the oaks that overshadowed the old school house, I used to pay my own court of love. She is now in heaven, and by the divine light which I see streaming down from the face of an angel through the opening gates I perceive that her soul rejoices up in paradise that I am still faithful to her first love. I wrote a beautiful poem about her, an anacreontic entitled *Ixion in Heaven*. When we get to your rooms, I shall recite it to you. It is indelibly written on the tablets of my heart. But first, while we have this moment of privacy, tell me about your own lady."

Poe stopped and began feeling in his pockets. "Damnation!" he said, "I seem to have dropped your ten dollars. We must retrace our footsteps and look for it."

"I haven't given it to you yet," Chivers said testily.

"Ah, thank heavens," Poe said. He held out his hand. "I'll take it now, please. And don't forget to remind me of it when I return home tomorrow."

Chivers was extremely reluctant. He had loaned a dollar and a half to Poe's mother-in-law on their very first meeting, and he was not eager to contribute more funds to the Poe ménage. But he was dying of curiosity about Poe's love scrape and, carried away, he counted out five two-dollar bills on the Bank of North America and saw them safely stashed in Poe's leather purse. "Now," he said, as visions of pearl-white teeth and a snow-white bosom made his brain race. "Now give me your confidence in return. Tell me—everything!"

Poe teetered a bit, and Chivers took his arm again. "Have you not met her?" Poe mumbled. "No, that's right, they're out of town. Her husband is a painter. Always away from home, and a damned fool at that."

"A married woman? Poe, Poe, the beautiful milk-white ship of your soul is driving into an infernal whirlpool, never to be reclaimed. Poe? Try to stand up, man! Be careful! You'll pull us both down in the street!"

But Poe's ship had already sunk for the afternoon. He spoke no more, or at least not coherently, and it was with the greatest difficulty that Chivers even managed to keep him upright. He thought of hailing a hack, but he reflected that here in Novum Eboracum, alias Sodom, it cost twenty-five cents just to get into one. Contemptuous of the stares they attracted, he half carried, half dragged the staggering Poe the rest of the way to East Broadway and the steps of his lodging.

One stare he couldn't ignore. Just as they were going up the steps, Poe's wife looked out of the window and saw them. Chivers tried to reach for his hat to raise it, but his arms were encumbered by the sagging body of the young lady's husband. She stared at Chivers a second from vast, sorrowful, violet eyes, then hurriedly withdrew her head. The window closed. When Chivers got Poe up the stairs to the third floor, she was nowhere to be seen, but the mother-in-law, Mrs. Clemm, beckoned from a door.

"Oh, Eddy!" Mrs. Clemm exclaimed tenderly. "Come here, my dear boy! Let me put you to bed!"

"Madam, I assure you—" began Chivers, but the tall old lady in the white widow's cap didn't let him finish.

"I know it isn't your fault, Dr. Chivers," she said. "Here, help me with his coat. No, his boots don't matter. Now to my bed. Easily now." She covered the prostrate Poe with a well-worn but immaculately white counterpane and looked at Chivers with tears in her eyes. "Oh, Dr. Chivers, how I have prayed that my poor Eddy might not get in this way while you were here!" she said. "But I knew, when he went away from here this morning, that he would not return in his right senses. Oh! I do believe the poor boy is deranged. His wife is now at the point of death with bronchitis and cannot bear to see him. Oh! Oh!"

Sorrowfully, the widow wept, and Chivers stirred uneasily, fearing what was coming next.

"Oh!" she said, now weeping freely. "Oh, my poor Virginia! She cannot live long! She is wasting away, day by day, for the doctors can do her no good. But if they could, seeing this continually in poor Eddy would kill her, for she dotes upon him. Would to God that she had died before she had ever seen him! My poor child! What will become of her? Eddy was to bring the five dollars today for her medication, but I know without looking that he has not a shilling in his purse. Eddy has no idea of the value of money, particularly when he gets this way. He's very charitable, and will empty his pockets to a beggar. Thank God I have you to turn to, Dr. Chivers!"

Chivers thought of the ten dollars—*his* ten dollars—resting right now in Poe's purse, and he flushed guiltily, as if he were the would-be adulterer, not Poe. But he could not betray another man to a woman, so he tightened his mouth in lieu of his purse strings and said hastily, "Alas, I wish I could be of aid, madam, but in truth I was hoping you could repay the small loan I had occasion to make to you earlier. My brother was to send me here in New York two hundred dollars he owes me for the sale of a farm, but not a penny has reached me. I am in sore distress for it."

The flow of tears down Mrs. Clemm's broad, wrinkled cheeks ceased. "My dear friend," she said, "how I wish he would send the sum to you immediately, to ease your distress—and mine. When it arrives, I most sincerely hope you will not think me importunate when I ask you to loan me fifteen or twenty dollars for a short time."

Chivers silently berated himself for choosing so large a sum to mention as being due him, but aloud he said, "Be assured, madam, of my desire to be of service to you." He bowed and started backing toward the door. "I shall go to my hotel immediately and see if perchance he has written me this very day." Bow again, back again. "I shall send a boy from the hotel if providence . . . er, luck is with us." His hand was now on the doorknob. He turned it with crafty stealth. "Be of good heart, madam." He opened the door. "Until later, then." He stepped out. "Until anon."

Chivers closed the door in back of him and strode hastily down the narrow hallway, thinking, once again, Good Lord. Had he stayed a moment longer, he would have been poorer by at least five more dollars, he was certain. And without having gotten the name of the woman. Oh well, what matter? He could surely pry that out of Poe, along with everything else he burned to know. Great God, to think that the woman was married! But, then, also, to think that she was no doubt fair. To think, with growing interest, of that milk-white bosom. To think of one's heart on fire, as fast as a woman's own heart beating, hers echoing one's desire, each pulse of one's own repeating!

Rather nice, thought Chivers as he reached the hot bricks of the street. Yet it wasn't nice to think of Poe, of all people, embarked upon such a shameful but engrossing affair. It wasn't as if Poe was far from home, where his wife and children need never know just what he might do in a sinful city. And it surely wasn't as if the streets of Providence, unlike the streets of New York, swarmed with milk-fleshed young women available for a modest price, milk-fleshed young women as agile as the bounding roe and as loving as the amorous doe. And it wasn't as if a poet shouldn't seek inspiration where he could find it. And, come to think of it, hadn't he saved five dollars not five minutes before?

Thomas Holley Chivers, M.D., of Oakey Grove, Georgia, bethought himself of a certain establishment at the corner of Broadway and Canal where, day and night, one always saw a set of hacks waiting and sundry gentlemen going in and out. He turned his steps back downtown.

To think, he concluded, as he walked rapidly, that Poe could even think of such a thing. If there was ever a perfect mystery on earth, the glorious Poe was one.

9

Toward four the next afternoon, Poe stood on the hurricane deck of the Providence packet, and watched for the first sight of the steeples of Providence.

Poe wasn't at all sure just where he had gotten the ten dollars he'd found in his purse, but the happy thought occurred to him that perhaps one of the magazines, so slow in paying for his writings, had sent him something. On impulse he had hurried off to board the packet, knowing that he was late by at least one day—or was it more? —but hoping that Fanny would still receive him.

Well, of course she'd receive him. The question was, was that husband of hers still away? And even that question was not of momentous importance, because he'd worked out a good excuse for being in Providence. He'd already tried it out on Muddy. It so happened that the Broad Street merchant who was enamored of Fanny had become so jealous of Poe that he invented an ugly rumor and passed it on to her. His story went that Poe had bilked another merchant by passing a forged check. Naturally, Fanny had told Poe about it, and naturally he'd been angry, but now Poe's young friend Thomas Dunn English was urging Poe to sue the fellow for libel. He had to check Fanny's recollection of the event before deciding whether to sue, he had assured Muddy.

No, the *real* question was, why had Fanny's letter with its command for him to come sounded so urgent? If only he had not made the mistake of having a glass of gin and water, no sugar, while talking with Cornelius Mathews yesterday. Had he had more than one glass? And had it been only yesterday?

Feeling tense, Poe made sure that he was among the first of the passengers to disembark at the pretty Rhode Island town, and he went immediately to the Earl Hotel on Main, opposite the foot of Thomas Street, to leave his carpetbag and brush up before seeking the address Fanny had given him. He combed his hair carefully and paused for a moment to stare at his reflection in the mirror, an unusual act since he had an aversion to mirrors, but Fanny would shortly be looking at that erect form, that pale, intellectual face, that romantic, perhaps weird expression of the eye.

Their "love scrape," as Chivers would have put it, had progressed mightily since their first meeting in March and the public exchange of poems in the *Broadway Journal*. Poe had gone to call a half-dozen more times on Fanny and her husband. Fanny had come to call a half-dozen times on Poe and his wife. Samuel Osgood had started a portrait of Poe, arranged by Fanny as an excuse to see more of him, and Fanny allowed her hand to linger in Poe's when they met and when they parted. At a second Saturday night reception at Miss Lynch's, Fanny had taken Poe's arm in the full sight of the world and allowed him to promenade her up and down the parlor, and out of the sight of the world, they hoped, they had later stolen a few meetings about the city. He had gazed into her eyes at Battery Park. He had put his Spanish-looking black cloak around her shoulders during a two-cent ride on the ferry to Brooklyn. He had let his hand brush hers at the establishment of Messieurs Tiffany, Young and Ellis among the imported perfume-burners, landscape-marble tables and Swiss osier-work. And, for both of them the keenest pleasure of all, she had thrice allowed him to slip his arm around her waist, once, daringly, behind the bookshelves of Bartlett & Wellford's bookstore and twice in the dingy hallway of his lodgings on East Broadway. On the last occasion she had let him kiss her, a swift, bungled kiss, his mouth landing on the corner of hers, her return kiss wasted on the dusty air, but even the thought of it still made Poe tremble.

Yet it was one thing to tremble deliciously during a forbidden flirtation, but quite another to let attraction slide into something deeper. He couldn't afford a serious involvement—could he? No, of course not, it was impossible. He was a married man, with responsibilities not only to his family but to his work, and here he was, lying to Muddy, playing truant at the office, spending passage money that he could ill afford, and all for the sake of what? No, it was dangerous, and to tell the truth, not altogether desirable.

Poe grew even more uncomfortable when he arrived at Fanny's address and discovered that it was her in-laws' house, but he could not suppress a thrill of excitement when he saw her. It was a sultry afternoon. Fanny was dressed in white muslin with white spots, trimmed with narrow Irish point lace. The white dress, the lightness of her step and the trimness of her waist as she hurried down the hall to greet him took him back fifteen years to the cherished memory of the walled rose garden in Richmond, and white violets and love. But Fanny's elder daughter, the ten-year-old, was at her side and an older lady at her heels. Poe greeted Fanny formally, intoning, "Good evening, Mrs. Osgood. I hope I haven't called at an inconvenient moment."

She grasped his hand and clung to it an instant, gray eyes meeting his gray eyes searchingly. Then she stood back and said, "Why, Mr. Poe, what a pleasant surprise. Mother Osgood, may I present a dear friend of Samuel's, Mr. Edgar Poe?"

"I would have recognized you anywhere from Samuel's portrait," the older lady said, perhaps inspired less by truth than by a desire to compliment her son's skill. "The portrait's nearly completed, isn't it? But how sorry Samuel will be to have missed you. He's still in New Haven executing other portrait commissions, and if you came for a sitting . . ."

"Oh no, madam," Poe said, and he trotted out his libel suit excuse, concluding, for the sake of both Mmes. Osgood, "You will naturally understand my zeal to investigate fully any slur against my name. But you can be assured that even in the unlikely event that the matter does come to court, there will be no mention of the fair name of Osgood in any connection whatsoever."

"I'm so relieved," said Fanny dramatically, taking her cue from Poe. "I shall of course tell you anything I can about the incident, but may I make a bold suggestion? There is a lecture and poetry recital tonight at the Lyceum, Mr. Poe, and I feared I would miss it for lack of Samuel to escort me. Could you, would you . . . ?"

He could. He would. The painter's mother invited Poe to tea, but Fanny shook her head unobtrusively, and Poe murmured that he had already taken an early tea on the steamer. He was next invited to supper, but Fanny mentioned a Mrs. Whitman to whose house she had been invited after the poetry recital and managed to excuse both of them. The elder Mrs. Osgood seemed taken aback by this and seemed unduly solicitous that Fanny not overtire herself. Poe feared for a moment that she was on to them, but the good lady occupied herself only with insisting that Fanny take a cloak against the possibility of any night chill. They were able to make their escape to privacy before the sun had yet waned—just the two of them and a whole town full of people sitting on front porches to await coolness and darkness and meanwhile, it seemed to Poe, deliberately to watch them.

He felt like a criminal as he escorted her decorously along the sidewalk, but her eyes, always more expressive than her words, reflected only longing. Poe tried to play his role properly. "Darling," he said softly.

"Edgar," she sighed in return. She bowed her head and looked away. "Oh, God, is there nowhere we can ever be alone?"

"You have something to tell me?" he said. "Darling, I was so worried when I got your message."

"I cannot tell you in the middle of the trottoir," she said. A deep pink suffused her white face. "Dearest, did you take a room at the Earl as I suggested?"

Poe was taken aback. "Why, yes," he said tentatively. "I suppose we could converse in one of the Earl's parlors. But, dearest, we might encounter someone you know. Might it not be better if we went to the library to talk? I have heard so much about Providence's library, I always wished to see it. Or the Athenaeum. I would dearly love to see the Athenaeum."

"There are always people there too," she said boldly, her voice strengthening. "The problem can be the same at the cemetery, but perhaps no one will be there this late. Should we not stroll in that direction?"

Poe suppressed a shiver, not of delight but of terror. Unlike everyone else in his world who found cemeteries an agreeably romantic site for sighs and sorrow and an occasional cheerful picnic, Poe hated cemeteries, or, rather, feared them, a legacy of his early childhood. Like all well-off children reared in the South, he had spent his early years under the care of a black nurse, and the John Allans' Eudocia often took him at night to the slave quarters, where many a gruesome story of graveyard ghosts was related. "They'll run after us and drag me down," a four-year-old Edgar cried out in nervous terror while chancing to pass a rural burying ground with an Allan relative. Later, a twelve-year-old Edgar, afraid of the dark and haunted by nightmares, nearly suffocated himself under the bedcovers to avoid the most horrible thing he could imagine, the feel of an ice-cold hand laid upon his face in a pitch-dark room. Now a grown-up Edgar, aged thirty-six since January of this year, still hated to be alone at night, and the thought of the sound of wind sighing through rank grave grasses was about as romantic to him as the thought of bloody murder. But he didn't dream of confessing his fear of corpses and graves to Fanny. He could only bring himself to demur to the point of asking, "You don't fear being late for the recital?"

"I fear nothing," said bold Fanny, "except . . ."

"What, dearest?"

"I will tell you when we're finally alone. Come, dearest, we will walk. Have you missed me? Terribly? As much as I've missed you?"

"More," Poe said tenderly.

They took the beautiful walk to Swan Point Cemetery, quite out in the country, and although Fanny could not yet bring herself to speak the words that she had asked Poe here to hear, they spoke of love, they spoke of what they were writing at the moment, they even spoke of money, for her husband's luck on commissions was still running against him, and, like Poe, Samuel Osgood had a habit of borrowing.

Beyond the hedgerows, the lazy clank of cowbells told of a dairy herd ambling toward twilight and distant barns. Fanny risked taking Poe's hand in hers. She asked, "Dearest, is something disturbing *you*? You know we can tell one another everything. We must. And we're alone now."

"Alone?" Poe said with a sharp little laugh. He withdrew his hand and gestured. A pony cart laden with children was coming down the lane. Fanny stiffened, feeling trapped.

Trapped, yes, that's how she had felt all week, trapped because of what the doctors had said: "We regret having to tell you this, Mrs. Osgood, but we have diagnosed a . . ." Ugh, she couldn't bear thinking of the word. Doctors, be damned! Why, she had only felt a bit under the weather for a time, a bit melancholy and overcome with lassitude. Ordinary tasks tired her, and she wondered if she were becoming lazy. Well, yes, and perhaps she had been a bit short of breath and had lost some weight, but that was because, inelegantly, she had lately been suffering from indigestion.

She had received the diagnosis in silence, eyes turned away from the doctors, hearing nothing after the one word she had not yet come to terms with. She wasn't going to argue with the fools. She pulled herself together, thanked the doctors for their examination and escaped.

Outside, the sun was bright and the street was filled with traffic. Fanny thought the trapped feeling would go away, but her fool of a mother-in-law had accompanied her and she was trapped afresh by the woman's tears. Good God, did she really believe it then? Why, the malady was as fatal as it was common. It sometimes moved in giant steps and sometimes in baby steps, but quick or slow, everyone knew what the end would be.

Fanny had never thought of death before. Was she ready to die? How could she tell Samuel and the girls? And, my God, how could she tell Edgar? Wild, playful, affectionate, witty Edgar, alternately as manageable and wayward as a spoiled child. He loved her so much. The news would kill him.

How *could* she die? It would mean that these hot streets and this weeping woman at her side and Samuel off in New Haven and the girls waiting at home were all there would ever be of life. This couldn't be life. No. Life was yet to come.

Maybe all of five years of it.

If she lasted that long.

But she would rather go out fast than flicker along half alive for years and years. "Ever" be damned. This was now. This was now!

Now, walking with Poe, she saw the cemetery just ahead. She had to giggle at the appropriateness of her choice of a trysting place. Poe looked at her nervously. Something surely was disturbing him, but she didn't know what. Perhaps it was the same thing that was disturbing her—so many people. Inside the cemetery, couples strolled between headstones of the usual white marble and pink granite, and to their left as they turned in a middle-aged woman was energetically weeding a plot marked by a double headstone, one half of which was occupied by a man's name and the other half empty, except for the shared motto, "Together Forever." She jibbed at the thought of the waiting grave and drew Poe off into a right-hand aisle, but there they encountered a family glumly planting a rose bush atop a grave which, from its lack of sod and its high-mounded earth, obviously dated to this season. The family stared at them, and Poe nervously said to Fanny, as if trying to give the impression they had been discussing innocuous literary matters all along, "Oh yes, speaking of Dr. Griswold's projected *Prose Writers of America*, have you heard how *The Town* sent him up? It announced, perfectly straight-faced, that Griswold will shortly publish a royal octavo entitled *The Advertisers and Advertisements of America.*"

Fanny gave him a cross look. Ignoring the watching family, she said, "Would you be interested to know that I saw Dr. Griswold not long ago?"

"He came here?" Poe said with prompt jealousy.

She nodded, pleased, and strolled on. "Yes. And he pleaded with me to run away from Samuel. To divorce Samuel, in fact, so I could marry . . . elsewhere."

"The villain!" Poe said. "Doubly a villain, for I have heard that Griswold is all but engaged to some lady from the South."

"Yes, his wealthy spinster," Fanny said. "She was why he came, to be quite truthful. He begged me to save him from such a fate, and swore he would marry her unless I could offer him hope."

"But of course you were scandalized by the mere suggestion. You turned him out. You did, didn't you?"

She fought back the urge to giggle again. Edgar looked like an angry eagle. "Of course," she said. "How could I not? Even if I did not have my good name and my little girls to think of, my . . . heart might be engaged elsewhere. But, dear Edgar, Dr. Griswold made it completely clear that he was all too aware of such a possibility. He warned me that people have started whispering about us, and begged me to break off our friendship. I lay all the whispering to your own admirer, Elizabeth Ellet. She's insanely jealous of me. Griswold said as much."

Poe's face flushed. "But, my dear, Mrs. Ellet has no cause to take any interest whatever in us," he said. "I've had nothing at all to do with the woman."

"She hasn't been writing you? She hasn't been coming to call every other day?"

"Oh, well, an occasional note, perhaps. As for calls, well, she has become great friends with my mother-in-law. It's not that she calls on me. Besides, she has left the city for the summer. That damnable Griswold was merely rumormongering."

"As is your Mrs. Ellet," Fanny said tartly. She hesitated, then added, "But he passed on to me another rumor, Edgar dearest, about which I am sincerely worried. May I speak frankly? He reported that it is being said that you have been, well, spending far too much of your time lately in bars. One acquaintance of his actually charged that you were a drunkard."

Poe looked furious, but Fanny knew that no charge can be more annoying than one which has a basis of fact. She concluded, "My dear, were it true that you have recently been giving yourself over to drinking sprees, such a circumstance could be ruinous for you. I will not speak of what excessive drinking could do to you personally, although that is my greatest care. Let me only say that society would shun you if such a tendency were to become common knowledge."

Poe burst out, "I, a drunkard? Very well, then, so be it, although I drink no more than the next man, and less than most. But it hardly surprises me that such rumors would flourish readily in literary circles. Literary, indeed! Let us give them their proper name and call them gossip circles! But I am happy to inform you, Fanny, that the fact that I may recently have taken an occasional glass has not affected the warm welcome I receive in these same circles. To the contrary, in fact. Surely you are aware that people follow every fad, and since the current fad is for temperance, they cluck over every sinner who falls into their clutches like a flock of hens chasing a June bug."

"Darling, please. I didn't mean to upset you."

"I'm not upset," Poe said stiffly. "At least it cannot be asserted that I have been the coward to deny the errors and frailties which I myself deplore. But if my pride or that of my family permitted, there is much—very much—there is *everything* to be offered in extenuation. I might even hint that the irregularities I so profoundly lament are the effect of a terrible evil, rather than its cause."

Fanny was both surprised and hurt. "I should have thought, Edgar, that you might confide in *me*."

Poe looked highly agitated, yet there was sincerity in his voice when he replied, "Of course, darling, to you I can do more than hint." He paused, as if gathering his thoughts, and Fanny seated herself on a broad headstone inscribed "Ernest Bouterlin, died March 28, 1823, of Stranger's Fever." As befitted the grave of a stranger, it was at the edge of the cemetery. Beyond a rusty row of spruces, wild growth began, and an indigo bunting noisily asserted its title to a copse of white pines and a thicket of underbrush. Poe started to sit beside Fanny, then apparently noticed that the stone was a gravestone. He shied back a foot like a startled horse.

"The world could never understand," he commenced, "but I know that you love my poor Virginia, and she loves you, and you, dear Fanny, will understand when I tell you that this 'evil' is the greatest which can befall a man. Consider: four years ago, a little wife who is as dear to me as if she had been my sister ruptured a blood vessel in singing. Her life was despaired of. I took leave of her forever and underwent all the agonies of her death. She recovered partially and I again hoped. At the end of a year the vessel broke again—and I went through precisely the same scene. Again in about a year afterward. Then again—again—again and even once again at varying intervals. Each time I have felt all the agonies of her death—and at each accession of the disorder I have pitied her even more and have clung to her life with a more desperate pertinacity. But I am constitutionally sensitive—nervous in a very unusual degree. I became insane, with long intervals of horrible sanity. During these fits of absolute unconsciousness I drank, God only knows how often or how much. As a matter of course my enemies referred the insanity to the drink rather than the drink to the insanity. I have nearly abandoned all hope of a permanent cure for my irregularities, but the thought haunts me that I may find one in the *death* of my poor little wife. This I know I could endure as becomes a man—it is the horrible, never ending oscillation between hope and despair which I can *not* endure. Some days I fear I will totally lose my reason. But in the death of what was my life I may receive a new—but, oh God! how melancholy!—existence."

Sweet heavens, how could she have overlooked the fact that Virginia had already spent long years in dying? Fanny stared at Poe. Slow tears began to well in her gray eyes.

Her tears and the setting seemed to make Poe gloomy, and gloomily he concluded, "Believe me, I do try not to drink, Fanny. It's just that sometimes I awake in the morning and the burden of apprehension I face daily comes crashing down on me, and I am goaded to a desperate effort to forget."

She couldn't tell him, she realized. She couldn't add to his burdens. Fanny willed herself to stop crying, courageously accepting her burden of concealment. There was only one more thing she could do for him, and she tried.

"You must resist the temptation," Fanny said. "Please, Edgar, won't you promise me? It's all I'll ever ask of you."

Poe sighed heavily. "So this is why you sent so urgently for me to come to you. Ah, how often have I heard those words from friends who only thought they understood. Fanny, I can't promise. Sometimes I'm maddened. Maddened. I wouldn't want to break my word to you."

He sounded completely honest. And what luck, that he, too, was capable of misunderstanding! If the tattered tail of life could still bring luck, perhaps it could bring yet more. Fanny nodded. "I understand, Edgar. But could you promise me that you would at least try?"

"Yes," he said reluctantly, "I can try."

"My poor Edgar, then let us say no more of it. Let us . . . let us try to be happy now." She drove her hands inside the folds of her cloak and clasped her elbows, cradling her breasts. She felt feverish and may have looked it, for Poe began to gaze at her worriedly. Quickly, she rose, and she stared wildly, head lifted, at the white-pine copse.

"You should have been winged," Poe said admiringly. "You look as if you wanted to fly."

"I do!" she said. "Edgar, have you ever in your life, just once, wanted something the world said you couldn't have?"

"Why, more than once," he said.

"Then come," she said.

She held out her hand to him. Poe rose, looking perplexed and, yes, she had to admit it, fearful. She grasped his hand with her small, hot hand and led him from the neat symmetry that was the cemetery toward the shadowed wilderness beyond.

"Uh, my dear, the people," Poe warned.

He gestured, and Fanny noticed for the first time that there were chatting voices from a hidden aisle not twenty yards from them.

Her chin went up, and she looked at him proudly, not letting go of his hand. In a moment, he followed her. A proper gentleman shouldn't, Fanny realized with a thrill of excitement mixed with intoxicating fear. But a true gentleman could do no else.

Amid a thicket of chokeberry and bayberry, trumpet creeper and wild morning glory, Fanny found a tiny greensward, no bigger than a grave. Perhaps it was one, a grave unhallowed, not fit for a cemetery approved by church and man. With a trill of grief-stricken laughter she sank down on her knees, resolutely ignoring the reaching green claws of vegetation that clutched at her white dress.

"Edgar, I love you," she breathed.

But Poe stood hesitantly, gazing about him as if wondering if anyone had heard her.

Incongruous laughter welled up in her because she found herself staring at her would-be lover's knees. At last Edgar's gawking appeared to be completed, and he sank to his own knees beside her.

"Dearest," he said, "we must control ourselves. I cannot allow you to sacrifice . . ."

Fanny cut him off with a gesture, and she saw that his eyes widened, with a flash behind them, but still he hesitated. She wondered, not for the first time, why this face among so many others? Why this hand that so slowly reached out to hold her own? But there it was, the simple magic. And how alluring he looked, even now, nervous sweat on his lofty forehead, head cocked, looking down at her.

Breathing shallowly, Fanny lay back on the rank grass and gazed back at him. "You said I looked as if I wanted to fly. And so I do, but I'm sure I'd fly only like that little bird to the top of some pine tree. But you—you're an eagle, Edgar. A caged eagle who desires the wind-swept sky and the distant eyrie."

His face softened, and she willed herself to see in his handsome features a glimpse of the other traits she loved—warmth, generosity, zealousness in causes that interested him, enthusiasm, boyish impulsiveness.

"Lovely little Fanny," he said. "But we really shouldn't be here. The grass stains . . ."

Should she scream? He was worrying about dirtying his knees, of all things. He was worrying, no doubt, because Mrs. Clemm surely had the duty of keeping his clothes clean and would frown in puzzlement, sponge in hand, gaping at his trousers. But to the devil with his mother-in-law, and with hers. Fanny waited to be seized by the grip of Nature, Nature the impeller, Nature the giver of dionysian madness, Nature who made the flesh. She raised her hands to his shoulders, wishing he had at least taken off his coat, feeling trapped by his layers and layers of clothing and by her own. Separating her from him were one white muslin dress, two petticoats, tight drawers with ruffles, one corset cover, one corset, buttoned shoes, stockings and, because she had been fool enough to listen to her mother-in-law's lamentations, even on a warm summer's day, one cotton union suit buttoned to the neckline from the ankle. Thank God it at least had the customary gaps.

"Kiss me, Edgar," she commanded.

It was hard not to laugh, because, again, he hesitated. The feeling of entrapment became stronger. She was trapped not only by her clothes but by his gentleman's code.

But, thank God and all the saints, and pity the vile sinners, he was at last laying himself down beside her. He was bending closer to her. His lips . . . ah, his lips . . .

The kiss was fleeting, but Fanny ceased to tell time. She said into an electrifying silence, broken only by the sunset song of the indigo bunting, "Ah, darling. If only just once . . ."

And so he kissed her again, and after a while yet again. A true gentleman could do no else.

10

When Poe promised the distraught Fanny that he would do his best to cut down on his drinking, he had not thought of how the promise would affect Virginia. He slunk home from Providence to find Virginia quiet and listless, given to sitting hour after hour before the open window of their small, hot bedroom and gazing out with unfocused eyes at the leafy branches of a tall old walnut tree that somehow had escaped the axes of corporate efficiency. But as the week passed and Poe daily succeeded in resisting the temptation to have just one Holland and water with ice, no sugar, she seemed to recapture a shadow of her old, childish joy at the sight of him returning sober and under his own steam every afternoon from the *Broadway Journal*.

It was just as well that he had promised. Harry Franco and the publisher, John Bisco, had declared open war on one another, and Franco caused the paper to miss an issue. He thought to force Bisco to sell out his interest cheap, then haul down Poe's name and issue a double number he had readied secretly with only his name and that of a new partner on it, but Franco's ploy merely caused Bisco to realize fully that, rather than the jealous, balky Franco, Poe even in his cups was the man with whom he would rather be associated. Bisco held out for so high a price that Franco temperishly challenged him to issue the paper by himself. So a sober Poe listened attentively to the publisher's proposition that Poe become the sole editor in exchange for half the profits. Although Poe silently cursed the fact that he had no money and therefore could not make the publisher a counter-offer to buy the paper for his very own, Poe accepted. More columns would have to be filled somehow, but Harry Franco was out. Poe decided to be happy about it, and he felt touched at Virginia's pleasure when he gave her and Muddy the news. Virginia even piped up with the suggestion that she and Muddy would copy all his old tales and poems to fill up the paper, and Poe watched her, smiling. She had seemed unaware for so long of his day-by-day business worries and occasional triumphs. Could it be that she was feeling better, even in this summer heat? He ran downstairs without his hat and bought them a watermelon from a leather-throated fruit vendor, and they all had a modest celebration.

So the days passed, and even though he had no word from Fanny, Poe worked busily and not unhappily. He tried to put behind him embarrassing memories of trousers at half-mast in a bed of morning glories, and the memory of their later wanderings through the streets of Providence, talking, endlessly talking, since indiscreet Fanny apparently was reluctant for the day to end. In the doorway of a house they saw Mrs. Whitman, the woman Fanny had used as an excuse for being out late. Dressed all in filmy, virginal white, unaware that anyone looked at her, she was romantically staring upward at the rising moon, and her distant, serene face made a chilling contrast to the feverish woman beside him.

Hoping to provoke a response, Poe wrote Fanny a discreet love letter, and when she still didn't reply he scarcely knew what to think. It occurred to Poe that he should write her a poem, but he was too busy. He saw occasional friends who hadn't abandoned the city for sandy Saratoga or cool Newport. He served as chief judge for a literary contest at the Rutgers Female Institute graduation events and chuckled heartily to himself when the Reverend Dr. Rufus Griswold, invited as one of the panel of judges under Poe, sent word at the last minute that he was ill and couldn't come.

Poe also endured frequent calls from Chivers. Chivers at first buzzed with questions about Poe's ladylove, and Poe realized to his dismay that during his last spree he must have said something he shouldn't have. But Poe vigorously denied that he was involved with any lady anywhere at any time, and Chivers soon settled down to nagging him about some ten-dollar loan he seemed to have dreamed up. The rest of the time Chivers gabbled about poetry and proclaimed daily bright ideas—yesterday, that Poe should come South to establish a paper and live with Chivers, today that Chivers would come North again next January and help Poe finally establish *The Stylus*. Poe's hours were crowded, but he good-naturedly gave of his time. He knew Chivers would leave for Georgia soon, and he could be patient.

When the long awaited day dawned, on July 19, it was doubly awaited, for *Tales by Edgar A. Poe* came off the Wiley & Putnam presses. The Georgia poet caught the packet ship *Independence*, Captain Hardy at the helm, with an affectionately inscribed copy of the book under his arm. Afterward, elated at the prospect of eight-cent-a-volume royalties, Poe so far forgot himself as to accept three cups of sangaree from barroom well-wishers, but then he thought of his promise to Fanny. Sprees were out, yes, but did that mean he was forbidden an occasional cup? He lost the argument with himself—or won—and went home tolerably sober to a relieved Virginia.

Both Poe and Virginia were loggy, he from the cold wine punch, she from the forty minims of laudanum that currently assured her of a comparatively quiet night's sleep, when at nearly four the next morning they were brought upright in bed by two nearby explosions in quick succession, explosions so powerful that they shook the house.

"An earthquake!" Virginia gasped. "Run, Eddy!"

He did, in his nightshirt, but only to the window. The white wake of the moon still shone, but dawn was just beginning to break. To the southeast, a huge column of red flame suddenly hurled itself upward, lighting the branches of the walnut tree outside with an eerie red glow. "Fire," Poe said. "A bad one."

Fires were so common in New York that the idle or the enthusiastic, hoping for a night's entertainment, could confidently plan on attending a fire somewhere around the town, but this one looked huge. Poe's view was obstructed by other buildings. The alarm bells of the City Hall watch tower and its satellites had not yet begun to pour out their tale of the magnitude and whereabouts of the fire, but from the direction of the column of flame Poe had to worry whether the whole southern tip of the island was kindled. The *Broadway Journal* offices were far downtown. Wiley & Putnam's publishing house too, with all those copies of his brand-new *Tales*. He dithered for a moment, ignoring Virginia's excited queries, then reached for his trousers.

"Are you going?" Virginia said.

"I'd better," he said. "If it's near the *BJ*, there might still be time to save the things in the office."

She stood up eagerly on her knees in the narrow bed. "Oh, Eddy, take me too," she said.

"Sissy, be sensible," he said. He grabbed his boots and struggled to jam his stockingless feet into them. "The fire engines would run you down, and the smoke would be fatal for your lungs. Listen to yourself. You're coughing right now."

"Then what difference would some smoke make?" she said simply. "I've never been to a big fire, Eddy. If I'm going to die anyway, can't I enjoy living just a little bit first?"

He was stuffing the tail of his nightshirt into his trousers, but her words shocked him into stillness. Fanny's words had been different, but the eager reaching out for life—that, he realized, was strangely the same. "Do you really want to go so badly?" he said. "Come then, we'll get you dressed. But be quiet. We don't want to awaken Muddy."

He scribbled a note for Muddy and propped it on Virginia's pillow against the event of their returning after she got up. Within five minutes they crept down the stairs together. By then, people were leaning out of windows. A few, like Poe and Virginia, were already hurrying toward the great glow that lit up lower Manhattan. There was a shouting and the blowing of a horn behind them and a cry of "Jump her, boys!" Poe pulled Virginia into a doorway just in time to clear the way for a fire-engine company rushing pell-mell down the street. Only six or eight firemen, booted and greatcoated but carrying their clothes in their hands, had arrived in time to direct the engine's start from the station house, and a crowd of boys and men from the streets helped drag the huge silver-plated vehicle as it flew to be in on the fire.

But there was no shortage of burning buildings to go around that dawn, nor any need for the no-holds-barred battling for precedence that often took place when two engines arrived at a fire simultaneously. By the time Poe and Virginia breathlessly reached Nassau Street and he reassured himself that the *Broadway Journal* was not in flames, they were treading on window glass shattered for blocks around the site of the explosion. Virginia stared wide-eyed after the other engine companies, the hook-and-ladder companies and the hose companies that were converging on Broadway and Exchange Place. Poe had only to nod before she laughed excitedly and dragged him after her.

The iron shutters on stores near Exchange Street were beginning to grow hot when they reached Broadway, and Poe made her retreat a half-block to watch from a point of greater safety. House fronts hissed as the volunteer firemen played water on them. All to the west of Broadway was flame.

They were forced back still farther as coy curls of flame licked out irregularly from new buildings catching fire at the back, and in the milling crowd Poe caught sight of a familiar face. It was Gabriel Harrison, his friend from the tea shop. Poe hallooed him. "What news, Gabriel? Have they contained the fire area?"

Gabriel's face was flushed and his eyes as wide as Virginia's. "Not by half," he said. "Have you heard? Three firemen were killed on Broad Street. The fire went every way at once, and the biggest stores on Broad are ravaged."

"Are we safe here, do you think? Oh, sorry, my dear, this is my friend Gabriel Harrison. My wife, Gabriel."

"Madam, should you be here?" asked Gabriel, more worried than polite.

"For just a while," she said in her shy voice. "What started it, Mr. Harrison? Have you heard?"

"They say it started in Van Doreon's sperm oil establishment on New Street, then Crooker & Warren's saltpeter warehouse exploded."

A man dressed like a country clergyman in rusty black with a white choker butted in with some asperity. "Not at all, sir," he said. "How could saltpeter explode with such dreadful effect? It was a gasometer that burst."

"Indeed!" said Gabriel hotly. "Next you'll be telling me it was gunpowder."

"'Twas gunpowder, gents," said a voice behind Poe, and they

turned to see a woman dressed in dirty finery, looking back at them boldly. "A thousand bags, I heard, and another gent just told me the Croton water's give out, so the fire will have it all its own way. The whole city's going up, and good riddance to it, I say."

"Yes, good riddance!" said Virginia. The excitement in her eyes was as bright as the four- and five-story buildings burning fiercely along lower Broadway, and Poe was dumfounded at her, not only for speaking to a harlot but for her obvious lack of fear. He and Gabriel exchanged looks. Every minute the crowds of fire watchers were growing thicker, and every minute it was becoming more apparent that this was no place for a lady. Poe took Virginia's arm and Gabriel offered his on her other side, and they drew her away, but she looked back over her shoulder all the way to City Hall Park. There the two men paused and worriedly regarded the smoke boiling up in the strengthening sunlight. But the fire was obviously decreasing, and Gabriel's urge to impart news promptly veered to matters as fascinating to him as the biggest disaster of the decade—literary gossip.

"Have you heard, Mr. Poe?" he said excitedly, and he bowed nicely to Virginia to include her. "Your friend the Reverend Griswold is going to get married. I have it from Henry Tuckerman, who says he could have grabbed off the same lady, or, rather, she would have grabbed off him, if he hadn't run away fast enough. She's of the Jewish faith, a Miss Charlotte Myers from the South, and they say she owns half of Charleston. And to put the icing on it, she's an old maid well into her middle forties, while Griswold's barely thirty or so, isn't he? I ask you, who would have believed it? The Reverend Griswold, with that Protestant quarterly he edits, planning to marry a daughter of Israel. How's that going to go down with all those clergymen he works for?"

Poe made a half-gasping, half-barking sound, triumph mixed with laughter. "I shouldn't think it would go down at all well," he said. He felt petty for doing so, but he couldn't help rejoicing at the prospect of Griswold's discomfiture. But Gabriel, looking delighted at the success of his news, chattered on.

"I must say I was as surprised as you look now, Mr. Poe. The story about town was that he had lost his heart to that Mrs. Frances Osgood. The poetess, you know? The one who flirts with everyone? But Mrs. Jane Locke of Lowell, her cousin-in-law, wrote Mrs. Mary Hewitt, who mentioned it to Mr. Halleck, that poor Mrs. Osgood has been handed a death sentence—galloping consumption, she has, and you know there's no cure for *that*."

Poe flinched as though he had been hit. Gabriel's cheerful voice faltered, but, carried on by his own momentum, Gabriel concluded, "D'you suppose Griswold threw her over because of it? I swear, it all makes a man wonder."

Virginia clutched Poe's hand. "Oh," she said sorrowfully. "Oh, poor Mrs. Osgood. She's a very good friend of ours, Mr. Harrison. I can't believe it. She always looked so healthy and gay. Oh, Eddy, couldn't you just cry?"

He felt as though he were suffocating, but both Gabriel and Virginia were looking at him, and he struggled for an outward show of composure. "This is . . . very sad news," he said. "I saw Mrs. Osgood only about two weeks ago, and I . . . never suspected. She said nothing."

Gabriel looked fearfully at Poe and at Virginia, perhaps recollecting that he had encountered speculative whispers about Poe and the same Fanny Osgood, perhaps recollecting reports about Virginia's own state of health. He said in a small voice, "I'm most awfully sorry. I suppose she just, er, didn't want it to, er, if you see what I mean, get around. Oh, not that there's anything *wrong* about having, er . . ."

He was silent. Virginia stood holding Poe's hand, her excitement over the fire apparently gone. Poe saw her swallow several times and duck her chin, and he groaned to himself. She was trying not to cough. That was to be Fanny's fate. Fanny!

He said to Gabriel, "I must get Mrs. Poe home now. Will you come with us for a cup of coffee?"

"No, I'd best get to the shop. Though I suppose there won't be much business done in the whole city this morning. I'm really *awfully* sorry about my tale carrying. If I'd thought, I . . ."

"No, Gabriel, you're not to blame," Poe said. "That's what we all do in our daily business—whether they're merry or whether they're miserable, we must tell the tales."

He wrote to Fanny late that same morning, a wild, lamenting letter, as firemen pumped river water over the smoldering ruins of the most valuable business section of the city and the local insurance jobbers began to announce, as always, that their offices were bankrupt and the fire policies therefore useless. Poe would have gone to Fanny, but it would have looked too obvious, even to the unsuspicious Virginia. Two days later, he received from Fanny a tender reply that gaily chided him for being, as always, so different from the rest of the world. Everyone knew that pallor and weakness were fascinating. What, would he rail against melancholy meditations over tombs? He would destroy all contemporary poetry.

Then she spoke of love, but that, too, only lightly. The letter smelled of pressed violets, and Poe was at a loss as to how he should respond to her. To write her a great poem, one of her very own, was what his mind and heart instructed him to do, but his pen would not obey. Mere verses could be written by the mind and the hand, but not a poem. A poem had to happen somewhere inside, somewhere in the oily tendrils of the intestines, somewhere in the pale jelly of the brain, or somewhere in the darkness of dreams, where a metaphor flashed like a sudden burst of lightning to illuminate some new dimension of the unexplored wilderness within.

And Poe was too numb with terror for his fair Fanny, his pitiable Fanny, his doomed Fanny, to feel the flash of the lightning.

11

In the weeks that followed, Poe had to struggle hard even to fill the hungry blank columns of the *Broadway Journal*. The weather waxed hot and mosquitoes flourished. One Saturday Alex the office boy, promoted to mail handler, fainted from the heat while folding the weekly edition and awoke to find himself stretched out on a table with his editor bathing his temples in cold water. Poe sent him home in a cab, and got the papers out himself, only to limp home wearily on sun-baked cobblestones to find that Virginia, too, had collapsed from the heat.

Poe and Muddy brought her around and worriedly began discussing a move. The board bill was past due anyway on East Broadway, and Muddy went that afternoon looking for new lodgings. Returning, she reported there were rooms available on Amity Street, not far east of where they had lived before.

"You know how much cooler it is near the square," she said hopefully, "and I vow, there are fewer mosquitoes too. And there'll be no skimping on the soap the way there is here. I told the landlady outright that I like to make my own, and she said to use the kitchen any time. My dears, I really think everything will work out beautifully there."

"We mustn't move just because of me," Virginia said from the bed where she reclined. "Really, Eddy, I'm all right. I'm going to be just fine."

He studied her chalky face. He watched her constantly these days, helplessly tracing the progress of Fanny's disease in Virginia's features. As he stared at the violet eyes shining forth from shadowed lids with sunken veins, and saw the eyes of another, he thought how little he had known, when once in his tales he had introduced a Ligeia, of the true dimensions of terror.

He brooded, too, over the way Virginia had acted on the day of the fire, and he asked her now, hesitantly, "Would you rather move back out to the Brennan farm for the rest of the summer if I could manage it? I wouldn't be able to come with you, except for a visit every Sunday, but—"

"Eddy, have you lost your reason in this heat?" Muddy interrupted. "We haven't the money. You'd have to keep lodgings in town for yourself. Why, it would double our expenses."

Virginia settled the debate. "No, Eddy," she said. "I couldn't bear for us to be apart, even to go out to the farm. The rooms on Amity Street sound lovely. Do you mind terribly if we just all move there?"

"Of course not," Poe said. "I was only thinking of you. Something gave me the idea that . . . Tell me the truth, Sissy. Do you hate living in the city? Would you really have liked to see it burn to the ground the morning of the fire?"

She laughed wanly. "Down to the last brick, and I'd come and help them grind it back to sand."

Muddy clucked, and Poe, taken aback, said, "My dear, I didn't know you felt so strongly."

"I don't," she said. "It doesn't matter. Besides, if someday we could really move to the country, wouldn't it be nice if we could have a house all to ourselves? We could take a cottage somewhere, and Muddy would make the soap, and I'd help with the cooking, and you and Catarina could take walks any time you wanted to. Doesn't that sound like a nice life? And then we wouldn't have a landlady and all sorts of other *people* always around."

Muddy clucked harder and said, "Shhhh. You're just upset about those letters."

"What letters?" said Poe.

"You shush, Muddy," Virginia said, daringly for her, as she was a loving and obedient daughter. "None of it matters in the slightest. Mrs. Oakes Smith says all women should have the ballot, and I think, all considered, that I'll cast mine for moving back to Amity Street." She turned her head toward the window and listened. An ice cream vendor, one that Poe particularly hated for the hullabaloo he made, sang from the street, "Tra la la, the lemon ice cream and *the* vanilla too," and Virginia giggled as Poe winced. "Why does he always sing, 'and *the* vanilla'?" she asked. "It throws the rhythm off, doesn't it, Eddy? But now that I think of it, the only other thing I'd really like in all this world, besides just having us three be together, is to have something cool. Eddy, dearest, do look in your pockets. Wouldn't we all feel cooler if we had a lemon ice cream? Oh my, I'll be so glad when it's fall."

Misfortune followed fast, and followed faster. Poe's friend Shea was the next to collapse suddenly, complaining of indigestion and terrible pain in his arm, and in less than an hour he was dead. Why? What could have happened? Walking behind Shea's bewildered, sorrowing family, Poe followed his coffin to the grave, and he wept upon learning that Shea had not forgotten to leave his friend a remembrance in his will—his favorite, crooked-headed hickory cane. Poe undertook the task of seeking a publisher for a memorial collection of Shea's better poems. It was nothing. It would help nothing. But it was the least he could do.

The heat of the city held, and Poe lost track of the long days spent soberly working, with only an occasional lapse, caused by his grief over Shea and the added burden of his despair for Fanny. These lapses he tried harder to conceal from Virginia. He was at home most evenings, for he could work in his shirt sleeves there, whereas even when the city temperatures rose over ninety and hung there for ten days, no gentleman could be seen outside his bedroom unless fully turned out in suit, waistcoat and ascot.

Then one morning he awoke feeling almost chilly and found Virginia already at the window of their newest lodgings, staring out delightedly at an extraordinarily clear, cool day. The heat wave had broken. The sun was rising a beautiful rosy red over red-brick buildings that suddenly looked clean and bright. The rivers had turned overnight from murky gray to deep blue. Someday soon it would be fall, and Fanny would return to the city. How would she greet him, after what had happened?

That same week, Poe learned from Wiley & Putnam that, pleased with the success so far of his *Tales*, the publishing house was willing to rush into print with his first collected book of poems in fourteen years. The famous *Raven* would go into it, of course, and any other poems Poe chose to include. It would mean having to hurry through a heavy load of final revisions. The publishers hadn't asked for them, but Poe compulsively felt the need to polish his poems to as perfect a sheen as possible if they were to be in a new book. The book was a personal triumph, and Poe felt so set up at the mere thought of it that he confided to young Thomas Dunn English, who hung around the office so much these days, that he thought he'd be able to get back to writing poetry again. With all the distractions of the *BJ* and, although he didn't say it, Fanny, he had been able to write little except prose since *The Raven*. It had been damned bad luck not to be able to take advantage of his high-flying reputation by amazing the public with a series of new, major poems. To make matters worse, the hoity-toity Boston Lyceum had offered him a fee of fifty dollars to lecture and present a new poem in October, and unless he could find the time and inspiration to write the new poem he would have to present something old out of his manuscript trunk. It had the makings of a fiasco, but now surely the fiasco could be avoided.

English congratulated Poe effusively, then went home to bed, complaining of a stomach disorder. Poe felt a pang of alarm. Another friend in danger? Perhaps cholera? City summers brought a plague of agues and nameless fevers that were dire enough, but at least less dreadful than a full-fledged cholera epidemic. Poe picked up a supply of paregoric after he left the office that afternoon, planning to bombard his lower intestines with the standard opiates, camphor and calomel at the first sign of the diarrhea that always presaged the disease.

Then he turned into Franklin's Ice Cream Parlor, a popular establishment favored by sweet toothed ladies, intending to buy a pint of peach ice cream to take home to Virginia. He was waiting to give his order when a woman's voice spoke his name, and he jerked and swung his head around wildly. It was the hour ladies favored for outings and the place was noisy and crowded, but he would know that voice anywhere. Fanny!

But it wasn't she. The voice, the smiling face and the elegant figure dressed in a trim piqué walking dress belonged only to Elizabeth Ellet, the member of The Starry Sisterhood whose attraction to Poe had made Fanny jealous. And at her side at a small, marble-topped table, looking nervously at Poe over a dish of vanilla cream, was the Reverend Dr. Rufus Griswold.

Poe wasn't sure which one to be more surprised to see. He had not heard that Mrs. Ellet or any of her crowd were back. And Griswold supposedly was married by now and living in Philadelphia with his new wife. Griswold rose and seemed to hesitate, then offered Poe his hand, murmuring, "What a coincidence."

"Yes, a wonderful coincidence," Mrs. Ellet assured Poe after greeting him. "This is my first afternoon back, and now I've run into both you and Dr. Griswold. I was planning to call tomorrow morning, and I hope you'll still permit me. How is your charming wife, and how is Mrs. Clemm?"

"Fairly well," Poe said.

"I'm so glad," Mrs. Ellet said, "though I don't know how they've survived the New York heat. We flighty birds who fled it have heard that the sycamore trees in Union Square are dropping their leaves and there's a touch of brown in the treetops at Battery Park, and so we come winging back. Dr. Griswold, as you can see, must love New York in the fall even more than I, for he has abandoned the nuptial chamber, if my informants are correct, in order to be here. Is it true, Dr. Griswold, that you've wed one of those Miss Myers of Charleston?" She glanced at Poe slyly, then back at the Reverend Griswold, and added, "My impression was you planned to wait for Samuel Osgood to be shot by one of his irate creditors, then offer your hand to the grieving widow. It shows you, doesn't it, that one shouldn't listen to gossip."

"Indeed, madam, nor repeat it as some so widely do," Griswold said sternly.

Mrs. Ellet's habitual haughty expression replaced her smile. "I trust you don't mean me, Dr. Griswold," she said. "I am of course interested in the welfare of those who are my friends, but anyone who chooses to be my enemy need never fear that I would sully my lips even with the mention of his name."

Griswold backed down immediately. As if to smooth her ruffled feathers, he insisted that Poe join them for a dish of ice cream, and his receding hairline was so bedewed with nervous sweat that Poe took pity on him and sat for a few minutes. Griswold's ingratiating ways and Poe's inquiries as to Mrs. Ellet's latest poetical production were to little avail, however, and Mrs. Ellet soon returned to the attack. "I don't know quite what to think of you, Dr. Griswold," she said bluntly. "We have so many friends all over South Carolina that you won't be surprised if I tell you someone in Charleston wrote me that you were to wed Miss Myers. Then someone from New York wrote that you had changed your mind, but the friends in Charleston swore that you and Miss Myers were married after all. What is the truth of the matter?"

"Why, I'm . . ."

"You are married?"

"Yes. No. Not exactly."

She laughed, a contralto chiming. "How can one be 'not exactly' married, Dr. Griswold? I really don't understand at all. Unless you mean you're married in South Carolina but not married in the North. How charming. You really must tell us how you've managed it."

Griswold put his spoon carefully into his ice cream bowl. "I meant to say that the lady and I *are* married," he said, "but that we have not yet gone to housekeeping."

"Ah, is that what it's called now?" Mrs. Ellet asked innocently. "But then I take it that you do plan to, ah, go to housekeeping. Will the new Mrs. Griswold move permanently to Philadelphia, or you to Charleston?"

Griswold was sweating again. "We contemplate spending at least part of the winter in Charleston. Miss Myers—Mrs. Griswold, that is —and my daughter Caroline plan to precede me to Charleston by a few weeks."

"Well, Dr. Griswold, it all sounds so delightful," Mrs. Ellet said. "The Myers home is charming, I understand, and you'll have stables and carriages and horses galore. I would add various humanities, black and brown, but as you have always been so outspoken about the evils of slavery I assume that now that your marriage entitles you to control your bride's property, you will immediately manumit the latter."

This Parthian shot seemed to satisfy her bad temper. She gathered up her gloves and reticule, and after pleasantly chatting a few moments more with Poe, arranging to call on "dear Mrs. Poe and Mrs. Clemm" at their new address, she departed, leaving Griswold hiding clenched fists under the table.

"Damn her!" he burst out to Poe. "Damn all women, and especially these literary women! How I detest them! Mrs. Ellet will be spreading her poisonous gossip all over the city. What can I do, Poe? Oh, damn them all!"

Women eating ice cream at nearby tables stared, and Griswold and Poe leaned closer together, two men in an enemy camp.

In a lower voice, Griswold pleaded, "You must help me with that witch, Poe. I shall have to find some way to placate her and win her silence. Won't you talk to her?"

"I'm afraid I'm the last one in the world to have any influence over the lady," Poe said.

"Nonsense," Griswold said. "She's set her cap for you. Can't you see that? Encourage her a little. And tell her . . . ." He hesitated, then burst out afresh, "Tell her as delicately as you can that there's a damn sight more to this Myers matter than can even be whispered by any decent woman. That should shut her up. And it's the sorry truth of the matter, worse luck."

Griswold looked at Poe so miserably that Poe reached out impulsively and patted his old enemy's shoulder. "There now," he said awkwardly. "The beginnings of any marriage can be a bit rocky. Surely it will all come out right with a little patience."

Griswold broke into a bitter laugh. "Patience. Angels above, will you listen to him? Patience, he says. Poe, you have no idea, you can have *no* idea, of the hideous trap these women have lured me into. They've entangled me in a snare made all the more horrible because any standards of good taste forbid me to cry aloud. Oh, God, how can I endure it?"

Griswold's lamentations, while not loud enough to be overheard by any of the ladies surrounding them, were still so loud that Poe squirmed uncomfortably. "I'm terribly sorry," he said. "If there's anything I can do . . ."

"There's nothing anyone can do," Griswold said unhappily. "People enough tried to talk me out of the marriage—Greeley, Hoffman, God knows who else. Poe, the woman to whom I have given my name is incapable even of being a wife!"

"Good Lord," Poe breathed. He was curious to hear more, but could think of no delicate way of inquiring.

"I should have suspected something," Griswold said. "Why else would those damned aunts of hers be so eager to catch a husband for her? Poe, I know that you are no gossip, but suffice it to say that on my . . . my *wedding* night, I learned, oh, God, Poe, I learned that I had been tricked into a marriage which should never have taken place."

"You mean . . ."

"I mean nothing," Griswold said. "I can say nothing, except that I have been betrayed." He sighed. "And to think that I once considered"— he looked at Poe gloomily—"love. It's a good joke, isn't it, Poe? Had not the affections of a certain lady seemed to have turned elsewhere, all the gold in the world could not have tempted me to pursue this alternate course."

"The . . . the sunshine which you sought may have had its own shadows," Poe said uncertainly.

"What do you mean?"

"The secret is not mine. But if you were to write or visit a certain lady, perhaps she herself would tell you."

"Go up to Boston?"

Poe blinked. "Is that where she is? She was to return to New York, the last word I had."

"Oh? Then perhaps my word is later than yours. It's to be Boston for a while, then perhaps Lowell. I thought the reason she was not returning immediately to New York was, well, you." He laughed, but a different laugh this time, and asked, "Well, Poe, is there some other suitor who has caught her eye? Are we both to be bereaved then?"

Poe hesitated a moment, then quietly replied, "Just so."

He would not say more, but Griswold seemed soothed by the sight of Poe's cheerlessness. Griswold asked a few questions about the progress of the *Broadway Journal*, and shortly claimed an appointment with Lewis Clark that he had to hasten off to. The two men parted, and Poe, after buying Virginia's peach ice cream, set off on his own. He was halfway home before it occurred to him that he had missed an opportunity he once would have delighted in—telling Griswold about his own good luck and the new book of poems by Edgar A. Poe that would soon grace the shelves of the nation's bookstores.

It was one thing to sympathize with an old rival about gossip and what appeared to be some kind of worrisome, regretted marriage, even to offer him a drop of consolation by implying that the laurel crown of Fanny's love was to be denied to both of them. But not to enjoy the jealous discomfort of a rival in literature was something else entirely, and too much to ask of any man.

12

Autumn is the true birth of each New York year. In the farms and orchards of the upper part of the island, such autumn migrants as phoebes, flickers and thrushes gleaned familiar fields before beginning their annual journey southward, but in the city proper the migration was in reverse as the population slowly trickled back from summer retreats. The pace of the city began once more to quicken. Daniel Webster came in from his estate and was seen striding along Wall Street in a bright blue satin vest sprigged with gold flowers. Old John Jacob Astor crept once more along lower Broadway, spittle drooling helplessly from his mouth. Miss Lynch resumed her Saturday night receptions and Mrs. Oakes Smith her fortnightly Sunday at-homes, and all The Starry Sisterhood took up Elizabeth Ellet's new habit of paying frequent calls on the Poes. Muddy made Virginia a crimson gown trimmed with homemade golden lace, Poe's favorite color combination. When she felt well enough she sometimes went with Poe to the literary salons that eagerly welcomed him, to sit silently, pale but smiling, while her Eddy recited *The Raven* to a rapturous company.

Finally, even Fanny returned to the city, but only for a brief visit, during which Poe met her twice at City Hall Park. She was thinner, and he stared at her so sorrowfully that her gaiety fled and she fled after it in only five or ten minutes. She soon went back to Boston, where her husband was painting at the time, and Poe had to content himself with her poems for the *Broadway Journal* and her letters. These both grew more intimate, and Poe hesitated a moment before sending to the compositors one poem which she signed by her own name and which all but named him outright as the object of her yearning, quoting as it did from *Israfel*, one of his own better-known poems.

I know a noble heart that beats/ For one it loves how 'wildly well'—who could miss that the flirtatious Mrs. Osgood meant the romantic Mr. Poe? But the *BJ* needed copy, and he was flattered besides. Bob the devil was soon at his typecase grabbing out the letters so fast that his agile hands were an inky blur. The poem demanded an answer. This time, this time for sure, Poe knew he could compose something magnificent, perhaps even something that he could also deliver at that damned Boston lecture that was fast approaching, but once again he ended up scratching out the dedication of an old but appropriate poem. Eight lines once titled *To Eliza*, after a flirtatious, lively young southern girl, became *To F——s S. O——d*, after a flirtatious, slowly dying New England woman. Along with every member but one of The Starry Sisterhood, young Alex the mail clerk shortly gave himself the pleasure of memorizing:

> Thou wouldst be loved?—then let thy heart
> From its present pathway part not!
> Being everything which now thou art,
> Be nothing which thou art not.
> So with the world thy gentle ways,
> Thy grace, thy more than beauty,
> Shall be an endless theme of praise,
> And love—a simple duty.

By now, Poe was carrying on the *Broadway Journal* almost alone, and he took to signing stories "Littleton Barry" to prevent his own name from appearing too often. The paper remained richer in promise than in profits. Poe had to regard it as a mixed blessing when the publisher, John Bisco, remarked that other irons he had in the fire were getting hot and if Poe really wanted to buy his interest, he'd let it go for a mere fifty dollars now and the balance the first of next year. Horace Greeley agreed to co-sign Poe's note for the fifty. The front page of the *BJ* soon carried the name of Edgar A. Poe as editor and sole proprietor. Poe slashed expenses. He kept Alex but let the printing staff go, including his friend the foreman and Bob the devil, and sent the paper out to a job shop for printing. He hit the streets himself to sell advertising. He borrowed money everywhere he could, knowing that if he could just remedy his urgent want of ready cash and obtain the most trifling immediate relief, the *BJ* would soon be on an excellent footing. If only Chivers would come through with a sizable loan at once, for now was his time of peril. If only. If only.

There was so much to do that time was gold itself, and gold more than time. The Boston poetry reading came and went, a fiasco as Poe had feared. Fanny returned to New York for a longer visit, but business made of Poe so great a slave that he had to postpone the pleasure of spending an evening with her for nearly a week. When he did arrive he found her in an angry mood, complaining that he apparently had ample time to shower attentions on Elizabeth Ellet but none for her. At their next meeting he was detained until after ten o'clock that night when the job shop misplaced three advertisements and Poe had to fill the unexpected gap in the *Journal* by writing a last-minute article. Fanny was so indignant at his tardiness that she refused to see him at all. It took only a final straw—the news that his friend Thomas Dunn English was sick again and asking Poe for copy, as he had in the past, to help him fill his own little journal—to send Poe to the nearest barroom. As a result, he felt sick, tired and discouraged late the next Monday evening as he dragged back to the *BJ* office from meetings to explain to the three advertisers whose notices had been misplaced why he had taken their money and not run the material on the week specified.

He hardly noticed when a swearing quartet of rowdies, out caterwauling under an unlighted streetlight, jeered at him as he passed by, nor did he notice when one member of their group suddenly darted toward a slender lad walking along in back of Poe, grabbed a package the youth was carrying and ran rapidly off. The rest of the gang deployed to keep the youth from following. He danced from side to side, hesitant to try to pass them, and finally piped, "Stop, thief!"

Poe turned. There were other passersby, but no policemen to be seen. Most of the pedestrians scuttled aside, but one, a tall, large, rough-looking young man in a broad-brimmed felt hat and an open-collared red flannel shirt strode toward the tallest rowdy and growled in a rich, deep voice, "Here, now! What's going on here?"

The rowdy swung his head so quickly that the heavily soaped curls plastered to his temples in proper street style swung free of his face. "Stick with your own business, fellow," he growled back. "This here is no concern of yours."

"That's right," chimed in another of the b'hoys. Lithely, he swooped across the path of the would-be rescuer and sent the big man's rakishly slanted felt hat spinning to the sidewalk. As the young toughs laughed, the big man picked up his hat, twisted it into a kind of rope, seized the taller of the rowdies by the collar and struck him with it four times on the side of the head. "Ouch," said the rowdy in a surprised but conversational tone.

Poe was no coward. He had been a first-rate boxer in Richmond during his youth and was a fair hand at wrestling besides. These Bowery toughs were reputed to carry knives, of course, but he didn't think of that. He only started walking toward them, not liking the odds the big man faced. Finding themselves confronted with yet another stranger coming to intervene, the other two rowdies retreated indecisively to the pavement, leaving their friend still in the big man's grasp. The man nodded in a friendly way at Poe and calmly proceeded to go through his victim's pockets until he came to what he wanted, a purse.

"What was in your package, son?" the big man asked the youth who had been robbed, a youth who could hardly have been more than five or six years younger than his rescuer.

"A papier-mâché work box for my mother," the youth quavered. "All fitted up inside."

"Cost?"

"Five dollars, sir."

"A pity," the big man said. "This villain only has four on him. Settle for that?"

"Well . . . yes, sir."

Looking inquiringly at Poe, the big man asked, "Fair enough? Or do you think I should catch another one?"

At this, the two rowdies still in the street took to their heels. Poe smiled faintly and nodded. He watched as the money went from the rowdy's purse to the youth's hand. It was a bit over four dollars, including the change, but the rowdy didn't stay to register any complaints. He took off like a pebble from a slingshot when the big man released him. The man turned to the youthful victim and demanded, "Stranger in town, are you?"

"Yc . . . yes, sir. I'm up with my father from Flat Creek, Indiana. We . . ."

"Never mind, I don't need your life's history. Just heed my warning: don't go wandering about the streets or parks unnecessarily in the evening here. The degrading confession is necessary that New York is one of the most crime-haunted and dangerous cities in Christendom." He waved airily. "Now scat, sir. Go buy another papier-mâché work box for your mother." He turned to Poe, dismissing the youngster as if he were already blocks away, and said, "Papier-mâché, ugh. Well met, Mr. Poe. I thank you for coming to my side."

Poe raised his eyebrows in surprise. "We know each other?" he said.

"In a manner of speaking," the young man said. "As a matter of fact, Mr. Poe, I was just coming around to see you about a small contribution I submitted to your paper. My name's Walt Whitman."

Even considering the constant parade of hopefuls through his haunts with their cartloads of manuscripts, Poe didn't see how he could have forgotten this particular neophyte. The fellow was built like a bull, with a muscular throat and fine, ample chest, and dressed like a carpenter. Hardly your typical scribbler. Poe had planned to spend the next couple of hours hacking together a column or two to help out English, but the scuffle in the street had formed a bond between him and this Whitman fellow, and he invited the man to accompany him to his office.

Only Alex was still there, scratching away at something on paper. From the way the boy quickly slid his arms over it and blushed when they entered, Poe inferred it was a new poem. He greeted Alex and ushered Whitman to a chair by his desk, wondering if the big man by some misfortune had called on one of those occasional days when he had taken a few drinks. He had a fuzzy memory of suddenly feeling fed up with the way these damn rhymesters pestered him and chasing someone out of his office with appropriate, or inappropriate, curses. Could he have attacked anyone this big? He said wearily, "Now, about this, uh, contribution of yours, Mr. Whitman . . ."

Whitman threw himself carelessly into the chair. It made a popping sound but held. He turned a fresh, ruddy face and singular eyes on Poe, eyes of a light, semi-transparent blue, with that sleepy look that comes when the lid rests halfway down over the pupil. "*Art Singing and Heart Singing*," he boomed.

"Oh *that* contribution," Poe said, less wearily. He remembered it very well. It had arrived by mail—a vigorous and well-reasoned essay appealing for the encouragement of native music. America has followed obedient and childlike long enough in the track of the Old World. Now it is time one heard the great, fresh voice of America singing. Or something to that effect.

"That and more to come," Whitman said confidently. "I will tell you frankly, as you probably do not know, that I'm a newspaperman like yourself. I'm presently writing for a Brooklyn paper, but I need a more influential outlet for my pen. Despite the fact that I don't care personally for your poetry, I still think it's both brilliant and dazzling, and your output has attracted for your journal an elite readership that would be very useful to me, just as I will be useful to you. Besides, if we can come to terms on payment, I could use the money."

Poe allowed himself one of his rare, genuinely amused chuckles. "So you don't care for my poetry, eh, Mr. Whitman?" he said, singling out the comment that interested him most. "Might one ask why?"

Poe expected the customary criticisms that boiled down to the fact that his work failed to exhibit the usual comfortable sentiments and moral lessons with which his contemporaries overflowed, but the young man surprised him once more. "I want for poetry the clear sun shining and fresh air blowing, with always the background of the eternal moralities," Whitman said judiciously. He studied Poe openly and without self-consciousness, and added, "But I must admit your stuff is powerful. In a dream I had once, I saw a vessel on the sea, at midnight, in a storm. On deck was a slender, slight, beautiful figure, a dim man, apparently enjoying all the terror, the murk and the dislocation of which he was the center. That figure of my lurid dream might stand for you, Mr. Poe—for your spirit and your poems."

"Well, perhaps for my storm-tossed fortunes," Poe said, becoming somber again.

"Then the rumors are right?" Whitman said. "The *Broadway Journal* will cease publication? Damn, and I was going to convince you I should write for you on a weekly basis."

"Rumors?" Poe said. "Is that what they're saying about the *Journal*?"

"I've heard it put about," Whitman said.

"So the jackals are already talking," Poe said. "Well, damn *them*. The lion isn't down yet."

Whitman looked around the empty office. "But he will be?" he asked sympathetically.

An impulse to confide in this unlikely-looking young scribe overcame Poe's normal reticence. "I fear so," he said. Then he thought that sounded too concerned, and he added lightly, "I suppose I could keep the *Journal* going if I were willing to take in new partners, but I am extremely reluctant to invite any interference in my aims. By that I mean my aims to elevate without stupefying our literature, to further justice and, a point with which you should find yourself in accord, to resist foreign dictation as to the directions America's literature should take."

"Commendable," applauded his visitor.

"Of course the format of a mere weekly literary paper was never to be regarded as fully suitable for the furtherance of my ideals," Poe said. "In fact, the one great purpose of my life, from which I have never swerved for a moment, is to establish a splendid monthly magazine in which men of genius may fight their battles upon some terms of equality with those dunces, the men of mere talent. It's to be called *The Stylus*. I shall probably establish it, in fact, soon after the first of the year."

Did the young man look skeptical? Poe thought so for a moment, then decided he was mistaken. But suddenly he was tired of his caller and wished he would go. Whitman sat heavily in his chair, his big body slumped and his odd eyes dreaming.

"Well, sir," Poe concluded, "perhaps you'll let me hear from you again one of these days when I have *The Stylus* pulled together and moving. I shall always be happy to consider your submissions."

Whitman thanked him. He fingered the broad-brimmed felt hat, which he had rested on his crossed knee, and said, "I'm sorry that fortune does not allow us to work together, Mr. Poe. You prefer storm and lightning and I sunshine, but through our poetry we both seek to cast new light upon the unknown regions of the soul. It would have been a good match."

As casually as if he had been discussing the market price of cod, Whitman thanked Poe for his time and departed, leaving Poe to shake his head, not for the first time, at the egotism of youth, which calmly assumes that the intention of becoming great is reason enough to behave as if one already were. But he liked the young fellow. His matter-of-factness, even his size and pretentiously unpretentious dress, were refreshing. A pleasant change from the usual soulful young men with their customary pastel imitations of the works of better men in whose footsteps they hoped to tread. No telling what kind of poetry young Whitman wrote, but better anything than one more *Ode on a Grecian Flute* or *Ode on a Grecian Krater*.

Better even a temperance poem from young Alex. Poe noticed that the boy had stopped writing. He looked at Poe nervously, then quickly looked away. The office was quiet, and the visitor's voice had been anything but. Poe feared Alex must have overheard the discussion about the future of the *Journal*. Well, poor youngster, he had to know sometime. Poe called him over.

"Alex," Poe said gently, "there's no rush, but I think we'd better start asking around for another position for you. *Sartain's* could use an intelligent young man, I think, and if I can't work out something for you there, I'll speak to other of my acquaintances. I'm afraid the *Journal* might not need our services much longer."

"No, Mr. Poe, don't sell it," Alex pleaded. "We've got such a host of advertising, the paper's bound to start making a lot of money soon."

"But it hasn't got a host of capital," Poe said. "It never did. That's the trouble. Mr. Bisco's note falls due the first of January, and if . . . Well, no matter. About the last expense I can cut is the office here. I may have to move into English's offices for a while, even to keep going until January."

Alex shook his head, then blurted, "Not him, sir. Not Mr. English. I don't trust Mr. English."

"But, Alex, he's a pleasant enough young man," Poe said, puzzled. "The point is, I want to see you safely settled somewhere. Do you think you'd like *Sartain's*?"

"No, sir," Alex said. "I don't want to work for anyone but you."

"Now, Alex, as men of business we must be practical," Poe said.

"It's all Mr. Franco's fault," Alex said, sounding sulky. "Ever since he had to leave the paper he's been writing and saying terrible things about you. He's trying to involve you in ruin, Mr. Poe, by destroying the *Broadway Journal*."

Poe sighed. "I suppose he's bitter," he said. "But that's the literary life for you, Alex. If one fights wars, one makes enemies. So the world wags."

"Doesn't one ever make friends?" Alex said wistfully.

"Yes," Poe said, "the best of friends." He smiled at Alex. After a moment, Alex smiled back. The boy was past due for tea at the ironmonger's widow's, but even though Poe protested he lit the lamps and sat back at his own table to work on the subscription list while Poe wrote. Their time together was coming to an end, but while it lasted, both cherished the light of the oil lamps and the still, stuffy warmth of the room and, for the time it remained to them, the light and warmth that were comradeship.

13

Now that the coughing had stopped, Virginia found her room cold. The room was small and on the back, and when the wind was from the north, as it was now, it rapped against the windows like a live thing that wanted in. It always got its way. Muddy had made heavy cotton curtains and neat miniature sandbags to barricade pane and sill, but as Virginia lay motionless, staring dreamily at the window, she could see the curtains puff out coldly like a ship in full sail, then flutter to brief stillness. Maybe later, when she got up, she'd look in Muddy's scrap bag for something to poke around the window frames.

But it was Muddy who always worried about drafts. Virginia rarely worried about anything at all. Every day, when she took her medicine, there was the warm, happy time, then there was the quiet, sleepy time, then it was early the next morning and the coughing time, followed by the calm, waiting time. Virginia stretched out her feet, nudging Catarina, who was curled up at the bottom of the bed. The cat, once aroused, stretched hugely, front claws kneading the quilt, and walked over Virginia's knees to settle in the crook of her arm. Catarina began to purr, and Virginia lay and listened to the big cat purring and the wind humming and banging, and she began to plan her day.

She deserved something nice today. Yesterday had been the doctor, so she had paid in advance for a nice day. She hated the doctor. She hated sitting there naked to the waist, and she hated it most of all when it was time for him to put his ear against her and listen. Dr.

Mitchell in Philadelphia always used a rolled-up piece of paper or a hollow stick and listened through that. She had told Muddy at least six times that she didn't need to go to the doctor, that she felt a lot better than usual, but that awful old Dr. Francis claimed that a feeling of vitality and vigor often came before an increase in her cough and higher fever.

But she would not think of Dr. Francis any more. When you were sick a lot, you learned not to think of things. When you were sick a lot, your world became your room and the warm fur of the cat and the wind rapping against the window and the seven-thirty pint of hot milk or the three slimy raw eggs that Muddy sometimes substituted. Catarina pawed at the covers. She wanted a tent. Virginia dutifully propped up her knees and lifted the quilt, and the cat slid underneath and turned around several times and settled and began to purr again.

From the next room, which Muddy and Eddy now shared, there was no sound. Since winter and the usual winter's coughing had come, Muddy had managed to buy a new cot for herself, and gave Eddy her old bed, and now he could get some rest. Virginia was always the first to wake up. She never really got back to sleep after each night's fever broke just before each day's dawn. Virginia would lie and watch Eddy's old drawing of the Lost Lenore begin to form in the dimness over his desk. She and Eddy called the girl in the picture Lost Lenore, but Muddy called the picture the Fatal Letter. Nobody called the girl Elmira, but that's who she had started out to be. A white-gowned girl with long black hair, her tearful face buried in a handkerchief, at her feet the fatal letter which told her too late that Eddy's foster father and her parents had been intercepting all of Eddy's letters to her while he was away at the university, and she didn't know until after she'd married someone else that he hadn't forgotten her and loved her still.

Virginia knew all about Elmira. She knew about all of Eddy's ladyloves. They wrote him letters, great bundles of them. Muddy would read them aloud, and she and Muddy would laugh. The funniest were from fat Mrs. Stella Lewis, the Brooklyn poetess who kept in her parlor a bust of Pallas with a stuffed raven sitting on its head. The longest were from that Mrs. Elizabeth Ellet, all full of sighs and jealousy and requests for favors—get her new poem published here, get her new article published there—and Eddy had quite enough to do without all that. The sweetest were from pretty Mrs. Fanny Osgood, but Muddy had taken up frowning and clucking her tongue about these, ever since the nasty anonymous letters had started coming more and more frequently, saying that Eddy had been sneaking around and seeing Mrs. Osgood in parks and places like that. Muddy had wanted to talk to him about the letters, but Virginia wouldn't let her. Virginia made her keep quiet because, after all, pretty Fanny Osgood exerted a good influence on dear Eddy. He'd only been on one real spree since way last summer, and that was recently when he had to close up the *Broadway Journal* and issued the Valedictory that he'd pinned to the wallpaper by his desk with one of Muddy's straight pins. He still stared at it somberly sometimes as he worked.

The light through the billowing cotton curtains had strengthened to the point that Virginia could read the brief Valedictory if she wanted to, but she'd read it so many times that she knew it by heart:

Unexpected engagements demanding my whole attention, and the objects being fulfilled, so far as regards myself personally, for which "The Broadway Journal" was established, I now, as its Editor, bid farewell—as cordially to foes as to friends.

Virginia turned her eyes away from it and watched the curtains flutter. Much as she hated it when Eddy got into one of his conditions, she couldn't blame him for that last spree. He'd worked so hard all year. He'd published *The Raven*, and the volume of tales, and the new volume of poems, and even in Europe they'd started writing nice things about him, and he'd become editor and finally publisher of his very own literary weekly, and it looked like now they were right back where they started, living in two tiny rooms and living off Muddy's begging basket. What was the use of being famous when you were still so poor? That nice Mr. Lane, the one who bought into the *Journal* at the last minute, had finally helped poor Eddy home, staggering and with a black eye. Mr. Lane had explained to Muddy that Eddy had got into a fight. It was with that nasty little Mr. English, and after all Eddy had done for him, helping him with his own journal. It was all Mr. English's fault for teasing Eddy when he was in a condition.

At least there'd been no conditions since, and it was nice to have Eddy working at home again. Soon he'd wake up, and Muddy would bring the nice milk or the slimy old eggs, and he'd sit at his desk and work on the new papers he was writing about the literati of New

York. And Virginia would go lie on Muddy's cot so he wouldn't be disturbed.

Today she would rest very conscientiously, and she'd take her medicine early. She wanted to be sure to feel good. They were going to go to Mrs. Hewitt's at-home that afternoon, before Eddy went to Miss Lynch's valentine party. She would wear her red dress with the gold lace, she decided, because Eddy liked it best.

Catarina suddenly plunged out of the tent of bedclothes and jumped off the bed. She always did things like that, and she always did them suddenly. Now she went suddenly to the door and looked at Virginia pointedly, as if to say, "Open it! Hurry up!" Catarina wanted her breakfast, but there was still no sound from next door, so Virginia shook her head and whispered, "You have to wait." Catarina never meowed. She only waited until she finally got her way, and she waited now as Virginia slipped out of bed and put an old black shawl of Muddy's around her shoulders and went to Eddy's desk.

It was a real desk this time, with a rolled top and seventeen cubbyholes. In the fourth cubbyhole from the left she found what she wanted—a poem. Oh, Eddy hadn't tried to hide it. There on the wallpaper was the mark of its own pin, next to the outline of chapter eleven of the literary history he planned to finish after he got the New York literati articles all done, and a review of Eddy's *Tales* in French and the Valedictory, which she wished he'd take down and put away. Once the poem had been finished and copied by Eddy himself in his beautiful handwriting, he'd simply put it away until today, because it was a valentine and today was St. Valentine's Day.

The problem was, it was a valentine to Mrs. Osgood. It was what Eddy called an acrostic. He seemed to think nothing of it, and even Mrs. Elizabeth Ellet, when Muddy told her about the valentine, had had to admit that poets were always writing poems to other poets, it was just a harmless pastime. But even though Virginia couldn't have figured out the riddle of the acrostic without Eddy's explanation, and even though the poem, from what little sense she could make out of it, seemed innocent enough, Virginia wasn't just utterly certain that she liked it.

"You've never written a poem to *me*," she had told Eddy.

"To the contrary, I write all my poems to you," he had answered affectionately.

After that, Virginia had felt better, but only for a little while. Then she got to thinking about a story of Mrs. Osgood's in *Graham's*, one that Mrs. Ellet had come rushing in one day to show to Muddy. Virginia had no trouble making sense out of the story, and it worried her. It was all about a coquette named Ida Grey, a desperate coquette, who appeared to be wild and reckless and wayward and often heartless, but everybody loved her anyway, because she was the veriest sunbeam that ever gladdened the weary world with beauty and light, and besides, she was a privileged person and not to be judged by common rules.

Now, what did that mean? Virginia didn't know, but she knew what Ida did. Ida was a young and beautiful widow, who had loved her husband in her way, but one night at a lovely party her gaze riveted on a remarkable-looking man in a distant part of the room, and she blushed deeply, and after a while the man came up to her, a man whose face once seen could never be forgotten and whose keen gray eyes bent with singular earnestness on her face, and though his manner and expression were coldly courteous, there was a peculiar depth in his tone which only some strong emotion could have given it. Sunbeamy Ida met him at last, him of whom she had read and heard so much, and she knew that he had heard much of her and had sought an introduction, and although they spoke but a few formal words and parted she knew instantly that their souls were as one forever and they would never truly part again.

Then came the part that worried Virginia. This man was married, but his wife, all of Ida's friends said, was cold and did not love him. Ida decided that if destiny had willed the man's wife to love him, he would have loved her in return, and then Ida decided that the man was *her* destiny, and the wife could just go away and find her destiny somewhere else.

Nasty Ida. Nasty girl who went around saying the man's wife was cold and didn't love him. Nasty Ida died in the story, and Virginia was deeply glad.

How could nasty Ida say the man's wife was cold and didn't love him? If pretty Fanny Osgood meant what Virginia thought she meant, how dare she write such a thing? How could she even think that Virginia didn't love her own dear Eddy? How could dear Eddy write a valentine to such a woman after that?

Virginia looked at the poem in her hand, and her black eyebrows, as black as her hair, drew together in an uncharacteristic frown as she read:

> For her this rhyme is penned whose luminous eyes,
> Brightly expressive as the twins of Lœda,
> Shall find her own sweet name, that, nestling lies
> Upon the page, enwrapped from every reader.
> Search narrowly the lines!—they hold a treasure
> Divine—a talisman—an amulet
> That must be worn at heart. Search well the measure—

And on and on it went, all about Gordian knots and challenging anyone to read the riddle. Well, of course, only Eddy with his marvelous flair for codes and ciphers could have figured out how to hide a name so well, tucked into the first letter of the first line, the second letter of the second line, and so on. But it *did* spell out Frances Sargent Osgood among all that sort of thing.

Virginia put the acrostic valentine back. The north wind was still shaking the curtains and her bare feet were cold, but she stood a minute longer by the desk, still frowning.

When Eddy decided he wanted to marry her, he didn't sit down and write some poem. He just wrote Muddy and begged for her to let them marry, and he never said a word to Virginia except for the time after that when he smiled and said, "Well, Sissy?" He never had to say another word or write some silly poem because he knew that she adored him and always had and always would, and he loved her, too, and still did, and she knew it because he wept in his sleep, not knowing it, every time she had some bad spell, and if the spell was very bad, poor darling, he couldn't stand it and got into a condition.

Virginia's frown disappeared, and her pale face regained its customary serenity. The darling. She suddenly knew what she would do. It would give her the nice day she'd earned by having to see Dr. Francis yesterday, and it would give Eddy something nice too. She would write him a poem of her very own, like all his ladyloves. Better still, she would write him an acrostic valentine. And best yet, she would surprise him and go with him that night to Miss Lynch's valentine party, because everyone read their valentines, and this time she would have one too!

Quickly, she took a few sheets of blue paper from his desk, and a pencil, and returned to bed. Catarina still sat by the door, waiting, but Catarina would just have to wait. Virginia hoped everyone would sleep late, late, late. Then she would have time to get a good start on her poem.

The poem took all day. It was hard writing poems. The rhymes, those were very hard. The acrostic part was hard too. Virginia consulted with Muddy in secret and chose the simplest way of riddling, starting each line with a letter of Eddy's name, but she couldn't make the rhymes come out with Edgar A. Poe and so had to use his name in full, Edgar Allan Poe. That worked better, but then came the hardest part. It was very difficult to keep truth out of a poem, Virginia discovered, and try though she might, the truth kept creeping in.

Although she had lain down to write, she was very tired by the time she finished. Muddy scolded that she should stay home from Mrs. Hewitt's and even went and interrupted Eddy while he was working and, despite Virginia's objections, said so. He came to the door and looked at her worriedly, but Virginia knew how to be stubborn, and Eddy finally said, well, he thought she ought to go because she was feeling so well and she wanted to go so badly.

They both thought she was feeling well because, all day long, she refused to allow herself to cough. Dr. Francis had warned her just yesterday that a girl who coughs all day works as hard as a man climbing a mountain. She mustn't expend the energy, and she was especially glad not to expend it so she could go to Mrs. Hewitt's at-home and then surprise Eddy by going to the valentine party. She asked Muddy to do her hair, and she thought it looked about as nice as it could, parted in the middle with a dark wing over each cheekbone and a big bun in back. When Eddy stopped working and she could go into her room, she put on the red and gold dress and carefully lay down to rest a bit more, and she was all ready to go when Muddy came in with the bottle of ruby-colored laudanum and the eyedropper and the glass.

"Give me sixty drops today, Muddy," Virginia said eagerly. "I want to be sure I feel good all evening."

Muddy clucked. "But, my poor little girl, that's far too much," she said. "You're already up to fifty minims a day, and Dr. Francis said no more than forty."

"It takes more now," Virginia said.

"But you'll fall asleep at the party."

"No, I won't. You feel very good for hours and hours, and by the time you feel sleepy you go to bed. Sixty drops, Muddy. Let's count."

After she swallowed the draught, Virginia could feel the pressure in her chest relax, and her tongue seemed suddenly very large. A warm serenity surrounded her like a cloud, and she scarcely noticed the chill of the north wind on the streets as she and dear Eddy walked the few blocks to Mrs. Hewitt's. Her poem was safely tucked into her muff, ready for later, and her silent smile was ready for the great ladies and gentlemen who had preceded them to Mrs. Hewitt's parlor.

Eddy seated her by the fire, her favorite place. From time to time he brought someone over to speak to her, but the rest of the time she could sit quietly and listen. Mrs. Ellet feared last fall's poor potato crop in Ireland would bring a dreadful new influx of Irishers to crowd the city come spring. Mrs. Oakes Smith feared the new rage, the polka, would lead to the final collapse of public morals. Mr. Bryant feared New York would capitulate instantly to Mexico, when war finally started, since the fortifications at the Narrows had nothing to recommend them except that they were picturesque of a spring afternoon.

Then there was a tiny pause in the talking, then a buzz, then several sly glances seemed to be turned to Virginia. She serenely wondered why and serenely smiled, until she saw that the hostess was greeting a newcomer. It was pretty Fanny Osgood. Virginia blinked. Pretty Fanny didn't look even as pretty as she had when she last paid a call at Amity Street about a month ago. She had lost more weight. Her neck was thin and flabby.

But Fanny Osgood's voice and smile were still determinedly gay as she flew about the room greeting various friends, entering with animation into conversation with some husband here, flying to hug the wife of some bookseller there. She acted for all the world like she hadn't seen the lady in years, while Virginia distinctly recalled that pretty Fanny was staying with the same bookseller's wife. It was with the same animation that, ten minutes later, she had made her way around the circle to Eddy. Virginia watched as pretty Fanny gave Eddy her hand, and she noticed that Elizabeth Ellet was watching too. But after all, now that she thought of it, so was everyone.

Well, but how could *they* think anything was wrong? Here came pretty Fanny gaily to the fireside, where Virginia sat, with Eddy following. Virginia allowed her cheek to be kissed by dry, hot lips and her hand to be grasped by a small hand as suddenly sweaty as her own. "How lovely to see you out and about," pretty Fanny said. "You've been such a stay-at-home this winter."

"Oh, I always stay at home," Virginia said uncomfortably.

Eddy knew she didn't like to talk, and he must have known she especially didn't feel like talking now, because he started talking poetry with pretty Fanny. Soon the usual group drifted up to hear what he was saying. Mrs. Ellet came with them, looking so jealously at Mrs. Osgood, looking so pale, so exasperated, that Virginia was suddenly seized with fright. How could Mrs. Ellet look at Mrs. Osgood like that? She'd give everything away! Virginia lifted her chin, bridling, ready to defend . . . whom? Herself? Eddy?

She wished now she hadn't taken so much of her medicine. It was hard to concentrate. She listened tensely as Mrs. Ellet spoke, and at first she was relieved because it was just poetry talk, but she tensed again as she caught a clear sentence from the angry face framed by quivering brown ringlets.

"Such a pity that you had to give up the *Broadway Journal*," Mrs. Ellet was saying to Eddy.

Eddy stiffened with the jab, but he answered negligently, "Ah well, I never regarded the *Journal* as more than a temporary adjunct to other designs. It fulfilled its destiny, so its demise is a matter of no great moment. As I may have mentioned to you, I now plan on a monthly magazine, although I'm so busy at the moment that it may not be out for a year."

"You create a hardship on your friends by leaving them so long without a voice in the literary world," Mrs. Ellet said. She glanced coolly at Mrs. Osgood, then said to Virginia, "For instance, our dear Mrs. Osgood had to go to *Graham's* to give the public her latest epic. I would have thought your husband had arranged its publication there for her, had I not chanced to notice the subject matter. I assume your husband showed it to you, Mrs. Poe?"

"N . . . no," Virginia said. "At least I don't remember . . ."

"Surely Mr. Poe pointed it out to you, dear Mrs. Poe," Mrs. Ellet said. "The poem in this month's issue?"

"I'll read it again when we get home," Virginia said. She compressed her lips to stop her chin from trembling. "Eddy dear, perhaps . . ."

Thank goodness, he understood. He made a few remarks, then bowed them out of the group by the fire. "Smile, Sissy," he whispered at one point, and she smiled brightly as he commented that his wife's health continued delicate and so she had tired quickly this afternoon. With dignified dispatch, he went to speak to the hostess, apparently with the necessary thanks and good-bys, and soon had Virginia bundled up and out on the front stoop. The north wind was still blowing, and Virginia shivered. She almost wished that she hadn't planned her poem and the surprise. At home in Muddy's room, the coal stove would be warm, and Catarina would be curled up in front of it. But she'd better speak up now, because Eddy had planned to go directly from Mrs. Hewitt's to Miss Lynch's.

"Eddy," she said feebly, "I'm going to go with you to the valentine party."

"What?" he said distractedly.

"I . . . I've decided to go to Miss Lynch's party with you. It's a surprise for you." When he only looked at her blankly, she added uncertainly, "I was invited, wasn't I?"

"Of course," Eddy said. "The ladies always invite both of us to these affairs. But, my dear Sissy, you couldn't possibly feel up to attending."

"I don't feel any tireder than when we left for Mrs. Hewitt's athome," Virginia said. "Please, Eddy, there's another surprise. A bigger one." She felt inside her muff. "I've written you an acrostic valentine."

He looked surprised, and not particularly pleased, although he claimed that he was both. He insisted that she had to go home immediately and concluded, "We'll read your poem together when I come in tonight."

"But I'll be asleep, Eddy," she protested.

He sighed. "That's true. Then we'll read it tomorrow."

"But tomorrow won't be St. Valentine's Day."

"Sissy, you're behaving very unlike yourself," Eddy said sternly. "Be a good girl and run along home now. It will be dark soon, and I won't have you out after dark by yourself."

"But . . . aren't you going to walk me home, Eddy?"

"Not this evening. I must return and escort Mrs. Oakes Smith on to Miss Lynch's. Not that I want to, you understand. It's necessary to show Mrs. Oakes Smith courtesy on account of her standing in literary society. Now, it's only a few blocks. You're not going to make a fuss about a little thing like that, are you?"

In the end, he walked her to the corner and promised to stand there and watch her until she was out of sight. Virginia was trembling so hard that she feared the poem would slip out of her muff, and she clutched it in both arms like a child guarding a kitten. Down the block a trio of scavenging pigs out sticking their snouts into every open gate looked at her burden alertly, and one cut toward Virginia, squealing loudly for the food it apparently suspected she carried. The two other pigs followed, squealing in deafening chorus.

Virginia began to cry, trembling harder with timid fear. She turned to call out to Eddy for help. But he was already gone!

"Oh," she sobbed. "Oh." A passing gentleman kicked the pigs and tipped his hat to her, but that only made her cry the harder and clutch her muff tighter. She closed her eyes, but that was a mistake, for she found her faces had begun.

Faces, faces dancing in front of her closed eyelids, strange faces of people that she had never seen before, one face succeeding the next with utmost rapidity, faces that usually came only when she closed her eyes to dream after taking her medicine. She opened her eyes quickly and there were still faces, faces of passersby, many of them staring at her curiously.

She wanted to run, but she knew she couldn't without starting to cough. She ducked her head and walked on as fast as she possibly could.

If only she weren't so afraid to be walking all by herself. If only she could stop crying. Then she could walk faster. Then she could be home to the haven that was Muddy's room with the warm coal stove and Catarina purring.

14

Poe's discomfiture was by no means assuaged when, watching Virginia start homeward, he was hulloed by his third admirer, fat Stella Lewis of Brooklyn. She puffed out of a cab, her husband behind her, calling, "Mr. Poe! Oh, Mr. Poe, wait! Has everyone already left?

We're shamefully late, but a poor girl jumped off the ferry, and it circled forever looking for her. Poor thing. Can you imagine, in this weather? You must come back in with us, Mr. Poe. Mustn't he, Sylvanus? Sylvanus is particularly anxious to talk to you. Aren't you, Sylvanus?"

Mr. Lewis docilely seconded his wife, and Poe cursed to himself as they herded him back to the Hewitt house and up the steps. He wasn't thinking of Virginia. He was worrying about Fanny and Elizabeth Ellet and the hostility in their tones when they spoke to each other. Here was Fanny so upset about gossip, and yet she couldn't keep jealousy off her face when she looked at the woman she fancied was her rival. Poe had done his best. He had even brought little Sissy out with him this afternoon, as Fanny had suggested, to remind the world delicately that he had a family. He still hoped to escort Fanny—not Mrs. Oakes Smith—to the valentine party, but these women's rivalries made everything so difficult, and the appearance of Mrs. Lewis augured well for additional difficulties.

The difficulties transpired as soon as he was back in Mrs. Hewitt's parlor, but not precisely in the form that he had anticipated. Mr. Lewis drew him to the side and Mrs. Lewis departed, and Lewis put to him a business proposition.

"Mr. Poe, forgive me if I say this poorly, but you know me. I'm just a busy lawyer, and not one of you literary chaps. The thing is, Mrs. Lewis does not feel she has received the acclaim she feels her poetry rightly deserves, and she asked me to—"

"My dear sir, please say no more or we will both regret it," Poe interrupted. "You know and I know that there are reviewers who write laudatory notices of books and poems and turn up to 'borrow' money or favors from their flattered authors afterward, but *I* am not one of them."

"Ah, you mean the likes of Dr. Griswold?" Lewis said shrewdly. "But you misunderstand me. I did not mean to suggest putting a price tag on your reviews. No, nor any such thing at all. I wish to propose strictly a business dealing, if tutoring qualifies as business. Or perhaps you would call it editing. I don't know much about poetry, but if writing it makes Mrs. Lewis happy, well, that's fine with me. But it occurred to me, what if she *does* receive the acclaim her stuff deserves, and what if it really doesn't deserve much? So I thought maybe you could teach her a little about how to write it better. What do you think, Mr. Poe?"

Poe was amused by the man's candor, but he shook his head. "I'm sorry, Mr. Lewis. I'd be delighted to work with your wife, but I'm just too busy right now to take it on. Might I suggest some other names to you?" He paused a moment, thinking. He'd bloodied young English's nose when they'd had that spat after the *BJ* closed, but what a nice way to show English he wasn't a man to hold a grudge. "I can highly recommend Dr. Thomas Dunn English. He's young and his fame still awaits him, but he has a firm grasp of poetic principles."

"I guess not," said Lewis. "Perhaps later on you won't be quite so busy, Mr. Poe. It's either you or no one with Sarah." He made a wry face and corrected himself. "Sorry, *Stella*. She hates for me to call her Sarah anymore."

They parted and Poe shortly saw him tell something to Mrs. Lewis, who looked reproachfully at Poe, pouting childishly. He took care to avoid her, and the evening began to go more successfully. The John Bartletts—the bookseller and his wife with whom Fanny was staying—were not invited to Miss Lynch's party, and he was able to volunteer his services as an escort without looking too utterly, utterly culpable. Fanny required that she be allowed to go to their home, on Amity Street not far from his lodgings, to change her dress to one suitable for an evening party, and they all left Mrs. Hewitt's together. Poe waited impatiently, talking books with the bookseller, until Fanny finally reappeared in last year's dove-colored satin and her furs. A cab was obviously indicated, even though the distance to Miss Lynch's was short, and he departed quickly to find one.

They were to be alone, alone in the smelly privacy of a rattling box jouncing through the cold city streets, but at least for a few minutes really alone, for the first time since that evening in Providence. Poe felt his throat tighten at the thought. No cabs in sight. Perhaps up at the square.

At the bottom of Fifth Avenue, the north wind howled from its narrow canyon and into the open parade ground of Washington Square with so gusting an effect that half the streetlamps had been blown out, and the smell of leaking gas whipped by on puffs of wind. Still no cabs. Perhaps he should have gone over to Broadway. Poe hesitated, shivering. Out of vanity, he had worn his black cloak instead of his heavier but shabby old West Point greatcoat. His hands would be too cold to feel Fanny's when he held them a few minutes hence. He shivered again at the thought, as he had shivered many times since learning of Fanny's illness. Fear and a frenzied sort of excitement bubbled through him every time he thought of her now, every time he remembered her delicate, childlike body heaving against him, her great, gray eyes closed by shadowed eyelids.

Poe located an empty cab on the southeast corner of the square, but by the time he took it back to await his lady in front of her door, he found an unpleasant surprise awaiting inside: W. M. Gillespie, the stuttering mathematical genius whose admiration of Fanny predated his own, had called in his absence to see if Fanny needed an escort to Miss Lynch's, and there was nothing for it but to invite him to accompany them. And Poe would have to pay for the cab!

Fanny slyly slipped her hand into his in the cab while chattering to Gillespie, and he could feel her fragile shoulder leaning against him, but his mood had turned dark and he brooded.

"You're so silent, Mr. Poe," Fanny chided at one point, and he replied grumpily, "I think I may be catching a cold."

"Everyb-b-b-b-body I know has one," stuttered Gillespie amiably. "You should b-b-b-b-buy yourself a lemon, Mr. Poe, and drink the juice hot with a little sugar."

"Pshaw," said Fanny, "it would only make Mr. Poe the sourer and would otherwise do him no good, as I can detect that he is in a sour mood tonight. We must try to cheer him up." She squeezed his hand and chattered on. "Lemon juice for a cold, I declare, Mr. Gillespie. Who comes up with these cures? Do you know what someone told me the other day? That if I put seaweed under my bed, it will cure my consumption. But someone else said that only cold bathing and breathing into a hole cut in fresh earth would put me back in the pink of health again. Do you know what I said? That I might try bathing in a mud puddle filled with seaweed, but only if they could assure me it would not give me a complexion like a turtle's."

She laughed, and Gillespie joined her, but Poe grimaced in the darkness. He hated the new way she had of constantly discussing her illness in tones of light-hearted gaiety, and he hated the fact that she did not seem downhearted as he about their crowded threesome. Could she possibly have arranged it deliberately? He knew his occasional displays of jealousy delighted her.

Poe gritted his teeth and wondered for the first time if that poem Fanny had just written for *Graham's*, the one Mrs. Ellet had made such a point of mentioning to Virginia, could possibly be sincere, instead of what he had assumed—a ploy to allay the ever increasing gossip about their "friendship." She had titled it *Caprice* and couldn't have referred to him more obviously if she'd tried.

The cab turned onto Waverly Place. One more block, and he wouldn't even be able to hold her hand, unless he was lucky and managed to escort her home alone. He would not leave it to luck, by God! He'd insist upon it, somehow. She was more desirable than ever, now that it had occurred to him that she might have meant those lines.

>Reprove me not that still I change
> With every changing hour,
>For glorious nature gives me leave
> In wave and cloud and flower . . .
>
>'Tis true you played, on feeling's lyre,
> A pleasant tune or two;
>And oft beneath your minstrel fire
> The hours in music flew . . .
>
>Be less—thou art no love of mine—
> So leave my love in peace!
>'Tis helpless woman's right divine,
> Her only right, Caprice.

Poe's gray eyes were so fiery, as he thought of Fanny's ridiculous poem, that the cabbie departed without grumbling for a larger tip, and the twelve-year-old maid who took their wraps at Miss Lynch's door quailed. A fine advance payment Fanny had made him, he concluded, for his charming valentine!

Poe was a great deal happier, but not much calmer, when he took the stairs two at a time at his boarding house toward eleven that night. He paused on the landing to compose himself, for he saw a light under Muddy's door and knew that she had waited up for him. He was sober, of course. Ah, how admiring all the ladies' eyes had been when, instead of the men's punch bowl, he partook only of theirs. But he was also intoxicated. Ah, Fanny.

Later, when he was in bed, he would dwell upon the enchanting memory of warm kisses in a cold doorway. Although his determination to take Fanny home alone had been thwarted, so very easily, by Dr. Francis's tedious insistence that he would take everyone within earshot home in his wife's carriage, a moment was all that it took for Fanny to whisper in his ear, and seconds for him to race on foot back from his own dwelling to hers once Dr. Francis's carriage had turned the corner.

He knew Muddy would have heard his footsteps on the stairs, so he waited no longer to tap lightly on the door. "Eddy?" her voice asked, and the bolt clicked immediately, without waiting for an answer. Catarina had been making herself comfortable on his bed. As Muddy took his cloak and cane, the cat came and wound around his ankles.

"Don't let her do that, Eddy," Muddy complained. "She gets hair all over your cuffs, and you know it won't brush off. I have to pick it off, a hair at a time."

"But, Muddy, she loves me," Poe said, and his throat tightened again at the thought. Yes, *she* loved him. There had not been a chance tonight to question her about that damned poem, but he would reassure himself tomorrow, for they had arranged to meet at the Historical Society. Not that he needed the reassurance. He smiled. It was not so much Fanny's kisses, he decided, but the memory of them that made him feel as if he had grasped the handle of one of those new electromagnetic machines for which the utilitarian purpose of curing headaches had recently been found. Curious. Why should the memory affect him even more strongly than the fact?

"I'm talking to you, Eddy," Muddy said.

"Oh, sorry, Muddy dear. I was woolgathering."

"Did you have a nice time?"

"Passably, passably," Poe said. He let Muddy help him off with his cloak, and he sat down by the coal stove to take off his still new-looking gaitered shoes. He would not remove his ascot, naturally, or the rest of his clothes until he was ready to step into the darkness of Virginia's room and change to his nightshirt.

"Did they like the poem?"

"Oh yes, it was rather a success. You know how people are about puzzles. In fact, we spent much of the evening talking about codes and ciphers." That memory was not electrifying, but it was at least very warming as Poe considered it. No doubt about it, he was a master of cryptography. Back in Philadelphia, he had once challenged readers to send him a single cryptogram that he could not resolve, and he solved all but one that was so messed up that it was incapable of solution. Difficult though it was, he could even solve ciphers in French, Italian, Spanish, German, Latin or Greek, and he had proved it.

"Virginia pinned her poem for you on your pillow," Muddy said. She gestured toward his single bed, in the shadows beyond the light of her candle. "I don't suppose you're interested in reading it, but do be sure to remove the pin before you go to bed."

"Why, of course I'm interested in reading it. What's wrong, Muddy? Are you tired tonight? You shouldn't sew so late, and by only one candle."

"I'm not tired," Muddy said. There was an acrimonious note in her voice such as he rarely heard from her.

"Something's wrong, I can tell," Poe said. "What is it, Muddy? If you think I've been drinking—"

"No, Eddy, it's apparent enough when you've been drinking," she said, even more sharply. "If you want to know the truth of the matter, I'm put out with you. Fancy propitiating Mrs. Oakes Smith at the expense of poor little Sissy. Timid child, she cried all the way home, and let me tell you, I had my hands full calming her once she got here. I even had to give her another dose of medicine."

Poe had forgotten his lie about escorting Mrs. Oakes Smith and he was confused, but he flushed guiltily. "Why, Muddy, I did nothing at Virginia's expense. I swear it, nothing at all."

"You left her to walk home all by herself," Muddy accused.

"But . . . there wasn't the least danger . . ."

"She was afraid," Muddy said. "But there, I suppose it was just her medicine. There's no need for you to get upset too, son. I know you'll be careful with her. I know you won't leave her to walk by herself again when she's so timid about these city streets. You will be careful, won't you, son? For my sake?"

"Of course, Muddy. And I'm really terribly sorry . . ."

"Well now, it's all behind us. I'm going to go to bed now. Just blow out the candle when you're ready, there's a good boy. And don't forget that straight pin."

"I won't. I'll read her poem now, and then I'll look in on Virginia for a moment. And, Muddy? Muddy, I'm really most terribly sorry."

She grumbled her way to bed, mumbling something about not telling him if she had known he was going to take on so. The ropes that served her cot as springs groaned as she lay down, and she sighed, perhaps unconsciously, but obviously with weariness. She sounded old and sad, and Poe felt even guiltier. Ostentatiously, he busied himself with fetching Virginia's poem and bringing it to the candle, and he arranged a pleased and interested expression on his face, for Muddy's benefit if she chanced to be watching.

Let's see. Written in a round, childish hand, but obviously Virginia's best effort, for there wasn't a single ink blotch on the page. Written lovingly, and the first letters of the lines, he saw at his first scan, spelled out Edgar Allan Poe. As for the verse, dear God! it seemed a pathetic enough first effort at a poem. When she was a girl he had taught her French, algebra and the harp. He might have been better advised to teach her something about poetry, because surely she was capable of more than these halting rhymes, these naïve expressions. Let's see:

> Ever with thee I wish to roam—
> Dearest my life is thine.
> Give me a cottage for my home
> And a rich old cypress vine,
> Removed from the world with its sin and care
> And the tattling of many tongues.
> Love alone shall guide us when we are there—
> Love shall heal my weakened lungs;
> And Oh, the tranquil hours we'll spend,
> Never wishing that others may see!
> Perfect ease we'll enjoy, without thinking to lend
> Ourselves to the world and its glee—
> Ever peaceful and blissful we'll be.

That was all, except for a carefully inked date, "Saturday February 14, 1846." Should have been a comma between "Saturday" and "February." And to rhyme "Tattling of many tongues" with "Heal my weakened lungs." Dear God.

Yet, dear God, did she really feel so? "Love alone shall guide us . . . love shall heal my weakened lungs." It was the cry of a grown, feeling woman. Those lines, those awkward, horribly pathetic, pathetically horrible lines: "Love shall heal my weakened lungs, and oh, the tranquil hours we'll spend, *never wishing that others may see.*"

Little Virginia. His own little Virginia, dying in the next room. She loved him, and she wanted him to herself. Could he, in her last days, offer her less?

"Don't cry, Eddy," said a soft voice from the darkness, and Poe jerked.

"I'm not crying," he said.

"Sissy didn't really mean to complain in her poem," Muddy said. Her voice seemed to smile in the darkness, as if she were trying to cheer him. "You poets, you all get carried away, now, don't you?"

He wiped his face with the back of his hand. "Right you are, Muddy. Anyway, it's a sweet poem. Listen, Muddy, would you remember to do something for me tomorrow? I want you to buy me a lemon. Somebody said to try hot lemon juice with sugar. I think I'm catching a cold."

She was all solicitude and wanted to get up and mix him a dose of cayenne pepper and turpentine to rub on his chest, but he put her off until the morning. He took his nightshirt to Virginia's room and stood for a long time, looking at her dim form, thinking, before changing his clothes in the chilly room.

In the morning, when Muddy went out, she could also drop a note by the Bartletts' house breaking his tomorrow's appointment with Fanny. When Muddy got back, maybe he could talk to her about new lodgings. It would probably be best to make a joke about it. A cypress vine, they were frost-tender, weren't they? They could tease Sissy about imagining cypress vines in the climate of New York. God knew where he could find a cottage in or about New York, but in the morning maybe he would think of something.

Tonight, Poe braced himself to face on the morrow one of the few completely unselfish acts of his life. He would break off with Fanny. For Virginia's atrocious little poem had broken his heart.

Book III

VIRGINIA

*An opiate vapour, dewy, dim,
Exhales from out her golden rim . . .*
  The Sleeper

1

To get to the little village of Fordham in the spring of 1846, one could take one's private carriage, or, failing that, board one of the New York & Hudson Railway cars that headed north nearly every hour from the depot near New York's City Hall. Disembarking at a stop called Williamsbridge, a country station too small to boast a post office or even stores of any kind, one then walked a mile and a half along an old stage road named the Kingsbridge Highway. Soon one could hear the chimes from a Jesuit school, St. John's College, sounding across the fields, and a few farmhouses began to appear, lining the highway at intervals. A woodcock might twitter overhead. Bees hummed sleepily.

This was the village, and here, on an acre of grassy land, Poe finally found Virginia's cottage. It had cherry trees and lilac bushes, if not her cypress vine. It was some thirteen miles from the city, and at first Poe thought with satisfaction that it should be amply far from tattling tongues. But prosperous husbands and carriages were common possessions of ladies with literary inclinations, and it was with only a familiar feeling of exasperation, not surprise, that he heard Muddy call to him, one morning in late May when they were still trying to get settled in the cottage, that another carriage was stopping at the gate.

Poe put down his saw and made a face. Virginia made the same face and giggled at him. They had been cutting off two of the posts of her bed. She had chosen one of two small rooms, in the garret, as always, as her bedroom, with Poe's room next door, but the eaves were so low that her bed would not fit next to the windows. Although the windows were small, like square-shaped portholes, she thought she would like to see the sunrise through them, hence the carpentering job.

"I'll bet it's Mrs. Lewis," Poe grumbled. He rolled down his shirt sleeves and picked up his coat.

"She took the train last time," Virginia said. "Maybe it's Mrs. Ellet again."

"She was only here a few days ago."

Elizabeth Ellet had, in fact, left in what looked like a huff, a circumstance which Poe put down to his having ignored her as much as possible, leaving her to be entertained by Muddy and Virginia. It was one way to try to discourage her. Poe and Virginia looked at one another in unspoken sympathy and understanding. They had never spoken of Fanny or the other ladies, and Poe had no way of knowing if Virginia realized he had let the affair with Fanny quietly trail off. No more stolen visits. No poems. Fewer letters and finally no letters, until one from Fanny last week thanking Poe belatedly but fervently for a glowing review of her poetry that he had written, as a last act of loyalty, before the move to Fordham.

It all seemed so long ago. Poe had been ill, first his invented cold becoming a reality, then a long siege of fever with headaches so bad that he had been near collapse. He had been able to write little of late, but he had made enough prior sales to be able to keep Virginia in medicine and buy simple furnishings for the cottage, and he would surely write more now that he was feeling better. Virginia, too, had had a hard spring, harder, he knew. It had been fever all day, day after day, and ice packs on her chest all night, night after night. He couldn't understand why it was happening in the spring—winter was always Virginia's worst time—until Dr. Francis turned his blood cold by confiding that consumption claimed most of its victims in March, April and May, when other respiratory diseases were at their peak.

But now Virginia was well enough for Poe to hope again. She was also well enough to follow him upstairs when he went to tackle her bedstead, and to follow him downstairs as he prepared to endure another tutorial session with Stella Lewis.

Stella Lewis. It was Muddy's fault that he had to put up with the fat, gaudily dressed fool. Well, no, it was no one's fault, except his for getting sick and halting the movements of his pen. Stella had been clever enough to realize that Muddy's begging basket might offer her an approach to the Raven, and Mr. Lewis had quietly seized the opportunity to contribute five dollars here, ten dollars there, to their Fordham household expenses. Lucky Mr. Lewis, Poe thought. The thirty or forty dollars he had placed in Muddy's open palm to date was a small enough sum to keep Stella out from under Lewis's feet, and under his own. To make matters worse, Stella couldn't seem to realize there was a difference between trying to teach her to write and actually writing the stuff himself—for her signature, naturally. With the childish pout that he found so repellent she even had begun nagging him to praise her work publicly, in exchange, no doubt, for a fee. Disgusting. His critical standards were not for sale.

Poe glanced quickly to see that the parlor was tidy. It was here that he worked with Stella at a big, round table that he had covered with green felt, tacked down with brass-headed tacks. Here he also would soon begin again on his great plans for *The Stylus*. The room was more than merely tidy, of course. Nothing in a house of Muddy's could be less than immaculate. The four simple chairs and the rocking chair gleamed with homemade polish Muddy had made from white wax, Castile soap and turpentine. The floor was scrubbed as white as flour where it bordered the matting with which the parlor was laid. Someone, either Muddy or Virginia, had put vases of wild bird's-foot violet and pansy violet in the windows. The room scarcely spoke of riches, but it was beautiful.

Poe's satisfaction with the cottage faded quickly, however, as he looked out the window to see whom Muddy was greeting. It was not loud, common Stella Lewis who had come to call after all, but the bluest of New York's bluestockings, Miss Anna Lynch, accompanied by none other than *Tribune* critic Margaret Fuller. Poe went into a brief panic. How would the simple cottage look to their critical eyes? He cringed as he realized the parlor was filled with the smell of stew simmering in Muddy's kitchen across the passage. The butcher's scraps he had regretfully thought so skimpy when she bought them from a grocery wagon that morning smelled so strongly that she might be cooking a whole cow. He stepped out with Virginia to the flagstones that served as a piazza and greeted the visitors there, hoping they would opt to sit outside in the shade of the cherry trees.

Then both ladies looked at him so strangely that he cringed again. His series on New York's literati, long since paid for and the money spent, had begun in last month's *Godey's*. While he had praised Nat Willis and Margaret Fuller in his first installment—attacking only that swine Harry Franco, who kept writing so many ugly things about him—perhaps he had been just the tiniest bit malicious in his remarks about Miss Fuller. It looked as if she had come to have it out with him. What a pity that Miss Lynch had seen fit to accompany her. Well, there was nothing for it but to face up manfully to the coming attack.

He greeted them, hoping he sounded sincere as he repeated the usual phrases: Unexpected pleasure . . . delighted to see . . . Miss Lynch responded with the usual remark about the cottage's charm. She seemed uncomfortable, and she added, as though seeking some further topic of conversation, "Mr. Poe, why have you a bobolink in a cage?"

She gestured. On the biggest cherry tree shading the piazza Poe had driven nails so that Muddy could put the parrot's cage outside on pretty days. The parrot now had a neighbor, a full-grown bobolink that one of the neighbor children had found with a broken wing and had brought hopefully to Virginia for mending. She mended their dolls and sewed them doll dresses. Why not a bobolink too? Virginia undertook the chore of explaining the bird's hospitalization to Miss Lynch, adding that it seemed to be making good progress. Margaret Fuller looked on impatiently, her prim mouth closed tightly. So Poe gave her her opening.

"Well, Miss Fuller, and what did you think of my sketch of you in last month's *Godey's?* Were you pleased?"

"If not quite that, neither was I displeased," the drawling Miss Fuller allowed. "It does not pertain to our errand, but since you have brought the matter up, I might add that I do not approve of passing literary chitchat off on the public in the guise of critical opinion."

"Come now," Poe said, "the discussions are not meant as full-fledged critical judgments. I am preparing a book on American letters which I assure you will go deeper than just these little impressions. They are designed merely to introduce the readers of our contemporary magazines to literary figures. Meanwhile, however, you must grant that I have contributed to your well-deserved fame. I have a letter from Mr. Louis Godey that you must see. The May edition with your sketch sold out in New York and Boston even before the first of May, and he is enlarging the printing for the rest of the series."

"It would be better if you would reserve your private letters for your own eyes, Mr. Poe, instead of showing them to all the world," Miss Fuller said.

"Now, Margaret, really," Miss Lynch admonished.

"No, Anna, it must be said. You see, Mr. Poe, it is about *letters* that we have come. Mrs. Poe, Mrs. Clemm, I hope you will excuse us. Mr. Poe, I think it would be better if we spoke to you privately."

"Just a minute," Poe said. "I can think of nothing about any letters that we cannot discuss in front of my wife and mother."

"Well, now that I think of it, I suppose not," Margaret Fuller said sarcastically. "In fact, to be specific it was a letter Mrs. Clemm showed Mrs. Elizabeth Ellet that sent us on this unwanted errand."

"What letter?" Poe said. "Muddy, did you show Mrs. Ellet a letter?"

Muddy said, "Well, I . . . there may have been a letter from Mrs. Osgood lying out."

Miss Fuller said, "Mrs. Ellet clearly told us that you read it aloud to her, Mrs. Clemm, while your daughter sat by and laughed."

Her voice was stern, and Muddy and Virginia both reddened. Seeing this, Poe reddened himself. "If what you say is true, Miss Fuller, then I'm very sorry to hear it," he said.

"I didn't read it aloud," Muddy said defensively. "She must have read it herself."

"Then I am even sorrier," Poe said. He chose Miss Lynch's long, intelligent face as the one to which he preferred to address his words. "I do hope you understand. Mrs. Osgood has long been a family friend, and the kind thoughts in her letters refer to all of us. Her last letter, for example, was written to thank me for a review, and of course she also asked about my mother and my wife. But I am sure that Mrs. Osgood did not expect her letter to be read by any passerby, and I am deeply disappointed in Mrs. Ellet that she would have stooped to reading other people's correspondence."

"I cannot debate that, Mr. Poe," Miss Lynch said uncertainly. "Especially since I fear that . . . that from what Mrs. Ellet said, the letter may have been unduly . . . well, *intimate*. Mrs. Ellet spoke to Mrs. Osgood, and Mrs. Osgood agreed that . . . that . . ."

"In short," Margaret Fuller concluded crisply, "we have been delegated to request that you hand over to us any and all compromising letters that Mrs. Osgood has ever written you. They will, of course, be returned immediately to Mrs. Osgood, unread."

Poe blinked, absorbing the insult. Fanny's last letter compromising? Effusive, maybe, but he had received far more intimate letters from Fanny in the past. And they hardly held a candle to those Mrs. Ellet penned. Incensed, he burst out, "Mrs. Ellet had better come and look after her own letters! 'Compromising.' Indeed!"

No sooner were the incautious words out than he regretted them. No matter that the woman might be as base, as perfidious, as the jealous Elizabeth Ellet. It was not honorable for a gentleman to betray a woman's confidence, or even to imply that there was anything to betray. Caught up in anger, alarm and in simultaneous shame, he looked bewilderedly at Muddy. But it was Virginia who came to his rescue.

"Mrs. Osgood's letters are in my husband's secretary, where he keeps all his correspondence," she said in a shy but resolute voice. "There is nothing even a little bit compromising about them, unless I mistake the way all poetical ladies address all poetical gentlemen, but they *are* Mrs. Osgood's private letters, and I scarcely see how we can deliver them to anyone else's hands. My husband will write to her, and if she wishes their return, they will be bundled up and sent off immediately."

Margaret Fuller looked as surprised as if a chickadee had flown down and pecked her. She said, "That's all very well, Mrs. Poe, but we were specifically instructed to bring back her letters in person. Perhaps she, ah, didn't wish to entrust them to the mails."

Virginia turned a flushed face to Anna Lynch. "You have offered us your friendship and hospitality often in the past, Miss Lynch, and I am aware that such bonds are sacred. Can you give me your word that this is Mrs. Osgood's wish?"

Miss Lynch bent her bonneted head. "It is her wish."

"Then . . . Eddy, shall I fetch the letters?"

"I'll get them," Poe said. He bowed with what dignity he could muster. "Ladies." He turned on his heel and walked back into the cottage.

Fanny's letters were where Virginia had said, in his sturdy wooden secretary. Poe was a methodical man, at least in small things, as writers must be, and the letters were neatly filed by date. They made a hefty stack. He had taught Muddy and Virginia never to dust or otherwise tamper with his notes, annotated books, private memoranda or other papers once they were put away, and he had

had no qualms about filing Fanny's least discreet letters alongside the merely imprudent ones. He made a package of them and addressed them, "Mrs. Frances Sargent Osgood," and glanced out the window. Margaret Fuller was standing next to Muddy, both looking red-faced and grim, both silent. Anna Lynch was staring up at the caged bobolink in the cherry tree, and she looked uncomfortable and sad. Virginia was where? Yes, here inside, standing in the doorway of the parlor. She was looking the other way, waiting to serve him, but, poor little darling, also trying to give him privacy. Beside her, the cat had appeared from somewhere, her fur smelling of bracken and lush grass and . . . blood? As he gazed at her, Catarina closed her beautiful gold-green eyes, heavy with undiscovered murders. He heard the first, faint beginnings of a purr.

"Here, Sissy, give these to Miss Lynch," Poe said. "And good riddance to them."

She risked a smile as she took them. "Isn't it horrid?" she said. "I do believe I hate all literary ladies."

"I'm not sure they deserve the title of ladies," Poe said. "But, one must be a gentleman." He turned back to the secretary and reached for Elizabeth Ellet's letters. His incautious remark about them would surely get back to her. There was only one way to defuse the diabolical malignity which would surely follow. He would package every letter she'd ever written him and take them to New York that very afternoon and deliver them to her house with his own hands.

Virginia still lingered. Poe smiled and indicated with a nod that she should go. "Good riddance," he said slowly, "to *all* of them."

2

To Poe's irritated amazement, the fragile sanctuary he was trying to build for Virginia at the Fordham cottage was next invaded by an angry gentleman who introduced himself as Mrs. Ellet's brother and demanded the return of the very letters that Poe had already left with a servant at Mrs. Ellet's door. There was obviously some mistake, and Poe packed the fellow off with the advice that he have his sister consult with the servant, whom he carefully described.

So he was doubly amazed and deeply shocked when, deciding to go to the city a few days later on literary business, he encountered a bombshell.

Upon leaving the depot, Poe first walked up to Gabriel Harrison's tea shop to drop three jars of wild strawberry preserves sent by Muddy to thank Gabriel for another present of coffee. "Mr. Poe!" gasped Gabriel, looking up from the tobacco counter at the tinkling of the bell at the front door. "What are you doing here? Don't you know that man is out looking for you with his pocket full of pistols?"

"Wha— What man?" Poe stammered.

"That Mr. Lummis," Gabriel said. In his distress he literally wrung his hands. "Oh, Mr. Poe, it was madness to come out of hiding! What if he walked by and saw you?"

"But I haven't *been* in hiding," Poe said. "And who is Mr. Lummis? I don't know a Mr.—" He paused and felt his face grow warm as he remembered. "Oh. You mean Mrs. Ellet's brother. But I saw Mr. Lummis only a few days ago, and—"

"I know, I know, the whole city knows," Gabriel said agitatedly. "Oh, Mr. Poe, they're saying terrible things. They're actually saying you demanded money from that woman in exchange for her love letters. Dr. Griswold said—"

"Griswold!" Poe said through gritted teeth. "I might have known his hand would be in this. He's back from Charleston?"

"Certainly, yes, that's a frightful scandal too. He's separated from the Jewish lady he married. She made him sign away his legal rights to all her wealth, but not before he demanded and got a round thousand dollars to reimburse him for his 'expenses' in contracting the marriage. They say— Oh! Where is my mind? Here I stand gossiping, and that Mr. Lummis might come shoot you at any moment. Mr. Poe, please, for my sake, you must return Mrs. Ellet's letters. She's circulating the most terrible stories about you and Mrs. Osgood, and—"

Poe was rapidly becoming as agitated as Gabriel. "I *did* return them," he burst in. "My God, Gabriel, how could you think otherwise? Oh, that woman! You mean she's actually still claiming she hasn't received her letters?"

Gabriel nodded excitedly. "And Mr. Lummis says that before he'd let her pay you a penny for them he'll shoot you out of hand. Did she lie to him? You really did return them?"

"Of course I did."

"Then perhaps he'll only challenge you to a duel for threatening to make her letters public. But, Mr. Poe, oh! You'll be shot one way or the other! And all because of a jealous woman's wrath!"

Gabriel's flood of terrified predictions was dammed by the tinkling of the bell. A young matron swept in and headed for the tea bins. Gabriel cast Poe a conspiratorial glance and went to serve her, obviously hoping to hurry her away again.

Left to himself, Poe struggled for breath. His heart was beating rapidly. The heavy smell of tobacco so prevalent in Gabriel's shop seemed suddenly suffocating. Poe stared about him for a moment, then rushed out the door. Gabriel called after him, but Poe hurried on down Broadway. He had no certain destination in mind, and he cursed when he discovered he was still carrying the three jars of preserves. What to do with the damned things? What to do about *everything?*

He'd have to have a pistol. Poe stopped abruptly, and three whispering shopgirls following hard on his heels all but ran into him. He started to turn back to Gabriel's. But no, a man like Gabriel Harrison couldn't be counted upon to have a pistol. Someone with a fiery temper. Someone given to quarrels. Who? Who, among his acquaintances in the city?

Poe rushed on, his brain caught in the whirl of the maelstrom, and he thought it only a happy accident that he found himself nearing the corner of Broadway and Duane Street. Thomas Dunn English and the pleasant young man who had briefly bought into the dying *Broadway Journal,* Thomas Lane, shared rooms there that served them as both offices and living quarters. Poe charged up the stairs. The servant knew Poe well and only looked surprised by Poe's haste as he ran in. The two men were not alone. A professor from New York University appeared to be paying a morning call, along with a nephew of former President Tyler. The professor turned to Poe with a welcoming smile, but Poe was too beside himself for good manners. He dropped his cane and the strawberry preserves on a table and blurted to young Lane, "Stand my friend, Tom, as I expect to be challenged!"

Lane's nose twitched like a startled rabbit's. "But who . . . what?" he sputtered.

"Be careful, Tom," English said sharply. He rose from his chair, his tall, well-built body tense. "Don't let yourself get involved in this affair."

"Ah, English, I'd hoped to see you too," Poe panted. "Loan me a pistol. There's a madman combing the streets for me. If he doesn't wait to challenge me, I must be able to defend myself from attack."

"I'll loan you nothing," English said. "Your surest defense against an attack from Mr. Lummis would be a retraction of unfounded charges."

It was like running into a stone wall at full gallop. Poe blinked at English, trying to grasp his meaning. "Come, English," he said, "are you still angry just because we had a quarrel? That's all forgotten, I assure you. I . . . I was given to spreeing upon an extensive scale when last I saw you. I assure you, I can't even remember why we fell out. Come, I apologize. Here is my hand."

"Which I refuse," English said smugly.

Poe's face darkened. "Is that your final word? While my friendship may be of small service to you, my enmity might be dangerous."

"I shun your friendship to the same degree that I despise your enmity," English said. He glanced at the trio of uncomfortable onlookers with a small smile that seemed to say, "There, didn't I insult Poe nicely?"

Poe felt himself begin to lose his temper and his head again. He tried to hold steady, but the arrogant young ass standing before him was exasperating him beyond endurance. Great God, English should be the last fellow in the world to condemn a man for hot words passed when one had had a glass or two. Hadn't he helped get out English's paper, not only here in New York but once back in Philadelphia when English was himself out on a spree? But wait. There was more than one insult here. What was it the ass had said first?

Poe began to tremble, but he still tried for self-control. "Pardon," he said stiffly, "but I was distracted a moment earlier. Would you kindly repeat what you said about 'unfounded charges'? I'm not sure I understand."

English gestured at Tom Lane and the two guests. "Really, Poe," he said, "no gentleman could possibly discuss the affairs of a great and blameless lady in front of others."

With growing anger, Poe said, "Great and blameless, is she? Do I take it that you have enjoyed a recent conversation with this 'lady'?"

"That has been my privilege," English said with a bow. "And now, Poe, I really must ask you to leave. You are interrupting—"

"And just what was it this lady told you?" Poe demanded. "That she had never received a certain packet of letters?"

English was obviously enjoying himself immensely. "You force me to speak," he said. "I cannot have my friends listening to your infamous implication that there ever *were* any letters. There's no use in trying to blacken her name, Poe, by continuing to claim that any letters were ever written to you that might be compromising to the reputation of the esteemed lady in question. Abject poltroon! If you have letters, produce them! Otherwise, leave instantly, before I'm tempted to throw you out or shoot you myself in defense of her honor!"

It was too much. Without thought, without plan, Poe threw himself on English, fists flailing. He landed a left square on his enemy's snout. English let out a squeal and swung back at Poe.

"Oh! Oh!" Tom Lane yelped. The President's nephew leaped out of his chair, but only to run behind it, while the professor and Lane rushed to try to break up the fight.

The professor grabbed English around the waist, but English shook him off and charged in again. Poe got three more good licks into English's face and shoulders before catching a hard blow to the chest. He went down, and English and the professor fell on top of him, English and Poe still grunting and punching. Fingernails clawed Poe's cheekbone, but he couldn't even gasp. His chest felt as if it had caved in, and breath came hard.

Wriggling, arms flying, Poe and English were pulled apart by the feet, and Poe rose shakily on one knee, fists doubled in front of him.

"Mr. Poe, oh, no, please, here now, gentlemen, control yourselves," the professor chanted, while young Lane grappled with the struggling English and sputtered, "Dammit, English, now, stop. Now, listen here. Now, stop this right now."

The quick exchange of blows had taken perhaps ten or fifteen seconds, but Poe felt as if he'd run ten miles at top speed. Shaking, fighting to breathe, he automatically tried to tidy his clothing. His collar. Had he lost a collar button? Careful, his cheek was bleeding. Surely he'd brought a handkerchief, where was his handkerchief?

"I'll kill you for this, Poe," English barked.

"You'll have your opportunity," Poe barked back. "The Weehawken Heights? Tomorrow morning?"

"Gentlemen, gentlemen, you know that dueling is illegal," the professor said.

"Only the survivor need concern himself with that," Poe said haughtily.

Tom Lane picked up Poe's cane. The table on which Poe had left it had overturned in the scuffle. "I'm sorry, Mr. Poe, it looks like your parcel has broken," Lane said. He retained the cane cautiously and poked at the leaking jars of preserves. "Is it . . . ? It's . . ."

"Nothing," Poe said. "A small gift for a friend. I regret the damage to your carpet."

"Oh, damn the carpet," Lane said. "Mr. Poe, *I'm* your friend. Or I hope at least you still regard me as such. And for the sake of our friendship, I beg you to forget this nonsense about a duel. English, if you say another word, I'll . . . I'll . . . You must apologize to Mr. Poe. There has been no challenge, do you understand me?"

"Apologize?" English snorted. "Never." But he had no further word to say about dueling.

Lane and the professor looked at each other as if despairing of a reconciliation between the two men. The quarters were English's, and it was obviously up to Poe to leave. His heart was still racing and his breath coming with so much difficulty that he allowed Professor Ackerman to lead him out into the hallway, and there Lane joined them with Poe's cane and a wet towel to clean the blood from his cheek.

"Mr. Poe, you must not fight Mr. Lummis, either," he said worriedly, dabbing at Poe's cheek. "I gather from what you said that Mrs. Ellet already has any letters that concerned her. I'll go talk to her brother. I'm sure there's a way to settle all this amicably."

Poe laughed hopelessly. "Amicably?" he said. "I'm afraid, Tom, that you don't know Mrs. Ellet."

"Nor do I care to," the young man said. His mouth tightened. "The interest she has lately taken in English can do him as little good as the interest she took in you. Someone should write her husband about the ruckus she's been kicking up, but I'm afraid only she is ignoble enough to write the kind of disgusting anonymous letter appropriate to the dissemination of such gossip."

The professor chimed in sympathetically, "Really, Mr. Poe, no one of any intelligence took her accusations against you seriously. 'Hell hath no fury,' you know. Surely everyone understands all this teapot tempest has blown up solely from her jealous rage. It's widely known that you, er, preferred another lady to her."

But their efforts to console him left Poe feeling as sick as before. Sicker. It was all too obvious that intimate details of his overly intimate affairs had become common knowledge to the whole of the city. What more were the gossips saying? What more would they say in the future? This set-to with English would only add fuel to the fire.

Wearily, Poe brushed off his hat and put it on. "I want to apologize to you for all this," he said. "My part in it has been none too noble either, I fear. But I'd like the two of you to know that I . . . well, you may not credit this, but I had turned over a new leaf. I thought I had put all these . . . these matters behind me. But I fear the tender green of my new leaf has . . . has . . ."

He couldn't go on. He felt too sick. He bowed and left, walking slowly down the stairs. It wouldn't be easy. He had to walk all the way down crowded Broadway to the depot, and then endure the long ride on the cars, and then the long walk from the station, and then he would finally be home.

Home. Home to Virginia's shattered sanctuary. For he knew now, all too dismally, that his bright new leaf had already withered and fallen in a dung heap.

3

Poor Eddy. Virginia was worried sick about him, because *he* was so sick. People just wouldn't stop writing letters and telling him what was happening, and none of it was good. Mrs. Osgood had fled the city, going to Albany. Eddy's foes said he fled too, for he came home to the cottage and to bed in the feverish state that all kinds of stimulants, whether bottled or emotional, often reduced him to. He felt so bad that he only listened listlessly to Dr. Francis when the funny old doctor rode all the way out to the country two days later to talk to him about Mrs. Ellet's brother and some terrible duel. Dr. Francis broke off the discussion to make a brief examination of Eddy. He listened all over poor Eddy's chest and asked gruff questions about pains in the head and chest, looking disquieted, and he looked no more satisfied when he rode away again with what he came for: a short letter, written at Dr. Francis's advice, to the terrible brother, excusing any incautious statement about any lady or ladies on grounds that amounted to a fit of insanity.

Muddy wrote the letter, of course, copying Eddy's handwriting. She and Dr. Francis decided that was best, and of course Muddy could copy Eddy's handwriting so beautifully that no one would ever know the difference. That way they didn't have to disturb Eddy with it, and some excuse was necessary, explained Dr. Francis, who had been in busy consultation with Mr. Thomas Lane. By having returned Mrs. Ellet's letters in a gentlemanly fashion, Eddy had deprived himself of the opportunity of providing any ungentlemanly proof of their existence. Virginia found it all too awful, and sighed to be quits with the subject.

But the subject would not be quits with Eddy. You'd think Mr. Gabriel Harrison and Mr. Lane and so many of Eddy's other friends would know better, but they kept writing him worried letters, telling him that new rumors were now circulating freely in New York circles, charging Eddy with being, at best, the most awful kind of a liar, and at worst . . . Well, she didn't like thinking of the worst. The nasty anonymous letters, addressed to her, had also started coming again. Virginia hated them most of all. Each time one came she told Muddy she wouldn't read the next, but then the next one came and she had to know, so she read it after all. They made her feel almost as sick as poor Eddy. But at least *he* didn't have to read them. He was upset enough as it was.

"The lion of last season is now a pariah," Virginia overheard him solemnly tell Muddy. Many former friends cut him. Editors began to avoid him. Almost worse to Eddy, some of the letters friends kept writing warned him that Reverend Griswold was insinuating himself into the social position Eddy had left vacant. Then he found out about the letter Muddy had written for him, and things were really terrible for a day or two. Eddy said it just seemed to confirm what a New York paper had already written about him, some ugly joke about Eddy's articles for *Godey's* on the New York literati, and how the students at Dr. Arthur's grammar school made a pilgrimage to Bloomingdale to gaze upon the asylum where Eddy was reported to be confined, in consequence of his immense mental efforts in writing the articles having turned his brain.

"Now people will start saying I'm mad," Eddy told Muddy grimly. He worried and worried over that and finally figured out that Dr.

Thomas Dunn English had maybe written the article. It was from the *Mirror*, of all places, but of course nice Mr. Willis and General Morris didn't run the *Mirror* any more. Eddy said the people who took it over were apparently his foes, like Mr. Lewis Gaylord Clark, who just kept on writing mean things about Eddy, and Reverend Dr. Griswold, who kept on saying them, and Dr. English, who now did both.

Eddy explained that he still had *Godey's* in Philadelphia and a few other outlets, but he lacked any powerful outlet in New York and was left voiceless in the face of new attacks. He was so upset about it that Virginia went to her room and cried. She had to take more medicine that night before she could stop coughing and go to sleep, and that upset Eddy all over again. He told her he had retouched his article on Thomas Dunn English and asked Mr. Louis Godey to run the piece in the next number and they'd see that the lion still had fangs. He seemed to think that would help her stop crying and coughing but she couldn't stop. They both had to stay in bed most of the next week, and Muddy had to run her legs off taking care of them. Only Catarina was happy. She liked the cottage and the woods, and she liked it when people had to stay in bed. Toward dawn, after the morning coughing, a blackbird would whistle and the bobolink in the cage would wake up and answer it and Virginia could see color begin to appear through her east window, and then Catarina would appear on the roof and want in to rest from her night's hunting. She would fall soundly asleep in the crook of Virginia's arm, her mouth open and her teeth all showing, and Virginia would put her finger on Catarina's chest to feel the fast, irregular heartbeat so she could make sure that Catarina wasn't dead.

Well, then things didn't get much better. Silly Stella Lewis stayed away for several weeks, and Eddy said that was one fair-weather friend he was happy to get rid of, but then she started coming back again. She would talk and talk to Muddy in the kitchen, then Muddy would talk and talk to Eddy, and Eddy would say he'd rather die than write reviews of her rubbish and try to get his friends to print them, and Muddy would go back downstairs looking worried, and Eddy would lie in his own room looking sad. Poor Eddy, he got sad sometimes. It wasn't like one of his conditions. It was something else. Nothing cheered or comforted him. He'd say that his life seemed wasted, and the future looked like a dreary blank.

But at least the sad spells, like his conditions, always went away again, and this one did. The weather got awfully hot and muggy, but Virginia started feeling better anyway. Before long Eddy could carry her downstairs to sit on the piazza to watch while Muddy knitted more purses and Eddy worked in the garden. Catarina delicately sniffed every spade of earth they turned over and committed naughty acts in the seed beds. Muddy said plant vegetables, but Virginia and Eddy said no, flowers. Eddy loved flowers. He loved to touch them, and it made him sad when they died.

At night, heat lightning danced over the granite ridge in back of the cottage where Eddy liked to walk, and heat lightning began to dance at the big round table where Eddy started back to writing. Dr. English wrote a lot of new insults about Eddy in the *Mirror*, and Eddy looked both outraged and happy. He said he would fix Dr. English and the *Mirror* and, to boot, Harry Franco, because it looked like Harry Franco was writing a lot for the *Mirror* now, and Harry Franco was one of Eddy's foes too. So Eddy wrote some insults back, but he also went off to the city and consulted a lawyer. Eddy and the lawyer decided to file suit for damages against the *Mirror* and Eddy said they'd win a lot of money because Dr. English had made the fatal mistake of repeating that old false charge that Eddy had bilked a merchant by passing a forged check. Eddy felt so good about it that he also wrote a new tale, all about revenge and retribution and a man who lured his foe to a deep, deep cellar and walled him up and just left him there. He called it "The Cask of Amontillado."

After that, Mrs. Fanny Osgood's husband threatened to sue Mrs. Elizabeth Ellet for libel if she didn't stop saying awful things about his wife, and Mrs. Ellet had to apologize in writing before he'd stop the suit. That tickled Eddy so much that things would have been just fine, if only the weather hadn't been so hot and if Muddy would only buy a two-cent bone instead of a one-cent bone from the grocery wagon for the soup. But Muddy said she'd better not, that the dandelion greens she dug were better for you and cleaned out your system at this time of the year. In addition to her basket, Muddy now had a bucket, and every day or two she'd walk across the fields and call on one or the other of the neighbors and come home and say, "Look, they made us a present of all this extra milk," so Virginia could count on hot milk in the mornings and the slimy old eggs rarely appeared any more.

But Virginia was hungry a lot of the time. "I just can't get filled up on greens," she told Muddy. She watched greedily as the cherries ripened and said, "Hooray!" on the day that Muddy told Eddy they were good and truly ripe and it was time to pick them.

Eddy looked considerably less eager. He was nibbling at his breakfast, some curds and an apple and a weak cup of twice-boiled coffee, and he said hesitantly, "I'd thought I might go to Brooklyn and call on Mr. and Mrs. Lewis today."

To Virginia's surprise Muddy's gray eyes glistened with sudden tears. "Oh, son," Muddy said gratefully. "I'll go brush your town clothes."

A little guiltily, Eddy said, "No, they've waited this long, they can wait until tomorrow. If we leave the cherries longer, the birds will take them all. How do you feel this morning, Sissy? Well enough to help me?"

"Yes!" Virginia said.

"No, Eddy, she might get overtired," Muddy said cautiously, but within five minutes Virginia had talked Muddy out of that and talked herself into Muddy's big white apron. She ran outside to sit on the grass under the trees and catch the cherries when Eddy threw them down.

It was a beautiful morning, drenched with light. Big, orange bumblebees buzzed all about them, and Catarina, who followed them out to the piazza, eyed them with bored disdain. Muddy brought out the parrot and hung it in the cherry tree next to the bobolink, which Eddy had decided to keep for the sake of its songs if it would only ever learn how to sing. Catarina watched with the same disinterest until the moment that Eddy chose a tree and stepped up agilely into its branches.

"Mouek," Catarina said, as if in sharp surprise. The fur of her cheeks swelled, and her whiskers twitched forward stiffly.

Virginia burst out laughing. "Look," she called up to Eddy. "Catarina is asking what in the world you're doing up in a tree."

"I'm exploring a new universe," Eddy called down. "It's green and crimson and brilliant blue sky above. Heavens, if this is what birds see all the time, I wish I were a bird."

"Then be careful, bird," Virginia laughed, "because here comes the cat."

Strong claws digging into the bark, Catarina followed Eddy up the tree. She disappeared among the leaves. Virginia could see Eddy's nice gaitered shoes standing on a branch above her, but she could see nothing else, and she started when a big bunch of cherries fell like a cannonball into her lap.

"Oh-o-o-o," she cried. "Oh, the sky is falling!" She gathered the cherries to her face. They were warm from the sun. Large, dark cherries, darker than crimson, redder than red. Virginia popped two into her mouth, and the sweet juice flooded her tongue and ran down over her chin.

"You're not supposed to eat them as fast as we pick them," Eddy's voice said from above her head, and she looked up to see his face smiling down at her. More cherries fell, bunch by sweet, ripe bunch as Eddy tossed them down to her, and despite her continued munching, the cherries gathered in Virginia's apron in an overflow of red.

A little neighbor girl, Susie Cromwell, stopped in the road in front of the cottage and appeared to be staring hard at the tree, and Virginia waved to her gaily and cried, "Good morning, Susie. Come and have some cherries."

The child approached a few steps, then stopped and peered some more. "Mrs. Poe," she piped, "I can see your cat up in the tree."

"Yes, she likes to climb," Virginia said.

"Will she throw some cherries down just for me?" the little girl said wonderingly.

Virginia burst out laughing again. "Oh," she laughed. "Oh, that's too funny. Eddy, did you hear Susie? She thinks it's Catarina who's picking the cherries. Oh. Oh."

She laughed so hard she had to stop eating the cherries. She laughed with her white face thrown back, eyes dazzled by the sun, mouth opened so wide that she thought at first Eddy had thrown a cherry directly into it when a new tide of warm crimson ran suddenly, wetly down her chin, as warm and wet and red as blood, as red as bright arterial blood.

The neighbor child, who had started toward Virginia, stopped abruptly and began to wail.

"Oh, my God!" Eddy said from above her head. Virginia looked at him guiltily. She started to pick up the hem of Muddy's apron to try to stanch the hemorrhage, but the white apron was filled with crimson cherries and already turning bright red from the stream of crimson blood.

Virginia began to choke, a tearing, suffocating sound, and she suddenly felt hot inside, and she saw Eddy spring down from the branches and felt him pick her up in his arms and saw the door of the cottage come closer as he ran, and she thought she heard him begin to shout for Muddy, but she couldn't concentrate on that because she was busy looking over Eddy's shoulder at Susie, who turned around and ran away, ran and ran, as hard as she could, but the little girl only got to run a few yards, because the universe wasn't green and crimson and brilliant blue anymore. Blackness overtook all.

4

It had been a massive hemorrhage. Virginia seldom was able to leave her bed through the rest of the hot, interminable summer.

Poe, shocked out of self-pity and the preoccupation with his own affairs, spent every free hour sitting by the side of her four-poster bed with the two knobs sawed off. If he worried that so many hours were free from the daily task of filling sheets of pale blue paper, he at least was able to be there to lift a glass of water to Virginia's mouth, to hold her hand during the attacks of knifelike pain that came now whenever she coughed hard or tried to breathe deeply, to cool with wet cloths her hot cheeks, which, no longer pale, were flushed with a pink that almost looked like the blush of health, but which was really a sign of the fever that was consuming her. Muddy's begging basket and the generosity of the neighbors in sharing fruits from their orchards and vegetables from their kitchen gardens kept the household from starving, but even though Poe surrendered to the new encroachment of Stella Lewis into his life, and sold everything he could flog himself into writing or rewriting for the loyal *Godey's* and a few small papers that were still willing to accept his material, money for Virginia's medicine grew shorter and shorter.

Muddy said it was all right, Virginia didn't really need all that laudanum. She unearthed reports of new cures. She fed Virginia butter made from the milk of cows fed in the Fordham churchyard. She poured large doses of olive oil down Virginia's throat for weeks, and when she could afford no more olive oil she brewed up her own medicine from ale, white honey and lousewort, and tried that. Coming home one evening from the high ridge in back of the cottage, where he had briefly immersed himself in contemplation of the wild Long Island hills far away over the East River, Poe found the cottage filled with the stench of burning cow dung, which Muddy was coaxing a feebly protesting Virginia to inhale through a reed. Poe put an end to that, and Muddy settled thereafter for steam from a croup kettle, which at least sometimes seemed to soothe Virginia's coughing. But nothing could soothe the intense perspirations, the palpitations, the writhing pangs in the stomach that came when they had to decrease her daily doses of laudanum to half, to a quarter, then to an eighth. It was a bad time.

That the curious paid occasional calls to stare at the outcast lion made matters no better. It was a struggle even to buy country cider to offer them as a simple refreshment. Poe groaned wholeheartedly the afternoon that Muddy wearily climbed the little winding staircase to Virginia's room to tell him that the Reverend Dr. Rufus Griswold, of all people, was walking with two other visitors through their front gate. Damn him. Of all the people in the world Poe least wished to see his straitened circumstances, it was Griswold. He had surely come to gloat. "You must offer them the grapes," Poe said to Muddy. He rose from the straight-backed chair by Virginia's bed. Poor little Sissy had managed to fall asleep for a while, and he had been near to nodding himself. "I'll go down to greet them."

"But the grapes are for your dinner, along with some nice buttermilk, my boy," Muddy protested. "It's been so long since you've had grapes, and they're your favorite."

"No matter. There will be plenty of grapes when the wild ones ripen. And honor demands it."

He hurried to the door, wishing he'd had more than a moment's warning. He could have changed to his town trousers and coat. These were old. But, like Muddy's parlor, Poe's clothes were never less than immaculate, and she had inked the seams for him only night before last. At least he chanced to be wearing his now aging gaitered shoes instead of the list slippers he sometimes wore around the house to save them.

A touch to his ascot to be sure it was straight, a hand over his curly, still raven-black hair to check its tidiness, and Poe opened the door to the party of visitors with as pleasant an expression as he could muster. He was genuinely pleased to see George Colton, editor of the *American Review*, to whom Muddy had delivered another new poem just the week before. Colton and Poe had had their spats about Poe's tough criticism, but it was the *American Review*, after all, that had first accepted *The Raven*, and Poe had warmed to the man. The idea that Colton might accept the new poem warmed him still further. The well-worn words of welcome were ready once again for use, with the invariable response from a young woman who had accompanied Griswold and Colton: Charming cottage.

Griswold looked at the plain plank floors and the inexpensive chairs of the parlor with a gratified expression. He waited, smiling vaguely and saying nothing, as if to see whether Poe would offer his hand. Poe did. With a guest, there was little option, although with a Griswold, who was always pleasant to one's face and always vindictive behind one's back, there was also little point.

Immediately, Griswold began to fawn. "Well, Poe, so you're speaking to us lesser mortals?" he said. "I hear you've had a letter from Miss Elizabeth Barrett Barrett of England, recently Mrs. Elizabeth Barrett Browning, that was highly flattering about your poetry. Is it so? Did the greatest of her sex really write you?"

"Why, yes," Poe said. "I have the letter somewhere about." It was, of course, in his inside pocket, next to his heart, where Poe felt a compliment from such a personage quite properly belonged.

The young woman, one of the lesser literary lights named Mary Gove, peeked all over the lower floor of the cottage, pronounced it "a perfect doll's house" and sighed, as all city dwellers did, over the delights of living in the country. Muddy came downstairs and offered fresh cider and the grapes, which they fell upon hungrily. Poe's dinner that night, he saw, would consist only of buttermilk. When Mary Gove went upstairs with Muddy to look in on Virginia, Griswold fingered over the last half-dozen grapes in the bunch and rejected them. "Well, Poe, what are you into these days?" he asked. "We hear so little about you any more."

"Oh, Poe is busy with poetry again," Colton said, answering for him. He gave Poe a puzzled look, then added, "We read the poem you sent the *Review* in conclave, Poe, and heaven forgive us, we couldn't make head or tail to it. What's it really about? One person who read it opined it was only a hoax you're passing off for poetry, to see how far your name will go in imposing upon people."

Griswold laughed, showing wolf's teeth, and Poe felt the skin tighten across his face.

"I would endeavor to explain to you what I really meant—or what I fancied I meant by the poem, Colton," Poe said, "if it were not that I remember Dr. Johnson's bitter and rather just remark about the folly of explaining what, if worth explanation, should explain itself. I shall leave the poem to its fate, therefore, and in your good hands." He turned to Griswold with a slight smile. Now to repay him for that laugh. "As for what else I'm currently working on, I am body and soul at my book on American letters. I may even discontinue my 'Literati' in *Godey's Magazine*. The unexpected circulation of the series suggests to me that I might make a hit and some profit, as well as proper fame, by saving the material for the survey of all the salient points of American literature that I have long felt the world so badly needs. You understand. Poetry, the drama, criticism, historical writing, versification, prose, et cetera. It will contain all my critical thought. I shall, of course, refrain from referring to previous opinions by *anybody*, and I shall probably publish a few articles from it as I go along. I have one in the works called 'The Rationale of Verse' that will give you an idea of the manner in which I am writing the whole book."

"Listen, Poe," Colton said, "be sure you give me a look at that."

"Gladly." And now to push the dagger in to the hilt. "By the way, Griswold, whatever happened to that book you were going to get up on American prose writers? Have your, um, recent distractions caused you to cancel it?"

Griswold glared worriedly. As Poe knew well, he regarded all books about American literature as his personal monopoly, and had no objection whatever to widening his grasp to include British, French and, if there were such a thing, Kickapoo literature.

"Oh, no," Griswold said, as if trying to sound casual, "the manuscript is coming along nicely. It takes a little while, of course, to get the appropriate material ready on such men as will naturally appear as my 'elect' prose writers. You know. Charles Fenno Hoffman. John Pendleton Kennedy. I suppose one just can't expect men of such well-deserved renown to be quick in answering questions of a biographical nature." He smiled.

It was Poe's turn to glare, but he also felt the urge to smile back. It was hard not to admire the neatness of the counterthrust, for Poe remembered he had been quite quick in responding to Griswold's request for material for the book.

The glare overcame the smile as Griswold continued, "As for my recent distractions, well, I suppose they're no worse than any other man's. But I admit that a sham marriage and half a divorce has been as unsettling as . . . Oh, I don't know. A half-dozen love affairs, with a few duels and lawsuits thrown in? But I'm back hard at work now in Philadelphia. Of course, it looks as though I may finally have to break down and move to New York. My *Prose Writers* will be coming out the first of next year, and there's the usual new edition of my *Poetry Writers*, and then Harper and Brothers are pestering me for some sort of biographical dictionary they want me to work on nearby so they can run over every couple of hours, I suppose, and make unnecessary suggestions. But it's not an unpleasant deal. They want six volumes, and they're willing to pay a thousand dollars a year for the work. I'm holding out for twelve hundred and fifty, and I'm confident I'll get it."

Griswold positively beamed at Poe, who was unable to choke out a response. Fortunately, Goerge Colton took up the slack in the conversation with the mandatory ahs and ohs. More than a thousand a year! And Virginia was lying upstairs in torment because he could not even afford to buy her full dose of opiates.

For once in his life, Poe was glad to see his blubbery pupil, Stella Lewis, arrive, towing along with her a niece and a nephew. Having purchased the Raven's further services, she had no compunctions about afflicting him with a steadily increasing swarm of her relatives and friends, whom she brought out with her on her now frequent trips to Fordham and for whose benefit she expected Poe to perform. It meant too much company to jam into the little parlor, and therefore no further exposure for Poe to Griswold's painful prosperity. They all went out for a walk in the woods. Poe was gratified to see Stella latch onto Griswold, whom she no doubt felt could also be of service to her. Let them suffer one another's company. They fully deserved each other.

Poe would have preferred to talk to Colton. When the wolf pack pressed one too ferociously, one could perhaps unbend long enough to drop a few words of explanation about a poem born of long nights of despair over Virginia's deepening illness, long nights spent listening to her tearing cough or, when one could bear it no longer, pacing the promenade at High Bridge, the great aqueduct bearing water southward to the city, and staring upward at the pallid stars. But Mary Gove moved up to walk with him, and Colton seemed to find ample consolation in the company of Stella Lewis's young niece, so Poe cast about in his mind for something to say to the dark, thin young woman strolling beside him.

Mrs. Gove was separated from her husband. There was even talk that she was considering divorce, so she was something of a pariah, like him. She wrote odds and ends for the magazines, but she was even better known for her daring lectures on physiology to classes of females, and for lectures on mesmerism. Deep into all the current fads, she was, he thought, a mesmerist, a Swedenborgian, a phrenologist, a disciple of Priessnitz and a homeopath, and she was even said to be a fine clairvoyant who diagnosed diseases with almost infallible intuition. Thinking of this last, Poe asked her, "And how did you find my wife, Mrs. Gove?"

Mary Gove had one fine feature—a pair of keen, intelligent black eyes. These she dropped quickly at Poe's question, as if to regard a clump of wild ginseng growing at their feet. "I found her looking wonderfully young and beautiful," she said. "Her pale face, her brilliant eyes and her raven hair give her an unearthly look. One almost feels she is a lovely illusion."

"And her health, Mrs. Gove?" Poe insisted. "How did you find her health?"

"Perhaps suffering a little in this extraordinary heat," Mary Gove admitted uneasily. She seized upon the topic of the weather and added in a lighter tone, "But relief is in sight, if relief it proves to be. The winter promises to be as cold as the summer had been hot. That is, if one is to believe my landlady. She is a country woman, and I found her quivering with alarm in the kitchen while counting the layers of skin on the onions this past week. One—two—three layers of skin. She says that means a hard winter."

"Then I dread the winter," Poe said gloomily. She looked at him sympathetically, and he couldn't resist confiding, "This summer has not gone well for us, Mrs. Gove. My wife so ill, and I . . . I misled Griswold and Colton just now. I've scarcely been able to write anything for months, except the poem I offered to Colton. What in God's name will it be like this winter?"

"Surely better," she said. "When a writer's pen dries up, it is not because he has lost the way to the secret spring. Springs, well, sometimes they dry up in the fire of summer, but bubble to life again in fall's cooling rains."

"I'll hope," Poe said.

"Poor Mr. Poe," Mary Gove said softly. "It's sometimes hard to live in this world, isn't it? You remind me of the bobolink you have imprisoned, and which, by the way, you really must let go. Little 'Robert of Lincoln Green' was not meant to be caged. Haven't you seen the way he springs continually from one side of the cage to the other in that fierce, frightened way? He is as unfit to live in a cage as his jailer is to live in this worldly society in which, perhaps to our dismay, we both find ourselves."

"I am quite out of it now," Poe said.

"But no," Mary Gove said. She gestured. Stella Lewis, panting from the pace, her pink silk skirts catching on the branches of a fallen silver willow, was striving energetically to keep up with Griswold, into whose ear she poured a steady stream of prattle. "The world comes to you, and perhaps, caring for fame, you go a little too far to meet it."

The hint of criticism cooled a bit of Poe's warmth toward his sympathetic visitor. Somewhat stiffly, he said, "Fame forms no motive power for me. I write from a mental necessity—to satisfy my taste and my love of art. If there are individuals whose judgment I respect, I would choose to have their esteem unmixed with the mean adulation of the mob."

"But the multitude may be honestly and legitimately pleased," Mary Gove said. "I am no great critic like yourself, but may I tell you the personal opinion I have formed through a decade of close readings of your work? You have blazed a path into the wilderness of American letters and have set standards, both by your criticism and by your example in your poems and stories, that we of the multitude can only gain by following."

"Heart-warming praise," Poe mused, softening again, "and I thank you for it. But the multitude should have an honest leader, and not a poor man who has been paid a hundred dollars to manufacture opinions for them and fame for an author."

"Do reviewers sell their literary conscience thus unconscionably?" asked Mary Gove uncertainly.

"A literary critic must be loath to violate his taste, his sense of the fit and the beautiful," Poe said slowly. "To sin against these and praise an unworthy author is to him an unpardonable sin. But if he were placed on the rack, or if one he loved better than his own life were writhing there, I can conceive of his forging a note against the Bank of Fame, in favor of some would-be poetess who is able and willing to buy his poems and opinions."

A shocked look crossed Mrs. Gove's face, and she looked as though she wanted to protest, but they were interrupted by a shrill, laughing cry from Stella Lewis, who called, "Mr. Poe? Mr. Poe! Dr. Griswold has just bragged to me that he was a splendid athlete when he was a lad in Vermont, and I've assured him you were a splendid young athlete in Virginia. I've challenged him on your behalf to a game at leaping. To the winner, I shall dedicate my next poem. Or shall I," she concluded daringly, coyly, "instead bestow a kiss?"

"Good heavens," Mary Gove said in quiet disgust.

Poe turned on her almost fiercely, his fine eyes piercing her. "Would you blame a man for not allowing his sick wife to starve?"

He left her, and went to join the leapers.

If the Raven sold his poems to be printed as the productions of another, or if he eulogized what he despised, then the offense brought with it sufficient punishment, Mary Gove concluded as she watched the men remove rocks and fallen boughs from the little grassy area they quickly chose for the site of their contest. Poe's beautiful, fine-featured face was the saddest she had ever seen, and Mary was glad when a little gladness and excitement seemed to creep over it at the prospect of this boyish game to see who could jump the farthest. Competition, even against unworthy opponents and even with an unwanted prize, seemed to stimulate him. But then, no man who was worth anything ever really grew up.

How intent they were, setting two stones to mark a jumping-off point, discussing how much of a running start to allow each contestant. Her friend George Colton, she was amused to see, was flirting madly with Stella Lewis's young niece, even though the girl showed promise of someday following her aunt into corpulence. Mary almost laughed aloud at George's expression when the niece, with feigned shyness, jibbed at his urgings that she use her foot to mark each jumper's landing spot, and Mrs. Lewis volunteered her own foot instead. So much for George's hope of peeking at a shapely ankle.

How hot it was even here in the shade of oaks and hickories, interspersed with occasional black walnuts. The massive old black walnuts, she was pleased to see, were heavy-hung with hard green husks that would ripen soon and let drop a fine crop of nuts that would make good eating for the Poes if they did not disdain such fare. A red-winged blackbird flitted high in the branches, and a rustling at ground level was . . . but what was this? A little girl in a gingham apron.

"Hello, there," Mary said calmly, and the child came closer. She held three blue feathers in her hand and, after appearing to consider for a moment, offered them to Mary.

"Look," the child said, "these here's a blue jay's feathers. Something got him."

"Maybe he died of old age," Mary said.

"In the poor house?" the child speculated. "You're visiting Mr. Poe, aren't you? The granny is always worrying to my granny that she'll die in the poor house. They're *awful* poor, aren't they? Are you poor, or are you rich?"

"Well, I suppose I'm poor," Mary said.

"How poor?" the child inquired. She seated herself comfortably on a big rock, wanderer in the woods, spectator at a sports arena.

It looked like a good idea, so Mary sat beside her. "I'm so poor that I shall have to make up for the few shillings it has cost me to come to Fordham," Mary said, quite truthfully. "I shall have to wear fewer clean shirts, or eat a less number of oyster stews."

"Oh, do you like oysters in stews? I like them in broils."

"Dear child, I never aspire to a broil."

The little girl nodded as if finding Mary's answer entirely reasonable. "Is Mrs. Poe down yet?" she asked. "Mrs. Poe *used* to come down with her cat and cut out clothes for my doll."

Mary thought back to the large and beautiful eyes that gleamed from the young invalid's face, eyes of an unnatural brilliancy. "No," she said slowly, "Mrs. Poe may not be down for a long, long time."

The child nodded again. "What is Mr. Poe going to do with those men?"

"He's going to out-jump them," Mary said. "I expect he'll jump so hard he'll fall over and get dirt all over his knees, because Mr. Poe can't bear not to be the best at everything he does."

"Then we'd better be quiet and watch," the little girl said, and Mary earned a frown by laughing. The niece came to join them, and they waited, relaxing in the scented air, for the contest to begin. Mary breathed deeply, so deeply that an underlying bitterness that was the green walnut husks bit at her nostrils. She sat quietly, pondering her conversation with Mr. Poe. Poor bedeviled man, she could have sworn he meant Dr. Griswold when he first began to speak in that low, melodious voice of selling laudatory notices. It was well known that Dr. Griswold allotted space in his anthologies on a basis of payment received, yet no sadness etched his face. Indeed, Dr. Griswold lived better and held his head higher than many who did more and better work. He was holding his head high now, backing up one step, then another, getting ready for his run, face intent. Now he crouched slightly, motionless, gathering himself like a big cat about to spring, and as suddenly as a cat he was off.

"A fault!" the nephew cried even as Griswold was in midair. "He overstepped the mark!"

Griswold landed with a heavy grunt, and with a flash of yellow stockings Stella Lewis ran unnecessarily to mark the hole his boot heels dug into the turf. "Nonsense!" Griswold said angrily. "I was right on the mark."

"Nay, Gris," George said firmly. "Your left foot was inches beyond the rocks. Jump again."

Back he went, none too happily, while Mr. Poe actually found it possible to look cheerful for once, and Stella Lewis pranced coltishly, if a creature approaching the size of an elephant and having something of the same shape could be said to have anything at all in common with a colt. And heavens, to wear yellow stockings and a pink silk dress topped with a Brussels shawl that must have cost in the neighborhood of seven hundred dollars on an excursion to the country!

But Mrs. Lewis was enjoying herself, and so was Mr. Poe, and Mary watched with happiness in her own black eyes until all cheer was extinguished by a small but grievous tragedy.

Poe jumped last. He gave his best, for their careful pacing off of each man's leap showed that while George, the clown, had fallen far short of Griswold's mark, the tall young nephew had exceeded it by almost a full pace. Beating the nephew couldn't possibly have meant as much to Mr. Poe as beating the Reverend Griswold, but he obviously couldn't resist a challenge. He backed up perhaps thirty feet, and it looked as though he were running twenty miles an hour when he neared the jump-off point, for he sailed, sailed, sailed, legs scissoring, arms flailing for every last quarter-inch of distance, to land with a wordless shout of triumph nearly a half pace beyond the nephew.

It was a prodigious leap. It was a leap of some fourteen or fifteen feet. It was a leap that landed him with such impact that, alas! his gaiters, long worn and carefully kept, burst on the spot.

The little girl beside Mary jumped to her feet. "Oh dear," she said in a mature and conversational tone, "I'm certain Mr. Poe has no other shoes. You'd better go away now, lady. He'll feel bad 'cause he's got no shoes to change into, and you're too poor to offer him money to buy a new pair."

The niece broke into a laugh, perhaps thinking this a quaint joke on the child's part. Mary and the little girl both frowned at her.

In the arena, dear old George looked uncomfortable too. Perhaps some glimmering of understanding had even come to Stella Lewis, for she named Poe the victor without insisting on kissing him. Griswold's sharp gray eyes darted at Mr. Poe's broken gaiters like a wasp, and a profoundly satisfied expression seemed to come into them. He hummed all the way back to Mr. Poe's cottage.

At the cottage, Mr. Poe's stalwart, queenly mother-in-law looked at Mr. Poe's feet with a dismay that Mary thought she would never forget.

"Oh, Eddy," the snowy-haired old woman gasped. "How did you burst your gaiters?"

"Why, I . . . I . . ." Mr. Poe stammered in sudden confusion.

The mother-in-law tried to pass her dismay off as mere surprise. Mary took advantage of the moment to speak quickly to George Colton. He as quickly began thanking the Poes for their hospitality and asking Stella Lewis whether, since she had apparently come on the train, she didn't want to ride back with them.

Mary's little friend had come no farther than the front gate, but she didn't need the child's warning to know that they must not go inside the Poes' cottage to force the shoeless unfortunate to advertise his poverty by sitting helplessly in his broken gaiters in their midst.

She made a move toward the gate, shooing the party before her, crying, "We really must go! My, we've consumed Mr. Poe's entire afternoon!" Stella Lewis ponderously began to move, and Mary turned a sympathetic smile on Mr. Poe and his mother-in-law to thank them for the afternoon.

Mr. Poe seemed to collect himself. "Come in a moment," he said to Mary. "You can overtake the others on the road. There's something I want to give you."

This something was a pretty presentation copy of Mr. Poe's poems. He took one down from a hanging bookshelf, wrote Mary Gove's name in it and gave it to her. Mary was touched. She could be of no advantage to him at all, as George Colton and Dr. Griswold could be, and she knew Mr. Poe had given her the book purely out of friendship. The mother-in-law nervously watched the little ceremony of presentation from the doorway. Mary held back for another second when Mr. Poe stepped outside to wave good-by to the other guests.

"Mrs. Clemm, there's a small but serious matter about which I must speak to you," Mary said.

"Eddy's gaiters?" the old woman said tremulously. "Here, come into the kitchen with me for a moment."

"No, it's about your daughter's nightgowns and bedclothes. You see, Mrs. Clemm, it has long been thought that consumption is caused by minute animals, or their seed, and that it passes from victim to victim by this method. Won't you boil your daughter's things twice in lye when you wash them? I so fear that you might yourself become a victim of this disease, and whatever would your two children do without you? And if Mr. Poe were to contract it . . . Ah, I shudder!"

"Well, I suppose I could do that," Mrs. Clemm said. "But please, Mrs. Gove, tell me about Eddy's gaiters. How could this have happened? Oh, my poor Eddy."

Mary related the cause of the mishap, and Mrs. Clemm grew confidential.

"Will you speak to Mr. Colton about Eddy's last poem?" she pleaded. "If he will only take the poem, Eddy can have a pair of shoes. Mr. Colton has it. I carried it last week, and Eddy says it is his best. You will speak to him about it, won't you?"

Mary, too, had read the poem, and it might have been written in one of the lost languages for any meaning she could extract from it. But George Colton had been actively instrumental in the demolition of the gaiters, so she made up her mind to intervene.

"Of course the *American Review* will publish the poem," she assured Mrs. Clemm, "and I will ask Colton to be quick about it. But, Mrs. Clemm, I'm afraid they're never able to pay very much."

"My dear, what does that matter?" Mrs. Clemm said wearily. "The *Review* only gave Eddy ten dollars for *The Raven*, and nobody else paid him anything at all for all the reprinting they did. But even five dollars for the new poem will give Eddy another pair of gaiters, and twelve shillings over."

Mary left after that, walking rapidly along the Kingsbridge Highway to catch up with her companions, thinking of Mrs. Clemm and the poet's gaiters. She felt a little guilty over her promise about the poem. She had to presume that Mr. Poe regarded it as genuine poetry, but poor George would be stuck with having to publish the incomprehensible thing.

What was its title? Oh yes, George had laughed helplessly about it. *Ulalume*.

5

Came autumn, and with it came heavy rains, frost and the melancholy sighing of the wind in the big cherry trees outside the Fordham cottage. In October, bright crimson bunchberries were beaten from their stems to rot on the sodden forest floor, food neither for birds nor man. By chill November, when the constellation Orion, the Hunter, appeared above the eastern horizon, most of the birds had flown south along the great Atlantic flyway. The slumber of those that remained huddled in the pines was stabbed all night long by the cries of the lords of the night—the hoot of the great horned owl, the catlike scream of the barred owl, the eerie, high-pitched ululation of the screech owl, which sounded to Muddy like someone laughing uncontrollably but sounded to Poe like the terrified cry of a woman dying.

For inside the cottage, a young woman was sinking rapidly into death by the feeble light of a few tallow dips; since the owl nights had begun, they could no longer afford even homemade candles. Nor could their neighbors be of much help. Rain at harvesttime meant a bad winter for everyone, and Susie Cromwell struggled over less frequently under the weight of a heavy hamper sent by her mother, then more rarely yet.

By early December, when the heavy snows had come and the birds began to starve, no hampers arrived at all. No visitors arrived from the city, for even ladies with literary inclinations, prosperous husbands and carriages could scarcely be expected to plow through heavy snowdrifts. But Muddy did. The trains still ran, and if there were no new manuscripts on pale blue paper to carry into the city, for a little time there were the pretty knickknacks she knitted for a notion store, then books for the second-hand stores, then a treasured collection of seashells and what few good dishes she possessed for the pawnshops.

Then, when there was nothing else to sell or pawn, Poe looked at his old West Point greatcoat and thought back to Room Number 28 in the South Barracks and a dark, cold drizzling night and drawing straws with Tommy Gibson just as the bugle sounded "to quarters" to see who would go down to Old Benny's and try to refill the brandy bottle. The lot fell on Tommy, and the coin was four pounds of candles and Poe's last blanket, but hadn't the sacrifices fetched not only brandy but a tough old goose to roast in their stove?

Poe's shriveled stomach filled with a ghost of remembered warmth as he thought of the brandy and his mouth with saliva as he thought of the goose. But they needed something more urgently now—more opiates for Virginia. Her voice had sunk to a whisper and her coughing was incessant. Her eyes were hot and glassy, her heartbeat staccato, her breathing shallow and jagged. Even worse, something was happening to her stomach, and she was beginning to suffer abdominal cramps and diarrhea. Opiates to ease the pain were mandatory. Muddy went into the city with their blankets.

There was still the greatcoat left to cover Virginia, but that meant Poe had to go without it when he left her dozing fitfully later in the day and went into the woods to look for firewood. Fuel, too, was scarce. It was impossible to heat the upstairs rooms, for only the parlor had a fireplace and only the kitchen had a stove, and Poe and Muddy had moved Virginia downstairs to a little closet of a room next to the parlor in which Muddy had formerly slept. He wept, he told himself from the cold, as he clumsily chopped down a young white poplar and dragged it to the cottage with hands that had lost all feeling.

Blown on the winter wind, a pair of snowy owls passed noiselessly over his head. He gazed after them, and the numbness crept over his heart. Snowy owls, day-hunters. Snowy owls, birds that flew this far south only in severe winters when they were starved out of their icebound homes.

He had learned about them once long ago from the great explorer Jeremiah Reynolds, to whom he had applied for telling details for an adventure narrative. "Your snowy owl is a true bird of the arctic," Reynolds had said, yearningly, but his tales of long winters, of frowning white mountains of ragged ice, had been peculiarly terrifying to Poe. The story he wrote of the journey toward disaster of a youth named Pym had somehow sucked up every nightmare Poe had ever had. Now, as in the story, Poe felt himself drifting with increasing velocity through a wide and desolate sea of winter, his companion a shy, sweet young wife with violet eyes whom he was helpless to save from the embrace of the chasm which threw itself open to receive them.

There followed six bad frozen nights and six dark winter days, the first three of which Muddy spent agitating two and a half ounces of bulk opium in a pint of water, the last three of which she spent agitating the mix with a pint of grain alcohol added. On the sixth day, in a French coffeepot borrowed from Father Doucet, a scholastic at the seminary with whom Poe was friendly, Muddy percolated the brew and added two more pints of grain alcohol.

Thus Muddy manufactured homemade laudanum for the sake of economy, and thus, as Poe watched the faint white fog of Virginia's breath in the cold room, Virginia regained her serenity. The coughing decreased. She no longer writhed with the pain of the abdominal cramps. Her face smoothed out, and even her breathing seemed to come easier. Watching her, Poe was so heartened that at first he could not understand the alarmed exclamation that escaped the lips of that now rare creature, a visitor—Mary Gove, who, cheeks flushed to the color of old wine, face stiff with the cold, had become worried after hearing nothing about them for many weeks and had braved the snowdrifts to come see them.

"Oh!" said Mrs. Gove. Poe followed her gaze with bewilderment.

He was sitting beside Virginia's bed, holding her hands so they wouldn't ache with the cold, and Catarina lay cuddled against Virginia's breast, as if conscious of her great usefulness in keeping Virginia warm. The wise cat was also keeping herself warm, but Mrs. Gove couldn't know that. Virginia had the dreadful chills that accompanied her hectic fever, and she lay hugging Catarina and shivering on a straw mattress, covered only by snow-white sheets and, now that the blankets were gone, Muddy's white spread and Poe's greatcoat. Of course, now that the opiate was working Virginia no longer suffered nearly as much from the cold, but Mrs. Gove couldn't know that either.

Poe rose unsteadily to his feet. "Why, Mrs. Gove," he said. Then he paused. He had forgotten the other words. How did it go? Unexpected pleasure?

"Mr. Poe, come away instantly," Mrs. Gove said. She turned to Muddy, who was wearily slumped in the doorway, and said, "Mrs. Clemm, your daughter and Mr. Poe are freezing in here. Can't we build up the parlor fire? Surely some of the heat would reach this room."

"There's no wood," Muddy said bluntly.

"Oh dear," Mrs. Gove said. "Oh dear, I'm a fool. I only brought some Everton toffee, having heard that Mrs. Poe was fond of candy. Mr. Poe, you must eat some of the toffee immediately. The sugar is digested quickly, and it will give you strength. And you must never sit so close to Mrs. Poe's face when she's coughing that way. Mrs. Clemm, I *spoke* to you about the danger. Didn't you warn him? Oh dear, why didn't I at least bring some beef tea? My friends, forgive me. I see poor Mrs. Poe with such a heartache as the poor feel for the poor. But I have nearly two dollars. Oh, Mrs. Clemm, haven't any of you been eating? Where can I go for food? And firewood?"

"The Barthursts . . ." Muddy began uncertainly.

"No, Muddy," Poe said. "The neighbors have already spared all they can for us. As for your kind offer, Mrs. Gove, I thank you, but we can—"

"Pooh!" Mrs. Gove said, then blushed a patchy red at her lack of manners. "Forgive me, Mr. Poe, but I will writhe on my own deathbed if you don't let me be of some small assistance. Mrs. Clemm, try to get him to eat some of the toffee. I'll be back as soon as I can."

She did return, within the hour, dragging with her Father Doucet from St. John's College and, thanks to his services, a sled loaded with wood, a beef joint, bread, milk, potatoes and a half-pint of brandy. Catarina leaped off Virginia's bed meowing loudly at the smell of the beef; Muddy had left her to hunt for herself in the snow-packed fields, but when field mice and chickadees starved, so did their predators. The priest stamped the snow off his boots and rekindled the fires while Mrs. Gove tried to persuade Poe to eat a bowl of bread and warm milk, but he refused, saying dazedly that it must go to Virginia.

"But there's plenty of food, Mr. Poe," Mrs. Gove insisted.

"No, no, we must save it," he said stubbornly.

"There will be more, I promise you," she said. "I am going directly to the city to enlist the sympathies and services of a lady I know whose heart and hand are ever open to the poor and miserable."

He drew up his sagging shoulders with a touch of his old hauteur. "Poor I may be, Mrs. Gove. It would be folly in me to deny it. But the concerns of my family must not be thus pitilessly thrust before a stranger."

The young priest intervened. "Come, Poe," he said gently, "I will not speak to you of Christian acts, for don't I know from the splendid hours I've spent in your parlor that you prefer the discussion of metaphysics to that of religion? But it's hubris to turn away the helping hand of man when an hour of desperation arrives. Poe, we've been friends. Couldn't you at least have told *me* that you've been denying yourself so many necessaries and suffering both cold and hunger to provide medicines for your wife?"

"There, you see?" Poe said. "They keep saying that I am 'without friends.' It's a gross calumny, as you yourself have just proved. Even in the city of New York I could have no difficulty in naming a hundred noble-hearted men to whom, when I felt it necessary, I could apply for aid with unbounded confidence and with absolutely no sense of humiliation."

Then, suddenly, he laughed. What was that he had just said? When he felt it necessary? But here he stood, shivering weakly in a barren room and, he suspected, exuding the distinctive smell of starvation, a little like the freshly baked bread Father Doucet had brought but unpleasant, the stench of a body that had begun to feed upon itself. There was an ironic artistry about the tragedies that dogged his life. They were almost as good as his better tales.

He laughed on. Mary Gove caught Father Doucet's eye and looked questioningly at the brandy bottle, and when he shook his head she went for Muddy's homemade laudanum.

Poe saw the wordless exchange and understood instantly. He would much rather have had the brandy, but he knew it must be for Virginia, so he did not protest the glass of laudanum and water that Mrs. Gove urged him to drink. He had taken opium derivatives before, of course, as had everyone else in the world, taken it once when a terrible earache had lasted for weeks, taken it for a summer fever he had feared was cholera, even taken it occasionally back in Philadelphia in preference to alcohol when one of his unutterable depressions descended upon him, but it was only a temporary remedy and alcohol was the best solace. He swallowed it now, for the sake of the grain alcohol he had longingly watched Muddy stir into it, and as he swallowed he still thought wistfully of the brandy bottle.

But laudanum, even in the modest doses in which he had always taken it, had its own peculiar benefits. It produced a long, serene glow; the powers of thought lay dormant, while the senses were keenly living and awake. Had any fire ever been so lovely and warm as the parlor fire in front of which they seated him once they had tended Virginia? Enjoying the fire, he tried to wave away the milk toast that Mrs. Gove seemed still to be talking about, but Muddy came and spooned it into his mouth, and for Muddy's sake he swallowed it too. As the laudanum took a firmer grip on him, he became conscious of indistinct things in the air, a heaviness in the atmosphere. There was also the smell of roasting beef in the atmosphere, and he smiled vaguely at the gods' little joke. Muddy must be cooking the joint. His knee sagged suddenly under an unaccustomed weight, and he looked at it carefully. Catarina had jumped in his lap and was energetically washing her face. Had Muddy fed her then? A great, warm roar filled his ears.

Soon Poe noticed that someone had lit the lamp. Was it night? With the approach of the winter solstice, darkness fell so early. Poe looked around the room. Mrs. Gove must be getting ready to leave. How thin she was, even in that heavy, ill-fitting coat tacked all over with coarse black braid. He shuddered delicately at the thought of such coarse stuff accidentally touching one's skin. Mrs. Gove and Father Doucet probably thought they were whispering so quietly there by the door that he couldn't hear them, but he didn't need laudanum to sharpen the acuteness of his hearing. Poe dreamily turned his eyes back to the fire and listened to their conversation without a qualm, but he was sorry that he was listening when he chanced to hear Mrs. Gove whisper, "I'm terrified that Mr. Poe may be stricken with his wife's ailment, Father Doucet. I understand that he is from known consumptive stock. They say he's just like Keats— that his mother died of consumption as did also his brother, who was nursed through to the end by Mr. Poe."

"What can we do, Mrs. Gove?"

"I shall ask everyone I can think of. I shall be back tomorrow with help."

Poe began to frown at the fire. He considered rising to his feet and objecting once again, but he was so very comfortable. He heard Mrs. Gove's light footsteps and Father Doucet's heavier ones go into the kitchen and their voices rise to a louder murmur as they talked to Muddy. There was still time to go in and tell them no, he and Muddy and poor little Sissy would rather all perish together than . . . how was it his foster father used to put it all the time? To eat the bread of charity?

But, in the cubbyhole of a bedroom, he could also hear Virginia breathing, lightly, calmly. It was this sound that stopped him.

Poor little Sissy. Poor little creature that he had all but created. He had dressed her, housed her, educated her, killed her, if not by his brother's disease, then by his inability to provide even enough food for her. The decent life for which he had striven all these years so fruitlessly and frustratedly—was it just for himself? No. No. No.

Poe sat back heavily in his chair, and the cat on his knee, disturbed by his small movement, woke up and looked at him, he fancied crossly. But he wouldn't disturb Catarina again. He wouldn't rise. He wouldn't protest. If he could not give Virginia comfort while she lived, he could at least keep quiet and accept with a beggar's smile any comforts that might ease her dying.

6

At the bottom of Poe's cup of despair lay the dregs of humiliation. Galvanized by Mary Gove, a gaggle of New York literary ladies rushed gabbling and honking to the rescue. With gall in his heart Poe accepted a feather bed and blankets from a Mrs. Louise Shew, sixty dollars from a public subscription, and dainty baskets of cherry wine, calf's-foot jelly and selected Smyrna opium from women to whom helping the poor, miserable Poes quickly became the latest fad. Of course, they did not refrain from discussing their errands of mercy once they were home in the city. Reports that Poe was dangerously ill of brain fever and his wife in the last stages of consumption hit the public print, and the papers did not fail to report, to Poe's chagrin, that he was without money. One repeated the talk that had already hurt both Poe's and Virginia's feelings—that he had no friends to whom to turn. The same anonymous hand that had tormented Virginia so long sent her the clipping, and she turned to the wall a sad little face, still round and full above a wasted body.

Poe, nurtured on John Allan's bitter bread, struggled again under a sense of inferiority mixed with outraged pride. Virginia, too, may have been none too happy about the return of tattling tongues. Even carefully and constantly dosed with opiates, she sometimes looked with troubled, violet eyes at the women who smoothed the fine linen that now covered her bed and urged her to eat the delicate foods with which, now that Virginia had a queer feeling of fullness in her stomach after only a few mouthfuls, the house now abounded. They acted like rival queens determined to outdo one another in kindness. Mrs. Louise Shew was the most helpful. Her father had been a doctor and she regarded herself as almost one, and she ministered to Virginia with a firm hand. But even her presence created problems. Mrs. Shew, whom Poe grew to like and called "Loui," didn't like Stella Lewis, who peevishly took it out on Muddy, who favored Mrs. Shew over Mary Gove, who had started the whole thing but who was soon jockeyed out of position. Through it all Poe fought his feeling of helplessness and waited, hoping to be of some solace to Virginia when she needed him.

But when she did need him, there was nothing he could do. As January came to a close, the winter's gloom was interrupted briefly by three afternoons of pale winter sun, which Virginia met with such joy and apparent return of strength that Muddy allowed her to sit up for a little in the parlor. Poe sat beside her, holding her hand. She asked him to turn her chair away from the fire so she could look out the window, but before he could do so, gray snow clouds cut off the sun.

With a small, rueful laugh, Virginia went back to bed. By evening she was failing fast and now suffering great pain. Summoned by a frantic note from Poe, Mrs. Shew drove out hurriedly in her carriage in the next morning's bitter cold. She joined Poe at the side of the bed, where he sat watching his young wife gasping, her destroyed lungs no longer bringing in enough air.

Until afternoon, Virginia was rational. In the afternoon, the snow resumed its fall, thickly now, thick heavy flakes falling straight down, and Poe sat holding both of Virginia's hands, waiting for the next spasm.

There was always another spasm. She died slowly, torturously, the spasms of choking coming again and again, with always less and less air. When they came, she jerked her hands from his, and since she didn't seem to want him to look at her convulsed face, he looked out the window. The snow still fell, white, covering everything in white.

Sometimes, between the spasms, Virginia spoke. Breathing with an effort, lying silent for a long while between sentences, she even rallied enough once to take from beneath the fine linen slip of her pillow a daguerreotype of Poe and an empty jewel case that Poe had been left by his mother and gave them to Mrs. Shew. Then another spasm came, and Poe felt her hands wrench themselves from his and watched them flutter toward her struggling throat, and he looked back out the window.

How thickly the snow was falling. It was almost impossible to see any gaps of air between the flakes. The world was snow.

"You'll have—to spend—the night, Loui," Virginia gasped after another while. "Wherever—can we—sleep—your coachman?"

She could hardly speak any longer, but as Poe turned to take the hands she tried to hold out to him, he saw the corners of her white mouth twitch up, the ghost of her old, merry smile.

"He can sleep in the kitchen," Mrs. Shew said practically, "and have nothing whatever to complain about. It's the warmest room in the house. Can you swallow now? It's time for your medicine, dear. Mrs. Clemm, brace her shoulders. That's good. Now swallow. Now try."

But Virginia started to choke again. Still the snow fell. Outside, not a bird track, not a cat print could be seen. Fresh snow covered everything.

It would soon be night. The falling snow whispered on the bed of dead leaves beneath the cherry trees. A faint roar like the distant boom of the sea arose above the house. A gale from the west. As Poe watched, the quiet, vertical fall of the snow became oblique.

Inside the little room, there was silence again, except for Virginia's labored breathing. He turned and took her hands again, but within seconds she wrenched them away. She gasped. Her face distorted into an ugly mask, and Poe started to avert his eyes, but Virginia's teeth ground together, and she struggled to speak. Her lips trembled. Finally a cry broke through. "Eddy," she gasped. "Eddy, help me! Help!"

"Oh, dear God!" he said. "Muddy, give her something. Give her the medicine! Oh, God, help me!"

But not one grain of sand could be saved from the pitiless wave. She couldn't swallow. At nightfall, slowly, excruciatingly, while the snow still whispered outside on the dead leaves of the cherry trees, she suffocated to death.

Book IV

THE LADIES

*. . . where the dames of Rome their gilded hair
Waved to the wind . . .*

The Coliseum

1

In his poetry, Poe could write with grieving pleasure, from his very first poems onward, about the death of a young, beautiful woman, but in the actuality of death there was only grief. No sooner was Virginia buried in the graveyard of the Fordham Dutch Reformed Church than Poe collapsed with a high fever, confined to the very bed where Virginia had died, muttering incessantly of the past and begging Muddy and Mrs. Shew to write down his mutterings for greedy publishers, who, he assured them, had been promised his next works and who would say all sorts of evil things about him if he should die without fulfilling his obligations. Wine, tonics or other stimulants brought on even more feverish ravings. Sedatives had to be administered with extreme caution. But the cause of his illness was hunger and grief, and the real cure was food and care and the slow passing of the chill days in his barren cottage until the sun and the beginnings of hope could come again.

It was a pale and shaky Poe who first walked the few feet into the parlor and gazed at his writing table, where Virginia's coffin had lain on the day of the funeral. It was a brooding Poe who put on the old cloaked greatcoat he had last worn on a cold, gray winter day in the company of a few neighbors, his landlord and two loyal ambassadors from the city, Nat Willis and G. P. Morris, to follow Virginia to the grave. With the sunshine of early spring throwing a long shadow before him, he turned his steps to his favorite high point on the granite ridge to gaze at the river and the Long Island hills beyond, accompanied by Catarina, whose idea of walking was to pause frequently to observe an early beetle, a new green leaf, then run swiftly to catch up, often dashing ahead and halfway up a tree trunk to bat Poe's shoulder as he paced slowly by. In time, Father Doucet joined them on the walks on the country roads about Fordham. If he found Poe nervous and strained and given to grandiose statements about a new work whose subject was to be no less than the nature of God, the universe and man's place in it, he gently refrained from pressing his own expert opinions on such matters to a man whose silent courage in the face of adversity he had long since come to admire.

So the weeks passed, and so Poe passed the weeks, spending much of his time out of doors. He couldn't bear the loneliness of the cottage. At night, when Muddy coaxed him inside, he found it almost impossible to sleep. Muddy sat with him late into the night, one rheumatic hand on his forehead, patiently waiting for the moment she thought he had fallen asleep, only to hear him whisper as she tried to leave, "Not yet, Muddy. Not yet."

Then, when the sunshine was ripe and the cherries were on the verge of blossoming again, Poe walked out into the garden at sunrise one morning and found the air smelling of lilac and the bitter leaves of spring and of dung that the grocery wagon's horse had deposited on the road in front of the house when it stopped the evening before. Muddy had bought pretzels and a whole pound of coffee and a bit of salt herring for his spartan but favorite breakfast. Poe had won his lawsuit against English and the *Mirror*, a total of almost two hundred and fifty dollars in damages, and there was real food in the house once more. Behind Poe, the front door opened, and Catarina appeared and slid into deep morning shadows cast by the lilac bushes. Muddy came a few steps out on the piazza and smiled hesitantly. Somehow she had managed to find or beg grain enough to keep the parrot and the bobolink alive over the winter, and she carried the parrot's cage in one hand and the bobolink's in the other. "It's warm enough for the birds to stay outside some now, don't you think?" she said.

The bobolink was highly excited. It dashed frantically against the sides of its cage, and Poe looked at it in some confusion. It looked different. It was different. Drab and sparrowlike all winter, the bird had put on its spring plumage—a solid black chest with white flashes on its back, like his own black coat and snowy-white shirt front in reverse. As Muddy hung its cage on its old nail driven into the trunk of the cherry tree, the bobolink burst suddenly into song, starting with a low, flutelike note and quivering upward, burbling, ecstatic. Poe felt his own mood lift with the ecstasy of the song. He stepped forward, swiftly, before he could change his mind, and opened the bobolink's cage. He stepped back and watched, but the bird, wary, only eyed the open door, so Poe turned and took Muddy's arm. "Come," he said. "Come walk with me in the garden."

"But the bobolink—you don't want it any more?"

"No, let it go. It has its own songs to sing. We'll keep the parrot. It would starve, dear Muddy, without you to look after it. Come, I want to tell you about my new discoveries, a matter of the greatest importance to the world. What I am going to propound will in good time revolutionize the world of physical and metaphysical science. I say this calmly—but I say it. I envision a great prose poem on the subject. No other format would be as fitting. I shall call the work *Eureka*."

So in time, sitting in the sun in front of the cottage or walking up and down the garden with Muddy or writing at night with Catarina on his knee and Muddy nodding in her chair beside him, safeguards against the cottage's now haunted solitude, Poe regained the use of his pen. He spent the year of 1847 largely as a recluse, his lofty dreaming brightened from time to time by the calls and guava jellies and sympathetic ministrations of the kindly Mrs. Shew, and shattered by the calls and pleadings and demands of the indefatigable Stella. The latter's calls became more frequent as the libel-suit money began to run out. In Muddy's kitchen, new promises were given that Eddy would rework this poem or write a complimentary notice for that magazine, and new expressions of thanks came out of a silk purse and were placed in Muddy's open palm.

In January of the next year, *Eureka* finished, Poe began to think again of re-establishing himself as a leader of the literary world. His health improved. Through all this time his mind was turning once again to *The Stylus*, and he arranged a lecture on *Eureka* with fifteen dollars borrowed for a lecture hall to try to build a campaign fund for a trip to the South to drum up subscribers. The weather was as usual—bad. The audience, more curious about Poe the man than able to comprehend the complex ideology of Poe the poet-philosopher, reacted to the lecture with confusion. What was all this? In the beginning, God created a particle without form, without emptiness, without individuality, glittering in infinite space? And then, oh dear, starting at the square of the distance between some surface and the center, some force of diffusion increases or decreases, and . . . oh, plague take it all. But newspaper reaction to Poe's lecture was favorable, and *Eureka* went to press. George Putnam, late of Wiley & Putnam but now a publisher on his own account, generously made Poe an advance payment of fourteen dollars, plus a shilling to take Poe home to Fordham. Poe's journey to the South had to remain only a hope, but it was a sturdy one. Poe was freshly resolved to be his own publisher. He confidently told Muddy that if he could but succeed in starting the magazine, he would put himself, within two years, in possession of a fortune—and, infinitely more, of power. The plan was simple, if he could but act upon it. All he had to do was go through the South and West and endeavor to interest enough friends so that he could accumulate a list of at least five hundred subscribers. With this list, he would be able to find the needed capital. "At all events," he told Muddy over and over, "*succeed I will.*"

Then one day, when the cherries had blossomed yet again and the first fruits were green with promise, Poe left his hermitage at Fordham. He went into the city to call on Nat Willis at the offices of Willis's new, extremely popular publication, *The Home Journal*, and the ever helpful Louise Shew, who had ministered so stalwartly to his dying wife.

The day was hot. Although all week rain had fallen on the flooding Kingsbridge Highway, the afternoon sun broke free of clouds, bright and clear, polishing mud puddles into mirrors and burnishing the brass doorknob on Mrs. Shew's prim, five-story house until it shone like a miniature of the sun itself. Poe found his friend Loui in a conservatory overlooking a back garden as narrow as the house. She told the young maid who showed him to the conservatory to bring tea. Trying to fathom his state of health, she peered at him closely.

She commanded, "Sit here, Edgar. No, not facing west. The glare will be in your eyes. Just move those papers from the green chair. You look exhausted, Edgar. Did you walk all the way from the depot? Regular exercise is fine, but there's such a thing as overdoing, especially when it's so humid."

To save the omnibus fare, Poe had indeed walked, despite the fact that Louise Shew's house was far uptown—Tenth Street, near Broadway—and Willis's office, which he had visited first, was far downtown. Poe's health was better by far than this time a year ago, but he still suffered from near constant fatigue. Today, in the steam bath that was the city, he confessed that he felt breathless as well.

"Then take off that hot coat immediately," Loui said. "Edgar, why must you forever stand on formality?"

He demurred. He even seemed to be looking worriedly at the tidy stack of letters and cards she had been answering, and said, "I'm interrupting you? I can call another time."

"Nonsense. Have you been eating properly, Edgar? I've concluded that you eat entirely too much fruit. You must eat fish, it's brain food. Fish and clams and oysters. They'll supply the brain power you use up in writing."

"Then give me fish instead of tea, Loui, for Willis has been lecturing me. He tells me I must write a new poem, to keep myself in front of the public. But I have no inspiration."

Loui never read Poe's poetry, unless it was addressed to her, and even then she read it less with appreciation than with apprehension of what people would make of his expressions of esteem and gratitude for all the help she had been, first to Virginia, and now to him. The foolish man had actually published one of the short poems in Willis's *Home Journal,* but Loui had succeeded in keeping another one out of the public eye by the simple expedient of paying Muddy twenty-five dollars for it and pointing out that there was now no need for Poe to sell it. Loui was an unprotected widow, after all, and had to be careful of what the world thought of her. Her friends had long looked askance at her relationship with Poe anyway. Particularly her women friends. They often asked her if she were not afraid of Poe—if, as persistent rumor now had it, he were not insane. But Willis's point that a poet must produce poems seemed sensible to Loui. She placed her pen and a fresh sheet of paper in front of Poe and said encouragingly, "Of course you have inspiration. Write about . . . the spring? All poets write about the spring."

Poe grimaced. He stared balefully at the piece of white paper in front of him. The sudden sound of church bells from up the block split the air. The maid who was bringing the tea tray started and set the cups to rattling. Poe grimaced again. He pushed the paper away. "I dislike the noise of the bells this evening," he said. "I can't write, I have no subject. Besides, you're right. I *am* exhausted."

"It's this heat," Loui said soothingly, pouring the tea. Despite her urgings, Poe would eat and drink but little. The bells kept ringing.

Loui picked up the piece of paper Poe had rejected and wrote on it, "The Bells, by E. A. Poe." Then she wrote a short line: "The bells, the little, silver bells." She handed it to Poe. "Now you have a subject. What rhymes with 'bell'?"

"Hell," Poe said glumly. But he pondered the line and took up the paper. First he crossed out his name and wrote, in his fine, copperplate handwriting, "By Mrs. M. L. Shew." Then he put parentheses around her line and studied it at greater length. Then, slowly, he began to write:

> The bells!—hear the bells!
> The merry wedding bells!
> The little silver bells!

"Oh yes!" Loui said. "That's much nicer." Poe smiled at her. He wrote on:

> How fairy-like a melody there swells
> From the silver tinkling cells
> Of the bells, bells, bells!
> Of the bells!

"Go on," Loui urged.

Poe shook his head. "It's not going right," he said. "It should sound the way bells sound to the ears. It should sing more. Ring more." He wearily put the paper aside.

"But then it only needs more bells," Loui said. She took up the sheet and wrote again: "The heavy iron bells."

"I'm really very tired, Loui," Poe objected. He consulted his watch. "I must leave soon if I'm to be in Fordham in time for supper."

But the new experience of the fever of composition was on Loui, and she urged and insisted until Poe returned to the poem. He wrote:

> The bells!—ah, the bells!
> The heavy iron bells!
> Hear the tolling of the bells!
> Hear the knells!
> How horrible a monody there floats
> From their throats—

> From their deep-toned throats!
> How I shudder at the notes
> From the melancholy throats
> Of the bells, bells, bells!
> Of the bells!

Looking dazed with fatigue, this time Poe put the paper down with finality. "I cannot proceed," he said. "But perhaps it's finished. I'll take the poem home and copy it for you. Shall I have Muddy send a copy to Willis? He'd be happy to have it for the *Home Journal*. I'll tell him he must print it for you."

"But no. It's your poem."

"No, yours, since you suggested so much of it."

"I insist, Edgar." She leaned across the table and scratched out her name. "The last thing I want to become is one of those dreadful literary ladies."

Poe gave in to her wishes and rose to bow his way out of the garden. He staggered slightly as he gained his feet, as if feeling light-headed and still breathless. Loui was immediately and solicitously at his side. He must not dream of going back to Fordham in his condition. She would send her brother to tell Muddy that her boy would stay in town. He must sup with her, and afterward would spend the night in her brother's room. No, no, it wasn't the slightest imposition. Didn't he wish to lie down now, until supper time?

It was apparent to Loui that Poe had not been drinking. And he had only come into town that afternoon—not long enough, surely, to account for such extreme exhaustion. She fussed over him worriedly, but he refused to lie down and instead sat in her music room, which he had always liked for its lavish use of crimson and gold. Reluctantly, she left him alone and at his request returned to her correspondence, only to find him dozing uncomfortably in a chair when she went to call him to supper.

She gave him stewed oysters and broiled flounder, true to her prescription, but to her increasing vexation Poe only picked at the food.

"Come now, you must try to eat," Loui said. "Cook will be upset. I sent her out specially for the flounder. It's blackback, fresh-caught."

Poe flaked a forkful from the fish and regarded it. "They tell me there's another species called the Baptist flounder," he said idly. "It goes bad shortly after it comes out of the water, whence its name."

Loui looked at him with sudden suspicion. No Baptist, she was nevertheless a devoted church-goer. Episcopalian, of course. One of her dearest friendships was with a young seminary student who lately had been warning her about the dangerous pantheism that Poe, if one took the trouble to read it and if one could comprehend it, had apparently been preaching in his *Eureka*. In fact, John Hopkins, the seminary student, had lately taken to warning her repeatedly about Poe's dangerous ideas. As a result, she may have gone a little less frequently to visit Muddy and Poe at Fordham. She may have been a little cooler in her attitude, may have discussed religion a little more often in Poe's hearing. Surely he hadn't taken it amiss. Surely he wasn't implying some comparison between a good Protestant and a flounder. Surely he wasn't just feigning this attack of illness. Was he?

She stabbed her own flounder agitatedly. "Edgar, you're as bad as a child," she scolded. "You won't even eat the things that are good for you, sick as you've been. I must tell you in all candor that nothing can or will save you from sudden death but a prudent diet and a prudent life of calm."

Poe looked alarmed. "Loui, is something troubling you?" he asked. "Has your unhappy and unfortunate friend and patient done something to displease you? No, don't turn away. I've felt for several months that something was wrong. You know how I depend upon your friendship. Tell me. Tell this lost soul what's wrong."

"How dare you refer to yourself as a lost soul!" Loui declared. "No soul can be lost unless its possessor turns his face from God!"

"My dear Louise, I beg your pardon. I would never willingly offend one who has been such an angel to my forlorn and darkened nature. But I *have* offended you somehow, haven't I? I've had premonitions for months that you were planning to desert me. Let me make amends. You must not vanish like all else I've ever loved or desired."

"Oh, Edgar, don't be so dramatic," she said. She pushed her plate of flounder back petulantly and rang for the maid with a smart tap of the ball of her foot on the bell push concealed beneath the table. "I'm only trying to advise you, as a disinterested party, that you need . . . you need . . ."

"Disinterested party?" exclaimed Poe. "My good spirit! My loyal heart! Must this follow as a sequel to all the benefits and blessings you have so generously bestowed?"

Loui could have screamed, but the maid was coming, but Poe was there, but Cook might have heard her in the kitchen, but ladies never raised their voices, much less screamed. "Please listen to me," she said. "I know I have little to recommend me in this world but common sense, and it is my common sense that advises you, that urges you to . . . to marry. Yes, Edgar, marry someone who can at once provide you with the means of existence and the care of a wife. Um, of course I don't mean the care of a mere friend like myself. You sorely require a woman who is both strong enough and fond enough of you to manage your affairs. And someone who has, um, the means to, um . . ."

Now Poe was beginning to look offended. "I believe I understand," he said. "You would have me marry for money. Like Griswold. But what did it gain him?"

"Edgar, no, not for money *only*. For happiness. And if happiness is accompanied by social position and enjoyment, must it then be condemned? You need, of course, the love and sympathy of a woman of kindred nature to your own, someone whose qualities of mind and heart can appreciate your genius. My dear friend, I would be the last one in the world ever to breathe a word against your lovely Virginia, but other friends say . . ."

Loui paused while the maid removed the plates. She inspected Poe with a keen look. His chin was sunk on his cravat, and his eyes were downcast. Was he even listening? The maid left, and Loui plunged determinedly onward.

"As your close friend, I feel it my duty to tell you that others have sometimes referred to your marriage as the greatest misfortune of your life and a millstone around your neck, holding you down against every effort to rise. What did it bring you? Years of incessant toil. A narrow and poverty-stricken home. No wonder you grew hopeless. Even reckless, though you've borne the humility of your poverty so patiently and uncomplainingly. Oh, Edgar, married to a true helpmeet, what a different life you would have led, and what a different man you still could be. I don't want to say a word against your faithful Muddy, but it is no secret that she made the match between you and her Virginia, just to keep you under her thumb. Such an unnatural marriage cut you off from—"

"Louise, you go too far," Poe said. His voice was low and polite, but his face was so pale and strained that Loui immediately stopped her tirade.

"Oh, but you're ill!" she cried. "You're really ill! You must lie down at once! I'll call Dr. Francis."

Poe protested, but with the help of both Cook and the maid Loui aided him up the stairs to her brother's bedroom. Cook took off his boots, and Loui worried the maid out the front door to run for Dr. Francis. She then waited discreetly in the hall until Cook informed her the gentleman was successfully bedded down, then rushed to his bedside. Poe seemed to be sleeping. She checked his pulse. It was alarmingly uneven.

The maid must have run the six blocks to Dr. Francis's home, for he arrived within the quarter-hour, smelling of cigar smoke and brandy. He patted Loui on the head and said in his loud, booming voice, "Poe drunk again? I'm surprised at you, Louise, calling me out for such as this. Not to mention at your receiving Poe when he's in such a condition."

"Shhhhh," Loui said anxiously, but Poe didn't stir. She reported her findings about his pulse and her conclusions about Poe's sobriety, and Dr. Francis grew more alert. He lifted Poe's eyelid, checked the pulse for himself, pushed back the nightshirt Cook had borrowed from Loui's brother and laid his head on Poe's chest to listen more closely.

"The pulse is very weak and irregular," Dr. Francis admitted, "and he seems in some sort of stupor. Have you seen him this way before?"

Loui nodded. "When he was so ill, after his wife died. I diagnosed a lesion on one side of the brain."

Dr. Francis snorted, but he only said, "And did you also diagnose heart disease? Yes, well, it's undeniable. Poor Poe. He'll die early in life. All right, don't look so shocked. I'm sure you've already come to the same conclusion. If his brain don't get him, poor devil, his heart will. But just let him sleep for tonight. Rest is the best thing for him. And the same goes for you, my girl."

"But what could have brought on this attack tonight, Dr. Francis?" Loui asked guiltily. "He . . . we worked a bit on a poem, and then we talked. Of course there's the heat, but . . ."

"I haven't the least idea," Dr. Francis admitted frankly. "Stimulants could have done it, but you say he's had none. Ask my illustrious colleagues. Ask yourself. Everyone runs around these days talking about congestion of the brain, lesions of the brain. What's that? God only knows. I only know that Poe is an unlucky fellow. Maybe that's cause enough. Now go to bed. And don't go dosing him with anything. He don't need opium and he don't need oil of elder flowers and he don't need anything. If stimulants are bad for that brain lesion you're so set on, what do you think opiates and those other messes you're always cooking up would do to him? Oh, and order your carriage for tomorrow morning, my wife's using hers. I'll take Poe home to Fordham. He shouldn't have to contend with those cursed trains. Rest is what he needs. It's the only thing I know to suggest."

"I'll drive him home myself," Loui said.

"No, you won't. You'd only lecture him. Or coddle him. Leave him alone. If an old friend could make a suggestion, Louise, I'd say to leave Poe very much alone. People are still whispering scandal about Poe, you know, and there's considerable antagonistic feeling toward him. You wouldn't want that to rub off on you, now would you?"

Loui stiffened. How dare he? The old man was skillful, but very odd. She saw Dr. Francis politely to the door, but she was pale with indignation when she closed it behind him. If she needed anyone's advice, she'd ask for it. The nerve of some busybodies, rushing around giving advice, trying to live other people's lives for them!

2

The day following, Poe did not remember he had been ill. He had slept twelve hours and awakened in a calm and pleasant mood, which brightened still further when Dr. Francis arrived after breakfast to take him home. They talked of the recent death of old John Jacob Astor, of the formal peace with Mexico, of generalities, and only as the carriage neared the cottage at Fordham did Dr. Francis bring up the subject of Poe's health.

"I'm not a man to preach, Poe," the old doctor said gruffly, "but I'm not content about the state of your health."

"My health is greatly improved," Poe said distractedly. He was thinking about Astor and all that money.

"Pshaw," the doctor said. "You're a sick man, Poe. Your vitality is dangerously low, and unless you give up all stimulants and excesses, the end is near."

"Why . . . why . . . Has someone been telling you stories about me? Why, damnation, it's false! I omit nothing of the natural regimen requisite for health. I rise early, eat moderately, drink nothing but water, and take abundant and regular exercise in the open air."

"Yes, and still go on drinking binges, I don't doubt. I'm only telling you, don't. Not if you hope to make old bones."

Poe drew himself up. "My dear sir, the causes which maddened me to the drinking point are no more, and I am done drinking forever. Whoever tells you otherwise tells a damnable falsehood."

Dr. Francis patted him roughly on the knee. "Good man, I hope your resolution holds. It must. We can't get along without you, you know. Louise tells me you're working on a new poem. The world needs its poems, so we have to put up with the men who produce them. Well, come to see me when you're next in town. You know I'm home nearly every evening, if not professionally engaged. We'll share a cigar and curse the Philistines together."

The carriage stopped in front of the cottage, where Poe and the doctor parted amiably. Poe was vaguely surprised when the driver turned the carriage and went back the way he came; he had assumed Dr. Francis had some errand in this direction, and did not realize the man had driven out the whole thirteen miles solely to deliver him safely to his door. Poe was less surprised, but far more unpleasantly, when Muddy hurried from the cottage and asked breathlessly, "Did you ride home with someone? I felt sure you'd take the train, and Stella Lewis has walked into Williamsbridge to await you on the cars. She's been here since breakfast with a manuscript, and she's very anxious to see you."

Poe jerked his head around like a man suddenly on the alert for marauding Indians. "I won't see her!" he exclaimed. "Don't tell her I'm home!"

He took to his heels, but Muddy grabbed his coattails. "Eddy darling, you must see her," she pleaded. "I told her you were eager to read her new poem."

"Oh, God, let me die, and rid me of literary bores!" Poe said. "Let me go, Muddy. I can't see her this morning. I'm working on a new poem of my own."

He fled into the fields, then fled further still, circling in back of the grounds of St. John's College. He avoided a favorite rock where he often went to sit, because Muddy had tracked him down there before when he rushed out to escape the ungainly Stella and her ungainly verses. But soon his breathlessness and a warning of fatigue slowed him down. He took refuge on the trunk of a fallen blackjack oak. It was still damp from the week's rains, but it would be Muddy's fault if he ruined the seat of his trousers. The thought brought him back to his feet, however, and he wandered on closer to the creek. The water was high and muddy. Poor Muddy, there must be no money again, or she wouldn't have been so anxious about his seeing Stella. Should he go back? But instead he leaned against an old, woodpecker-ringed apple tree, and felt in his pocket for the poem Dr. Francis had mentioned. Bells. Of course, he'd only forgotten for a moment. Why in the world had Loui suggested a poem about bells? The subject was so hackneyed. And yet—it could work. What was that word he had tossed into the columns he did for the *Columbia Spy* when he first got to New York? *Tintamarres*—the noise of the charcoal wagons that infested the city streets. Pliny, on the bells the pagans used, wrote *tintinnabula*. He had the clipping somewhere in his notebooks. *Tintinnabulation*, a delicious word. But the real trick would be contrasting closed vowel sounds with open vowels. The poem would take a lot of revision.

All poems took a lot of revision. Poe put the rough draft back in his pocket and looked toward the fields through which he had made his escape. A hen pheasant, followed by a brood of . . . twelve? thirteen? . . . walked sedately out of a patch of pokeweed. Poe waited a moment longer, until the hen and her brood disappeared, before dutifully turning his steps homeward. He still had Muddy to look after, as she had him; unless he saw Stella, there might be no dinner.

But Stella was gone by the time he got back to the cottage. Alone in the kitchen, Muddy was getting out her basket and a clasp knife. Poe looked at her apprehensively. Her broad, wrinkled cheeks were shiny. Tears? Muddy said nothing to reproach him, merely commented quietly that Mrs. Lewis had had to leave but hoped, since the master was feeling well enough for trips to New York, he might soon come to Brooklyn, as well, to call on her and Mr. Lewis, since she always seemed to miss him on her visits to Fordham these days.

"I'm sorry, Muddy," Poe said ruefully. "I didn't want to alarm you, but I felt a little ill while I was in the city. I just didn't feel up to Mrs. Lewis this morning."

"I know, my dear," she said. "I would have been terribly worried about you had Loui's brother not reassured me last night. Why don't you rest in the parlor? I'm just going to go out for a little while."

Poe eyed her basket. Not begging from the neighbors again, he hoped. As she left the cottage, he was reassured, but freshly depressed, when he heard Muddy exchange greetings with a passing neighbor woman, and, upon the woman's inquiry, reply that she was going out to look for dandelion greens.

"Greens can be took too often, Mrs. Clemm," the neighbor woman warned.

"Oh no," Muddy said defensively, "one of my good friends who's almost a doctor says they're very good for you. Besides, my Eddy likes them so."

They must have walked on together, for their voices, murmuring, faded, and Poe was left alone, staring at the whitewashed walls of the parlor. Last evening he had sat beside windows draped with crimson, double-curtained in gold; here his favorite crimson blossomed only in the gay flowers of a big geranium Muddy had put in the empty fireplace. Last evening he had admired the scroll-figured pile of a luxurious carpet, not these white-scoured plank floors. Last evening he had pushed aside costly foods on a Wedgwood plate, and this evening would probably dine only on wild greens dished up on one of the dozen pieces of common crockery that, aside from a treasured tea set she had bought with part of the *Mirror* libel-suit proceeds, were all Muddy had. And she might not have them much longer. Unless he could begin to make some money regularly, the few little things she had accumulated since Virginia's death would inevitably find their way back to the city and a pawnshop.

As would the ring he was wearing. The ring, also a fruit of the successful libel suit, was made of Virginia's and Muddy's wedding rings, intertwined, and since the day he had gotten it from the jeweler, it had never left Poe's finger. Not yet, at least. Money. Always there was the problem of money. It seemed so little to ask of the world:

decent food, a decent place for Muddy to live, a decent life. If only he could ever get his hands on some modest but regular income.

There was still *The Stylus*, of course. It would require such a small sum to take him southward to try for the subscriptions. Home, home to the South, away from these contemptible material values of a metropolis that honored only commercial prosperity, away from these ranting fools who condemned their own populace to a subhuman life in their ever increasing factories, while yet piously attacking the South and slavery. He remembered again Dr. Francis's talk about the death of old Mr. Astor. The heir to all those millions, Charles Astor Bristed, had almost become interested in *The Stylus* once. Might Bristed be good at least for a loan?

And Poe remembered something else. What was it Loui had been saying last night? Marry. Marry some sensible but sensitive woman with an income of her own. The idea wasn't completely without merit.

But what were his prospects? Poe passed over the thought of Stella Lewis with a shudder—she was married already, thank God—and lit briefly on Anna Lynch. After the new spurt of public attention about his *Eureka*, Miss Lynch had sent him notes that Muddy had put somewhere, apologetic notes, conciliatory notes, and he had called on her not long ago while running other business errands in New York. But an old maid like Miss Lynch? Never. If not some fresh young woman, better a widow.

There was one widow, Fanny Osgood's cousin-in-law, as it happened. Where had he put her letters? Jane Locke, that was her name. Wanted him to come to Lowell, where she lived. To lecture, she said. People there were anxious to hear him, she said. She would make all the arrangements, she said. But he knew enough about women to read between the lines. And she must have some means. She had been among the ladies who had sent not just guava jelly but, graciously if somewhat gushingly, cash, in the bad days of the worst winter of his life.

His poor Virginia. But that was a thought not to be dwelled upon. Onward, then. He had never met the Widow Locke. If he didn't like her, whom else could he turn to? Fanny, no. That was over. Married, besides. Poor, besides that. And sick, worst of all. He could never go through that again.

There was that poetess in Providence, Sarah Helen Whitman, another widow. Mrs. Whitman had written a valentine to the Raven only this past February and had sent it to Anna Lynch's annual valentine soiree, to which he, Poe, had not this year been invited. Miss Lynch had forwarded it on, once she had apparently decided to unbend toward him. He knew of Mrs. Whitman, of course. She was the very same woman he and Fanny had glimpsed gazing up at the moon that time in Providence, the woman Fanny had used as an excuse for them to be alone. Poe knew Mrs. Whitman's poetry, too. It was real, at least in part, not this drivel so many poetesses turned out. And the valentine had been pleasantly flirtatious. He had responded, hadn't he? Oh yes, because her middle name was Helen he'd ripped out his early *To Helen* from his Wiley & Putnam edition and sent it to her.

Poe went to his secretary, planning to look through the recent crop of letters. There might be other prospects he was overlooking. But he would try the Widow Locke first, and if she wanted to arrange a lecture for him in Lowell, well, let her. It wouldn't do any harm at least to meet her and look her over. Pursue his perennial hopes for *Stylus* he would, but he had to be practical. It would do no harm to have a second string for his bow.

To marry. The thought stirred his mind like a sudden, warm wind. Virginia had been so ill for so long. There was Fanny, but even that was so long ago. Perhaps . . . Oh, the dimly remembered poetry that was the curve of a buttock, a pair of round, naked breasts crushed to his naked chest.

Animal, he called himself. Animal. That had never happened. Like any gentleman, he had never made love clothed in less than his shirt or his nightshirt, and to women whose nearest state of nakedness had been a voluminous nightgown, or, at minimum, a little chemise. Yes, animal. But to suppress animality and yet to fall in love . . . ?

He would write Mrs. Locke this very day, yes, and Mrs. Whitman too. Willis had told him firmly that he must write a new poem. What about a second, original *To Helen*, just to be polite? There was the bells thing, an interesting technical problem, but it would have to ripen in the back of his mind, nor did it interest him today. Something easy. Blank verse. Something very, very romantic. A woman glimpsed only once, on a summer night, standing in a rose garden . . . Well, there were no roses. If he remembered correctly, Mrs.

Whitman had been standing in a mere barren courtyard, but there should be roses, the rose garden in Richmond, the garden where he and Elmira so often met. . . .

Poe's eyes wandered to his old "Lost Lenore" drawing, which Muddy had hung in the parlor, as always close to whatever served him as a desk. Elmira, the gentle incarnation of youth's fleshly passions. Elmira, her expressive eyes. Elmira's sensitive lips, trembling, moist with his trembling kisses. Elmira, who was torn from him as an arm caught in an insensate machine might be ripped from one's living body. Love and Elmira. The two words had always gone together in his mind. Strange, her full name was Sarah Elmira, just as Mrs. Whitman's was Sarah Helen.

He didn't feel it in his viscera. It wouldn't be a very good poem, but the devil with that. Taylor at *Union Magazine* would pay adequately for it, and he'd first send a draft to the poetess in Providence. Anonymously. No sense getting her too stirred up until after he had gone to Lowell for a look at Jane Locke. But a man should be practical and explore all possibilities.

He sat down at his desk and found a piece of his favorite blue paper and began to write:

I saw thee once—once only—years ago:

After a while, Catarina jumped onto his knee and began to sharpen her claws on his trouser leg.

Muddy came in with her basket, filled with wild greens. She smiled a little and sighed a little. At least Eddy was writing again, and home again under her wing after becoming ill in the city. He could get in no trouble that way.

3

It was July of 1848, a year and a half after Virginia's death, when Poe set forth in quest of a woman, a romance, a wife. He traveled in a fire storm of sparks showering all about him: puffing steam packet from New York to Boston, fuming train out of Boston and deep into the Massachusetts countryside, past villages, past the spires of meetinghouses, past woods, past broken-windowed farmhouses abandoned to decay as their discouraged inhabitants turned their eyes and then their feet from the rocky soil of New England to trails West.

Poe's pilgrimage was to him no less of an adventure. He hadn't felt like this since he was a boy. Adrift. Tingling with anticipation. The grief and despair of the recent years seemed to evaporate with each passing mile. En route if needs must to the world's edge, his baggage a clean shirt, a few dollars scraped up by Muddy, a lecture to be delivered in Lowell and intriguing speculations.

What would this woman be like, this Jane Locke? Since writing her, he had been deluged by letters and samples of her poetry, and he had written her outrageously flirtatious letters in return. As the world raced past him through sooty train windows at speeds of fifteen and twenty miles an hour, Poe felt alert and on edge, the way he had been when he was first wooing Fanny, or, long ago, the dreamy-eyed Elmira. Now the old game would begin again, its prize unknown, and all the more prized because it was unknown. Perhaps the most marvelous woman in the world was waiting for him, all unknowing, in Lowell. Each stop at each small station along the way only prolonged the delicious agony, the soft exaltation of anticipation. And at each stop, the locomotive, like Poe, trembled and fretted to be gone, its bell clanging out the warning to make haste, make haste, because trains and life do not wait, but rush onward.

So, onward to Lowell, unlikely showplace of America. It was considered a showplace by some because of its huge, seven-story, belfry-capped mills, and by others because of the snug white dormitories in which the mill workers were comfortably housed and sternly chaperoned against any taint of immorality. But to any drummer, lecturer or cotton broker lucky enough to have business in the town it was a showplace because of the ripe and laughing little "nuns" of Lowell—thousands of splendid, blooming young Yankee farm girls who thronged the streets in obedience to the factory whistles. "The prettiest women in America, by the Eternal!" Andrew Jackson had called the daughters of New England farmers who came to spin cotton in Lowell for a few years, much as their brothers all went to sea, to learn the ways of the great world and amass a tidy nest egg.

But immigrant labor now came cheaper than country lasses, and as every man on Poe's train crowded to the windows to stare when they rolled into Lowell, a sprinkling of Irish red and Italian black was already sprouting among the brown and blond heads in this flower basket of young American womanhood. Being a gentleman, Poe stared more discreetly than some, but he stared, and it was a deep shock to him when the only middle-aged woman in sight, a pinch-faced little woman with thin hair parted in the middle and dressed in two sparse ringlets over each ear, approached him at the station. A gentleman was with her, and she turned white with emotion when Poe confirmed, in answer to the gentleman's query, that he was indeed Mr. Edgar Poe and was expecting to be met by Mrs. Locke. *She* was Jane Locke. She was forty-three years old and showed every dreary year of it. She was not even a widow; the gentleman with her was her husband.

Poe struggled to control his disappointment. He bowed over her hand and was horrified to see that, from pasty white, she went lobster red, as if scalded. What in God's name had he indiscreetly written in those letters? She had obviously convinced herself, sight unseen, that she was deeply in love with him.

The Lockes drove him off at once in a rattling cab to their home, Wamesit Cottage, a Gothic vulgarity with gardens running to the Concord River. There, Poe found that in addition to a husband Mrs. Locke had four children. Still blushing incongruously, she murmured that she feared some friends and neighbors were so eager to meet the Raven that they would be calling before he delivered his lecture that evening. Perhaps he would like to rest now after his journey?

"I've left my own copy of your *Collected Poems* in your room," Mrs. Locke said with yet another blush. "Would you sign it for Mr. Locke—and me?" Her voice was choked with emotion, as if she were imploring him to save her life. Mr. Locke looked irritated, and kept glancing at the four children and the waiting servant, quite obviously wondering what they were making of his wife's behavior. Poe gained the sanctuary of the bedroom to which the servant showed him, closed the door behind him and leaned back against it, shuddering like an overworked horse.

Those ringlets! That long, thin nose! Those thin, wrinkled lips! For this he had traveled such a long way? For this he had so keyed himself up with anticipation?

The room was jammed with heavy mahogany furniture. Some hand—Mrs. Locke's, he did not doubt—had left a blue pitcher of water, snowy towels, a huge vase stuffed with snapdragons, red poppies and overblown yellow roses. Poe threw himself on the bed and contemplated the bouquet. After a while, unable to do else, he began quietly to laugh.

Poe laughed not at this pathetic woman, but at himself. By teatime, when he went downstairs to meet the assembled guests, he thought he had himself under firm control. The parlor was crowded with people, and he was his usual grave self as Mrs. Locke introduced him to this swarm of strangers with obvious and heartfelt pride in having Poe, her literary lion, at her side. Mrs. Locke's husband still looked disturbed; not jealous, actually, but apprehensive, stern, embarrassed, like a man who sees someone close to him make a fool of herself, and fears the world will hold him responsible. Poe made a small public ceremony of returning the inscribed book of his poems to Mrs. Locke, and he praised her own poems (sentimental nothings though they were) to the eagerly listening assemblage. Then, in an effort to lighten her husband's frowns, Poe included him in a public expression of thanks "for the great kindness, the great generosity these two chivalrous natures showed me in the saddest moment of my life."

Everyone sighed and looked wise. Obviously the Lockes had made no secret of their donation to Poe in the winter of his despair. Mrs. Locke's pale face beamed, but Mr. Locke still wasn't satisfied.

"My dear," he said to his wife, "our guests will want their tea. Aren't you going to pour?"

She went reluctantly to the teapot, and Poe was soon pounced upon, with simulated shyness, by a laughing eighteen-year-old who called to a pair of late arrivals, "Nancy darling, you and Charles must come and meet Mr. Poe. And then you'll recite something for us, won't you, Mr. Poe? Oh, how we'd love to hear *The Raven* from your very own lips!"

"Mr. Poe must save his voice," gloomily said Mr. Locke, who had lingered beside him. "He has to lecture this evening."

The woman addressed as "Nancy darling" said gaily, "We're coming to hear you, Mr. Poe. We wouldn't miss it for the world," and Poe turned to greet a slender young woman with curly, light chestnut hair and deep-set, dreamy eyes with an expression in them that instantly reminded him of his lost Elmira.

"This is my sister, Mrs. Nancy Richmond," the eighteen-year-old said. "And this is Charles, my brother-in-law. You must be very nice to Nancy, Mr. Poe. She's president, vice-president and director of absolutely everything that goes on in Lowell, and we can have you again and again to lecture if you make a good impression on her."

"Behave yourself," the young woman told her sister. "What will Mr. Poe think of us?" She laughed up at him with serene self-confidence, inviting him to think her charming. Poe did indeed. Here was someone very much to his tastes. Slightly above medium height. Perhaps ten years older than her schoolgirl sister, but still delightfully young, with a face as pretty and delicate as a pansy. His first impression of her was that of perfect natural grace. His second impression, even more vivid, was that of charming enthusiasm. Why, oh why did she have to have a husband standing at her side? Of course, this husband was quiet and fondly smiling and—indifferent? Good-naturedly indulgent of his wife? He certainly exhibited no disapproval as she gave her hand to Poe and pressed his warmly.

Poe decided to be charming in turn, if only to reassure Jane Locke's husband that he had no intention of encouraging the blushes of the sad-eyed Mrs. Locke. "Nancy?" he said contemplatively to the young woman. "I would have thought—Annie. Somehow you look more like an Annie."

She took back her hand and pouted, a mock pout. "Is that good or bad, Mr. Poe? 'Annie' sounds so plain. But I mustn't say that, must I? You'll promptly tell me it is your mother's name, or someone close to you."

"Indeed not," Poe said truthfully. "But wait, there was an Ann once who made a deep impression on me, although I never knew her, only of her story."

"Tell!" the young woman commanded. "It must be a romantic story."

It was, all too much so. The woman Poe remembered was Ann Cook, a southern lady of good family who was seduced by an over-ardent admirer and who consented to marry a second admirer only if he killed her seducer before their wedding day. And so he did, with scandalous results. It was a celebrated case in its time, and Poe had tried his youthful hand on a verse drama based on the story. But it was hardly appropriate for parlor conversation with a lovely young woman whose husband, even if complacent, was standing by her side.

Poe bowed to Mr. Richmond and addressed his refusal to him. "I will tell you when I know you better. But I can tell you that I began a play about the lady once when I was very young." He smiled. "I renamed her the Lady Lalage. She was wooed in a moonlit Roman garden with all the usual trappings dreamed up by young poets. Counts, earls, duels, that sort of thing."

The husband, Charles Richmond, brayed with laughter. Across the room, by the teapot, Mrs. Locke looked up, her eyes burning, her face once again a strained white.

"The Lady Lalage?" young Mrs. Richmond said. "Oh no, I don't think I like that. I shall settle for Annie. Roman gardens and earls wouldn't suit me at all."

Mrs. Locke could bear her exile no longer. She left the teapot and rustled anxiously to join them. "Won't you share the jest with all of us?" she said. She was in no way mollified when Mr. Richmond explained that her honored guest had just given his wife a new name. Her fevered eyes stabbed so jealously at Nancy Richmond that Poe broke into hurried questions about Wentworth Hall, where he would give his talk, his usual one, on American poets and poetry. Yet still Mrs. Locke slew pretty Nancy Richmond with her eyes, and Mr. Locke slowly turned bright red. "Ring for the maid," he said tightly. "It's time to clear. And time to go. You'll want to wash your hands, Mr. Poe. Melvin"—he summoned one of the four children—"show Mr. Poe where."

Feeling like a clumsy thief who has stolen something that is of no earthly use to him, Poe followed the boy through the back rose garden, past a berry garden, past a pigsty to the "little house." Even his guilty sense of propriety was outraged when, returning in the growing dusk, he found Mrs. Locke lurking by the pigsty, waiting for him.

She was weeping. "Oh, Mr. Poe," she gulped. "I don't know what's gotten into Mr. Locke. I had planned a simple supper for us here after your lecture, no guests, just us, *en famille*, you understand? Now he says you must go on to the Richmonds'. They want to have a few more people in to meet you."

"Why, that's, er, very nice," Poe said. "Very kind of them. I, er, trust you're coming too."

"He won't let me," she wailed. She tried to check herself. "I'm not . . . in the best of health, you must understand. So he tries to keep me from overdoing. Kind . . . considerate . . . oh! Oh, Mr. Poe, won't *you* be kind to me?" She reached her hands out to him, but Poe stepped back.

"My dear friend—"

"You called me 'sweet friend' in your letters."

"Then, my sweet friend, my dear, sweet friend, to whom I am forever most gratefully indebted—"

"Oh—damn the debt!" She came close to him. The air was heavy with the oriental scent of roses and the stench of pig manure. "Kiss me," she pleaded in a low voice. "Please, kiss me."

"But, sweet friend! I must not! Not that one's heart would not yearn to clasp you to one's bosom, but—but you are a wife. Your womanly honor—"

"Damn my womanly honor! One kiss. Oh, please. One kiss, and I shall be consoled for a lifetime."

Poe cringed back. He was shocked at her, but he was also deeply sorry for the poor, beastly woman. He steeled himself. He then leaned forward and with cool, closed lips briefly but gently kissed the hot, wrinkled mouth held out to him.

She clutched his lapels for another moment, then, with an effort, drew back, sighing. "Oh my," she said. "Oh my. My goodness, I suppose we should be getting back to the house. Perhaps you'd better go first. I—I'll just take a moment to compose myself. If Mr. Locke asks, I'll be right there. We mustn't make you late for your lecture." She paused, and a note of pride came into her voice. "All of Lowell's intellectuals are attending, you know. I assure you, I've seen to that!"

Poe left her by the pigsty. One kiss, she had said, and one kiss she had settled for. He felt a little contaminated, but a little proud of himself for his charity. And he felt a small, growing admiration for Jane Locke. Perhaps there was, after all, such a thing as womanly honor.

4

Poe spent the night and part of the next day with his new friends, the Richmonds. He returned to Fordham with a disturbing vision of a pair of deep-set, dreamy eyes before him. It was as if Elmira had come to life all over again. But now she was named Annie. "You must try to say 'Aunt Annie' now instead of 'Aunt Nancy,'" Nancy Richmond told a niece in Poe's hearing, and threw him a smiling glance over the top of the child's head. The lecture, yes, that went well enough, he reported to Muddy when he arrived at the cottage in Fordham. The crowd could have been bigger, but he was not displeased. No, the purse wasn't large enough for him to make the subscription-raising trip to the South he hankered for, and off Muddy must go to the city to bring back Thomas Chivers, who was up from his Oakey Grove estate in Georgia for a long-threatened visit. This time, by God, Poe planned to squeeze some money out of the wealthy skinflint to finance the southern expedition.

But it was Annie, Annie, on whom his thoughts revolved tremulously, like a butterfly impaled by a pin. Annie, with a pansy's pretty face and Elmira's eyes. Annie, simple, sympathetic and naturally sagacious. Even her family was charming—with the possible exception of that husband, but Mr. Richmond was at least cordial, pleasantly deferential to Poe and apparently too engrossed in his paper-manufacturing business to pay much attention to the lovely Annie. Poe had described the Lowell adventure to Muddy in detail. But not all the details. He failed to mention actually kissing the frog princess who obstinately had remained a frog, but they laughed together heartily over her obvious infatuation and Mr. Locke's ensuing fury. While Poe mentioned that he had spent the evening at the Richmonds' home reminiscing, he refrained from mentioning just what he had said. Annie and her sister had been so eager to know everything about his life. Perhaps he had improved on it a little: toddling Edgar Poe, the offspring of a runaway match, adopted by a wealthy "uncle" who wished to make him his heir, driven from his home by a cruel, jealous stepmother when "uncle" married again. While a tall old clock on Annie's wall ticked to the rhythm of his halting delivery, he had even spoken of Virginia, in a low, deep voice. Tears ran down Annie's cheeks as he spoke. The sight of her emotion so affected him that Poe wept, himself.

Yes, Annie was lovely. But married. Even if Poe had no need of a rich wife—or, alternately, the successful embarkation on *Stylus*—he must not spend his hours dreaming of a married woman. He must spend them working his way out of his financial difficulties. He must get rich. Ah, to get rich—to triumph—for Annie's sweet sake. At least, then, he would not have to marry some rich woman he did not love. The thought, now that he came to think of it, was disgusting. To sell himself into a marriage, merely to provide an income, like a pretty but poor woman who must get on in the world—ugh. Disgusting. *Stylus*, then. *Stylus*, at last, it absolutely had to be.

But Chivers, when Muddy delivered him like a faithful bird dog retrieving a downed duck, only wanted to blather. He strode excitedly through the door and to the parlor fireplace, a matter of three steps for his storklike legs, then strode back, talking ninety to nothing. "I've just sent off a play to Edwin Forrest," he proclaimed. "You know of his contest, of course. He's offering three thousand dollars for the best original American tragedy in five acts. Think of it, three thousand dollars! I had to keep Mrs. Clemm waiting while I sent off the manuscript. Sorry. But it's your own fault. You should have written me before you went on this excursion to Lowell. My dear friend, what a joy it is to see you! You've been well? Mrs. Clemm said you'd been well."

"Well enough," Poe said. Chivers's familiar, Georgia accent was balm to his ears, but what was this new costume? All black, funereal black from his ascot to the tips of his boots, as black as Poe's own clothing. Even Chivers's forehead looked taller and more imposing above his piercing, narrow-set eyes, but in Chivers's case it was from progressive balding. He was even carrying a crooked-headed hickory cane amazingly like the one Shea had left Poe. It was like seeing oneself walking through a door in front of one's astonished eyes. A conscious imitation on Chivers's part? If so, why? Poe was on the verge of commenting on the transformation, but he thought better of it. Instead, he said politely, "So you've written a new play? Splendid. But I hope you've not become so engrossed in the drama that you've lost interest in the idea we've so often discussed of your joining me in *The Stylus*."

"*The Stylus?*" Chivers said. "But I was telling you about my play. It's not exactly new. I sent it to you a couple of years ago. You'll remember. *Leoni, or the Orphan of Venice*. You spoke of it very highly. And of course I've been improving on it. It should be a great success as an acted play. Ah, Forrest! Forrest! Have I not spent some of the most joyful hours of my life in the theater listening to his able outbreathings of the genius of the immortal bard of Avon? Forrest will play my Alvino, of course. He is not yet too old for the role, do you think?"

Poe vaguely remembered the play, a rework of an even earlier play that, now that he came to think of it, was based on the same Ann

Cook tragedy on which Poe had based his own *Politian*—the very Ann Cook about whom he could not, in politeness, tell his lovely new Annie. But even in the instant Poe had paused to think, Chivers had dashed on to a deluge of description about . . . poetry? Yes, but he also seemed to be talking about some sort of mill machinery he was in the process of inventing, and in the next breath was off on the folly of allowing foreigners to vote.

"It is, therefore, obvious that no Roman Catholic foreigner should be allowed to vote until after the expiration of twenty-one years!" Chivers concluded roundly.

"Uh—" said Poe.

"Yes, enough of this chitchat," said Chivers. "Let us get down to cases. I want you to write down for me how to pronounce M-e-l-p-o-m-e-n-e. Mark the accents. Also C-a-l-l-i-o-p-e. There has been a dispute among my poetic friends in Georgia about the true pronunciation of them. I know you know and will therefore abide by what you say. Besides, I may want to use them in a poem. Ah, Poe, the embers of enthusiasm are still glowing with a quenchless heat in the center of my heart. Poetry is my chief delight. And speaking of poetry, I could tell from your last letter that you completely misunderstood *my* last letter. I did not wish you to *sell* the poem I sent you. I only wished you to *supervise* it, and then if it were *worthy*, to have it published. I know very well that poetry will not sell. Nothing, in a corrupt age, will sell but corruption."

"Ah—" said Poe.

"Nevertheless," Chivers said, "your letter was an intellectual delight. I studied it for a full week after receiving it. I believe it was strawberry time. I had just been eating strawberries and honey, such a delicious compound, it is the nepenthe of my life. But I'm astonished, Poe, that you don't write me more often. If you knew how much pleasure it gives me to receive a letter from you, I know you would write me every week. You must not mind the half sheets of paper on which I write you back. I don't live in a city, you know, and I write on the first thing I can get hold of. I know you know my heart, and why should I get thin French paper to pour it out to you?"

"But, I—" said Poe.

"I was sure you understood," Chivers said. "But you must also understand that I'm much too busy to do more than just scratch out a note to let you know that I am still in the land of the living. You must believe me that I am the true friend of Edgar A. Poe, and if you don't believe it, it will make no difference. I will still be *your* friend. And it is as a friend that I tell you, Poe—"

But Poe firmly seized the conversation. "It is because you are my friend that I am so anxious to talk to you," he said loudly. Chivers wriggled like a bored child forced to sit through a three-hour sermon, and Poe went on even more firmly, "It is about *The Stylus*, Chivers. My magazine."

"Oh yes," Chivers said eagerly. "I've been thinking of forming a magazine myself. I've even drawn up a frontispiece for it. It is going to be called *The Swan*."

"But, Chivers," Poe said bewilderedly, "surely you remember our discussions of *The Stylus*. You have always indicated that it might not be impossible that you yourself may have both the will and the ability to join me in the enterprise."

Chivers waved his hand airily. "I must have overlooked that part of your letter. Now, *my* magazine—"

Poe said, "*My* magazine would long since have been under way if I could only procure a little seed money for it. Now, Chivers, we have discussed this many times, and not just in one letter. But let me make it utterly clear. You see, as I have no money myself, it will be absolutely necessary that I procure a partner who has some pecuniary means."

"Well, how did I know this?" Chivers said. "But, no matter. I have no money either, being at this time in a business which places me above the use of it. You will ask me, 'What business?' but of course you already know the answer—poetry! Listen, Poe, I am working on a beautiful new poem I have tentatively titled *Chinese Serenade for the Ut-Kam and Tong-Koo*. It begins with the effect of a plectrum plucking on two strings. Just listen to the beginning. No, now, listen:

> "Tu Du,
> Skies blue—
> All clear—
> Fourth year,
> Third moon,
> High noon
> At night;
> And the stars shine bright . . .

"Now! What do you think of that!"

Feeling dog-weary, Poe said, "I think—"

"No, don't tell me yet. The ending is even more superb. Of course, I don't have the middle yet, but at the ending the beautiful queen leaves her balcony, and the sound of a bronze gong orchestrates the despair of her lover as the poem dies away:

> "Bo-aw-awng, ba-ang, bing!
> Bee-ee-eeing, ba-ang, bong!
> So-au-awng, sa-ang, sing!
> See-ee-eeing, sa-ang, song!
> Bing, bang, bong!

"There! Now. Now tell me what you think of it."

After all, there were worse things than finding a rich wife. Poe said sincerely, "I think it's abominable."

Chivers's thin mouth tightened to a tiny slit. "Well!" he said.

"I dislike discouraging another poet," Poe said, "but I really think, Chivers, that the sound is carried a little to extremes. Could you, rather, concentrate upon perfecting some of the effects you attained in your *Lost Pleiad*—"

"Yes, of course, you would prefer that," Chivers said icily. "You should, considering the fact that you stole so many things from my beautiful poems in *The Lost Pleiad*."

Poe was astounded. "I beg your pardon?" he said.

"Do you deny that you have stolen everything that is worth anything from me? Why, you stole all your *Raven* body and soul from my *To Allegra Florence in Heaven*, which you *know* you did if you know anything at all. The same is true of your lectures on poetry—besides many other things."

"Why, you're mad," Poe said wonderingly. "My *Raven* has nothing whatever in common with your *To Allegra Florence in Heaven*."

"Oh no? I'll grant you, Poe, that you're the greatest poetical critic who has ever lived, but you must grant that I am the man who has taught you all the things for which *you* have become famous, while *I* sit in Oakey Grove being called a crazy and a Yankee by every fool in Wilkes County, Georgia, just because I pay a visit to the North every once in a while. There's no way to talk your way out of it, Poe. Why, you bodily lifted your refrain 'Nevermore' from my lament on the death of my mother containing the beautiful refrain 'No! never more!' And I need surely not remind you that it was published long before *The Raven*."

"Do you dare accuse me thus?" Poe sputtered. "Make up your mind, man! Not that being considered a good imitator of Thomas Holley Chivers, M.D., wouldn't be quite honor enough for *me*, but if I lifted *The Raven* bodily from your *Allegra Florence*, how could I also have lifted it from your *Lament*?"

"You took the refrain from my *Lament* and the rhythm from my *Allegra Florence*, that's what!" Chivers said. "You've stolen my very style, which I alone originated! The very rhythms of my beautiful poems cost me years of study. It is a task which few have ever attempted, to originate a style, and it's *mine*. Furthermore, what of this *Ulalume* the *Review* printed? Someone has been writing you about me from Wilkes County, haven't they? For how else could you have heard of my brand-new *Lord Uther's Lament for Ella*? See, you did it again, stole from two of my beautiful poems. You bodily took over the mourning of my lost beloved, Nacoochee, from my beautiful *Nacoochee, or, the Beautiful Star*, and you *stole the very words* from my new *Lord Uther's Lament for Ella*, which begins, 'In the mild month of October/ Through the fields of Cooly Rauber/ By the great Archangel Auber—'"

Chivers's eyes were burning like brown fire in twin black caves. Poe rose. "My friend," he said quietly, "I think you'd better go."

Chivers blinked. "Oh," he said after a moment, "are you not feeling well after all? I could have sworn Mrs. Clemm told me you were feeling well."

"I'm afraid it's up and down where my health is concerned," Poe said smoothly, soothingly. "You understand?"

"Oh yes. Of course." The brown eyes blinked some more, and Chivers also rose to his full, lanky height. He patted Poe's shoulder. "I understand perfectly. You know, Poe, you *really* shouldn't live in the North. It'll be the death of you. You know, it's peaches-and-milk time now in Oakey Grove. Think how you'd thrive on peaches and milk! I have a really marvelous idea, Poe. If you will come to the South to live, I will take care of you as long as you live—although, if ever there was a perfect mystery on earth, you are one. However, come to the South and live with me, and we will talk about all our beautiful new poems at our leisure."

"It sounds wonderful," Poe said.

"No, I mean it," Chivers said.

"So do I, but I'm afraid I have pressing business that must be attended to just at the moment. However, I hope to make a trip to the South soon, and perhaps we can have at least a short visit."

"I'll hold you to that, Poe. Where did I put my cane? Oh yes. Now, let's see. The train station is . . . ? Oh yes, that way. Well, I must say I've enjoyed our sublime conversation. Let me know when you're going to be in from the country, and we'll resume it. I should be in New York for at least another two weeks. Pressing business, you know. If you don't come to see me the very first hour you're in New York, you may expect to be passed in the street without being recognized by me. Remember! I give you warning, and if it should be the case you can't blame *me*, for it's your own doing."

It took another five minutes, but Chivers finally muttered his way out. Poe waved him out of sight, then came back into the cottage and sat slowly in the rocking chair in front of the empty fireplace, not knowing whether to laugh about Chivers or grieve.

"Now, what was that all about?" Muddy inquired mildly, coming in from the kitchen.

"Nothing," Poe said, rousing himself. "You know how Dr. Chivers carries on. Muddy, do we have any money? I'm thinking of making a little trip to Providence."

"Whom are you going to see there?" Muddy said with quick suspicion. "Mrs. Osgood—"

"I believe Mrs. Osgood is in Albany or somewhere," Poe said. "No, I'm thinking of paying a call on another lady, a widow named Helen Whitman. Muddy, what would you think if I were to marry again someday?"

"Why, I'd . . . I'd be glad for anything that made you happy," she said. But she turned her eyes down to the cup towel she held in her painfully rheumatic hands. "Are you considering it?" she asked in a small voice.

"Only if you promise that you and Catarina and the parrot will never, never leave me. For we must stay together, Muddy. I could never live another day if you weren't with me. You know how I rely on you. You wouldn't get tired of taking care of me?"

Muddy raised her eyes quickly and smiled. "No, my boy. Never."

"Well, then, that's settled. Now go look in your sugar bowl and tell me about the money. I don't have to go to Providence immediately—but I see that go I must."

5

It was September when, preliminary skirmishes conducted by mail behind him, Poe embarked upon his formal joust by presenting himself and a letter of introduction to Helen Whitman at the door of her mother's red brick house on Benefit and Church streets in Providence. It was eleven in the morning, the most fashionable hour for calls, and as he waited in the entry hall he heard feminine voices softly rising and falling in the parlor like the churring and cooing of doves. But the elderly woman who emerged from the parlor to receive him looked more like a butcher-bird than a dove—large nose with a slight hook at the tip, cross expression, her dress molting from the full mourning of black to the half-mourning of gray. She stared at him with unblinking, hostile eyes even as she said courteously, "My daughter, Mrs. Whitman, is not down yet. I am Mrs. Power. Won't you join us in the parlor?"

Outside, the sun was bright, but this dovecote was so dark inside that Poe stumbled against a settee as he entered the parlor. A loud voice instantly said, "There, Mother! I told you Helen must let us open the curtains. My lands, it's like living at the bottom of a coal mine!"

It took a few seconds for Poe's eyes to adjust to the subdued light. By that time he had already been introduced to the speaker and several other ladies, so he knew that one was Helen's sister and the others were callers, but he wasn't sure which was which until the sister, Susan, spoke up again.

"I understand you're a poet like Helen, Mr. Poe," she said. "Well, I'm one too. Did you know that? Here's one I wrote about my father:

> "Mr Nicholas Power left home in a sailing vessel
> Bound for St. Kitts,
> When he returned,
> He frightened his family out of their wits."

The sister ended her recitation with a scream of laughter. "You see," she explained to Poe and the round-eyed visitors, "Daddy got captured by the British in 1812, and he hated being away from us so much that even after they let him go, he didn't get around to coming home for nineteen years. What do you think of that?"

She screamed again with laughter and seemed not to expect a reply. It was just as well, for Poe was speechless. Was the sister going to turn out to be as eccentric as Chivers, and Helen as eccentric as her sister?

Poe was the only man present in the parlor, and whereas he normally would have been pleased, he found himself feeling markedly uncomfortable. They seated him. They gave him some beastly syrupy mixture that might have been chocolate-flavored mineral water. They discussed in tedious detail the time it took to go by train from Providence to New York. It was a full fifteen minutes, time limit for the normal courtesy call, before an odd, deathly sweet odor tugged at his nose, and he glanced at the parlor door to see a woman flitter, birdlike, into the room.

Helen Whitman was forty-five to Poe's thirty-nine. She was dressed in white silk, with double skirts flounced over unfashionably narrow hoops. A white organdy fichu fluttered about her shoulders, fastened in front with a tiny wooden replica of a black coffin, and a thin, gauzy white veil covered her head. As she entered the room, a white shawl knotted carelessly about her waist slithered to the floor. It was hard to tell under all the layers of drapery, but her figure looked slight. Raising to her nose a handkerchief that reeked of the odd odor, she murmured to her frowning mother, "Pray pardon my tardiness. I am oppressed at heart today." Then, pale, timid, hesitating, she turned her eyes appealingly to Poe for one brief moment, before pausing to greet the visiting ladies.

He had risen to his feet, of course, and he tried not to stare as, finally, she fluttered toward him with rapid but uncertain movements. A lace fan clicked to the floor, joining the shawl, but the lady did not seem to notice that she was steadily shedding bits of her costume.

"Ah, Mr. Poe," she said falteringly, seeming scarcely conscious that she addressed him at all, "am I at last to hear your voice? I have heard the veteran Landor, called by high authority the best talker in England, convey his political animosities by fierce invectives on 'the cunning knave, Napoleon.' I have heard the Howadji talk of the gardens of Damascus till the air seemed purpled and perfumed with its

The Ladies 279

roses. I have heard the racy talk of Orestes Brownson in the days of his freedom and power, have treasured up memorable sentences from the golden lips of Emerson. Yet I am told that unlike the conversational power evinced by any of these is the earnest, opulent, unpremeditated speech of Edgar Poe."

"Madam, you have tied my tongue," Poe said, but he flushed with pleasure.

She gave him a small, nervous hand. Her eyes gazed over and beyond but never directly at him. Heavens, she had her mother's nose, though not as large and not as hooked at the tip, and her pale, eager face was irregular. Yet the brow was broad and noble, the mouth full and promising, the hair dark and worn with ringlets clustering about the face in a beguiling frame. Not bad at all. But, ye gods, what *was* that sickly sweet scent she obviously used all too abundantly?

"Mr. Poe," she said, "I was overcome with the most extraordinary sensation just now as I entered the room. I believe in the stars and in the great truths of the occult sciences, and I have been so fortunate as to have received many messages from the beyond, but none so strong as this. I *distinctly* received the impression that the names Poe and Power were once one. Can it be? Can it possibly be that I am, many times removed, your sister?"

"All too possibly," Poe said gallantly. "I too was overcome with a most extraordinary sensation as you entered the room."

"Then it must be so!" the lady said. She clapped the handkerchief to her nose and breathed deeply, murmuring, "My heart. The senses reel."

Was she fainting? Poe reached out to support her, but her sharp-eyed old mother was there first. "Really, Helen," she scolded, "there's not a thing wrong with your heart. It's that nasty ether you're forever inhaling."

Helen drew herself up, while simultaneously her filmy white veil joined the fan and the shawl on the floor. "Mother, my frail hold on life demands that I shield myself from the too savage light of reality. Mr. Poe, I am too unwell to speak with you further now, but we must explore this revelation that has been sent to us simultaneously. Won't you come to us again this evening? Ah, but you may be bored. Just a few friends, a glass of lemonade and my own unworthy self. It will be—"

"A dream, into which I yearn to melt 'as the rose blendeth its odor with the violet,'" Poe said daringly, quoting Keats.

The lady understood. She blushed. The lines, after all, described the most passionate moment in a most passionate poem. "'Sweet solution,'" Helen murmured, capping his quotation with the next phrase. Then, as if overcome with shyness, she fled, this time leaving her handkerchief to float gently to the floor like a falling leaf of autumn.

That evening, flitting to and fro about a room dimly lighted by a coal fire, Helen discussed music and French literature, and presented Poe with the opinion they were both descended from a splendid ancestry dating back to an ancient Norman family named L'Poer. Upon questioning Poe as to his birthday and learning that both she and he were born on January nineteenth, she had to have another handkerchief freshly soaked in ether brought to her. The stars had obviously fated their meeting.

The next evening, now sitting by his side, now standing with her hand resting on the back of his chair, Helen discussed painting and German literature, and confided to him that, under psychical influence, she had transposed the letters in the name of Edgar Poe and had been astonished to produce the anagram "A God-Peer." Furthermore, she could clearly distinguish a strange spiritual emanation ensphering him, which she assured him acted upon those who were en rapport with him to enhance and intensify their spiritual faculties of insight and intuition.

On the last evening, disregarding her mother's obvious displeasure, she arranged for Poe to come early, and, all unchaperoned, went out with him for a walk, trailing the inevitable veil, peeping at the world through the inevitable fan, accompanied by the inevitable scent of ether. It may even have been stronger this evening than usual, and her wandering gaze had something troubled in it. Poe experienced a frightening feeling of déjà vu when she murmured that there was something she wished to ask him about and proposed that they stroll out to Swan Point Cemetery so they could talk in privacy.

Whatever could she have in mind? And why the cemetery? It was the very same cemetery where he and Fanny . . . where they . . .

But there seemed no way to duck the cemetery. Down the same country lane they trod underfoot the falling leaves of the autumn catalpas whose summer corollas, two years ago, he and Fanny had trod, and soon came in sight of the same cypresses, the same pines, the same wildwood copse where . . .

At the entrance of the cemetery, Poe tried uncomfortably for a tone of levity. "Receiving, as you do, messages from the beyond, do you not fear cemeteries? It will soon be dusk. What if there were ghosts?"

"That would be fascinating," Helen said eagerly. "I have never seen a ghost, although I once saw a beautiful, luminous hand write three initial letters for me, which I still have."

Strange lady. He never knew what she was going to say next. Sometimes her conversation was sparkling, even witty, and sometimes she veered off into strange fancies, as now. So he wasn't terribly surprised when, seating herself on a low gravestone, she said, "Edgar, is it true that you have met the great seer Andrew Jackson Davis? I have lately received a report that you once had an interview, and I am compelled to ask you about it."

"Why, yes," Poe said, all at sea. "I had heard him lecture, and someone introduced us. But we only chatted for a few moments. I don't even recall what we discussed."

"Ah, it's not what Mr. Davis says, but what he sees. Perhaps you're not aware that he is able to look through people. And, Edgar, here's what troubles me: he has told people that all about you he saw a background of very dark hills, with a mystic and dolorous landscape about your head, and . . . and . . . I am sorry to be the one to tell you this, but he also saw a strange, dark shadow that always lay before you."

Poe was amused. "I have seen that shadow myself from time to time, but I prefer to think that it is in my past, not my future."

"You must not cast Mr. Davis's vision aside so lightly," she said. "This dark shadow augurs ill for all that lies in front of you. It troubles me, Edgar. It truly does."

"Helen, dear, is that all? If that is the only worrisome report you ever receive about me, then I foresee a long and delightful future for our friendship."

Helen's full lips compressed for a moment into a tight line that strengthened her resemblance to her mother. "Oh, I have received other intelligence," she said tartly. "For instance, we have a mutual friend in Fanny Osgood, who chanced to write me a few days before you came to Providence."

"Oh. Um," Poe said. "I hope Mrs. Osgood is well, and that she gave you a good report of me."

"I fear Mrs. Osgood's health worsens continuously," Helen said, "yet she is courageously going on with her poetry."

"Then she didn't . . . speak of me?"

"Only briefly. Only to call you a glorious devil with a great heart and a great brain. Although perhaps she did laughingly call upon the heavens to protect me if a certain Raven were to swoop down upon me. She admires you, Edgar, and obviously wishes you the best. But, my friend, you should give greater heed to the possible meaning behind Mr. Davis's vision of you."

She looked sincere. She looked solicitous. Here in the gathering dusk she even looked astonishingly pretty. Poe decided to take the plunge. He sat beside her and said, "Even in the darkest shadows, a sun might yet shine. Might there not be hope for me both as a person *and* a poet? Even great hope? Helen, I have implicit faith in first impressions. I perceive that your interests and mine are infinitely similar. Would it not be glorious to establish in America the sole, unquestionable aristocracy—that of intellect—to secure our nation's place in the literary sun, to lead it and control it? I am ambitious, I admit it. And all this I truly believe I could do, Helen, if only there were someone at my side to bid me do it—and to aid me."

Her gaze fluttered downward. "Heavens, what a burden of responsibility that 'someone' would have to bear," she said.

"Sweet Helen, I speak not of responsibility. I speak of inspiration —and love."

She didn't reply. He sat close beside her and, trembling slightly with nervousness that she might repulse him, encircled her waist with his arm. Struck with a sudden inspiration, he said, "I have not told you this, Helen, but from the first moment I saw you I have had such strange dreams. It is as though I had known and loved you ages ago."

"Past loves should not be spoken of," she said in a low, faltering voice.

"But, Helen, I love now—now—for the first and only time. I love *you*. My darling Helen, make me the happiest man in the universe, and tell me what I most want to hear—the happy day when we shall be married."

"Please," she pleaded. "Say no more." She rose, leaving her shawl behind on the gravestone and dropping her fan. "You are not, perhaps, aware that I am many years older than yourself. I can only say to you that had I youth and health and beauty, I would live for you and die for you. But, Edgar, I am aging and ailing. Were I to allow myself to love you, I would enjoy a brief, brief hour of rapture— and, perhaps, die."

"Ah," Poe said sadly. "Beloved Helen, may God forever shield you from the agony your words have occasioned me."

"Please, Edgar, have pity on my heart. It is too frail to bear the burden of either agony or love."

Poe's eyes brightened. Oh, so that was it. She feared the carnal side of love. He cast about frantically in his mind for soothing words to serve up to her. He settled on, "But, dearest, it is my diviner nature—my spiritual being—that burns and pants to commingle with your own."

For a woman who couldn't keep from dropping every garment that wasn't buttoned on, she was surprisingly well organized. From a pocket, she produced a tiny flask of ether and sprinkled it onto her handkerchief and breathed deeply. "Edgar, my heart disease," she warned again. "From what the doctors tell me, I can give you no hope."

"No hope? None?" Poe said, talking fast. "May not this terrible disease be conquered? Frequently it has been overcome. Just as frequently doctors are wrong. Darling Helen, they've talked and talked about my own heart being diseased, but I stand before you, perfectly well."

"I assure you, *my* doctors are *not* wrong," she said.

"How can you be sure?" he said. "Nervous disorders, especially when exasperated by ether, can give rise to all the symptoms of heart disease. And even if your doctors are not deceived, isn't that all the more reason to reach out for the kind of devotionate care which I would bestow? Listen to me, Helen. I would comfort you—soothe you—tranquilize you. My love, my faith, would instill in your bosom a preternatural calm. On my own bosom I could still the throbbings of yours. You would rest from care, from all worldly agitation. You would get better, and finally well. And if not, Helen, if not, if you must die, then at least I would clasp your dear hand in death, and willingly—oh, joyfully, joyfully, joyfully—go down *with* you into the night of the grave."

She sighed. "You overwhelm me."

"I want to overwhelm you," he said. "I want you to say those coveted words that would turn earth into heaven."

Wandering—but perhaps not utterly dazzled—eyes peeped at him over the clutched handkerchief. "You must not press me for an answer now," she said. "I am utterly dependent upon my mother, and could give no promise without her consent and good will."

That brought Poe up sharply. "I . . . I see," he said.

"Of course, I have a few monies and mortgages of my own," she said vaguely, but very much to the point. "Still, were I to act against my mother's wishes I might find myself . . . cast adrift . . . only a burden to you . . ."

Poe knew the duties of a gentleman. "Sweet Helen," he said, "you have confided in me, and I can be no less frank. Before coming here, I *dreaded* to find you in worldly circumstances superior to mine. So great was my fear that you were rich that I almost didn't come. I have seen affection made the subject of barter and it has inspired me with the resolution that under no circumstances would I ever marry where riches and property could be suspected as the object of any marriage on my part. Now you tell me that you are dependent on your mother. How glorious! Come to me, beloved! Penniless? Cast adrift? I laugh in the face of fortune. We will make our fortunes together!"

Now the wandering eyes did look dazzled. But still she demurred. "I must have time to think," she said.

"But you will at least *consider* my proposal?"

"Yes," Helen breathed. "Yes, I will consider it."

She gave him her hand to kiss. There was nothing more to be won in the deepening shade of the cypresses of Swan Point Cemetery.

The next morning, before catching the Stonington train to New York, Poe walked out to the same cemetery and sat on the same gravestone. No thoughts of ghosts even occurred to him. He was too preoccupied.

He hadn't lied. Had he?

He was sincere when he told Helen that worldly goods were, if not *a* consideration, at least not *the* consideration in entering a marriage. Wasn't he?

It looked as if she was going to say yes. And he couldn't marry unless he were genuinely convinced he was in love with the lady. Could he?

He had asked discreet questions about her before ever coming to Providence, not wanting to repeat the fiasco with the unwidowed Widow Locke in Lowell. And his prior research had revealed that the "monies and mortgages" Helen had spoken of so vaguely amounted to some eight thousand dollars.

With a mere thousand, he would be well on his way to *The Stylus*. And, my God, what more could he do with a lovely, well-educated, wealthy, witty—even if somewhat eccentric—lady with whom he was madly in love at his side!

6

But *did* he love her? Even as Poe sat in his parlor at Fordham rough-drafting the first obligatory love letter to Helen, he realized that something was very, very wrong. Muddy had just returned from the West Farms post office, where some of their mail was addressed, with a new invitation to lecture again in Lowell—an invitation issuing this time not from the frog princess, Jane Locke, but from the fairy princess, Annie Richmond. A pair of deep-set, dreamy eyes that looked at him frankly and laughingly, not a wandering gaze that only fluttered in his direction, kept coming between him and the page. . . . *The divine trance of passion . . . the crystal heaven of your eyes . . . think of my lips pressed fervently and lingeringly upon your own* . . . To whom, Helen or the adorable Annie, did he think he was writing?

Poe leaned on his elbows and considered. He must not make love so passionately, even in a letter, to Helen. While she might desire it, she obviously also feared the passionate side of love.

"Colder than a widow's kiss . . ." The old wheeze floated through his mind. Would Helen be cold? Gentleman he might be, but in addition to gentle he was also, after all, a man. *She* would be passionate, that other she, Annie. He could tell from the expression of those eyes. To think that he would soon see her again! And that was the problem. If he truly loved Helen, why did the prospect of seeing Annie excite him so?

Muddy walked in from the kitchen carrying a vase of stiff, golden chrysanthemums, harvest of her walk.

"Aren't they pretty?" she said. "That Miss Marvin who runs the post office picked them for me. She's got some letters for you that came postage-due, Eddy, but I told her I'd pick them up another time."

"Yes, let them wait," Poe said. Getting his mail was a chronic problem. Even when people paid their postage, they often did not pay enough. Some of his mail was sent to him in care of the city post office in New York, some was sent to West Farms and some still languished at boarding houses from which they had long since moved.

Muddy smiled at the sight of his growing pile of pale blue paper, and Poe smiled back guiltily. Poor Muddy, she probably thought he was writing a new article. Wooing a potential wife, like all other enterprises, stole time from writing.

But it was for Muddy's sake, too, that he had gone a-wooing. Hmmm. Might be a problem there. Since Helen (not Annie, *Helen* —one had to keep one's mind straight) lived with her mother, Muddy might not be welcomed too wholeheartedly were they all to domicile together. And damned if he cared to live in close proximity to that butcher-bird of a mother or cuckoo of a sister, anyway.

Poe watched absently as Muddy began to sweep the hearth. He and Helen, and of course Muddy and Catarina and the parrot, would have to set up housekeeping elsewhere. New York? All well and good, especially for the sake of *The Stylus,* but there was no compelling reason why it had to be New York.

He leaned back and examined this thought. How extraordinary. He actually faced the prospect of financial security. That meant he would at last be free. He could live anywhere he wanted to, and not just where the next job led him. Richmond, for example. Home. The slow, sweet poetry that was the South. Turtles basking in the yellow river. Summer roads deep in mud. What he wouldn't give right now for one fistful of that very mud! If only one *could* end the long, weary exile and go home again.

Poe sighed, a small, wistful sigh. Regrettably, he had to take into account the fact that he was not exactly loved in Richmond. The old, old trouble with John Allan, from whose house he had angrily flung to go out into the world and make his fortune, had seen to that.

But, on the other hand, there was the other lovely Richmond—Annie Richmond. The thought tugged irresistibly that he and Helen could even go and live in Massachusetts near Annie, but he put the temptation firmly out of his mind.

What was it? What was wrong? Why did he keep thinking of Annie? He did love Helen, didn't he? Somehow he must probe that question more closely. This new Lowell lecture would help. He would stop in Providence and see Helen on the way to Lowell, to remind his heart and gladden his eye. Then, once he had wrung a yes from her, he would continue on from Providence to Lowell, where he could put his tenuous emotions to the test, to look at Annie more objectively and perhaps push her from his mind. There was room for only one love in his new life. The ethereal Helen.

But still, *did* he love her? He thought so when he left Fordham on a mild, sunny Indian summer kind of morning. He thought perhaps not when he arrived in Providence under dull, slowly gathering clouds and found Helen stretched out on the parlor settee in the company of her mother and her sister with the ether-soaked handkerchief over her face, complaining that she could feel a change of weather coming, and therefore felt heavy and depressed.

He was even more uncertain when, at her mother's proddings, Helen removed the handkerchief, sat up and, casting intimidated glances at the butcher-bird and antagonistic glances at the cuckoo, falteringly began to question him about reports she had received that he was a drunkard. The old stories, surfacing once again, rising from his past to haunt him. And she was apparently willing to believe them.

"I am greatly disappointed," Poe said sadly. "Not because a few people have dared to—"

"Many people have dared, Mr. Poe," the mother interrupted with icy politeness. "Helen has lately been tortured by a flood of adverse reports about you."

"I am not surprised," he said. "I have, unfortunately, made many enemies during my professional life. But I was about to say, I am not so deeply hurt that the stories continue to follow me, but rather that you choose to give them weight that they do not deserve. The stories are an exaggeration, Helen. A base exaggeration, growing from a time in my life when an occasional cup served perhaps too often and too well as surcease from the sorrow of my dear Virginia's illness."

"And yet, Mr. Poe, we have also received reports that you have announced to the literary world that you and Helen are engaged," the mother said, "when she has never, never agreed that you are to be wed. How do you explain that?"

"I have announced nothing," Poe said. "I have said nothing. Good God, Helen, I— Beg pardon, Mrs. Power, Miss Power. I did not mean to use unseemly language. But, Helen, I severed myself from the literary world nearly two years ago, and even were I still entangled in its spider web, surely you don't believe I would have said anything?"

"See, Mother, I told you," Helen said. "It's not Edgar's fault if the eyes of the world are upon him. I told you and told you, people have simply jumped to conclusions."

"That may be," Mrs. Power said. "But there is still the drinking problem. Go on, Helen, tell him."

Helen looked sulky, but she obeyed. "I must warn you, Edgar, that if even our friendship is to continue, you must swear to me that you will never again drink a single drop."

Poe was offended. He looked at the handkerchief Helen clutched in her hand. Were these women sane? How could anyone who constantly drugged herself with ether dare to criticize a man who had hardly even tasted wine since the day his poor wife died? He refrained from mentioning the former but icily told Helen the latter, at which point the butcher-bird put in another squawk.

"Now that you have raised the point of your wife's death, Mr. Poe," Mrs. Power said, "I feel compelled to tell you that at least one of Helen's acquaintances has gone so far as to suggest that your late wife died of your deliberate neglect and unkindness, that by her death you might gain inspiration for your poetry. I hope you realize that my daughter is delicate, and—"

"What?" Poe exploded. The blasted woman had gone too far. He rose to his feet angrily and started for the door, then remembered himself, and turned to bow, wordlessly, before leaving.

The cuckoo laughed loudly. "My lands, Mother, you're scaring him away," she said. "Don't go, Mr. Poe, or Helen will do what she's always threatening us with, and dematerialize on the spot. Mother didn't believe that foolish story. All she's really worried about is the state of your bank account. You look mighty fine, but what if you're one of those fortune hunters who's out to grab off a wealthy widow?"

"Susan!" Helen cried sharply. "Mother, I think Susan needs to go lie down now."

"Foo," said the sister, "I'm not a bit tired. After the way you two have treated him, I'd rather stay around and see if Mr. Poe wriggles off the hook."

"Mother!" Helen all but screamed. "Mother, Susan must leave the room immediately, this very minute, or I'll . . . I'll . . ."

"Dematerialize?" the sister suggested. Her manic laughter rang out, and the mother, anxious, clucking, darting dubious looks at Poe, was forced to lead the sister from the parlor, leaving Helen trembling with embarrassment and Poe trembling with fury.

"Just tell me one thing before I depart," he said through clenched teeth. "Did you entertain, even for a moment, the thought that there was truth to the allegation so wretchedly suggested by your mother?"

She inhaled deeply from the handkerchief. "Please, Edgar, you mustn't speak to me like that."

"And what about the way your mother spoke to me?"

"My dear, she's only worried about me. Dr. Griswold came to Providence to ask permission to include me in his *Female Poets of America*, and—"

"You discussed me with Griswold? He is the source of these infamous 'reports'?"

"No, no, Edgar, no. We hardly discussed you at all. Then, out of the blue came a most disturbing letter from Mrs. Elizabeth Ellet, and—"

"Ah!" Poe said.

"And a very curious one from a lady I only know slightly, a Mrs. Jane Locke of Lowell. She wrote some very odd things about some other lady named Mrs. Nancy Richmond, or a Mrs. Annie Richmond. I couldn't quite get the straight of it. But, Edgar, Mrs. Locke appears to conceive herself to have been deeply wronged by you. I hardly know what to think."

Good Lord, did he now have *two* harpies on his trail, along with Griswold and all his clique? Poe hardly knew what to think either, but he said stiffly, "If you knew me better, Helen, you would know that I have wronged no one—that I am incapable of any maliciously harmful act. If you choose to believe persons who vilify me, what can I say? I will, of course, investigate. I cannot allow such criminal slanders to be spread about."

"No, Edgar, please," she said faintly. "If you love me, you must not even think of involving yourself in a public scandal. Let them say what they will, but don't pursue it. My mother would never forgive such a thing becoming public."

"*If* I love you?" he said. "If you loved *me*, Helen, the opinions of others could not possibly be of importance to you."

"But I do lo . . . lo . . ."

"Dearest! Say it!"

"But, Edgar, dearest," she burst out, "how often have I heard men and even women say of you, 'He has great intellectual power, but no principle—no moral sense.'"

Poe ground his teeth. "I would not have believed it possible that such opinions could exist, even less possible that you would attend them," he said. "Helen, by the all-divine affection I bear you, and by the God who reigns in heaven, I swear to you that my soul is incapable of dishonor, that—with the exception of occasional follies and excesses which I bitterly lament, but to which I have been driven by intolerable sorrow, and which are hourly committed by others without attracting any notice whatsoever—I can call to mind no act of my life which would bring a blush to my cheek. Or to yours. If I have erred at all, it has been on the side of what the world would call a quixotic sense of the honorable and the chivalrous."

She took her nose out of the handkerchief. "And these follies of which you speak," she said. "You would promise to overcome them? To be firm?"

"If your answer depends on my firmness, all is safe," he said.

"You must give me more time. Only a few days, Edgar. Return to me after you give this lecture you mentioned in Lowell, and I promise you I will then give my answer."

"Answer me now, Helen. Don't keep me any longer in this cruel suspense."

"Then my answer . . . my answer is . . ."

"Speak!"

But the ether bottle came out of her pocket and tremblingly spilled its sweetness upon her handkerchief.

7

And, by God, he did *not* love her. How unbelievable, Poe thought with wry moroseness as he dressed for breakfast at the Earl Hotel in Providence two days before Christmas. How awkwardly appropriate, that by the time he realized he loved the lady not, he was stuck with her anyway. If sometimes his life seemed straight out of his tales of horror, at other times it was the stuff of his farces.

Not that his tales of horror and farce were so far apart. He'd known that since his apprentice days, when he'd made a careful study of what published readily in the magazines. The ludicrous heightened into the grotesque—the fearful colored into the horrible—the witty exaggerated into the burlesque. It was all in dubious taste, of course, but it was beginning to look as though life was as dubious as literature.

Going downstairs, he hesitated at the door of the dining room. The smell of food was almost as nauseating as his thoughts. Three acquaintances of Helen's, prim bachelor brothers who lived at the hotel, looked up from their plates and nodded to him, and Poe bowed. Thank God no seats were vacant at their table. He didn't feel up to talking to them, not with another visit to Helen's house already clouding his day. Better hurry up and have breakfast now, lest he get stuck with someone else Helen knew. The way his luck was running, it was bound to happen.

The place was packed with guests, and the guests were packing their stomachs with tea and coffee, wine and ale, biscuits, butter, creamed cod and cod chowder, fried potatoes and baked potatoes, pickles, conserves, apple sauce, prunes, blood sausages, deviled sausages and fried eggs, fried liver, fried steak, fried pork chops and fried ham. Simultaneously, they talked at the tops of their voices, trying to make themselves heard over the din of pots rattling in the kitchen, silver rattling against plates in the dining room and loud chomping sounds from their neighbors. Poe chose a table near the kitchen, the only one that offered a few empty seats. He asked a waiter for coffee, ham, applesauce and ink, and tried to ignore the chatter of his tablemates: three young men across from him, deep into deviled sausages and discussion of a fast rising gold mania caused by reports that some great gold strike had been made in California; two older men at the end of the table, drummers from the looks of them, who were deep into cod chowder and cholera, thanks to reports that cholera had broken out in Edinburgh and London and was on its way to U.S. ports.

When the ink came, Poe pushed aside his napkin and drew from his pocket a few sheets of paper, and with a grimace of distaste began to write:

> To the Reverend Dr. Crocker—
> Will Dr. Crocker have the kindness to publish the banns of matrimony between Mrs. Sarah Helen Whitman and myself, on Sunday and Monday. When we have decided on the day of the marriage we will inform you, and will thank you to perform the ceremony.
> Resp^y yr. Ob. S^t
> Edgar A. Poe

The ham arrived. It looked cold, and the waiter had forgotten his coffee. Poe grimaced again, still feeling nauseated, and put the plate aside. He'd have to write Muddy. Today was Saturday. Now that Helen had finally wrung every last concession from him ("You haven't forgotten your promises about drinking, have you, Edgar?") and answered "Yes," she seemed eager to answer "I do." She had spoken pointedly about being married on Monday, Christmas day, and it was now Poe who was stalling. But why not get it over with? As a gentleman, he was now committed. He began slowly to write:

> My own dear Mother—
> We shall be married on Monday, and will be at Fordham on Tuesday, on the first train.

He should say something else. Some cheerful word. But, God, he felt so far from cheerful. He'd just sign it. Muddy would understand.

But his pen hesitated even at the signature. Yes, the ludicrous heightened into the grotesque. It fit. The fates had presented him a ready-made plot, with all the ridiculous exaggerations and sudden turns any writer could desire.

He had gone to Lowell, as intended, to push Annie forever from his mind. But after Helen had kept him dangling, and after the way she and her mother had hurled the old tales in his face, plus new tales, villainous tales, he found himself angry and frustrated. Rather than wiping Annie from his memory, he grew more indecisive, and he became increasingly charmed. If love there was in his soul, then it was love for Annie, not Helen. But the love, which probably would have remained forever platonic, a distant worshipfulness, was startled to the surface by more letters, more tales, this time directed to Annie, so many sneaking tales spread by two other ladies in love with *him*, that Annie's doltish husband became alarmed. And Poe, just as doltish, just as foolish, just as alarmed, forgot himself long enough to plead with Annie to run away from her husband and marry him, to save him from having to marry Helen. The stuff of fiction? Yes. Only Annie, sweet Puritan with the pansy face, had come out of it looking well. Though it grieved him, he would adore her all his life for her gentle, worried answer: she loved him, loved Poe, but she must honor her commitments and he must honor his, and she would always be a loving sister to him.

Then, as with all his better farces, the tale turned to horror. For it was with sudden and overpowering horror that he realized his own ready-made plot was not even original. The first thing requisite to a tale of the sensation stamp is to get yourself into such a scrape as no one ever got into before. And yet with horror came the recognition that he was behaving exactly like the Reverend Dr. Rufus Griswold before Griswold's unhappy marriage. Substitute Fanny, whom Griswold had loved, for Annie, whom he loved. Substitute Miss Myers, to whom Griswold had then been all but engaged, for Helen, to whom he was the same. The cast was different, but the protagonists's speeches were so hideously alike.

He had returned to Providence after the unhappy scene with Annie, meaning to do as she bade him and resign himself to Helen. But he was so ashamed. Of all people, to emulate Griswold. He could *not* turn into a Griswold. Yet honor insisted that he follow his commitment to its end, as long as there was breath in his body. Knowing he did not love Helen, he had wandered the streets of Providence and steeled himself to face her. In the cold, keen air the demon of despondency tortured him still. Rather than turn toward Helen's house, he turned into a pharmacist's shop and bought two ounces of laudanum. Better to die near Annie than, Griswold-like, live with Helen.

But even there, the farce took over again, most appropriately combined with horror, to draw the tale together. Poe had far too little experience with drugs to know that even one ounce of laudanum was entirely too much. The embarrassing tale broadened into a splendid, comic scene. Poor, doltish Poe. How was he to know that the stomach would reject such a giant dose of opiates? He succeeded not in killing himself, but only in getting abominably sick to his stomach.

Still, the foolish tale had not ended. The ludicrous plot called for him to be alive a few days later when horror and farce intermixed once more to forge a dizzying climax. Helen, benignly and belatedly, accepted his proposal. Yes, she would marry him.

End of farce? No, there was one final laugh to bring down the curtain. It might have been considered anti-climactic, had it not been so perfectly engineered. One last grisly joke, which had come yesterday. For the poor, foolish protagonist, Poe, after all his talk of not wanting Helen's money, had been gravely handed, only yesterday, in the presence of witnesses, a document for his signature. The document transferred the entire assets of Helen's estates—some $8,300, lock, stock and barrel—to her butcher-bird of a mother. Poe, without an honorable exit left to him, signed. The last laugh rang out. The curtain came down. Now Poe would not only have a wife, but a penniless wife, whom he would have to take home on the day after a cheerless Christmas to share the barren cottage where he had once tried to make a home for a child-wife with violet, loving eyes.

"Good morning, Mr. Poe," someone said, and he jerked to attention and half rose, bowing. Some other acquaintance of Helen's? It didn't matter.

". . . join the rush to California?" asked a sausage-eater.

". . . stay home when the weather gets hot and the cholera cases pick up," answered a chowder-eater.

Poe looked at his ham. He would never be able to eat it. If only he could catch the busy waiter's eye, perhaps he could at least have his coffee. Ah, here came the waiter at last.

"Check," ordered the sausage-eaters.

"More wine," ordered the chowder-eaters.

"A cup of coffee," ordered Poe, but the waiter had no more than taken one hurried step away before a brilliant idea occurred to Poe. There was surely more than one way to end the farce. At least it was worth a try.

"Waiter!" Poe called commandingly and quite loudly, so that across the room the three prim bachelor brothers turned their eyes to him. "Waiter, I've changed my mind. Instead of coffee, bring me a glass of wine for my breakfast."

For a while it looked as though fate and farce would still win. His stomach had been so queasy in the hotel dining room that he'd had a hard time choking down even one glass of claret. He'd hoped to reek of the stuff when he called to take Helen for a morning drive in a rented rig, but neither she nor her mother, in whose face he carefully breathed, noticed anything at all. Apparently a single glass of wine had not been enough. His heart sank. By afternoon, when Helen suggested they visit the library, his faint hope had died. He watched with dull disinterest as one of the librarians tiptoed to Helen and handed her a note that had apparently been left for her.

But when, upon reading the note, Helen dropped shawl, fan, veil *and* the ubiquitous handkerchief smelling of ether, his hope revived.

"Take me home, Edgar," she said.

"But, my dear, what is it?" he said, gathering up her belongings.

She would not answer. She would only insist that he take her home.

And it was there—glorious!—in front of the butcher-bird that she announced, "Mother, Mr. Poe has dispatched a notice to Dr. Crocker regarding a matter of banns. The order must be countermanded immediately."

"Helen!" Poe said in his most deeply shocked tones.

The mother glowered at him and rushed to the side of her forty-five-year-old nestling. "What's happened?" she demanded.

"Mr. Poe has . . . Mr. Poe has . . ." The bottle of ether came out of her pocket, and its sickly sweet odor filled the room. After inhaling deeply, Helen was able to continue, "Mr. Poe has broken his promise and infringed upon the one firm condition set upon our marriage. I have it upon authority not to be questioned that he called for a glass of wine this very morning in the Earl Hotel."

"Traitor!" shrieked the butcher-bird. "Helen, you must not go through with this ill-fated marriage!"

"Nor shall I," said Helen staunchly, handkerchief to nose. "Mr. Poe, my good influence on you has proved unavailing. I bid you farewell, with feelings of intense sorrow thus to part from one whose rare and peculiar intellect had given a new charm to my life. But if we ever meet again, it will be as strangers."

She went to gather the letters he had written her and books he had given her, and left him thereby to the mercies of her mother, who was far from merciful. When Helen returned with the papers clutched in her trembling hands, she collapsed upon the settee and draped the handkerchief across her face.

What role to play? The despairing lover. It was only honorable. Poe rushed to Helen's side and knelt.

"Dearest Helen, speak to me!" he said.

"You must go, Mr. Poe!" the mother said.

"One word before I leave!" he said. "But one, final word!"

"Mr. Poe, the next train for New York leaves in half an hour," said the mother. "I hope fervently that you will not miss it!"

Then Helen's voice whispered dazedly from under the handkerchief. "What can I say?"

"Say that you love me, Helen."

He pressed close. Closer. From the ether-soaked handkerchief floated the last words she would ever speak to him: "We must never meet again, but . . . I love you."

As he left the house, Poe patted his ascot, straightened his coat, lightly touched his hair to see if it was tidy. He also tried to tidy his thoughts. What intolerable insults the butcher-bird had seen fit to throw at him! And poor Helen. Had he done the right thing? Would he live to regret it?

But his one, overwhelming feeling was that of relief. If he hurried, he would just have time to catch that train. And from this day forth, he would . . . Good God, what? What next could the wayward fates have in store for him?

Well, at least one thing was sure. From this day forth, he would shun the pestilential society of literary women!

8

There was no way he could have foreseen fate's last joke. He had to apologize to Muddy when, back home in Fordham, back home to the pale blue paper and impoverishment, he startled her one day after she had been again to the West Farms post office by bursting out with a long, loud roar of helpless laughter.

"Oh, Muddy," he laughed, gasping. "Oh, Muddy, you've got to listen to this." He picked up a letter which had long languished in the post office for lack of a shilling to pay its forwarding charges. "I am in receipt of a communication from one Edward Howard Norton Patterson of a settlement called Oquawka, or Yellow Banks, in Illinois. Muddy, he proposes . . . he wants to . . ."

He had to stop, he was laughing so hard, and she rustled toward him anxiously, but he got control of his voice again and said, "No, I'm all right. Muddy, listen to this. Young Mr. Patterson wrote this four months ago. He has just come of age and seems to have inherited both literary ambition and rather a lot of money. Muddy, he wants to put up the money, and I'll put up the brains for . . . for . . ."

"Good heavens, son, whatever is it?" Muddy said as Poe burst again into helpless laughter.

It took a full minute, but as soon as he could, he gasped the words out:

"Don't you see, Muddy? I'm going to have *The Stylus!*"

He need never have gone a-wooing after all.

Book V

HOME AGAIN

> "Over the Mountains
> Of the Moon,
> Down the Valley of the Shadow,
> Ride, boldly ride,"
> The shade replied,—
> "If you seek for Eldorado."
>
> Eldorado

1

Home, wailed the whistle of the steamboat as it wallowed up the yellow, winding James River. *Home*, pattered the warm rain that began to fall at the same moment Poe's eager ears picked up the deep-voiced mutterings of the falls. *Home*, cried the terns, circling, now white, now gray, above the tangle of spars and masts that lined the black warehouses of the rapidly nearing docks. "Home," Poe whispered to himself, looking up at the graceful hills of Richmond, the green hills of home.

It was Saturday, July 14, 1849, and Poe at last was on his long-anticipated trip to the South to gather subscriptions for the magazine he had wanted all his adult life, the splendid magazine that would form the literary taste of the nation. His future partner, Edward Patterson, the twenty-one-year-old crown prince of Oquawka, Illinois, was zealous to issue the first number of *The Stylus* no later than January next. While Patterson first proposed that it be published in Oquawka, Poe did not regard a settlement consisting of a grocery, two taverns, two warehouses, sundry dwellings and a weekly newspaper that Patterson had also inherited as the best possible choice of locale for a magazine that would exercise an influence never previously felt in America. They compromised. It would be issued simultaneously in the old, petrifying East and the new, wide-open West, New York and St. Louis.

So now for the subscriptions Poe had always known he could gather—and how much easier it would be, thanks to Patterson's money. He need not try to convince this old college friend, that old West Point acquaintance that they should pay their subscriptions in advance, but merely collect names of interested parties pledged to pay when the first *Stylus* rolled off the presses.

First, Poe made a short trip to the North, where perhaps he did not work as hard as he should have on the subscriptions, but, even better, had the comfort of sitting in Annie Richmond's parlor. Listening to the ticking of the tall old clock, he gazed with an affection he assured her was brotherly at the deep-set eyes and chestnut hair of a sweet Puritan pansy who for a while had reminded him of an old dream of southern violets and roses.

Then it was time to travel South. Poe cleaned out the overflowing cubbyholes of his secretary. So many rough drafts of manuscripts to be thrown away now that they'd been published. The arrival of his fortieth birthday—or was it the departure from his life of the idea of finding a wife?—had brought on a sudden wave of rich productivity. Bushels of miscellany, six stories, a major critical article on poetry, and poems, many poems. There was a greatly enlarged and possibly perfected version of *The Bells*. There was a short poem, *Eldorado*, that came upon him one day after he'd been into the city and learned that, of all odd events, Fanny Osgood's husband had given up his canvas and easel and had joined the Irish and German immigrants, the Bowery b'hoys, the wealthy young men from Fifth Avenue, the editors, the hordes of men who seemed to be rushing off to hunt for gold in that far land, California. Then there was a poem to Annie. There was also a sonnet *To My Mother*, dear Muddy. And, remembering a shy, sweet voice that once said, "You've never written a poem to *me*," he wrote a ballad to which he gave his sorrowing best, *Annabel Lee*. He hadn't tried for a publisher yet for the latter, but after thinking a moment he had copied it off and included it with a group of poems Rufus Griswold had requested for yet another edition of Griswold's disgustingly successful poetry anthology.

Everything tidy at last, Poe and Muddy temporarily closed the cottage at Fordham. Off went Muddy to stay with Stella Lewis in Brooklyn, off went Catarina to be fed by Susie Cromwell, off went the parrot to lodge with Father Doucet and off went Poe on an itinerary that reversed the years and the years' long journeying: Philadelphia, Baltimore, then Richmond. He left feeling optimistic but a shade depressed. Poor Muddy, how she hated to see him go. She had wept, even when he assured her he'd be good all the time he was away from her sheltering wing, and would soon return to love and comfort her.

Farewell, then, in the last days of June, to the spire of Trinity Church, seen for a final glimpse through the masts and across the bows of anchored California clippers in New York harbor, for New York was raging not only with a severe cholera epidemic and a screaming heat wave, but with the mad excitement of the great California gold rush. Hello in soft twilight in the middle days of July to the snaggled black teeth that were the docks of Richmond, and hot summer rain, and no doubt the same gold fever that was infecting every other port city he'd passed through.

As the steamboat thudded against the dock, Poe was caught up in a sudden gust of excitement and apprehension that felt ridiculously like stage fright. He clutched his flowered carpetbag tighter with his left hand and clutched his black coat tighter around his neck with the other, trying to keep his white collar from melting in the rain and wishing fervently that he had a fresh one in the carpetbag. This was Richmond, hallowed capital of Virginia, hallowed home, and a gentleman should look his best.

But he didn't really feel at home until a voice called, "Edgar! By God, Edgar, is that you?" Poe turned on the rough wooden planking of the docks, trying to locate the speaker amid the dockside clangor and shouting. From behind, an umbrella slid over his head and a big hand eagerly grasped his shoulder. Poe turned again, and he gasped with pleasure.

"Rob!" he exclaimed. "Well, by God! Little Rob Sully!"

The friend of his boyhood, once a fragile, blue-eyed, fair-haired little boy whom Poe had helped with school lessons when the younger child found them hard and whom Poe had protected with casual condescension from the bigger boys' bullying, stared back at him with the same delighted blue eyes, ignoring the rain that began to plaster his fair, curly hair to his forehead. "I can't believe it!" Sully said happily. "Edgar Poe, in the living flesh!"

A man striding rapidly from one of the tobacco warehouses stopped at the mention of Poe's name and stared at him alertly, then veered over to speak to Sully. "I most surely beg your pardon, Sully," the man said with elaborate southern politeness, "but did I hear you right? Is this Poe the poet?"

"Get along with you, Petticolas," Sully said with a grin. "Your damned old paper will have to wait. Poe's friends get a shot at him first."

The man grinned back. "At least introduce us, Sully. Then I'll give you fifteen minutes or so."

Sully sighed with mock annoyance. "Mr. Edgar Poe, may I present Mr. Arthur Petticolas, of the Richmond *Examiner*? Now shoo, Petticolas! Edgar, you old scoundrel! Are you home for good, or just passing through on your way to the gold fields?"

Poe's spirits began to lighten still more at the interest shown in him by the press. "No gold fields for me," he said. "I'm just here to conduct a little business, Rob."

A notebook and pencil appeared in Petticolas' hands, and, standing in the dwindling rain with pencil poised, he said, "Might one ask, what kind of business, Mr. Poe?"

"Shoo! Shoo!" said Rob Sully. "Edgar, you're coming with me to Sadler's for turtle soup and a full report on what you've been up to. Oh, all right, Petticolas, you can come too, but only if you promise to be quiet. Edgar, by God! I just can't believe it's really you!"

Poe had meant to go out to Duncan Lodge, the home of old friends, twice dear because, when he had been taken in at age two by the John Allans, they had taken in his baby sister, Rosalie, but once he had been hauled away by Rob Sully and the *Examiner* reporter, he changed his mind and left the flowered carpetbag at the old Swan Tavern on Broad Street. Once fashionable, the hotel was now at least respectable, home to many bachelor businessmen of the town.

To Sully's good-natured impatience and Poe's growing elation, every man in the house came up to him, courteously curious, curiously courteous, to shake his hand as he made the arrangements for lodging. Poe did not fail to notice delightedly that those who could say, "Well, Edgar, it's been a coon's age; I guess you don't remember me, but we did French together at Master Burke's," or "Why, Edgar Poe, of course, I remember the time you swam six miles from Ludlow's wharf to Warwick; bet you weren't more than twelve," looked with sly pride at those who could only say, "Pleasure to make your acquaintance, Mr. Poe; we sure kept reading a lot of things about you when you were up North."

Word spread quickly. The standard method of communication in Richmond in 1849 was to send a boy. Given a penny, any boy within calling distance, black or white, who was not otherwise occupied, would run anywhere in town to deliver a message, for he could usually count on getting an additional penny at the other end. Rob Sully chose a big boy to send to Duncan Lodge to tell the Mackenzies and Poe's sister that Poe had arrived and would be out to see them the next day after he had rested. Then, over Poe's insincere objections, Sully chose a little boy to run tell Poe's other favorite Rob, Rob Stanard, that their old chum was back home and to drop everything and hie himself to Sadler's Restaurant for a gala supper.

But the news that Edgar Poe was in town spread even without the services of errand boys, and en route to Sadler's his progress turned into a triumphal procession. How warming to see the startled looks, to return the bows. He was home. How gratifying to be halted by fervent greetings from John Thompson, editor of the *Southern Literary Messenger*, and then, within the block, envious greetings from hawk-eyed John Daniel, editor of the *Examiner*. He was home. How touching to see a little boy run out of a house and peer wide-eyed up into one's face to inquire, "Are you really Edgar Poe? My uncle just said, 'There goes Edgar Poe.' " He was home!

But he felt his stomach tighten—oh, God, if only he had a fresh collar—when a passing carriage suddenly stopped, and a face leaned out to put him to the hardest test of all. It was Mrs. Julia Mayo Cabell, whose family, the Mayos, and their home, the Hermitage, were golden memories from his years as the loved and petted future heir of the wealthy John Allan. All that was gone now. Mrs. Cabell was a cousin of the second Mrs. John Allan, his dead foster father's antagonistic second wife, and had automatically sided with the foe on the day when John Allan's angry threats, so often repeated, to cut off the supply of the bread of charity finally became a reality. Mrs. Cabell was the old, old trouble in the stringy, aging flesh, peering at him out the window of a carriage.

"Good heavens," Mrs. Cabell said flatly, "so it's true. Someone said you were in town, Edgar."

Poe had to fight to keep his breathing calm, but he bowed and said what a man reared in Virginia must always say: Unexpected pleasure.

"Edgar just got here, Miss Julia," Rob Sully said gaily. "We're taking him off to stuff him with terrapin and canvasback duck. They don't feed him too good up North. Look at him, skinny as a rail."

Mrs. Cabell peered at Poe more closely. All gentlemen drank in Richmond, but Poe's drinking habits were widely known and widely thought of as ungentlemanly by Richmond society. It was all Poe could do not to turn and flee, not because he had been drinking but because of the bedraggled state of his clothing. With the rain, with a spell of sickness in Philadelphia and without Muddy to valet him, he was far from his usual immaculate state. But he must have passed Mrs. Cabell's inspection, both as to his sobriety and his attire, for she only said, suspiciously but not as coldly as she had spoken before, "You don't look at all well, Edgar. Have you been ill?"

"I fear so," he said, quite truthfully. "I had what was apparently a mild attack of cholera in Philadelphia on the way down. The cholera is terrible there."

"Why, bless your heart," Mrs. Cabell said, now warmly indeed. "You're lucky to be alive, my boy. Take care of yourself. And . . . yes, I'll do it. Come call on me when you have time. You've been away so long, half my friends have never had a chance to see you. I might have a few people in some evening to meet Mr. Poe—or do you not have time for silly hometown parties now that you're famous?"

He really *was* home! Poe glowed with relief. "Nothing would give me greater pleasure than to meet your friends, Miss Julia," he said.

She leaned back in the carriage with a satisfied expression. "I'll count on you, then," she said. "Drive on, Belmour."

"So," teased Rob Sully as Mrs. Cabell's carriage rumbled noisily up the brick street. "With Miss Julia taking you up, we'll be lucky if we ever catch another glimpse of you. Come on, you old scoundrel. Rob Stanard'll be there by now, and supper's getting cold."

It was a long, leisurely supper, filled with laughter, with explanations about the coming debut of *The Stylus* and, after the man from the *Examiner* left, with exchanges with Rob Sully and Rob Stanard beginning, "Remember the time we . . ." Rob Sully called for port, and even though he knew he shouldn't, Poe accepted a glass.

Rob Stanard laughed at Poe for his obvious hesitation. "What's this, Edgar?" he said. He was a plain-faced man with a shock of unruly dark hair. He was the son of the first and loveliest Helen, Helen of the hyacinth hair and classic face, but in Stanard's blunt features Poe could only look in vain for any trace of his friend's beautiful mother. At least in Stanard's smile there was the same lovely light, and Poe smiled back, even as Sully teased, "What's happened to the old boy whose favorite toast used to be 'To him who drinks deepest'?"

"Oh, nothing, nothing," Poe said. "I'm still just a little off my feed from that business with the cholera in Philadelphia."

"You were serious about that? You really had a touch of the stuff?"

"I can't think what else it might have been," Poe said. He passed a hand over his stomach, wondering if he was beyond it even now. It had been a frightening experience. On the very afternoon that his boat left New York for Amboy and connections south, Poe had seen the alarming spectacle of a young Englishman go into a fit not ten feet from him on the passengers' promenade, screaming and shouting and struggling in the grasp of two frightened men who seemed to know him. People edged away, scandalized, thinking the Englishman was drunk, but one glimpse of the corrugated, blue look of his hands and the strings of ropy saliva in the Englishman's mouth told Poe the true nature of his affliction: the dreaded cholera. There was no doctor on board. Poe and a New York stockjobber whom he vaguely knew instructed the Englishman's friends to bed him down in a cabin. The poor fellow soon was dosed with laudanum bought from the bar, camphor contributed by a lady passenger and a mustard plaster rigged by a steward to try to relieve the abdominal cramps with which the unfortunate Englishman was convulsed. By midnight, when Poe reached the steaming hot Philadelphia waterfront, his own abdomen was in spasm. Cholera? Over a week later, when he had finally been able to hold a pen and write Muddy, he still hadn't been sure. Either cholera, or something quite as bad.

Stanard dug into his pocket. "If you're still worried about it, then I've got just the thing for you," he said. He spilled a handful of opium pills on the table. "Fire away, if your stomach is bothering you. Dr. Carter said start on them the minute your lower intestines show signs of acting up."

"Thanks, no," Poe said. "I'd better stay away from those things. I took some in Philadelphia, and I had a terrible time."

Stanard nodded. "I see snakes every time I take opium. What'd you see? Dragons?"

"Oh, God, everything," Poe said. "It was horrible." So it was, but sitting so cozily with old friends, slowly sipping the port, the memory began to lose its peculiar terror. How wretchedly lonely and afraid he had felt. How sick, and the opium pills he bought on the last ferry only made him more wretched, for he couldn't get his mind off Virginia, and then there arose a frightening idea that he couldn't get rid of—that Muddy was dead too. He couldn't remember a tenth of what happened, but he'd had the delusion that he'd been carted off to the county prison, where a radiant female figure, all in white, appeared on the battlements of the prison and whispered to him across a great distance, whispered something he couldn't hear, and he knew that if he didn't hear her it would be the end of him. It was only a nightmare, he knew, and it was the opium's fault, but it had been as terrifying as though it were real.

There was more. A cauldron of burning spirits from which he was invited to sip, but he declined, yes, because if he had accepted he would have been lifted over the brim and dipped into the burning liquid, up to the lips, like Tantalus. Thinking of this, Poe put down his wineglass. During the long nightmare the ghouls had also brought out poor Muddy, and, as a last means of torturing him, sawed off her feet to the ankles, then her legs to the knees, then her thighs at the hips. And somewhere the radiant white figure of his delusion took him on a flight over the rooftops of Philadelphia, and as he looked down, down, down, the figure turned into a black, evil bird that told him it was the cholera. Poe felt uneasy talking about it, but he told the latter to his two old friends, and Rob Sully burst into laughter.

"Just like you, Edgar," he said, "to dream your own *Raven* into your nightmares."

Poe laughed too, but he insisted, "It was no joke. Thank God I have friends in Philadelphia. They looked after me, and found my valise. It was missing a week before it turned up at the depot, but wouldn't you know, my money was missing and the two lectures I was going to use to pay my expenses through the South."

"You have friends here too, Edgar," Rob Stanard said firmly. He reached for his purse, but Poe stopped him.

"No," Poe said, "my credit appears to be good at the Swan, and I can rewrite the lectures. If I need a loan, I'll know where to come, but when you're a poor devil of an author you get accustomed to living from hand to mouth."

Both Robs laughed, evidently not believing him. Their famous friend was surely as wealthy as he was renowned. But Rob Sully pursued the subject long enough to say, "If we had any sense we'd all join the gold-hunting emigration to California and make our fortunes. Billy Benson is going, and I saw John Marsh off just this evening. Looks like there's not going to be a man left on the whole Atlantic Coast."

Poe shook his head. "No, gold hunting might be adventurous, but I guess it's not for me. I have too many things I still want to write. It looks as if I'm stuck with literature, and it with me."

"Then you're going to go on writing? I mean, aren't you going to be too busy, running your magazine and all?"

Poe was astonished. "Of course I'll go on writing. I shall be a littérateur, at least, all of my life. Nor would I abandon the hopes that still lead me around by the nose for all the gold in California. Hasn't it ever struck you that all that is really valuable to a man of letters—to a poet especially, be he a poor-devil author or not—is absolutely unpurchasable? Love, fame, the domination of intellect, the consciousness of power, the thrilling sense of beauty, the free air of heaven—these are all a poet cares for. Answer me this: *why* should he go to California?"

"Bravo," applauded Rob Sully. "Quite a speech. Stanard, refill Edgar's glass."

With a shock, Poe realized that it was empty. He put his palm over the wineglass to indicate he did not wish more. When he started making speeches, he'd already had too much. And if two such old friends as Stanard and Sully could forget that not all men could partake freely, then southern hospitality and conviviality were going to present problems.

"I notice you started off your list of wants with 'love,'" Stanard teased, pouring for himself. "Are you going to go see Elmira Shelton while you're home? She's a widow now, you know. And quite a wealthy one at that. You used to be mighty sweet on her, weren't you?"

"No, thank you," Poe said emphatically, "no rich widows for me." But his mind buzzed gently with remembered excitement. Elmira. His very own Elmira, the love of his young manhood. The memory was like a rejuvenating breath of the cherished past eddying softly into the present.

"Well, if you won't have a rich widow," Stanard said, "how about a poor one? Come on, Sully, help me think. We ought to get Edgar married off to a hometown girl before one of those cold Yankee women grabs him off."

Sully obediently began inventorying possibilities, but he yawned as he did so, and the yawn was catching. Stanard put down his glass instantly and apologized for both himself and Sully in keeping Poe up so late when he had so recently been ill and even more recently ended a long and wearisome journey. The two Robs walked Poe back to the Swan and left him after much back-thumping and planning for future meetings.

Poe was tired when he reached his room. The room was hot, and a June bug, attracted by his candle, flew through the open window and ardently began to buzz and bump around the flame, and Poe swatted at it listlessly with his hat. He missed, and was not unhappy that he had. Poor bug, let it live. Maybe a bug's life was as important to it as a man's life was to him. After all, life was all one had.

Poe wandered to the window, too tired to go to bed, and looked out into the darkness. The strident, summer song of a cicada burred somewhere nearby, and he could smell the river, an odd, musky smell, a smell of fever, a smell of decaying vegetation, swept along toward the sea by the dark, living waters. Home.

A few lines from one of his earliest poems bubbled up in Poe's memory:

> O craving heart, for the lost flowers
> And sunshine of my summer hours . . .

Yes, those were the happiest days, the happiest hours, when the splendor of the southern sunshine had competed on equal terms with the intense glow of his pride and ambition. Poor ambitious Tamerlane, his hero, himself. How much lovelier might life have been had he just stayed at home. To have bent the knee to John Allan and inherited the kingdom. To have become the conventional Virginia gentleman, bride named Elmira, plantation in the country, red brick house in the town, summer dust rising from the heels of one's blooded horse as one journeyed in between. Fewer poems, perhaps no poems, but in their place—home.

Suddenly, Poe wondered if he ever really wanted to leave again. Oh, he'd have to, of course. There were the subscriptions to gather, the lectures to give, a meeting planned with Patterson in St. Louis in the fall to work out the final details for *The Stylus*. There was even a nagging worry about Catarina and the parrot. What if Catarina wandered lonesomely back home to the cottage at Fordham instead of staying with the neighbors? Who would feed her? And there was

Home Again

Muddy, always dear Muddy, whom he could never in this world abandon.

But couldn't *The Stylus* be published simultaneously in St. Louis and Richmond, just as easily as in St. Louis and New York? Couldn't Muddy and Catarina and the parrot be brought to Richmond? Once back to his native shore, might not a weary, wayworn wanderer find . . . ? What? Failing happiness, perhaps peace.

Poe shook off the thoughts that buzzed and bumped around him like the June bug. He opened the carpetbag, took out a sheet of pale blue paper and sat down next to the candle to write a note to Muddy to tell her he had arrived. He had hoped to lecture in Philadelphia and send her expense money from the proceeds, but the cholera or whatever it was had taken care of that. Well, he had two dollars. He would send Muddy one of them.

Poe sat, the ink drying on the point of his lifted pen, contemplating the future, and as if it blew through the open window he felt a little gust of his old, youthful enthusiasm.

Home, buzzed the June bug, flying stubbornly at his candle. *Home,* burred the strident cry of the cicada as it sang its summer song. *Home,* purled the lazy yellow river, the undying voice of a dead time. "Home?" whispered Poe to himself.

He wasn't really home yet. Home was unalterably intertwined with the ghost of a lovely young girl with large, deep-set eyes from which her parents—once they had received John Allan's tight-mouthed assurance that a blackheart named Edgar Poe, once briefly called Edgar Allan, would not, after all, become his heir—had kept his loving letters.

Tomorrow he would walk by the old walled garden in which they had once wandered together and see if it still harbored roses and white violets. If the spring of youth had slipped away so quickly into fall, was there not such a thing as Indian summer? He might, later on, just might go see Elmira.

2

On a Sunday morning two weeks after, Elmira Royster Shelton was upstairs in her bedroom, staring drearily at the odd, barège-covered protuberance in the region just below the small of her back and thinking that she sincerely loathed her new dress. It was quarter-mourning, mauve-and-black skirt in a small flower pattern, black basque, which was all good enough, but how she hated the new shape of skirts. Who was it that decided women's backsides should puff out? Could her dressmaker possibly think women looked better shaped that way? No man had ever known it, but—if only for the comfortable trousers the world allotted them instead of crinolines so wide that one woman filled a carriage to capacity—Elmira often envied men.

She jerked impatiently at her undersleeves of embroidered muslin, making sure that, as was proper, her wrists were completely covered. So much bother to dress for church. God would surely not care that she was wearing a new cap-crown bonnet trimmed with this year's mandatory flowers, lace and ribbons, but her milliner would. Possibly Mrs. Poitiax, Mrs. Lambert and Mrs. Cabell also would, and possibly, if her day were unusually exciting, they could be caught looking at her with less than their customary bland, bored smiles.

From long habit, Elmira was only faintly offended at the silent proof given her daily that her friends found her boring. Elmira was bored herself. She sometimes thought she had been bored all her life. The protected daughter of a comfortably well-to-do Richmond family, she had been married off at seventeen to a comfortably well-to-do merchant, who had given her comfort, protection, a son who had lived, two infant daughters who had died, and an all-enveloping boredom scarcely alleviated by his own death. It was a woman's lot, but it was not a lot to live for if one were a woman.

Elmira gazed one last time at her mirror, and on impulse she stuck out her tongue at her reflection. Instantly, there was a firm knocking at her bedroom door, and Elmira's eyes widened guiltily. From the firmness of the knock, she knew it was her black butler, creaky old Dabney Bradford. Heavens, what if Dab had caught her?

"What is it, Dab?" she called, and the door opened immediately to his disapproving stare.

"Gentleman caller downstairs," Dabney said. "Come right before church. Now, what kind of time is that to come calling?"

"Well, I didn't invite anyone, Dab," Elmira said. "Who is it?"

"Say his name Mr. Po'."

"*Who?*"

"Mr. Po'," Dabney said testily. "Po'. Mr. Edgar Po'."

Elmira rushed back to her mirror to gaze with dismay, not at her loathsome dress, but at large, deep-set eyes that gazed back from . . . Dear God in heaven, what had happened? Where was the wistful, round little face? Where had this cold-eyed, boringly practical expression, these sunken cheeks come from? The mirror relentlessly marked the passage of the years that the mind's eye always forgot.

So many years. The last time she had seen him, with an indescribable feeling, almost agonizing, she had glimpsed him on the streets almost thirteen years before, a very new, very young wife on his arm. Only a few months before that she had met him on the stairs at a Richmond party to which they both had chanced to be invited. Alone, she was ascending the curving, double stairs. Alone, the handsome young man whom she had loved as a beautiful boy stood at the top, and for one moment his eyes brightened, burned, as they looked into her own. But other footsteps climbed the stairs behind Elmira. Her husband. After a single look at his wife's face, Elmira's husband had abruptly retrieved her wraps and hurried her away from the party. She and Poe had not met since.

Old Dabney loitered in the open doorway, his stare more disapproving than ever. Having told her a gentleman was downstairs, he clearly expected her to descend immediately. A feverish, pinkish tinge crept from the base of Elmira's strong neck and rose to the hollow cheeks she found so objectionable. She turned from the mirror.

"Thank you, Dabney," she said in a voice she was gratified to note sounded neither breathless nor trembling. She followed the old servant obediently to the stairs.

Even had Dabney not already given her the caller's name, she would have instantly recognized the man who waited at the foot. The dark lock of curling hair on the broad forehead, the easy, graceful attitude, one hand resting lightly upon the newel of heavy, carved oak, the brooding eyes that suddenly brightened at the sight of her—it was Edgar, it was Edgar, it was Edgar after all these humdrum years.

"Why, Mr. Poe," she said. "What an unexpected pleasure."

"Mr. Poe?" he said. "Unexpected? Surely you knew as well as I that I would come. I've been trying to get up my courage from the moment I set foot on the landing."

Elmira could feel herself flushing, and thought how ridiculous she must look, a woman of thirty-eight simpering like a young girl. "Edgar, you haven't changed a bit," she said, then flushed again at the triteness of her words. "Come into the parlor for a moment. I'm on my way to church, and . . ."

"Of course. I've chosen a bad time. You must never allow anything to interfere with church."

There was something strange about his manner. Was he sneering at her? Elmira's flush deepened still further, and she said astringently, "Quite right. I'm afraid you must call again."

"I shall," he said. "But first, give me that moment in the parlor. Oh, Elmira, what a miracle you are to my eyes. How absurd one is at nineteen. I suppose I thought I'd never see you again."

"That will be all, Dab," Elmira said sharply. How boldly Edgar spoke! She couldn't possibly risk the servants' overhearing him. And then, after she led him into the parlor, all she could do was stare shyly at the tips of the flat-heeled, light-brown boots that the bootmaker had wished off on her.

"You have a piano," Edgar said, looking about. "Do you remember how we . . . ?"

He sounded so uncertain, so timid. Why, of course, that was it. He was obviously as nervous as she. She regained a smidgen of her poise and said, helping him, "How we sang together when we were young. Or I would play the piano, and you would accompany me on the flute."

Edgar smiled, but his eyes—heavens, what incredibly long lashes, how she'd envied them as a girl—looked sad. "And now, we are no longer quite so young," he said.

She smiled back and quoted to him:

> "And boyhood is a summer sun
> Whose waning is the dreariest one—
> For all we live to know is known
> And all we seek to keep hath flown—"

She added, "Perhaps you don't remember the lines. They're by one of my favorite poets."

"Remember!" he said. "Elmira, I'm flattered. Why, I was thinking of *Tamerlane* on the very night I got to Richmond. But I'm afraid it was not one of my better poems."

Elmira looked helplessly at the tips of her boots again. "It was a very nice poem," she said. "I chanced across the volume one day at Sanxey's Book Store."

"Dear old Mr. Sanxey," Edgar said. "I would never have gotten to read much of anything if he hadn't loaned me so many books. He's too feeble to go out now, you know. I called by his house to see him."

"How sweet of you, Edgar," Elmira said, touched. "That must have delighted his old heart. He must have been honored that so famous a poet would even remember him."

"Not so famous, I fear," Edgar said. He smiled wryly. "Not so famous by a tenth, not by a thousandth, as I thought I was going to be as a boy. But you remembered. Remember also the line, 'I saw no heaven but in her eyes'? The girl I wrote about in that poem, Elmira, was you."

Old Dab came to the door of the parlor and looked at her pointedly.

"I must go," Elmira whispered.

Settled in the carriage five minutes later, going up the hill to church, Elmira gazed unseeing at the familiar streets of Richmond and had not a single thought to spare for the display, so fleeting but so all-important to her dressmaker, her milliner and her bootmaker, that she would make as she rustled down the aisle of the church.

The beautiful boy she had loved as a girl, the man that, given his genius, his burning ambition and not incidentally his trousers, she might have wanted to have been, had handed her into the carriage murmuring that he would soon call again. He meant it. She could tell. But alas, what about the poem that neither of them could help remembering? Did he really feel now as he must have felt when writing the last two lines of the very stanza that she had quoted to him? *Let life, then, as the day-flower, fall/ With the noon-day beauty— which is all.*

Noon's bright beauty may have faded, but she wondered, as the carriage stopped in front of the church and Mrs. Poitiax, Mrs. Lambert and Mrs. Cabell turned upon her their customary bland, bored smiles, if Edgar could possibly come to believe that the beauty of evening might, after all, be very beautiful itself.

3

They came quickly to an understanding. When it became known to Richmond that Poe was engaged to marry his first sweetheart, the wealthy Mrs. Elmira Royster Shelton, more doors opened to him, and old doors opened wider. When, as a defense against overly generous hosts, Poe joined the Shockoe Hill Division Number 54 of the Sons of Temperance, the doors opened wider still. Courted by the local society and the press for the next two months, Poe found it hard to do his own courting at leisure and in privacy, but on the evening of the last Saturday in September, when Poe left Elmira's house after paying her a farewell visit, he had a white violet pressed in his notebook and a gold wedding ring in his pocket, ready for his return from the North, from whence he would fetch Muddy, Catarina and the parrot.

Sweet Elmira. Poe sighed gently as he started the long walk down the hill, thinking about her. If his youth was gone, and a lovely girl with it, then ripe maturity had its compensations. How solicitous she'd been, feeling his pulse, worrying that he had a fever. How she'd fretted over his determination to depart on the 4 A.M. boat for Old Point Comfort and connections north, as he planned. How shyly she'd smiled when he reminded her that the sooner he left, the sooner he could return. There'd been no chance to kiss her good-by. That stiffly proper old butler of hers, a relic of her first husband's, had seen to that. Mayhap they should retire the old man. But, then, that could be decided later between Muddy and the new Mrs. Poe. Household matters would be their domain, while he threw himself into *Stylus*. And poems. Ah, the new poems he would write.

Poe quickened his steps. He had a great deal to do. He had to get a dress coat somewhere for the wedding, but maybe he could find a minute for that in Philadelphia when he stopped there. Yet another poetess, Mrs. St. Leon Loud, had read about him in the Richmond papers and had her husband look him up to offer him a round hundred dollars to edit her poems, and of course he accepted, especially since the whole labor would not take him three days. Yes, he would postpone the dress coat. There were so many friends to say good-by to, especially Rob Sully and Rob Stanard, and he must not forget to go by the *Southern Literary Messenger* and leave his surprise for

Home Again

John Thompson. Thompson had been so kind to him that he surely deserved a little trifle in return. Poe had copied out his final revisions for *Annabel Lee*, and would leave the poem with Thompson so the dear old *Sou Lit Mes* could print it first.

But he had to hurry. There were so many, so very many things he had to do. He could stop at the office of a new friend, Dr. John Carter, conveniently located midway between Elmira's house and the Swan, to attend to another good-by and catch his breath before continuing on to the rest of his errands. Poe tilted the broad brim of his new Panama hat, which matched his glistening new white linen suit with the black velvet vest, and hurried on down Church Hill.

Carter was alone when Poe entered. He wrung Poe's hand heartily and spoke of *The Stylus*, the Inspector's Weekly Report on Cholera in New York, about which he had just been reading in a newly arrived newspaper, and steamboats, advising Poe to stick to bread and coffee while aboard to avoid poisoning himself on their filthy fare.

"You'll be making a connection downriver?" Carter asked.

Poe nodded and picked up Carter's new malacca cane to examine it. "The *Columbus*. I'll probably stop in Baltimore for one day about subscriptions, then go on up to Philadelphia for a few days before wrapping up my business affairs in New York," he said. "Handsome cane, Carter. I lost mine on the trip down, when I got sick in Philadelphia. Maybe I should get a malacca when I replace it."

"Borrow that one," Carter said.

"No, no," Poe said. "I know how men feel about their canes." He missed his own sorely. It was the crooked-headed hickory cane that had been Augustus Shea's loving legacy to him.

"Nonsense," Carter said. "Take it. You can give it back when you're home again. When's the big day going to be? I'm planning to come dance at your wedding, you know."

"Right after I get back, I expect," Poe said. He looked up at Carter and smiled. "Damn business anyway. If it weren't for fetching my mother home for the wedding, I'd never leave."

"You watch out for yourself in Baltimore, hear?" Carter said, gesturing at the newspaper he had been looking at. "They're getting ready to elect congressmen and state legislators, and the town's boiling with excitement. Don't get yourself cooped."

"Not I," Poe said. "I know Baltimore like my own backyard. It's strangers who have to be wary."

Poe looked at the paper for a few minutes, resting, then left for his errands, telling Carter he ought to step over to Sadler's and have supper with him later on if he could manage the time. At Carter's insistence, he accepted the cane. "I'll guard it with my life," he said. "You just don't realize how attached a man can become to his cane. You'll be hobbling around on this one when you're ninety."

"No, you will," Carter said. "Come home quick, and I'll give it to you as a wedding present."

Later, at Sadler's Restaurant, Dr. Carter didn't show up, but Poe met another friend, and Mr. Sadler came to join them, and then some other acquaintances came in and sat at their table, and a cheerful party soon developed. There were wine bottles aplenty, but a newly pledged member of the Shockoe Hill Division Number 54 of the Sons of Temperance quite obviously could not indulge, and Poe remained sober, even when the drinking and the conversation went on and on.

It was near dawn when Poe remembered the time. He snatched up his palm-leaf hat and Dr. Carter's malacca cane and rushed off to the Swan for his trunk and carpetbag. Since everyone insisted on accompanying him to the landing to see him off, Poe was glad that the future held Church Hill and Elmira's comfortable house, not continued residence at the Swan, for they made so much noise that they awoke every boarder in the place.

By sunrise, Poe was on the river, and the hills of Richmond had already given way to swamps on the north side, drained plantation fields on the south. Somewhere across the fields, the mournful lowing of a conch sounded; breakfast time for the hands. The steamboat bell would soon sound the same call, and Poe looked forward eagerly to his coffee. Bread and coffee, Dr. Carter's prescription for him. Well, he'd stick to it. He wouldn't risk coming down sick again. Not now. Not when life finally was giving him what it owed him.

The Stylus. Richmond regained. And a gentle, unhoped-for present from the past—Elmira. Mosquitoes whined sluggishly about him, losing strength and enthusiasm as the sun increased in strength and the shadows faded. For a moment, Poe's thoughts went to Annie, sweet phantom, brief hope unrealized. But the eager fist that holds to youth must sometime loosen. If Annie had been the last of youth and lightning, then Elmira was warmth, sweetness, tenderness.

Home Again

A new season that succeeds the old. And who could say, when there was no need to say at all, which was the sweeter?

One thing was certain. He would not return for even one glimpse of the cottage at Fordham. He had written Muddy, many times, telling her about Elmira, and a final time telling her to give up the cottage and start getting ready to come on to Richmond in the packet. Fordham was beautiful, but Fordham was inseparably tied to another memory of another time, a time painful but beautiful which should rest undisturbed and thus intact.

4

Smell of pitch-soaked oakum and garbage; rake-masted China and California clippers through which little skipjacks and bugeyes skittered, bringing to the city their cargoes of crabs; long slips bordered by red brick warehouses—it was forty-eight long hours before Poe saw the docks of Baltimore, for the Norfolk–Baltimore steamer stopped at seventeen regular stops en route and at every plantation landing that chose to signal it. It was four in the morning and Poe was tired, so he hired a man from the boat to carry his trunk to Bradshaw's Hotel on Pratt Street and guiltily decided, once again, that *Stylus* subscriptions could wait. Elmira might like to accompany him for a more leisurely visit to Baltimore after the honeymoon. Right now, he had to get a few hours' sleep.

By noon, he was on his way to Philadelphia by train, impatient to get his editing job over with and hurry on to meet Muddy in New York, happily impatient to get started on the return trip to Richmond. He was dismayed when the train reached the Susquehanna River to discover that a northwest wind, bearing on it the cold reminder that the calendar had turned to lonesome October, was churning the river to a white, choppy foam.

There was no bridge. Passengers had to be transferred by boat to a train that should have been waiting on the other side, but there was no sign of the other train, either. The wind was rapidly becoming a blowing storm. One boatload of passengers got across, but the second boat turned back at the hysterical insistence of a seasick steam-valve manufacturer. Poe resigned himself to staying on the cars for their return trip to Baltimore. While the minor politicians of the city canvassed frenziedly for votes, he would, after all, canvass for *Stylus* subscriptions.

There was more time consumed in rehitching the engine to the front of the train. Then a bitter hubbub broke out over whether passengers had to pay extra fare for the return trip to Baltimore. The conductor maintained they must pay. The passengers maintained it was the railway's fault, not theirs, that they had to turn back. Once, a matter of an extra dollar's fare would have meant eating or going hungry for Poe, but now he sat back quietly and watched these poor dolts howl at each other and savored the extraordinary feeling of not having to care. Amazing, when fortune has finally smiled, how much less reason one finds to frown.

The conductor seemed to appreciate Poe's non-partisanship, for once the train finally got under way, he stopped to pass the time of day with the fine, white-clad specimen of a gentleman who paid so indifferently once the decision over the fare had been handed down —in favor of the railway, of course.

"Day's turning right nasty," said the conductor.

"Do you mean in here or outside?" Poe said with the faintest hint of a smile.

"Well, out," said the conductor. He gestured discreetly. "Those two men down from Philadelphia or New York or wherever, I don't care much for their looks, but they said the river was calm as glass when they came down on the eleven o'clock to meet the Baltimore connection, but they had to wait a couple of hours and it started whipping up before their very eyes."

"What happened to the train that was supposed to pick us up?" Poe asked.

"Wreck, sir. Bad 'un. Those damned Pennsylvania farmers just won't keep their damned cows off the track. Maryland men, now, they know better."

"I take it you're a Maryland man," Poe said.

"Yessir! Baltimore City, that's me. You'll be staying there the night, I suppose."

"It doesn't appear I have much choice," Poe said.

"Well, you'll want to be careful," the conductor said. "Election day tomorrow. Lots of ruffians in town." He gestured again at the two men who had come aboard the train from the other side of the river. "Not that a gentleman don't have to watch out anyway, traveling. Those two, now, sharks by the look of them. They've been giving you the eye since they first sat down. Like as not they'd cosh you in a minute, just for your collar stud. You'll want to keep your eye out."

"The world is full of sharks," Poe said.

"Yes, I reckon you're right," the conductor said. He glanced out the window at the darkening sky and said, "There'll be rain tomorrow at the polls. That'll mean a light election turnout." Then he touched his tall black hat and rolled on down the aisle in his rocking, seaman's gait. Poe gave himself over to patience and the pleasure of wondering whether Elmira had anything against gold and crimson, and whether they should redecorate her house.

Due to the delay at the river, it was almost eight that night and dark when the train returned to Baltimore. Poe hired another porter to carry his carpetbag and trunk back to the hotel he had left only that morning, and he turned his own footsteps toward the docks. It was awkwardly late to be calling on any friends, and he had bethought himself of a plain but respectable eating house he had once frequented when he was a young, hopeful writer living just a short walk away on Wilks Street in Mechanics Row with his Aunt Muddy and little Cousin Virginia. The Widow Meagher's, the place was called. The proprietress was as Irish as her name but the black cook was Mississippi-born. The plain boiled crabs would be subtly seasoned with hot red pepper, thyme and allspice, and the roasted oysters on the half shell would come from the oven sizzling with butter and fragrant with lemon juice. He'd had a hard day's traveling. He would give himself a small treat.

Mm, mm, mm. He'd quite forgotten, it had been so long, but those oysters would also be lightly sprinkled with toasted cracker crumbs, topped by a turn of freshly ground black pepper from a pepper mill. If Richmond was the rediscovered home of his heart, could it be that Baltimore was the rediscovered home of his stomach?

Poe was still smiling to himself over his little joke and thinking of nothing more profound than the hot biscuits that the Widow Meagher's cook would give him with his crabs and oysters when the two men caught up with him.

The streetlights had been lit, and the two rowdies glimpsed Poe's meditative profile as he passed beneath the light at the corner of Pratt and Light streets. Attracted by the glistening white suit, the planter's hat, the handsome malacca cane, the obvious prosperity of an obviously southern gentleman, they had followed him from the train, not very hopefully at first, but with delighted astonishment as he turned down Pratt Street and walked toward the noisy rum palaces, the gambling hells and the dark, crowded warren of the docks.

"Je-e-sus, easy pickings," whispered the bigger of the two men as Poe walked through the soft pool of light cast by the flickering streetlamp.

"Somebody else'll spot him in a minute," panted the other man nervously. "Quick, before he gets to the next lamp! Let's get him now, or we'll lose his purse to the locals!"

The bigger man took a half-dozen long steps forward and, drawing from his pocket a black woolen sock filled with gravel scooped up from the spume-washed banks of the Susquehanna River, sapped Poe neatly at the base of his skull, just below his new Panama hat.

Poe sagged instantly. The big man smoothly slid his arm around Poe's chest and held him upright, but the Panama hat slithered off his head and fell into the filth of coal ashes, discarded tobacco wads and slop that filled the gutter.

"Je-e-sus!" the big man muttered as his companion slid to Poe's other side and helped support him. "I wanted that hat!"

The smaller man looked around quickly. Three toughs lounged in front of a seaman's boarding house, but they only watched with critical professional interest and made no move to intervene. "So he gets to keep the hat," the smaller man chuckled. "We still get his clothes and his pocketbook. Come on, help me. Into that doorway."

But great expectations can't be carried in a worn leather purse with a snap on it. The two men were disappointed in the money, just a little over fourteen dollars, and they cursed each other, briefly and indifferently, as they went through the rest of Poe's pockets.

"The cheating bastard," muttered the big man. "Fourteen lousy dollars. We ought to dump him off the wharf."

"No, wait, dammit," the smaller man said. "I've got an idea. My cousin says the Fourth Ward Club's paying four bits a head for voters. Let's take him over to High Street and sell him to the coop."

"Ah-h, what's four bits?" the bigger man said.

"It's a pound-and-a-half T-bone," the smaller man snapped. "That's better than nothing. Careful now, don't get him dirty. That suit should fit me fine. Christ, is he still conscious? Get that cane away from him. A cane like that, that's worth another fifty cents any day."

"I can't. He won't turn loose."

Struggling feebly, mumbling incoherently, Poe had just enough strength left to keep a death-grip on the cane. There was something about the cane that was important. As they dragged him through the dockside streets, moving as unobtrusively as possible, Poe's hat, filthy from the gutter, kept falling off his lolling head, but he stubbornly clutched the cane.

This sign of life was encouraging to the boss of the Whig coop on High Street in back of an old engine house. He wasn't about to pay fifty cents for any dead man. Didn't those two rowdies from Philadelphia realize a man had to be able to mark his X in the proper place, conscious enough to hold up his hand before an election judge and take the oath that he was a citizen, if he was going to be voted? He almost told them to take their chicken elsewhere, but when they started stripping off the man's clothing and replacing it with a stained, sleazy, black alpaca coat, worn and baggy cassinette pantaloons and a pair of worn-out shoes, he saw the chicken rouse himself and fight to hold onto the cane, so he nodded and agreed to accept him for the coop.

The fellow bucked and spat when they poured the usual opium-dosed whiskey down him to keep him happy until the polls opened in the morning, and the coop boss was almost sorry he'd bought him. Damned fellow wasted at least a pint. But finally he got his dose and quieted down, and the boss had him chucked in back with the other chickens, maybe a hundred thirty, hundred forty of them now, that he had all ready and waiting to be dosed again in the morning and then voted at every poll they could be herded to in order that a sweeping Whig victory might be assured.

It was dark in the big back room of the old engine house. The place reeked of poverty, cheap whiskey and vomit, but most of the men were unconscious, so it was quiet.

Poe was thrown across someone's legs, and as he struggled to sit up, someone stirred next to him and clumsily struck a match, sticking it in his face. "My God, Johnson," a voice murmured with groggy indignation, "so they got you too?"

"Mm—M'rmm," Poe said, trying to tell the man that his name wasn't Johnson. He held tight to the cane.

The match flickered out and Poe's neighbor struck another. "They got me and three of my friends. It was the police who nabbed us. Right off the streets."

Poe's mouth worked briefly, trying to form words. After a long while, he said, "I don't feel very well."

"For God's sake, don't throw up on my legs," the voice said, and the legs moved jerkily. "Listen, Johnson, how can we get out of here? Can we break the lock?"

The man continued to talk, blithering soddenly, but Poe stopped listening. It was too hard to concentrate. Too difficult to understand what was happening. The man had him mixed up with someone else. His name wasn't Johnson. What made the man think he was Johnson, anyway? Oh, the cane. Of course, the man thought that it belonged to somebody named Johnson. But no, it was the cane Shea had given him. He had to keep the cane. Poor Shea, it had brought *him* no luck, but it was a lucky cane, and he had to keep it or he'd lose his luck.

The legs under his head succeeded in squirming out from under him and Poe's hat, so clean, so new, now so filthy, so battered from its many falls, fell to the filthy floor along with his head. Poe thought about it a long time, even though the irritating voice kept droning beside him and threatening his concentration. Then finally the voice trailed off and Poe remembered what it was he'd been trying to think of. He was beginning to feel even worse, but . . . cooped, was he? That would mean being dragged about the streets, being voted tomorrow from the moment the polls opened until they closed. Slowly, slowly, holding tightly to the cane with one hand, he reached out and grasped the hat with his other and shifted it to his head. A gentleman couldn't be seen in the public streets without his hat.

5

The next day, the other stupefied men—derelicts, unwary travelers, a few stray citizens—participated in the democratic process by being prodded from poll to poll and voted at thirty different places. Most went quietly, too dazed from the whiskey-and-opium mixture to know what was happening. Some even went happily. The whiskey they poured down you every few hours was raw and cheap and the quality of the crude opium with which it was liberally laced was dubious, but if you were down and out on the docks of Baltimore, there were worse ways to earn a highly potent potation. When you'd had enough, well, you'd had enough, and your keepers would abandon you where you fell and leave you to sleep it off.

Edgar Poe, sometimes and some places known as the Raven after a poem most of his unknowing keepers knew by heart, fell in the ashen afternoon, stumbling on a skid, as the long, wide boards stretched across barrels in lieu of a proper wooden sidewalk were known locally. He fell from the skid into oozy mud; true to the train conductor's prediction, election day was adrip with a thin, chill rain. Poe chanced to take his fall on Lombard Street in front of a liquor shop named Gunner's Hall, and one of the chief cooper's helpers grumbled, "Oh, shit, there he goes again. What's the use of dragging around a dead man?"

The boss cooper turned Poe's body over with the tip of his boot. "Hell, he's not dead," he said worriedly. "Reynolds is election judge at Ryan's poll. He'll let us vote him."

"Not if he can't stand up, he won't," the helper argued. "Come on, I've had to carry him on the last three rounds. Let him go. I'm too damned tired to drag my own feet, much less him."

They left Poe in the gutter. He lay there for over an hour, object of indifferent gaze of passing pedestrians—not that any citizen of Baltimore wouldn't have halted promptly to aid him had they realized he was ill, but the sight of a discarded voter near a well-known party coop on election day was too common to attract their attention. Besides, from his filthy, ragged clothes and tattered, almost brimless Panama hat, anyone could tell that the man in the gutter was just another wretched derelict.

Toward three o'clock, however, Joseph Walker, a compositor at the Baltimore *Sun*, hurried past from Ryan's Fourth Ward Poll, where he had just exercised his franchise, and chanced to notice that the ill-dressed derelict was tightly clutching an expensive malacca cane. Walker paused. The derelict wore neither vest nor neck cloth, and his shirt front was as filthy as his face. But what was there about that bloated, dirty face that seemed familiar?

Walker stooped beside the man, careful to keep his pants cuffs from the mud and said, "Say there. You, fellow. Come on, now, you're going to get sick lying about in this rain. Come on, now, fellow, try to get up."

The man muttered incoherently and raised large, lusterless eyes to Walker's face.

"Come on, you can sit up if you try," Walker said. "Are you sick or something? Sa-a-a-y. I know you. Don't you recognize me? I'm Joe Walker. I used to work at the *Saturday Courier*. You used to write all them stories."

The man struggled to a sitting position, still clutching the cane. "Sorry," he said faintly. "Unexpected pleasure, Walker."

"Poe!" Walker said. "Good God in heaven! Poe, that's who you are! Poe, the poet! Why, man, what are you doing here?" He glanced at Gunner's Hall in back of him and thought he knew the answer, even when Poe seemed unable to supply one, but the saloon was the closest refuge from the cold, drizzling rain. Sacrificing his cuffs and sleeves, Walker succeeded in pulling Poe out of the mud, holding him up for the few necessary steps to get him inside Gunner's, and propping him in an armchair. Poe lapsed into more incoherent mutterings. He seemed more unconscious than conscious.

"Had a drop too many, eh?" said one of the habitués of the saloon who indifferently watched the proceedings.

Poe muttered something, and Walker dithered indecisively. "Maybe he's sick," he said. "Mr. Poe? Mr. Poe, are you sick?"

Poe seemed to rouse. "Sorry," he said. "Yes. I'm very ill."

One of the eavesdroppers snorted with laughter, but the barkeep leaned over the bar and said, "Better get him a doctor. He looks damned sick to me."

"Yes, a doctor," Poe whispered. "Dr. Snodgrass. On High Street. He's an acquaintance. Please . . ."

With paper borrowed from the barkeep, Walker wrote a hasty note to Dr. Snodgrass and sent it by the pot-boy, but Poe lapsed again into full unconsciousness, broken only by a sobbing breath, a moan, a mutter, and Walker panicked. He couldn't wait until Snodgrass arrived. He had to get back to the *Sun*. They'd only let him off to vote, and he'd already been gone far too long. Upon advice of the saloon's patrons, who obviously didn't want a sick man around while they were drinking, Walker stopped a hack outside and loaded into it the filthy, muttering form that still clutched tightly a handsome malacca cane. He gave the driver a card with a hastily scribbled note on it bearing Poe's name, and sent the hack off through the rainy streets of Baltimore at five in the afternoon to Washington Hospital.

The Washington College Hospital was a busy place. Students daily traversed its wards, peering at the patients in 250 beds, seldom less than 150 of which were occupied. Dr. John J. Moran, physician-in-charge, was a busy man. When the porter came to notify him that a hack was at the door containing a man in a stupor, Moran was writing a letter. It was important, so Moran said, "I'll be along soon," and returned to his writing. The letter was a complaint to Washington about the sailors who were regularly sent to the hospital by the government and the fact that the lye soap which they used there should be supplied by the government and not by the hospital. Washington Hospital was not a charity hospital, and Dr. Moran's support and the support of his family, who lived with him on the premises, depended on the hospital receipts. The sailors used far too much soap and were cutting into those receipts.

When the porter came again to tell him that the man in the hack looked pretty bad, Dr. Moran threw down his pen in disgust. He never had a moment to himself. He rose and followed the porter outside, and suppressed a grimace of annoyance when he looked into the hack.

"Where did this man come from?" he asked the driver.

"Near the Light Street wharf, sir."

"Dead drunk, I suppose?"

"No, sir, he's a very sick man. A very sick man, sir."

"Are you sure he isn't drunk?"

The driver began looking miffed. "He didn't smell of whiskey, sir, and he was too white in the face. I had to pick him up in my arms like a baby to get him in the back."

"All right, all right, who sent him? Who pays?"

"You have the ticket," the driver said. "Gave it to your man there, I did."

Dr. Moran snapped his fingers impatiently at the porter, gesturing for "the ticket," whatever that was. He was handed only a plain, cheap card with something scrawled on it. A name, it looked like. Very poorly written. He turned a scowl on the driver. "What's this?" he demanded. "I can't even make it out."

"Well, now, don't look at me," the driver said. "All I know is that's what the man gave me, the man who said to bring him here."

"We can't take in every derelict on the streets," Moran said. "The usual charge must be paid in advance. You just turn right around and take this man back where you found him."

"Now, you look here, sir," the driver said. "This here is a hospital, and they said take him to a hospital, and I done that, and that's that. Now who's going to pay my hire?"

"Your hire?" Dr. Moran said. He turned to the porter. "For the love of heaven, will you listen to the man? Now he wants us to pay the hire."

"That's right, my hire, I earned it. I did proper, sir, and now it's up to you to do the same."

Nothing more exasperating had happened to Dr. Moran during a long, exasperating day. It was with ill grace that he finally gave in to the driver's stubbornness and handed him two shillings, and he wouldn't have done that had he not chanced to notice the cane that the derelict was clutching. It seemed a nice one, and might fetch five shillings or so, so he could always get his money back. He ordered the porter to take the derelict straight up to the drunk room, a small room on the third floor in the turret part of the hospital building, iron gates on the window, where they regularly put patients who were in liquor, and he soothed his ill temper by snapping at the porter, "For God's sake, get those dirty rags off him before you put him to bed. They must be crawling with lice."

"I can't tend him," the porter complained sulkily, "I got the fever ward still to sweep."

"You do what I tell you!" Dr. Moran stormed, and he went back to his office and his letter, which took a long time to finish. The government simply had to understand the hospital's position. The reason the sailors used an inordinate amount of soap was not that they had any penchant for washing, but rather because they persisted in filling their convalescent hours with the wasteful habit of carving soap up into little whales, elaborate ships and certain, selected portions of women's anatomies, generally those existing between the neck and the knee. Moran was laboriously finishing a clean copy of his masterpiece when one of the nurses, male, of course, from the drunk room knocked at the door and entered to complain about finding a man on a stretcher dumped in the hall and left there.

"What?" Dr. Moran said. "Still there? I told Nat two hours ago to put him in a bed, damn his eyes." But the letter was nearly done, and this time Moran tried to keep his temper. He sighed. "Well, just find a bed for the fellow somewhere. Wasn't one of the beds vacated this morning? Ridge died, didn't he?"

The nurse nodded, but said, "Ridge peed all over the bed and we haven't got any clean sheets."

"So?" said Moran indifferently. "What do you think the new patient will do? Just put him to bed. Is he still unconscious?"

"Mostly. He comes out of it from time to time. He's groaning quite a lot, Dr. Moran. He appears to be in some sort of pain. He keeps muttering his head hurts."

"Oh, hell," said Dr. Moran disgustedly. But he was only a busy doctor, not a bad one, and he began to feel a little guilty about the patient's having been forgotten and ignored for almost two hours. Despite the strain on the budget, he was strongly adverse, as he frequently told his students, to having a patient suffer unnecessary pain. "All right," he said, "administer hydrochlorate of morphia and apply a cold application to his head. I'll be up in a little while to look in on him and the others."

Then, for a few blessed minutes, Dr. Moran had peace and quiet and was able to finish copying off his letter, secure in the knowledge that the penniless patient who awaited him would shortly find some relief from the monstrous hangover that surely tortured him. Hydrochlorate of morphia, or morphine, was a white, crystalline powder, as all good physicians knew, that was the chief active principle of opium.

6

Poe remained unconscious in the turret room of the college hospital from five in the afternoon of Wednesday, October 3, until three o'clock the next morning, when he threw the covers off his chest and looked groggily at the night nurse, who sat reading by the light of a candle. Poe asked weakly, with complete triteness, "Where am I?"

The nurse made no reply. He stepped into the hall and sent another attendant for Dr. Moran, who had left orders that he was to be called when the patient regained consciousness.

Dr. Moran came quickly, in his dressing gown, for by that time Poe's identity was known. Dr. J. E. Snodgrass and a cousin of Poe's, having deciphered the note from the Baltimore *Sun* compositor, finally tracked Poe down at the hospital a few hours after he was admitted and announced that the Washington College Hospital had in its care not the nameless derelict they thought, but rather Edgar A. Poe, the famous poet. Moran was startled and felt a bit sheepish when he heard. To think that he had worried about who would pay the hospital bill. Edgar Poe? Why, he was famous across the country. And undoubtedly as rich as he was famous. Moran immediately had the sheets changed on the drunk room bed, though Poe was unconscious at the time and couldn't appreciate it.

As the word spread around the hospital, all sorts of people came to peer at the well-known poet, including such long-time admirers as a medical student named Albert Grey from Virginia, and a young resident physician, George McCalpin from Alabama. Dr. Moran, knowing he would be plagued by questions from them in the morning, looked closely at his renowned patient and drew a chair by the side of the bed. He took Poe's wrist in his left hand, checking his pulse, and with his right hand pushed back the black locks of hair that covered Poe's forehead.

"How do you feel?" Dr. Moran asked.

"Miserable," Poe said.

"Do you feel sick at the stomach?"

"Yes, slightly."

"Does your head still ache? Have you pain there?"

"Yes."

"Mr. Poe, how long have you been sick?"

"Can't say."

"Where have you been stopping?"

The patient gazed around the prisonlike room, with its wired inside windows and iron grating outside. "In a hotel on Pratt Street, opposite the depot," he said. "Where am I? Is this prison?"

"No, no, you're at the college hospital, and we're going to take very good care of you," Dr. Moran said. But he frowned. Mr. Poe's pulse was very slow, and he seemed extremely weak. A stimulant to give him strength, or another opiate to give him sleep and rest? Dr. Moran tried to decide.

"How did I get here?" his patient asked wearily.

"We were hoping you could tell us, Mr. Poe," Dr. Moran said. "Don't you remember?"

Poe moved his head restlessly on the flat pillow. "Did they throw me off the dock?" he said fretfully. "I think I remember starting for the boat, and then . . . I don't know . . . I think . . . Were they trying to kill me? I remember a horrible dread that I would be killed, and they'd throw me off the dock. Poor Elmira. Poor, sweet Elmira."

"You have a wife, Mr. Poe?"

Poe nodded. "In Richmond."

"When did you leave Richmond, Mr. Poe?"

But the patient was slipping away again. His incoherent mutterings revealed some worry about a trunk: where was his trunk of clothing? He muttered and muttered for a few more minutes, then seemed to doze, and Dr. Moran rose with a sigh.

"Sponge his body with warm water, and add spirits to it," he instructed the nurse. "Apply sinapisms to his stomach and feet, and continue the cold applications to his head. I think I'll try . . . yes, beef tea and a stimulating cordial. Make sure he drinks them both. I'll send the cordial right up. Let me know if there's any other marked change in his condition."

"You want me to wake you up again, Doctor?" the night nurse asked.

"Yes, I suppose so," Dr. Moran said with another sigh. When you were a doctor, there wasn't much point in going to bed.

By four in the morning, when Dr. Moran's famous patient next awoke, there was a change, but not for the better. Moran found

Poe's breathing short and oppressed, and he seemed much more feeble. He was even less able to answer questions coherently.

By five in the morning, when Moran had risen, dog-tired, to start his daily rounds, Moran noticed that the color was deepening on Poe's cheeks and lofty forehead, and the blood vessels at the temple were enlarging slightly. His pulse, which had been as slow as fifty heartbeats a minute, was rising rapidly, but it seemed very feeble, very irregular. Was Moran giving him the right medications? It was so hard to know, without being aware of a patient's medical background. He decided to have the stimulant continued and left to attend to other patients, but upon next looking in on Poe he found the man trembling violently and in quiet but rapt converse with some sort of spectral and imaginary objects on the walls. The patient's face was pale and he was drenched in perspiration. Good God, what now?

Dr. Moran was not a great deal older than the students he taught, twenty-seven, and acting as administrator and physician-in-charge of a big hospital was a heavy responsibility. It was not that he doubted his own medical acumen, but he stopped and wondered again for a minute—stimulants to encourage the faltering heartbeat, or opiates to induce tranquillity? He thought of asking the opinion of the oldest, most experienced professor on the medical faculty, Dr. J. C. S. Monkur, but he was tired, so tired, and he couldn't decide. Yet he had to decide.

Damn it all, that's what came of never getting enough sleep. Moran concluded he had been wrong in ordering the stimulant. Opiates it must be. Opiates and tranquillity.

Dr. Moran worried still more when, despite the opiates, Mr. Poe continued to thrash and struggle all day Friday, all day Saturday, until Saturday evening he entered a new phase and commenced to call out for someone named "Reynolds."

"Reynolds!" Mr. Poe called loudly. "Reynolds!" He called for hours. It disturbed every patient on the floor.

When the chief nurse from the second floor came to his office to complain, Dr. Moran had suddenly had enough.

"Is Dr. Monkur by any chance in the house?" he snapped to the nurse, cutting the man off in mid-complaint.

"Yes, sir, he dropped by to see Mr. Peabody in the fever ward, and

I might tell you, sir, Dr. Monkur himself has commented about this disturbance."

"Please ask him if he can step upstairs and give me a minute of his time in the drunk room," Dr. Moran said. "I'll go up immediately and wait for him."

The pale man on the bed looked exhausted. He sounded it too, hoarsely calling, still calling, "Reynolds! Reynolds!" at irregular intervals. Dr. Moran went quickly to the bed to check his pulse and found it feeble and variable. He rose quickly from the bedside chair when the elder physician came in and bowed courteously.

"Hope I'm not imposing, Dr. Monkur," Dr. Moran said. "Got a case here that's got me plenty puzzled."

Dr. Monkur raised white eyebrows as shaggy as a sheep dog's. He took the chair by Poe's bed and leaned over him briefly, then looked back up at Dr. Moran. "There's no puzzle to it," he said. "This man will die. He's dying now."

"Well, sir, but he's been raising a ruckus since just about the day he got here, Wednesday. Maybe he's just enfeebled by the exertion."

"Nonsense, look at the way his eyes are dilating and contracting. Death is approaching, rather rapidly, I'd say."

Dr. Monkur rose and clapped his hand on the younger physician's shoulder. "This man will die," he pronounced, "from excessive nervous prostration and loss of nerve power. Found somewhere in a gutter, wasn't he? The condition is the result of exposure, affecting the meninges, which in all probability have been attacked by a low grade of inflammation. In short, my boy, brain irritation. What have you been giving Mr. Poe?"

"Uh, beef tea," Dr. Moran said.

"Good. That's about all you can do."

"And . . . uh . . . well, I did order an opiate when Mr. Poe was first admitted, but he went off into incoherence, and I ordered, uh . . ."

"A stimulant?" Dr. Monkur said mildly. "Tsk-tsk. Alcohol in the slightest quantity can set up serious irritation among morbid matter in the delicate and sensitive membrane of the brain. Of course, opiates might do the same. Well, when in doubt, stick to beef tea. That's my prescription. You can't go wrong with beef tea!"

Dr. Monkur took his colleague with him when he left. The

exhausted man on the bed followed them with wide, staring eyes, but he didn't really see them at all. He was adrift on a wide and desolate ocean, drifting, drifting out of space, out of time, and he had lost something that might have helped him very much as he felt a tug, a tug, then a harder tug catch his drifting craft. He had lost . . .

Oh yes, yes, he knew, he remembered again now. It was not something, it was someone.

"Reynolds," he whispered with dry lips.

How thirsty he was. To die of thirst, surrounded by a sea of water . . .

But he would not die of thirst. In the days, the days, the long, weary days in which he had drifted, all alone, until the edge of the irresistible current caught his helplessly drifting craft, he had realized that the polar winter appeared to be coming on. It was evident that he was hurrying onward to some exciting knowledge—some never-to-be-imparted secret, whose attainment might be destruction, but . . .

"Reynolds," he whispered again. On all sides rose mountains of ragged ice, one precipice arising frowningly above the other, and in front there shimmered a range of white vapor, like a limitless cataract rolling silently into the sea from some immense and far-distant rampart in the heavens. One should not go forward into this white wilderness without Reynolds beside one, without Reynolds the experienced explorer. One could not go into the dazzling distance without a guide.

He was hot. Despite the numbness of body and dreaminess of sensation that had come over him—when? at the start of this journey?—he knew that the heat of the water still increased, and he now saw that the range of vapor to the southward was beginning to assume more distinctness of form.

"Reynolds!" he tried to shout. One more journey. He could not make it alone.

But then, oh, then someone put a small lump of delicious ice in his mouth and gave him a sip of delicious water from a glass. Poe revived a little and gazed up at the dolorous face of Dr. Moran, but he did not recognize him, and he fixed his eyes upon the window. There was wire over it. It was . . .

And then he realized that Reynolds had answered his summons. He looked back at the face.

"Reynolds," he tried to say, but his attention was diverted by the fact that he noticed suddenly that his craft was now helplessly approaching, with hideous velocity, the embraces of the cataract, where a fathomless chasm threw itself open to receive . . .

Oh, God, in his pathway, at the brink of the chasm into which he rushed, there arose a radiant, white, shrouded human figure, very far larger in its proportions than any dweller among men, and it opened its arms and whispered . . .

What? What? He couldn't hear it, for all that damned talking. What were they saying to him? "Mr. Poe? Mr. Poe, can you hear me?"

He would rest for a short time. He moved his head minutely on his pillow, how soft, how . . . The pillow? No, the prow of the craft that swept in a great, descending circle, toward the figure . . . No, toward the chasm . . . No, it was . . .

"Well," said Dr. Monkur when he ran across his younger colleague in the hallways of the hospital at eight o'clock Sunday morning, "and how's that patient of yours?"

"Since five this morning, either very well off, or very poorly, depending on how you look at those things," Dr. Moran said morosely. "He died."

"Hmm, h'rumm," Dr. Monkur said. "Well, don't take it too hard, my boy. I expect it went easily enough for him."

"Yes," said Dr. Moran, brightening. "I think it did. He seemed to rally a little right at the end."

"Any last words from the great poet?"

"Yes."

"Well, what'd he say?" Dr. Monkur prodded curiously. " 'Nevermore'?"

"No. He said, 'God rest my poor soul.' "

EPILOGUE

October 8, 1849

ii

"... better get home, or she'll be irritated," Horace Greeley was saying when Dr. John Francis looked up from the last sheets of Edgar Poe's death notice handed him five minutes before, somewhat reluctantly, by the Reverend Dr. Rufus Griswold. At the rustle of paper in the now quiet office, the *Tribune* publisher glanced at the old physician almost challengingly, for the lengthy account of Poe's career painted a dark and denunciatory picture of a writer whom Dr. Francis's personal experience had always painted as more gentle and gracious. But Francis said nothing, and the publisher concluded his remark to Griswold, "My wife complains that I'm never at home enough. Can you imagine what she's taken up doing when she decides I'm not paying enough attention to her? She grabs up whatever manuscript I'm working on and throws it in the fire."

Secure in his status as a semi-bachelor, Griswold laughed. No one disturbed *his* manuscripts. He saw his estranged wife only during her rare visits to New York, and the rest of the time he lived the life of a highly popular man of letters, always in demand to squire the city's women of letters to this soirée and that at-home; if the Reverend Dr. Griswold paid overly frequent calls on a poetess whose husband had traded his paintbrushes for a pick in the California gold fields—well, after all, the lady was in the last stages of consumption and, besides, there was the little matter to be considered of one's position in future editions of the reverend doctor's anthologies.

Francis handed the sheets of foolscap to the publisher in silence. Griswold looked as though he badly wanted to ask Francis's opinion —he was a man who always sought approval—but he also was silent for a moment, then apparently decided to laugh again and rise.

"Well, that's that," he said to Greeley. "When do I get my pay?"

"Writers," snorted Horace Greeley. He turned and yelled into the speaking tube on the wall by his desk, "Boy! Copy!"

Downstairs in the editorial offices, there was a commotion and cries of "Copy's coming down from Mr. Greeley!" Greeley rose too, and absently straightened his black cravat, which had slipped off the collar and worked its way to the side of his neck as his nightly literary battle came to a climax. The publisher looked weary. Another edition of the New York *Tribune* was ready to go to press, and he had a distracted look and a twitch visible in his left temple. He smiled at Griswold and Dr. Francis and said wistfully, "Got out to the country for a few hours yesterday. I love October. Maple leaves down. River grapes ripe. The country's looking lovely, even in despite of the filthy encroachments of suburban deformity. Well, gentlemen, shall we call it a night?"

Small boots thudded up the stair, and a copyboy appeared in the doorway. Greeley thrust the obituary of Edgar A. Poe at him, and they all followed the boy downstairs, though far more slowly, while straightening coats, putting on hats.

Out front on the street, the Reverend Dr. Griswold breathed deeply, sniffing the faint scent of leaking gas, ink and ancient grime as though it were incense. "Plague take your country, Horace," he said to the publisher. "Give me New York. It's the ideal city, to the man of taste as well as to the man of action."

"Well, it took you long enough to make it here," Greeley said, but he smiled at his friend as he said it, and, smiling wearily, said his farewells.

It was a perfect New York autumn night, though chilly, and Dr. Francis shivered a little, feeling cold around his knees. On the sidewalk grates that let hot air out of the pressroom, three newsboys huddled, sleeping, and Francis smiled, admiring the ingenuity of his city's citizens.

The smile must have given Griswold courage, or else he could stand Dr. Francis's silence no longer, for he said abruptly, "Well, what do you think? I didn't do such a bad job on Poe after all, now did I?"

Francis didn't respond. What was there to say? The Raven was dead. The pack would gather to gnaw the bones of his reputation. What matter whether Griswold or another claimed the crown as king of the jackals?

"I wonder," Dr. Francis said finally, "what will become of Poe's old mother-in-law? Poor woman, I can't count the times she's wept to me that she feared she would end in the poorhouse. And I guess she will."

"Bet you can't count the times she's put the bite on you, either," Griswold said sourly. "She's been pestering me with her standard pitiable notes ever since Poe left town, begging for a 'small sum' until he could send her some money."

"Did you answer her?" Francis asked.

"Good God, no," Griswold said, looking startled. "You know what an old beggar she is. Give her an inch, and she's there whining for a mile. I know for a fact that Stella Lewis invited Mrs. Clemm to stay with her in Brooklyn for a few days, and she's been there for weeks."

Dr. Francis raised his bushy eyebrows, but again he made no comment. How utterly typical that Griswold would have been seeing Stella Lewis. Since the Raven had flown away, many eyes that formerly followed his every move had turned to the Grand Turk, as Griswold was now flattered to be called.

Griswold shrugged his shoulders uncomfortably in the wake of Dr. Francis's silence. "You know, perhaps I *could* do something for Mrs. Clemm," he said. "After all, I suppose there might be some small demand for an edition of Poe's collected works now. He might even have a few new manuscripts among his papers. I expect Mrs. Clemm could lay her hands on all of them."

"But surely a man with Poe's morbid concern for his future place in literature has already appointed a literary executor," Francis said.

"Oh, of course," Griswold said smoothly. "Mrs. Lewis confided in me only recently that Poe has long been in the habit of expressing a desire that, in the event of his death, I should be his editor. After all, as you've pointed out, we've had our quarrels, but whatever else he thinks of me he has . . . he *had* a proper regard for my abilities as an editor. I am sure Mrs. Clemm would tell you the same."

"By which I take it you mean there might be a little money in a collection of his works," Francis said.

Griswold laughed nervously. "What a skeptic you're becoming, sir," he said. "Naturally the entire proceeds would go to Poe's mother-in-law. Would you really rather see her go to the poorhouse?"

"No," Dr. Francis said quietly.

"Well, then," Griswold said. Two policemen walked past them, ostentatiously swinging their clubs, trying each door they passed to be sure it was locked. The sidewalks were empty, except for the two policemen, the street urchins sleeping on the grate and, reappearing from the shadows behind the policemen, one of the army of harlots who also patrolled the city at night. "Getting late," Griswold said. "Come along. I'll go with you to Delmonico's for that beef and brandy. It's still open, isn't it?"

"I believe so," Francis said. "Yes." He was one man, old, tired and powerless in the face of inevitability. Poe had made too many enemies in his life for them not to descend upon him now that he was dead and powerless to defend himself. And after all, it wasn't as if Edgar Poe were a Halleck, a Percival, much less a Professor Longfellow.

"Yes, go along to supper," Dr. Francis said with a hint of a regretful sigh. "You've had a hard night's work. You've earned your beef and brandy."

"You're not coming?" the reverend doctor said.

"No, thanks, not tonight," Dr. Francis said. "I seem to have lost my appetite."

As their footsteps faded, going down newspaper row toward Broadway, there was a deep rumble within the basement of the building that housed the New York *Tribune*, and the big presses started to clank. Horace Greeley the younger awoke instantly and turned on the grating, through which warm steam began to rise, to punch the Wandering Jew.

"Paper's coming off," he mumbled sleepily. "Bet we could sell an armload on the early ferries."

"Ain't got two cents for the ferry," said the Jew, and he went back to sleep.

It was five the next morning, when, more or less awake, Horace Greeley the younger, the Wandering Jew and O'Neill the Great conferred long enough to effect a compromise. O'Neill had a dime given him by a drunk the night before for a shine, and they invested it in ten copies of the *Trib*, sold to them at half-rate, and hurried off to the foot of Christopher Street to the oyster boats, or boat stores, that lay anchored there.

"He-e-e-re's your *Tribune*, get the *Trib*," O'Neill and the Wandering Jew cried shrilly, but Horace the younger was coughing hard that morning and couldn't join them for a minute or two. It was then that he heard a reeking oysterman who had just bought a paper from O'Neill say to a companion, "Well, looky here. Sez in the paper that Edgar Poe's died. You remember him. He's the gent they called the Raven. Used to see him all the time. Always dressed in black, he was, and bowed just like you was another gent. Must have been mad as a hatter, from what the *Trib* says here."

Horace Greeley the younger cried a little. He was about the only one.

AUTHOR'S NOTE

On the raw, rainy afternoon of the same day the New York *Tribune* carried the prejudicial story characterizing Edgar Poe, thenceforth known as Edgar Allan Poe, as a sordid degenerate, a single carriage followed a hearse drawn by black-plumed horses through the streets of Baltimore to the Presbyterian burying ground at Fayette and Green streets. The carriage contained only four shivering mourners, Poe's cousins, Neilson Poe and Henry Herring, Dr. J. E. Snodgrass and an old classmate of Poe's at the University of Virginia, Z. Collins Lee. The hearse contained a plain, unlined poplar coffin stained to imitate walnut, hidden under a neat muslin covering sewed by the wife of Poe's attending physician and a few neighboring women, for when the news that Edgar Poe was dead made the rounds of Baltimore and many onlookers came to view the body, Mrs. Moran feared there might be criticism of the plainness of the coffin. Out of pity, Moran paid the cost of the coffin, and would have bought a better one if he could have afforded it. Out of pity, medical students at the hospital raised suitable clothing for Poe to be buried in. Dr. Moran contributed a vest and white cravat. The resident named George McCalpin from Alabama gave the black pants and Albert Grey, the student from Leesburg, Virginia, gave the coat.

It was October, the month which tolls like an iron bell in *Ulalume*. It was a most unpleasant day in Baltimore, a cold, cheerless one, accompanied by drizzling rain nearly all day. Poe was buried in a grave near that of his grandfather. Neilson Poe later ordered a simple marble gravestone, but fate continued its grisly jokes and the stone was broken before it could be erected, victim of a runaway railroad car that jumped the track in front of the stonecutter's shop and ran over only one tombstone, that of Edgar A. Poe. As Poe did have an active sense of humor, the macabre detail would probably have delighted him, but it worried others. Until twenty-five years later, his grave remained unmarked, and the Reverend G. W. Powell of Baltimore took it upon himself to pepper the world regularly with pronouncements such as, "Poe did not die drunk as the world believes. His grave is level with the earth, with only a stake driven down at his feet to mark the spot. Shame!"

Poe's small, beloved household fared little better. Catarina was found dead outside the cottage in Fordham when the grieving Muddy eventually returned there to close it. No record exists as to the parrot's fate. Muddy escaped the poorhouse, but not by far, dying in 1871 in the Church Home Infirmary in Baltimore, by coincidence then housed in the building that, on October 7, 1849, when Poe had died there, had housed the Washington College Hospital. Muddy died as she had lived, in poverty, having been paid for Poe's collected works only in a few sets of the books. For the rest of her wandering, hard-pressed years she tried to eke a few dollars by begging Poe's acquaintances to buy them. The Reverend Rufus Wilmot Griswold, editor of Poe's collected works, swore he never made a penny from them, but they sold quite well, so somebody did.

Verbally and in print, Griswold continued his posthumous attacks on Poe. He enlarged upon and repeated in his biographical "Memoir" of Poe, published with the collected works, much of the article he had first written anonymously, over the signature "Ludwig," for Poe's obituary in the New York *Tribune*. It was an article in which details were carefully selected to present Poe's life in the most unfavorable light, and according to Professor Arthur Hobson Quinn, whose biography, *Edgar Allan Poe* (New York: Appleton-Century, 1941), is still regarded as the definitive Poe biography, the article did incalculable harm to Poe's reputation. There it was, in cold print, in one of the best papers in the United States, Horace Greeley's New York *Tribune*—Edgar Poe was a base, bitter, dissipated, gibbering loony. The article was republished in the *Weekly Tribune*, Greeley's widely circulated weekly wrap-up of the most important news covered in the daily *Trib*. It was accepted as authoritative and was widely copied—standard practice permitted the verbatim pirating of news stories—by even those many newspapers that sided with Poe in the literary spats that typified his career. Moreover, as Professor Quinn points out, Griswold's article "created that *first* impression, so hard to efface." Inclusion of the "Ludwig" article as a biographical note in the collected works led to the worldwide acceptance as fact of Griswold's account of Poe's life, as early scholars had no other widely published "facts" to turn to.

Poe did have friends and even foes who rushed to his defense in print, but the mythical picture the public now has of Poe has developed from the Dorian Gray portraits first painted by Griswold and his ilk: that of a black-clad madman walking the streets in a drug-induced nightmare, lips moving in indistinct curses, heading for the nearest cemetery to dig up a corpse upon the stroke of midnight, while a raven squawks dismally from a lightning-blasted tree. Exactly what this mythical Poe might do with the corpse is in controversy, as those critics who indulge in the dubious practice of writing psychobiographies have variously characterized Poe as necrophilic, oversexed and impotent, all more or less due to an obsession with his beautiful young mother's early death. The reading public—didn't we all at least read and adore Poe as children?—would probably settle for a bit of post-mortem dentistry, à la the protagonist who pulled his dead (he thought) beloved's teeth in Poe's tale "Berenice," for, as it was pointed out even soon after his death, we have insisted upon confusing Poe the man with Poe's tales, forgetting, if we ever knew, that Poe was simply a hard-working journeyman writer who carefully studied the magazines of his day, wrote what he hoped would publish and, through the genius that even the Griswolds of his world could not deny that he truly possessed, succeeded in elevating much of it to the status of literature.

Poe undoubtedly had his obsessions and his problems. Chief among the latter was a galloping drinking problem, for a careful study of the mass of conflicting material written about Poe turns up report after report that he was given to spree drinking, alternating with periods of strict sobriety. There *is* controversy as to his being an habitual taker of drugs. This claim was slow to develop, as even Poe's most bitter enemies neglected to make the charge in the period immediately following his death, and one eager enemy, Thomas Dunn English, whose one fragile claim to fame is that he presented to posterity the old song "Ben Bolt," is on record as denying that Poe indulged in anything stronger than the one-too-many rum toddies, pointing out that he had known Poe intimately for years, had a medical degree and therefore should know what he was talking about.

Author's Note

That Poe was unfamiliar enough with the effects of laudanum to overdose himself—"I had not calculated on the strength of the laudanum," as he put it in a letter—during his depression over discovering he was in love with one woman while semi-engaged to another, has also been frequently cited as evidence that Poe was not a drug addict. It is safe to infer, however, if only from the familiarity Poe shows in his tales with certain psychological and physiological states accompanying the taking of opium, that Poe, like the rest of his age, had at least run to the corner drugstore for his thirty minims of laudanum or a few opium pills if he chanced to have a toothache. Opium was common, uncontrolled and cheap.

As Poe's defenders have pointed out, more damaging to his life, if not to his posthumous reputation, was his fatal knack for wasting high-quality vituperation on small literary hacks the world has long since forgotten. After his death, Poe became good copy, and persons who had seen him even once happily gave interviews to this magazine or that newspaper. They frequently changed their stories, improving upon their reminiscences in later years, and much of the conflicting information extant on Poe is due to this tendency. Poe's literary enemies, too, were glad to make money by slashing away at him for the rest of their lifetimes. Of all people, Harry Franco, as Charles Briggs was known when Poe helped oust him from his co-editor's spot on the *Broadway Journal*, somehow came to be regarded as one of the Poe experts, and by 1858 was writing about him in a British edition of Poe's collected poems, "Some of the biographers of Poe have been harshly judged for the view given of his character, and it has naturally been supposed that private pique led to the exaggeration of his personal defects. But such imputations are unjust: a truthful delineation of his career would give a darker hue to his character than it has received from his biographers. In fact he has been more fortunate than most poets in his historians. Lowell and Willis have sketched him with a gentleness and a reverent feeling for his genius: and Griswold, his literary executor, in his fuller biography, has generously suppressed much that he might have given." Early British critics proceeded to repeat such material.

Thus Poe's black reputation was embellished upon and thus it grew, but if a petty foe such as Harry Franco hated Poe enough after his death to go on blackguarding him, what of the biographer whom Harry Franco defended, Rufus Griswold? Did Griswold really suppress anything? Perhaps, if only by accident. According to the memoirs of a close friend of Griswold's, Charles Godfrey Leland, Leland one day found in Griswold's desk a collection of letters and other material of a nature unfavorable to Poe and others which Griswold intended to publish. Leland burned it all. He liked Griswold and Griswold liked Leland enough to forgive him, but Leland's act was daring, for he characterized his friend as one of the "most vindictive" of men.

Griswold was indeed vindictive enough to publish portions of Poe's letters with conveniently chosen deletions and forged additions, all designed to make Poe look bad, except where they were designed to make Griswold look noble and good. This was suspected early by such staunch defenders of Poe as Sarah Helen Whitman, to whom Poe was so briefly engaged, and proven conclusively by Professor Quinn in the Poe biography previously mentioned. Quinn's discoveries on the forgeries make interesting reading.

And where did Griswold's vindictiveness end? There is no documentary evidence to prove or disprove Griswold's frequently made claim that Poe requested him, at least indirectly, to write his biography and act as his literary executor, although Stella Lewis and, for a short while, Muddy both claimed that was Poe's wish. Stella had literary ambitions and Griswold was an influential critic and anthologist. Muddy was poor. This may have colored their statements. After a time, Muddy changed her tune and tried to retrieve the letters, papers, annotated books and manuscripts that she had delivered to Griswold at his request, but once in Griswold's hands they were lost to her. The manuscript of the critical literary history which Poe often said he was working on through his years in New York somehow disappeared, if it ever existed. One worried writer on Poe has gone so far as to suggest that had not *The Bells* already been in type and *Annabel Lee* in other hands, two fewer Poe poems might have been known to the world, but Griswold appreciated poetry, even though—or perhaps because—he could not write it, and this suggestion seems unduly harsh.

It is sufficient to understand the success of one single Griswold thrust, the bitter "Ludwig" memoir that was reprinted with most sets of Poe's works and letters, while contemporary newspaper and magazine articles defending Poe were lost to the public eye for many years. So myths begin. Weaving my way through the maze of conflicting reports, no doubt becoming guilty of something of a psychobiography of my own, I have presented, as fiction, the Poe whom I believe to have existed as fact. Many of the words here put in the mouths of Poe's acquaintances and in his own mouth have been taken from his writings, his letters and the more reliable reports by those who knew him. I have sought not isolated "facts," but, like any applauder of scientific method—which I firmly believe could be utilized with happier results than the intuitive and (one might as well say it plainly) haphazard methods so often preferred by students of literature—I have sought a "cluster of facts," those which seemed logically to stick together.

For these facts I am indebted to so many collectors of Poe lore, both his contemporaries and ours, that it is difficult to acknowledge and thank them all. Scholarly footnotes have no place in novels, nor do detailed bibliographies. Basic among my many obligations, however, is that to the painstakingly thorough work of John Ward Ostrom, editor of *The Letters of Edgar Allan Poe* (New York: Gordian, 1966). Quotations from Poe's works are from the versions used in *Complete Stories and Poems of Edgar Allan Poe* (New York: Doubleday, 1966).

To the reader who might enjoy making up his own mind about Poe and his times, I recommend from the mountain of material that has been produced on Poe the Quinn *Edgar Allan Poe*; a somewhat newer and much shorter biography by William Bittner, *Poe* (Boston: Atlantic Monthly-Little, 1961); and, if you'll read it with a grain of salt, remembering that the extent of Griswold's forgeries had not yet been discovered at the time, *Israfel: The Life and Times of Edgar Allan Poe* by Hervey Allen (New York: Farrar, 1926, 1934). Allen, it will be remembered—well, no, maybe it won't—is the author of the huge and once hugely popular novel *Anthony Adverse*, and he crams his treatment with the kind of colorful, closely observed detail that would appeal to both the reader and writer of fiction, not to mention the man who invented that astute, close observer of details, M. Dupin, and thus is often credited with inventing for the world the detective story. For other treatments of the times, go straight to the diaries of New York's two famous nineteenth-century diarists, George Templeton Strong (New York: Macmillan, 1952) and Philip Hone (New York: Dodd, 1927). For a critical approach to Poe's work, read Daniel Hoffman's sound and delightfully written *POE POE POE POE POE POE POE* (New York: Doubleday, 1972).

Lastly, if it is Thomas Holley Chivers or the Reverend Dr. Rufus Griswold who attracts you, consult S. Foster Damon's *Thomas Holley Chivers* (New York and London: Harper, 1930) or *Rufus Wilmot Griswold* by Joy Bayless (Nashville: Vanderbilt Univ. Press, 1943), who defends ably this man whose wish to have a monument placed on his own grave was never carried out and who lies in an unmarked lot in Brooklyn's Green-Wood Cemetery. He outlived Poe only eight years, years which he certainly did not spend hard at work all the time vilifying his old rival or sighing after the memory of Fanny Osgood, but falling in love again, then again, divorcing, remarrying, being charged with bigamy, undergoing illness, undergoing financial success and producing books. They are now as forgotten as his grave. He almost found a niche in the English language by a suggestion made in the Providence *Journal* in 1875 that "in the future when we wish, in one single, stinging word to stigmatize a being who has exhausted all his resources of malignity, falsehood and dishonor against a dead man who trusted him, we will say that he 'griswoldized' him."

But "griswoldization" did not stick. Baudelaire said it better when, growling about Griswold's treatment of Poe's character—the treatment that we still think of today when we think of Poe—he wrote:

"Does there not exist in America an ordinance which forbids to curs an entrance to the cemeteries?"

BARBARA MOORE

PS
3563
.O57
F4
1976

$18.95

PS
3563
.O57
F4

1976